P9-DHL-091

For my friends in
STAR and the members of
the Hard Lemonade Science
Fiction Society, with thanks
for your encouragement
and support.

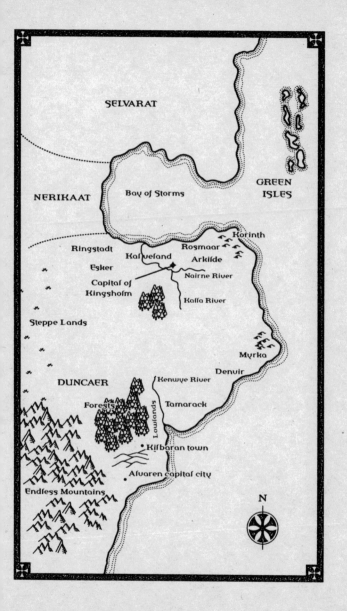

One

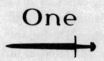

DEVLIN OF DUNCAER, CHOSEN ONE OF THE GODS, Defender of the Realm, Personal Champion of King Olafur, King's councilor, and General of the Royal Army, muttered to himself as he strode through the corridors of the palace. The few folk who saw him took one look at his face and discovered urgent business elsewhere. It was not just his appearance that gave them pause, though his green eyes and black hair—now streaked with white—marked him as a stranger here: the first of the Caerfolk to enter into the service of their conquerors. Rather it was his reputation they fled, for it was well-known that the Chosen One had little patience for fools, and his power made him an enemy few wished to have.

As Devlin reached the chambers that served as his offices, the guard on duty took one look at his face and swiftly opened the door, forgoing the formal salute. Devlin slammed the door shut behind him.

Lieutenant Didrik looked up from his papers. "The council meeting went as expected?"

Nearly four months ago, when Devlin had been

named General of the Army, Lieutenant Didrik had been detached from the City Guard to serve as Devlin's aide. Some thought the lieutenant too young for the task, but his age was offset by his proven loyalty and friendship. And Lieutenant Didrik knew him well enough to know when Devlin was truly angry and when he was merely frustrated, as now.

"The council sits and talks and does nothing," Devlin said, unbuttoning the stiff collar of his court uniform. "And the folk in the palace flee like frightened sheep whenever they catch a glimpse of me."

Lieutenant Didrik nodded. "It would be easier to convince them you were tame if you did not growl."

"I do not growl."

"Yes, you do."

Devlin gave a wordless snarl and began to pace the small confines of the outer office. Lieutenant Didrik remained seated, his eyes following Devlin's restless movements.

Devlin paced in silence for a moment as he tried to shake off the frustration of that afternoon's council session. Four hours, and little enough to show for it. He was not made for such. In his past he had labored as a metalsmith and a farmer. Both were hard trades, but each carried the reward of being able to see the fruits of his labors. But now the Fates had conspired to turn Devlin into a politician. No one knew better than he how ill suited he was for the task. Court politics was about compromises and alliances, jockeying for influence and trading favors. It took skill to navigate the treacherous waters of the court, and time to get anything accomplished. Time they did not have.

Worse, Devlin's voice was but one of sixteen, and no

matter whether he whispered or shouted, he could not bend the council to his will. Instead he had to reason, cajole, flatter, and bargain, and try to be content with the smallest of victories.

Such as the victory he had achieved today. "There is some news," he said, dropping into a wooden chair across from Lieutenant Didrik's desk. "The council approved the proposal for recruiting trained armsmen. Word is to be sent to all the provinces at once. With luck we should have a hundred before the snows, and perhaps a thousand by springtime."

Lieutenant Didrik leaned back and smiled. "That is excellent news. Why did you not say so at once?"

"Because it is a victory, but at a cost. I had to agree not to urge the King to train the common folk who live in the danger zones," Devlin said, running the fingers of his good hand through his short-cropped hair. He was still not convinced that he had done the right thing, and yet there had seemed no other choice. Even those councilors who normally supported him had been united in their opposition to his proposal that the common folk receive weapons training, as was the custom in his homeland. To Devlin it was simple logic: make use of the people that had the most to lose in an invasion; teach them to be effective fighters rather than see them slaughtered.

But the councilors' concerns were not for the present dangers but for their future power. A peasantry that was trained in the arts of warfare would be far harder to control. The common folk might even take it into their heads to rise up against those they perceived as unjust. Devlin acknowledged the risk, but had argued that those who ruled wisely had nothing to fear. His words had fallen on deaf ears.

"Perhaps there will be no need. Since Major Mikkelson and his troops repelled the landing force in Korinth, there has been little trouble along the borders. It may be that the worst is over," Lieutenant Didrik said.

Devlin shook his head. "I do not believe our enemies will give up so easily."

They were still not even sure who their true enemy was. The invaders in Korinth had been a mercenary troop, in the pay of someone they could not even name. It was only chance that had led Devlin to discover the plot in time to repel the invasion. The Royal Army had made short work of the would-be invaders, but Devlin knew better than to suppose that this was the end of the threat.

Yet where would the enemy attack next? Devlin and his advisors had wracked their brains trying to divine the strategy behind the enemy's seemingly random attacks. Without knowing whom they were facing, they were reduced to guessing.

The trouble was that Jorsk had grown into an empire whose very size made it difficult to defend. The Royal Army could not be everywhere at once. Devlin had to deploy his troops carefully, which was why he had proposed arming the common folk to serve as a first line of defense.

"The armsmen will help," Lieutenant Didrik said.

"Aye. Draw up a list of those provinces most in need and a plan to allocate the armsmen. I will want to see it tomorrow." He closed his eyes and leaned his head back. The council sessions wearied him in a way that hard labor never could, for it was an exhaustion born of frustration and a sense of his own inadequacies. "Anyone would make a better councilor than I."

"Do not speak such folly," Lieutenant Didrik said. "Without you, the soldiers would have sat idly in their garrison rather than meeting the invaders on the shores of Korinth. And you were the one who sent the Royal Army out to patrol the highways and survey the border fortifications."

Comforting words. But such actions were only a fraction of what Devlin had hoped to accomplish when he had accepted his position. Then he had been sure that with the King's backing he could set this Kingdom to rights. But he had not counted on the numbing effects of court politics, or that his influence would wane as memories of his heroism faded.

Now he was left to struggle as best he could. A lesser man might have given up hope, but Devlin was the Chosen One, bound by Geas to serve the Kingdom as long as breath remained in his body. He could not conceive of surrender. He would not rest until he had fulfilled his promise and made this Kingdom safe.

The last chords faded away into silence, and Stephen lifted his hands from the harp strings. A scattering of applause broke out from the assembled guests, and Stephen felt a warm rush of pleasure as he bowed his head, acknowledging their praise.

It was seldom these days that he had a chance to play for an appreciative audience. Not that he was lacking in offers. Quite the contrary. If he accepted only half the invitations that came his way, he could have filled every night and most of his days. It had taken a while for him to realize that the invitations were proffered not in appreciation of his musical skill, but rather because of his well-known friendship with the Chosen One.

At least tonight he need have no such fears. Soren Tyrvald was not a member of the court, but a wealthy wine merchant. On several occasions over the past two years Stephen had played for him, entertaining his guests. Tonight was just another such gathering.

Stephen caught his host's eye. Merchant Tyrvald nodded, then rose and signaled to the servants standing in the back of the room, who began circulating among the two dozen assembled guests, offering chilled wines and sweet pastries. During the interval the guests would refresh themselves, giving Stephen a chance to rest before the second half of his performance.

Stephen bent his head down to the harp, plucking lightly at the strings as he retuned them. The old harp was a lovely instrument, but the worn pegs meant it couldn't stay in tune for more than an hour.

"A delightful performance," Merchant Tyrvald said.

Stephen lifted his head, startled. He had not heard the man approach.

Setting the harp back on its base, he rose to his feet and gave a short bow. "Your praise honors me, Merchant Tyrvald."

The man smiled, his round face and bald pate giving him the appearance of an indulgent uncle rather than the shrewd trader that his reputation held him to be. "Please, I have told you before. I am Soren to my friends."

Stephen inclined his head but said nothing. It was a fine line he trod. Stephen, son of Lord Brynjolf, Baron of Esker, could well address a wealthy merchant as an equal. Stephen of Esker, the as-yet-undistinguished minstrel, could not afford such familiarity.

"Come, walk with me a moment," Merchant Tyrvald said. He took Stephen's arm and led him in a circular path around the drawing room, nodding and smiling in acknowledgment of his guests. "The tune you played at the end, that was a new one, was it not?"

"Yes," Stephen said, feeling absurdly pleased that Merchant Tyrvald had been paying such careful attention. "It is a new composition I am crafting."

Stephen had composed songs before, writing lyrics, then setting them to music. This time it was the melody that had come to him. He had tried in vain to find words to fit the haunting tune, until he finally realized that the melody needed no words to convey the emotions he felt.

"A pleasant tune, yet at the same time unsettling. Does it have a name?"

"I was thinking of calling it 'Waiting for the Storm.'"

As they reached the back of the room, Merchant Tyrvald nodded to one of the servants, who drew aside the silken hangings. They stepped into a small chamber, and the hangings fell back into place behind them.

Stephen's heart sank. There was no reason for Merchant Tyrvald to take him aside for private speech unless what the merchant had to say had nothing to do with Stephen's performance.

"I need to give you a message for the Chosen One," Merchant Tyrvald said, the affable smile melting from his face.

"I will not be used this way," Stephen said, turning on his heel to leave. "I am here as a minstrel. Speak to me of my music or not at all."

"Hear me out," Master Tyrvald said. "Five minutes, in return for all those times I gave you employment before anyone knew your name."

Stephen took two more steps, then his feet dragged to a halt. Merchant Tyrvald had been a patron to him, in those days when Stephen had been reduced to singing for his dinner in dockside taverns. If any other had made this request, Stephen would have continued on. But he owed the man, and so he turned around.

"Five minutes," Stephen said slowly. The elation he had felt moments before had vanished.

"Your friend is causing quite a stir. Even the merchants of the city can talk of nothing except the Chosen One."

Stephen's eyes narrowed. "Devlin. His name is Devlin."

"Lord Devlin, then," the merchant said. "The reforms he proposes have frightened many, and they begin to wonder if the cure is worse than the ailment."

Was this some kind of warning? Devlin had been the target of assassination attempts before, but none since he had vanquished Duke Gerhard and exposed his treasonous plots. "Do you threaten us?"

The merchant shook his head. "Not a threat. Say rather some advice. One with my reputation often finds himself consulted by merchants and nobles alike. These days I hear strange whispers. Voices saying that Devlin of Duncaer is not the true Chosen One."

"What nonsense is this? Has he not proven himself a dozen times over? Where would we be if Devlin had not risked his own life challenging Duke Gerhard to a duel and exposing his treachery for all the world to see?"

"The late Duke was a traitor, none will deny. But

now many also say that the Gods had turned against the Duke and that anyone could have slain him. Your friend was merely a convenient instrument."

Hot anger surged inside Stephen. "Devlin nearly died that day," he said, his fists clenching at his sides. He would never forget what he had witnessed. Devlin bleeding from dozens of wounds, cradling his maimed hand to his chest, staggering slightly as he fought to stay upright until he was sure that justice would be served. In his worst nightmares Stephen revisited the horrors of that day, watching a friend come within inches of the Dread Lord's realm.

"Memories fade," Merchant Tyrvald said. "And heroic deeds are soon forgotten. Now the courtiers worry about their future, and the Chosen One frightens them, as do his plans. So they gather and whisper. They say that he is not the true Chosen One. That if he were truly anointed by the Gods, then they would have given him the Sword of Light as proof of his calling."

"The Sword of Light has been lost for two generations," Stephen pointed out.

"And there has been no true Chosen One for as long. Not one to measure up to the heroes of old. You know it as well as I."

"Why are you telling me this?" Stephen asked.

"Because I believe the Chosen One is right. There will be war, and sooner rather than later. Though if you speak those words outside this room I will deny having said them. This new rumor is a clever attempt to discredit the Chosen One, for he draws much of his power from the belief of the common folk. And it is these folks who cling most tightly to the old legends. Soon, they, too, will begin to ask why he does not wield the Sword of Light. I thought it best he hear this first from a friend rather than an enemy."

Stephen ground his teeth in frustration. So much for his vow not to be used as a pawn in these games of politics. But he could not ignore the information the merchant had given him. Devlin would have to be told, and Stephen would once again find himself sucked into the political quagmire he had tried so hard to avoid.

"I will give him the message, Goodman Soren," Stephen said, with pointed lack of courtesy. "And now I will collect my instruments. You may make my excuses to your guests."

He strode out of the room, fumbling his way through the silk curtain till he found the opening. But even knowing how foolish he must look could not blunt the edge of his anger. He was angry at Soren Tyrvald, and at the court for treating him as a tool rather than as a musician. And he was angry with Devlin, for putting him in this position, though he knew this was petty of him. What matter if there was a price to Devlin's friendship, and that the price might well be the end of Stephen's dreams to be recognized as a serious musician? It was not Devlin's fault. His friend would never demand such a sacrifice. If there was any fault, it belonged to King Olafur and his courtiers, for not being able to recognize an honest man even when he stood in their midst.

And with the Gods, who had sent this most unlikely of heroes to a people who could not measure his worth.

Devlin threw the scroll across the room in disgust. By all the Seven Gods, how could one man be so stupid?

His orders to Troop Captain Poul Karlson had been blindingly clear. The troop captain was to take his hundred men and patrol the Southern Road, ensuring that it remained open to all lawful travelers.

Halfway through his first circuit, the troop captain had encountered an ingenious band of outlaws who had imposed their own form of tolls upon travelers. Rather than pursuing the outlaws and arresting them, the troop captain had halted his advance and sent a messenger to the capital, asking for instructions.

The scroll had been dated over a fortnight ago. By now the outlaws would be long gone from the province, no doubt laughing at the expense of the Royal Army.

Still, what was done was done. It was now up to Devlin to set things right. "Didrik, who is the next senior troop captain?" he called out.

He heard the sound of shuffling papers, then the scrape of wooden chair legs across the floor, as Didrik rose from his desk. He leaned his head into Devlin's own office. "There are no senior troop captains in garrison, except those you have already designated as free from duties. However there is a junior troop captain, Rika Linasdatter."

"She will do. Send a messenger to the garrison, and tell her to report to me at once. I am sending her out to replace that useless worm Poul Karlson. If she succeeds in clearing the highway, then I will raise her to senior troop captain."

"Do you wish me to scribe the orders?" Lieutenant Didrik asked, his gaze touching lightly on Devlin's maimed right hand.

Devlin shook his head. "No, I can do this. I need you

to finish the muster lists, and the allocation for the provincial armsmen."

He waited until Lieutenant Didrik returned to his own office before he pulled out a blank piece of parchment from the center drawer of the desk. Taking the pen in his hand, he dipped it in the inkwell and began to write. "Troop Captain Poul Karlson, you are instructed to turn over your command to the officer bearing this scroll and return with all haste to the capital garrison. . . ."

The official wording came easily to him, for he had written such orders several times in the three months since he had been named General of the Royal Armies. It was a post for which he was far less qualified than even Lieutenant Didrik, yet when the King had offered the honor, Devlin had not been able to refuse.

Only later did he realize that the post was more punishment than reward. Unlike the City Guard, where officers such as Didrik began in the ranks and rose by merit, the Royal Army drew its officers from the noble families of Jorsk. Political influence had been far more important than skill in advancing the careers of its officers. This alone would have caused problems for any new general. But Devlin had been named to his post when he had defeated the former general, Duke Gerhard, in a duel, and exposed the duke as a traitor.

Many of the most senior officers owed their positions to their friendship with Duke Gerhard, and they felt little loyalty to their new general. They blamed Devlin, as if he were somehow responsible for the Duke's treachery. And those who were not bitter over the death of the Duke resented Devlin for his humble origins.

And Devlin, as a stranger to the army and its politics, had no clear means of separating out those officers who were merely incompetent from those who were actively disloyal. Left to himself he would have purged the officer corps, but he could not do so. Not when the army might be called upon to fight a war at any time. And not when he needed the support of the very same noble families whose kin made up the corps.

In the end, the officers were given a chance to prove themselves. So far, many had performed well. Those like Poul Karlson who showed themselves unfit were swiftly dealt with. Upon his return to Kingsholm, the failed senior troop captain would be strongly encouraged to resign his commission. Should he refuse, he would find himself permanently assigned to the garrison, his name on the private list of those who were never to receive another command.

Devlin scrawled his name at the bottom of the orders, then stamped it with the seal of his rank. He folded the parchment but did not seal it. The new troop captain should see the orders she was carrying to ensure there would be no misunderstandings.

He pulled out another piece of parchment and began to write a separate set of orders for the new troop captain. "Junior Troop Captain Rika Linas—"

His right hand spasmed, and the pen seemed to leap out of his grasp, flying across the desk until it landed on top of a stack of unread reports. Black ink ran from the pen, staining first the reports, then his left hand, as he picked it up and set it back down on the blotter.

"Blast!" he swore, as his right hand spasmed again. This time it twitched and fell off the desk to hang uselessly by his side. There was a moment of blinding pain as the muscles cramped. Then, mercifully, the pain was gone, replaced by a tingling numbness that ran from his fingertips to his shoulder.

Since his right arm no longer obeyed him, Devlin used his left hand to reach down and lift it up, placing his maimed hand palm side up on the desk as he tried to rub feeling back into the arm with his other hand.

He stared balefully at the two fingers and thumb that were all that remained on his right hand, and the angry red scar that cut across his palm. He willed his fingers to close, but they stubbornly remained open. At least they had stopped twitching.

He continued massaging his arm, even though he knew from bitter experience that it would be hours before sensation returned and the hand was once again his to command.

"I should feel lucky."

"What did you say?" Lieutenant Didrik called.

"Nothing," Devlin replied. He had not realized he had said the words aloud. He *should* feel lucky, he reminded himself. Lucky that the healers had been able to save as much of the hand as they had. Though he had lost the two smallest fingers and a chunk of his palm, the rest of the hand remained. And he had use of it, after a fashion. Even these spasms afflicted him less often than they once had. In time, Master Osvald had assured him that the spasms would cease all together—although the master healer had been vague over just how long it would take. Instead, the healer had urged patience, as if Devlin had naught to do but wait for his traitorous body to heal.

Devlin had thanked the healer for his advice, then set grimly about the task of discovering what he could and could not do. It had taken nearly a month for him to gain even rudimentary control of his fingers. Then the real work had begun. The transverse bow proved no difficulty, for the left arm bore the weight, and only two fingers were required to load and fire the bolts. The war-axe was more of a problem, for the grip of his right hand lacked the strength it had once had, and thus the full force of his right arm was not translated into each stroke. Where once he had been able to deliver killing blows, now he would only maim. But muscles could be strengthened, and in time he would learn to compensate.

The sword was another matter. His grip was clumsy, even when he tried using a two-handed long sword. The few practice bouts he had attempted had all ended in ignominious defeats. Master Timo, the Royal Armorer, was experimenting on different grips for the hilt of Devlin's sword, but so far the armorer's craft had failed to produce a workable solution.

Devlin would just have to try harder.

Two

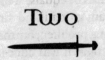

"Then we are agreed. The armsmen will be used to reinforce the border with Nerikaat," Devlin said, leaning over the map and tapping the northwestern corner of the kingdom with one finger. "The southern provinces will have to wait until the next wave of reinforcements in the spring."

He looked up from the maps spread over his worktable.

"Agreed," Captain Drakken said. Lieutenant Didrik merely nodded.

Devlin began rolling up the map. "Lieutenant, I will need to inform the senior army commanders of my decision. Send a message and ask that they meet with me on the morrow."

"There is the council meeting in the morning," Lieutenant Didrik reminded him.

"Shall I ask the officers to meet you at the first hour past noon?"

"That will serve." Devlin placed the rolled up map inside the wooden tube, then fitted the cap back on.

"Captain Drakken, I thank you for the courtesy of your time and counsel."

Captain Drakken dipped her head in the show of respect between friends or equals. "I am at your service."

"And for that I am grateful."

Strictly speaking, as the commander of the City Guard, Captain Drakken was concerned with security for the palace and maintaining order within the city. The defense of the realm and disposition of provincial armsmen was more properly a matter for the Royal Army. But Devlin could count on his remaining fingers the number of folk in Jorsk whom he could trust to give him honest advice, and only one of them was a member of the Royal Army. And Major Mikkelson was far from here, having been dispatched to lead the defense of the coastal province of Korinth.

Thus Devlin had become accustomed to consulting Captain Drakken, taking full advantage of her more than quarter century of experience. Once he had determined his course of action, he then informed the Royal Army officers of his decisions, allowing him to appear a decisive leader. Only he, Lieutenant Didrik, and Captain Drakken knew this for the hollow pretense it was.

Today they had debated how best to allocate the armsmen who would soon begin to trickle into the capital in response to the summons of the King's Council. The needs were many, but rather than sending a few armsmen to each of the trouble spots, Captain Drakken had convinced him that the best course of action was to pick one place where their numbers would be enough to tip the balance. That decided, the choice of Ringstadt was simple. Even in peaceful times the border with Nerikaat was a trouble spot. And in these past years

Ringstadt had been hard hit. Half their original complement of armsmen had been killed in the past three years, and new recruits often perished before they completed their training.

He heard the sound of the outer door opening, then footsteps, as a voice called "Devlin?"

"We are in here," he replied.

Stephen paused in the doorway. "I do not wish to interrupt . . ."

"No, we were just finished our deliberations. And as I have not seen you in some time, it would be poor courtesy to turn you away."

Stephen was the first friend Devlin had made in this strange place, though it had taken him time to acknowledge that friendship—and to accept its burden. Stephen had shared many of Devlin's adventures, but in these past months they had seen little of each other. Devlin had been consumed with his new responsibilities, and Stephen had made it plain that he wished to pursue his music rather than be caught up in the games of the court.

Yet somehow the court must have found Stephen, for there was no other reason for him to look so unhappy, or to have sought Devlin out in his offices rather than his private quarters.

Captain Drakken glanced at Stephen, then back at Devlin. "I will leave you now."

"No," Stephen said. "You and Lieutenant Didrik will want to hear this as well."

Devlin perched on the corner of his desk, wondering what had brought Stephen here. He nodded encouragingly.

"I played last night for a wine merchant, Soren Tyrvald."

"I know of him," Captain Drakken interjected. "He has a reputation for shrewd dealing. Shrewd, but honest."

Stephen nodded, his narrow face pale. "A respected merchant, not one to get himself involved in political schemes. Or so I would have said before last night."

"And now?" Devlin prompted.

"Last night Soren drew me aside for private speech. He claims to have heard rumors that certain nobles are objecting to your claim to be Chosen One. That if you were the true Chosen One, then the Gods would have given you the Sword of Light."

"Is that all?" Devlin asked.

"Merchant Tyrvald asked me to make sure you knew of this rumor, and that it was likely an attempt to diminish your influence with the commoners," Stephen said. His shoulders slumped as if he had given up some great burden.

Devlin could see that Stephen felt used, but his message was hardly unexpected. "I have heard this tale before," Devlin said. "Over a week ago, it became clear that there was some new rumor circulating through the court. It took only a day before a helpful soul felt compelled to tell me what was being said."

Captain Drakken rubbed her chin thoughtfully. "I wonder who gave this news to the merchant? Lady Vendela's faction would not stoop so low. Or would they?"

Devlin shrugged. "It could be anyone. Even the palace servants have heard the tale, so I am surprised that you had not learned of this before now."

"It is a clever ploy, I will grant you that," Captain Drakken observed. "At the very least, it may cast doubt on your stature. At best, they may succeed in convincing the King to have you search for the sword."

"Thus removing me from the court and from the deliberations of the King's Council," Devlin added. He had expected this rumor to die out, but instead it seemed to be growing stronger with each passing day.

At least there was one mercy. Though he had not voiced it aloud, Devlin was convinced that those who plotted against him had yet another goal in spreading this rumor. They hoped that the Geas that bound him would compel Devlin to seek out the Sword of Light, whether he wished to or not. Some could have argued that such was his duty as Chosen One. But this time the Gods were merciful, and the Geas had not stirred from where it slept at the back of his mind.

"And how do they expect me to search for this sword?" Devlin asked, trying for a mocking tone. "There must have been dozens of copies forged over the years. Now they are scattered around the Kingdom, rotting alongside those that bore them."

"There are no copies," Stephen said. "There was only one Sword of Light. When Lord Saemund perished and the sword was lost, they forged a new sword for the next Chosen One. But it was not a duplicate. The armorer felt it would be impious to make a copy, since the Sword of Light had been forged by a son of Egil."

Devlin snorted in disgust. "They say such things of all great swords. Why not claim the Forge God himself made it?"

"It is what is said," Stephen insisted.

Devlin forbore to argue. Stephen's passion had been

the lore of the past Chosen Ones, and he knew more of their history than any other in the Kingdom. If Devlin objected, Stephen might feel compelled to share more of the sword's supposed history. There might even be a song or two of its forging, which Devlin was in no mood to hear.

Still, the part of Devlin that had once been a metalsmith was intrigued. What had the Sword of Light looked like? Had it been a two-handed great sword? A long sword in the more modern style? Or something entirely different?

"Are there any descriptions or drawings of this sword?" he asked.

"There is a hall of portraits, little visited now, but in there is a portrait of Donalt the Wise. And I seem to recall he is holding the Sword of Light," Captain Drakken said.

"Can you guide us there?" Devlin asked.

"Of course."

Captain Drakken led them from the western wing where Devlin had his offices to the older central block of the palace. The hallways grew progressively narrower, and the stones beneath their feet more worn as they made their way up to the fourth level. They traveled down a corridor, with rooms branching off either side. Through the open doorways Devlin glimpsed marble sculptures, a room filled with decorative porcelains, and another room that held boxes or perhaps furniture hidden beneath white shrouds.

At the end of the corridor, an archway led into a long room that ran the full two-hundred-foot length of the tower. Light streamed in from windows set high up on the three exterior walls. Devlin paused. The wall before him was covered with paintings of various sizes and styles, hung from high above down to the very floor. He turned around slowly and saw that the other three walls were equally covered. A battle scene with life-size figures hung next to a jumbled collection of small portraits. There were gilt frames, tarnished silver frames, and those of plain wood, and the mix of subjects was equally diverse. There seemed no rhyme or reason to their placement.

"Where do we start?" Lieutenant Didrik asked.

Captain Drakken went over to the northern wall. She leaned forward, peering at the pictures as she walked down along the line. Then she straightened up. "Here," she said.

Devlin came over, with Lieutenant Didrik and Stephen following.

Captain Drakken pointed to a medium-sized portrait. "Donalt the Wise."

Donalt, often called the last of the great Chosen Ones, was shown as a man in his middle years, with long blond hair done in a warrior's braid. His features were harsh, and his blue eyes stared directly forward, as if they could see into the viewer's soul. Across his back he wore a baldric. Only the hilt of the sword was visible above his shoulder.

It couldn't be. And yet . . .

Devlin swallowed hard. "Is there a better picture of the sword?"

"My age is beginning to tell, for I had remembered this differently," Captain Drakken said. "Still there must be another portrait in here. We should keep looking."

They split apart, one to each of the four walls. Devlin took the southern wall, the one farthest from the portrait of Donalt. His eyes scanned the pictures, but he was not really seeing them. It could not be, he told himself. His mind was playing tricks.

He craned his neck upward, and then he saw it. A young woman, who bore an unmistakable resemblance to Donalt, held the sword extended in front of her as she fought off an armored warrior. Behind her, crouching next to the uncertain shelter of a boulder, was a young boy. The artist had been truly gifted, for he had managed to capture not only the boy's fear, but also a sense of the woman's fierce determination. One knew that she looked her own death in the face, and that she was not afraid.

But any admiration for the artist's skill was lost when Devlin contemplated the Sword of Light, which had been depicted with equal skill. It was clearly a long sword, with a tapering blade. The grip was unusual, for instead of a single curved crossbar there was a double guard of two straight bars, one longer than the other. And in the pommel was set a stone that shone with red fire.

"The stone is wrong. It should be dark crimson, so dark it seems nearly black," Devlin whispered, though a part of him felt like screaming.

"It is dark," Stephen said, and Devlin jumped. He had not realized that the others had joined him. "The stone glows when the sword is wielded in battle by the Chosen One," Stephen explained.

But Captain Drakken had understood what Stephen had not. "How do you know of the stone's appearance?"

Devlin took a step back from the wall, then another, although his eyes did not leave the painting.

"Because I have held that sword in my hands." He tasted bile and for a brief moment he fought the urge to vomit. But there was no denying the truth of what he saw, or of what he knew.

Devlin had thought the Geas an evil thing, for it replaced his will with its own. But had there ever been a moment when his destiny was his own to command? Or had his feet been set on the path that led him here from the moment he first beheld the sword of the Chosen One?

"How is that possible?" Captain Drakken asked.

Devlin did not answer. He turned on his heel and began to walk away. He needed to get out of here. Quickly. Before he gave in to the urge to smash something.

But he could not flee fast enough to escape his friends. Stephen caught up with him and grabbed his sleeve. "You have seen it? You know where it is?"

Devlin shook his arm free. "The Sword was lost at Ynnis, was it not?"

Stephen nodded. "During the final hours of the siege, when Lord Saemund was killed."

"During the massacre," Devlin corrected. His people had their own memories of Ynnis, and none of them were kind to the Jorskians. Lord Saemund may have been Chosen One, but he deserved to suffer in the Dread Lord's realm for all eternity for what his troops had done. Men, women, and even children had been slaughtered, and those not killed by the soldiers perished in the flames as the army set the city to the torch. Those who survived were too few to bury the dead, and to this day Ynnis remained a ruin, inhabited only by her restless ghosts.

Still, Ynnis had been a small city, and the destruction

there had not befallen the rest of Duncaer. Most Caer-folk, including Devlin, had done their best to put the siege from their minds. The war was long over, and there was no sense in brooding about the past.

But now the past had come back to haunt them.

Devlin ran his left hand through his hair, trying to think of a way to explain. "When I was a boy, my parents apprenticed me to Master Roric, a metalsmith. Like my parents, Master Roric was a survivor of the massacre at Ynnis."

"You say massacre, but that is not how it is recorded," Captain Drakken said.

"I care not what tales you tell, or what the minstrel sings," Devlin said, his clipped tones revealing his anger. "My parents were both children who were lucky to survive, for all their nearkin perished on that day."

His parents had been cared for by other refugees until they reached Alvaren and found shelter with kin so distant they could scarcely even be called farkin. And yet they had taken the children in, raised them, and in time found trades for them. But those who survived Ynnis had a special bond that kept them a closely knit community within the teeming capital city. Kameron and Talaith's friendship had ripened into love, and they had married when they became adults. When it was time to apprentice their youngest son, it was natural that they turn to one of the other survivors of Ynnis.

"Master Roric was already a journeyman smith in Ynnis during the siege. He never spoke of how he managed to survive, or of what he had lost on that day. But he did have one reminder of the battle."

"A sword," Captain Drakken said.

"A sword," Devlin agreed. "A sword so fine it was

surely the work of a great master, made of steel that shimmered in the light, flexible and yet stronger than any blade I have seen before or since."

Master Roric had kept the sword in a chest, for it was both an object of great value and one that seemed to hold painful memories. From time to time he would bring it forth and let the best of his students study it as an encouragement to them in their own craft.

"So you know where the sword is?" Lieutenant Didrik asked.

"No. But I know where it was," Devlin answered.

Three

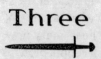

AFTER HIS UNCANNY REVELATIONS, THE CHOSEN One had stalked off, and so plain was his anger that none dared follow. Captain Drakken exchanged a glance with Lieutenant Didrik, who raised his eyebrows, but said nothing.

Only the minstrel Stephen seemed oblivious to the tension. His face was transfixed with wonder as he murmured, "The Sword of Light."

"He has seen the sword," Lieutenant Didrik echoed.

"But what does this mean?" Stephen said.

"It may mean nothing. Only that by some strange twist of fate, the Gods have sent us the one man who can return the sword that was lost," Captain Drakken said, trying to reassure herself as much as the others.

But Devlin had worn the look of a man faced with painful memories, and she did not think he would be able to banish them as swiftly as they had come. And she could not risk this new revelation damaging the frail alliances that they had begun to build in service of the Kingdom.

"Didrik, send word to the watch commanders. I

want every guard to keep an eye for Devlin and let me know when he is found. He may try to slip out of the city quietly, without telling anyone."

"You think he will go after the sword?" Didrik asked.

"I do not know what he will do," she answered honestly. "But I know he is angry now, and that may drive him to some foolish action, perhaps even leaving Kingsholm in the heat of his anger, ill equipped and unprepared for a winter journey."

It took the guards less than an hour to report back that Devlin was in the practice yard, methodically destroying one wooden target after another with his great axe.

Captain Drakken spent the rest of the day busy with her own duties, inspecting the watch at the city gates, meeting with a delegation of merchants from the great square who complained about an outbreak of petty thievery, then approving the watch schedules that Lieutenant Embeth had drawn up. But even as she went about her tasks, a part of her mind kept returning to the Chosen One and the mystery of the Sword of Light. She realized that it was only a matter of time before Devlin would have to go after the sword, for the sake of the Kingdom.

And once his anger cooled, the same thought would occur to him as well.

She worked through the dinner hour and late into the night. Each time she heard footsteps outside her office, she looked up, expecting to see the Chosen One. But he did not come. Finally, in the middle of the night watch, she decided she had let him brood long enough.

Donning her cloak against the night chill, Captain Drakken left the Guard Hall and made her way across the great courtyard to the north tower. The guard on duty at the base of the tower saluted as he saw her approach.

"All quiet?" she asked, returning the salute.

"Yes, Captain. All is at peace," the guard, Behra, said, in the traditional response.

Her eyes glanced upward to the battlements and Behra's glance followed hers. "He is still up there," Behra said.

The guard opened the door to the tower and Captain Drakken made her way inside, then up the narrow circular stairs that led to the battlements. As she opened the door at the top, she was struck by a chill blast of wind. The night air, cold enough in the protected courtyard, was positively glacial up here.

She walked the perimeter battlements until she found Devlin on the south side. He had chosen the most dangerous perch, for he sat on top of the narrow railing. She was reminded of that night over a year and a half ago when she had sought out the new Chosen One and given him his first quest. Then Devlin had been a stranger to her, a tool that had yet to prove its value. His past had been of little interest to her, or to any other in the city.

Now they entrusted him with the safety of the Kingdom. And yet they still knew little of his people, or of Devlin's past. He had volunteered few details, and there had seemed no reason to be concerned. Until now.

The conquest of Duncaer had taken place over fifty years ago, before she had been born. As a novice guard, she had known grizzled veterans who had been young soldiers at the time of the conquest. And though these veterans often boasted of their heroic deeds, they were strangely silent regarding the events at Ynnis.

What she knew of that battle was the history that all children were taught. Ynnis was a small city, located deep in the south of Duncaer. The last free city in Duncaer, it had been doomed from the moment the siege began. The people of Ynnis recognized the futility of their struggle, and with supplies running low, they agreed to surrender the city.

Lord Saemund, the Chosen One, had led his troops into the city, only to discover that the surrender had been a ruse. Without warning, the Caerfolk had attacked. After a bloody struggle the trained soldiers of the Royal Army had won the day, but not before Lord Saemund had been killed. In retaliation his troops had put the city to the torch.

It was not a pretty tale, but armies had been known to do far worse when confronted with the loss of a beloved leader. The accounts she had heard all said that the folk of Ynnis had been allowed to leave their city before it had been destroyed. When pressed for details on the battle, those who had been there had always demurred, claiming that it was too painful to remember the loss of the Chosen One.

There had been no whisper of a massacre in the tales she had heard. Yet it was plain that Devlin had been told a far different story, one that gave him little reason to love those who had conquered his people.

Not for the first time, it occurred to her to wonder if Devlin would still be as eager to serve as Chosen One, were it not for the Geas that bound him to his duty.

Devlin's head turned as he heard her approach. In

the flickering torchlight she saw that his eyes were bleak, and his face shuttered and unreadable.

"You must go after the sword," she said, without preamble.

"I know," Devlin said. "Even now, the Geas tugs at my will. Soon I will not be able to ignore its call."

He turned his face away from her, back to whatever had caught his attention. She wondered what he saw.

"Winter is not far off, but if you start now, you can be well south before the heavy snows. You will need an escort. I can have a squad of guards ready to travel in a day's time, or you can send to the army garrison should you think it more politic."

Devlin shook his head. "There will be enough difficulty over my return to Duncaer as things are. I do not need an armed escort and the trouble it will bring."

"But you cannot travel alone," she argued. Especially not if he was retreating into the darkness that had gripped him when he had first arrived. In that mood, Devlin might well be careless of his life, and the Chosen One was far too valuable to take foolish risks.

"I will take Didrik. And Stephen, if he has lost his taste for the comforts of city life."

It was less than she had hoped, but better than nothing. Lieutenant Didrik was a trained warrior, and the minstrel had proven his courage in the past.

There was a long moment of silence, then Devlin asked, "Do you believe in fate?"

"No," she said firmly. "From the moment we are born, each of us makes our own path and our own luck."

"So I once thought," Devlin said. "Yet there are only a handful of folk who have seen the Sword of Light in the years since Ynnis. It passes all belief that my presence here as Chosen One is mere coincidence."

There was nothing she could say to that.

"Perhaps they were right to name me kinslayer," Devlin added, in tones so low she could scarcely hear him.

"What do you mean?"

Devlin leaned back, swung his legs around so they were on the inside ledge, then stood to face her. "If my family had not been killed, I would still be in Duncaer. I would never have become an exile, never have heard of the Chosen Ones, never been foolish and desperate enough to journey to this place. The Gods wanted a tool to return the Sword of Light." He took a quick breath, his fists clenched by his sides. "Cerrie was killed because she loved me, and because I never would have left Duncaer were she still alive."

"No," Drakken said swiftly. "You must not think that. I do not believe the Gods would be so cruel."

"Then you have more faith in the Gods than I," he replied.

"So what will you do?"

He laughed mirthlessly, and the sound made her flesh crawl, for it was the sound of a man who stood again on the edge of madness. "I have no choice, do I? The Gods set my feet on this path, and now the Geas binds me to their will, regardless of what I think or feel. I will fetch the sword as they command. But one day I will face Lord Haakon, and I will demand a reckoning."

His eyes glittered darkly, and such was his intensity that she had no doubt that in time Devlin *would* demand such a reckoning, regardless of the consequences.

Four

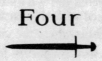

DEVLIN SHIVERED AS THE NORTHERN WIND GUSTED through the battlements, tugging at his cloak, and chilling his exposed flesh. The late-afternoon sky above him was leaden gray, filled with the promise of rain. From the shelter of the southern watchtower the guard eyed Devlin warily, but knew better than to question his presence. The Chosen One had made it clear that he was not to be approached. The battlements were his own private retreat, the one place he could be certain of solitude.

He needed this time to reflect. The past two days had been a blur of activity as he made ready to leave on this quest. Once Devlin would have been able to slip out of the palace unnoticed, but those days were long gone. Now he was a King's councilor and the General of the Royal Army, and neither role could be easily abandoned.

The cold outside was a fitting match for the chill within his soul. Tomorrow he would leave this place and return to his homeland. Yet this thought brought no joy. When he had left Duncaer, he had sworn never to return. Now, less than two years later, the fates had conspired to prove him a liar.

He gazed toward the southwest, his eyes tracing the path as the city of Kingsholm gave way to smaller settlements, interspersed with tidy farms. In the distance there was a darker blur where the cultivated farmland began to give way to forests. And beyond the forests were hills, and that would be but the start of his journey.

It would be a long trek, made worse by the season, for winter was nearly upon them. And there was the knowledge that this effort could all be for naught. He might waste months traveling, only to find that the sword was no longer there.

What would he do then? Would he spend the rest of his life hunting for the cursed object? Could he bear to be in Duncaer and yet not part of it? To his family and friends he was as one already dead. He would be a ghost to them, a walking phantom, his isolation made even more complete by the uniform he wore. The uniform of their conquerors.

He would give anything not to go on this journey. To stay here in Jorsk while someone else went to fetch the sword. But the choice was not his. It had never been his, really, and the bitterness of that knowledge ate away at his soul.

He closed his eyes and leaned back against the wall, feeling the chill of the granite seep into his bones. Lost in silent contemplation, he did not move until he heard the sound of booted footsteps approaching. Devlin opened his eyes, his gaze fixed on the distant horizon as the intruder approached.

"I thought better of you than this. If you leave now

on this fool's errand, all that you have done here will be wasted," Solveig said, coming to stand in front of him and blocking his view. She was dressed in a rabbit-fur cloak, with the hood pulled up over her head against the wind, but there was no mistaking the anger in her gaze.

"How did you find me?" Few people outside of the guards knew his habit of retreating to the battlements when he needed to be alone. Even Stephen had never followed Devlin here, so his sister's presence was a surprise.

"I have been hunting you since morning, when I first learned of this folly. Finally, I went to the Guard Hall and persuaded Captain Drakken to tell me where you could be found. She was reluctant, but I convinced her I needed to see you before you left."

"You have seen me," Devlin replied.

"And I tell you, you must not go. This is a ruse to divert your attention from Kingsholm. We have spent months building our coalition, but without you at its center it will fall apart. The conservatives will dominate the council, and the borderlands will be left on their own. Again."

"I know this," Devlin replied. The trip to Duncaer and back would take four months in good weather, six months if the weather was poor. And there was no telling how long it would take to retrieve the sword once he was there. By the time Devlin returned to the capital, his deeds would be long forgotten, and his influence with the King would be nil.

Besides there was no certainty that he would return at all. It was common knowledge that the borderlands were dangerous places. He might well be walking into an ambush, his death conveniently dismissed as just one more victim of the unrest. Either way, dead or exiled on this fool's errand, his enemies would win.

Solveig threw up her hands in apparent disgust. "Then if you know this, why do you go? Stay here and do what you have sworn to do. Help us strengthen the Kingdom so we are ready for the war that we all know is coming."

If only matters were that simple. If it were his choice, he would let the damn sword rot in Duncaer. He did not need a fabled sword to prove his worth. He had defeated Duke Gerhard and foiled the invasion of Korinth on his own. Holding the Sword of Light would not make him stronger, or wiser, or more brave. Crippled as he was, he could not even use a two-handed sword.

And he had reasons of his own for not wanting to return to his homeland.

But all this meant nothing against the pull of the Geas. Even now he could hear its song in the back of his mind, urging him on. For now the voice was faint, but it was growing in strength. The longer he resisted, the stronger it would grow until he could think of nothing else.

"If I had not volunteered, King Olafur would have ordered me to go after it. He has been looking for any excuse to send me away. You know how much he loathes conflict. He is tired of the bickering of the King's Council, tired of my constantly urging him to decisive action. With me gone, he can follow his own inclinations, no matter that they may lead him to his doom."

"You may have given up, but I will not. We will go to the King and convince him that this is madness. The sword has been lost these fifty years; there is no reason to look for it now. You could spend the rest of your life hunting it."

Devlin hesitated, wondering how much to tell her, then decided she deserved to know the truth. Solveig was a staunch ally whose advice had served him well in the murky realm of court politics. She needed to know that this was not some foolish whim.

"If the sword were truly lost, then I would indeed stay here and refuse even the King's orders to leave. But the sword is not lost. I have seen it, though I did not know what it was at the time. Only yourself, Captain Drakken, Stephen, and Didrik know this truth. The rest believe that I am off on a fool's errand, which may be our only protection, for my enemies dare not let me succeed."

"You have seen the sword? How can that be?"

"When I was learning my craft as a smith, I had the chance to study a sword that had been wrought with great cunning. I spent hours studying the design, and marveling at the composition of the steel. I did not know that it was the Sword of Light, of course. Neither did the man who owned it. All he knew was that this was the sword that had killed his brother, and yet it was too beautiful for him to destroy." Devlin swallowed against the bitterness that rose up in his throat. "I had long forgotten the sword until Captain Drakken showed me the portrait of Donalt the Wise. And from that moment, I have been fighting the Geas that urges me to seek out the sword that belongs to the Chosen One. So you see, it does not matter what you say, or the council, or even the King. I have fought off its bidding for two days, but I can delay no longer. We leave tomorrow at dawn."

Solveig's pale blue eyes widened in comprehension, and he turned his head away, unable to face the pity he saw there.

"If you are determined to go, you must take great care. Stephen told me he is to accompany you, and Lieutenant Didrik, but he would not say anything else about the arrangements. How large is your escort?"

"None. There will be enough difficulty over my return as it is. I do not need to add to that by bringing along a company of soldiers."

Difficulty was a mild word for his troubles. Devlin had left Duncaer under a cloud of suspicion so black that even his friends and kinfolk had turned their faces from him. Now he was returning, having sworn an oath to protect the very Kingdom that had conquered his people. They would call him traitor and kinslayer. And these were the very folk he must convince to turn over the Sword of Light.

"But you must take an escort. Here in the city the guards can protect you. But once on the road, there are many dangers to fear. Once you are dead, what does it matter if it was the work of common bandits or hired assassins? The result is the same and we cannot afford to lose you."

He knew her true concern was not for his safety but for that of her youngest sibling, and offered what assurance he could. "If we are attacked, I will do my best to protect Stephen. But I can make no promises. Not for his safety, nor for my own."

He was silent as he considered yet again whether he should refuse to let Stephen accompany him on this trip. For all his courage, Stephen was a minstrel, not a warrior. And he was young both in years and in experience, possessing an innocence that Devlin himself had lost years ago. But Stephen was also a friend, and had proven himself stubborn. If he forbid Stephen to go with him, no doubt the minstrel would simply follow on his own.

"A small party can elude ambush far better than a large one," Devlin said. "And there may not be any trouble. My enemies have already accomplished their aim by sending me on this quest. It will take nearly two months to reach Duncaer, and once there I must find the sword. The man who owned it has since died, and the sword may have changed hands many times since. I will be lucky to make it back in time for the spring council."

"And without your prodding, the council will revert to their old habits. They will bicker among themselves and take no action to shore up the Kingdom's defenses. Your influence will wane as your allies find themselves outnumbered and outvoted."

His enemies did not need to kill Devlin. Simply getting him out of the capital would be enough to serve their ends. Devlin's power and influence were newly acquired, and could be lost just as easily as they had been gained. By the time he returned, no doubt King Olafur would have found another chief advisor, and Devlin would once again be relegated to the position of useless spectator.

"The King has agreed that Lord Rikard may hold my seat on the council, but he is not allowed a vote," Devlin said. Even this concession had taken him hours to achieve. Lord Rikard had not been his first choice, but the King had flatly refused to consider Solveig. True she was the heir to a Baron, but many considered that her family already had too much influence over court politics through their friendship with Devlin.

"Rikard is a good man, but his hot temper may do more harm than good," Solveig observed.

"Rikard has promised to restrain himself." As a border noble himself, his insights would balance those of the more conservative members. Still, it was an imperfect solution at best. Rikard would have only his eloquence to sway the council. And a great deal could happen in four months time.

"You should delay this. Find some way to stay until springtime, until we are certain that the threat of invasion is gone. Then it would be safe for you to travel, and in fair weather your journey would be much faster," Solveig said. "What of Master Dreng? Can he not ease the Geas spell so you can remain?"

"The spell is beyond his talents," Devlin said.

Ever since the fateful duel, Master Dreng had been experimenting on ways to lift the Geas that bound Devlin's will. He had gone so far as to ensorcel dogs with a lesser version of the spell, then try his skills at breaking it. Three dogs had died in his tests, and when Devlin had learned of this, he had forbidden any more experiments. The dumb beasts did not deserve such a fate. No creature did.

"The spell may be beyond his ken, but perhaps someone schooled in a different form of magic may hold the key to understanding this spell. My mother has family in Selvarat, and could find a trustworthy sorcerer."

"No," Devlin said, instinctively rejecting the offer. It

was enough that his friends knew of the Geas spell, and how it bound him like a witless slave. He did not need to share his shame with strangers.

"No, I thank you, but I do not need their help," Devlin repeated. "I will endure as I must, as those before me have done."

The wind strengthened, bringing with it the first drops of rain. Fat drops darkened the stone railing, and he could see beads of moisture on the fur of Solveig's cloak.

"It is late and there is nothing more to be said here. Go to Stephen, he would welcome your company," Devlin said.

Solveig nodded, then stepped forward and embraced him as if he were one of her brothers. He returned her embrace awkwardly. "I wish you safe journey and a swift return," she said.

Then she released him and, turning, made her way across the narrow walkway to the guard tower. He watched as she departed, then he began to walk in the opposite direction. He greeted each of the guards on sentry by name, urging them to remain alert. It was foolish, he supposed, but he needed one last inspection, to reassure himself that the palace was as safe as he could make it. When he had completed the circuit round the battlements, he could delay no longer, and reluctantly he went inside, to face those that waited for him within.

As he turned down the corridor that led to his quarters, Devlin was surprised to see a guard standing watch outside his door. As he drew near, he recognized Signy, one of those who had journeyed with him to Korinth that spring. She saluted, thumping her shoulder with her right hand. "Chosen One," she said, nodding in respect.

He noticed that she wore the short sword of one on city patrol instead of the spear that was used for strictly ceremonial duties.

"Signy. To what do I owe this honor?"

"Lieutenant Didrik assigned me to this post, with orders to keep the corridor free from distractions," she replied.

"And have there been many of these distractions?"

"A few," she answered, a faint grin ghosting across her features. "It took them a bit to realize that I was serious, but the sword helped."

Devlin chuckled, wishing that he had been there. No doubt the courtiers and their lackeys had been surprised by her enthusiasm for carrying out her orders. In many ways the guards considered him one of their own, and they protected him zealously. He was grateful that her presence had spared him from having to waste these last few hours dealing with fools who would merely irritate him with their demands.

"Lieutenant Didrik is within," she added.

"See that we are not disturbed."

"As you command," she said, then opened the door for him.

Devlin entered the outer chamber and closed the door behind him.

Didrik was sitting at the table, his pen scratching across parchment. There was a stack of neatly folded missives before him and a jumble of scrolls piled in a basket to the side. "I was beginning to think you had left on your own," he said. His tone was light but his eyes betrayed his worry.

"I needed time to think," Devlin said, stripping off his gloves, then unfastening his rain-sodden cloak. He hung the cloak next to the fire and placed the leather gloves on specially designed hooks so they would dry out before the morning. He stood in front of the fire, rubbing his hands together, watching as the pale flesh grew pink once more and feeling the chill begin to leave his bones.

He indulged himself for a moment, savoring the warmth, and turned to face his aide.

"The sentry was a good idea."

"There have been messengers here all afternoon," Didrik said, waving his right hand at the wicker basket, which held at least two dozen ribbon-bound scrolls.

"Anything of importance?"

Didrik shook his head. "I haven't had time to read them all, but I can guess what they say. They profess good wishes for your journey and offer useless advice. Your allies hope you return swiftly and in triumph. Your enemies are pleased to see you go, and urge you to great diligence in your search, meaning that they hope you will stay away and never return. The fence sitters send their wishes for your success, so they will be remembered as your friends should you actually succeed."

"Dispose of them as you see fit," Devlin said. He felt no urge to read the letters himself. After four months as Devlin's personal aide, Didrik had developed an instinctive sense about what was important and what was not.

Devlin glanced through the open door that led to his

sleeping chamber. At the foot of his bed there were two full saddlebags, and a third one lay open on top of the banded wooden trunk, waiting for him to add any last-minute items.

"Are all the arrangements made?" he asked.

"Yes. A coach with the royal crest and a baggage cart will depart at the third hour past dawn, and leave the city through the south gate. There will be an escort of six riders from the Royal Army, who will accompany the coach as far as Denvir."

"And the others? The horses are at the stable behind the Singing Fish?"

"Yes. Stephen will meet us there at the first hour before sunrise."

"Good." The carriage was a ruse, meant to deceive anyone who might be watching and planning a potential ambush. While all eyes were on the palace, Devlin and his friends would already have left the city through the eastern gate. They would travel lightly, forgoing their uniforms to pass as simple travelers. Hopefully this would throw any would-be ambushers off their trail.

It was a child's trick, yet that was the very virtue of the plan. With luck, no one would suspect him of trying such an obvious ploy. Every league that they traveled undetected increased the difficulties that their enemies would have in picking up their trail. At worst they would gain several hours head start. At best, they might lose their shadowers altogether.

Unless his enemies had decided there was no reason to shadow him. Devlin was doing exactly as they wished, after all. They might well be content simply to see him leave.

Didrik finished writing and put his pen in the metal holder before slipping the paper from the wooden frame. Then he placed this final sheet on top of the stack of similar papers to his left.

"You need to sign these orders," he said.

Devlin bit back a sigh. Before becoming a general, he had naively imagined that the head of the Royal Army spent his days preparing for combat and inspecting fortifications. But in his brief tenure he had come to realize that paperwork was the bane of the army's existence, and all of it seemed to end up on his desk. In many ways, he was nothing more than a glorified clerk.

He took his own seat across the table, and Didrik slid the stack of papers to him. Picking up the pen with his left hand, he dipped it in the inkwell and positioned it carefully between the two good fingers of his crippled right hand. He swiftly scanned the text before scrawling his name across the bottom. He passed the signed document back to Didrik, who folded it and sealed it with the crest that proclaimed it came from the General of the Royal Army.

There were a dozen orders in all, dealing with everything from ordering supplies for the western garrison to a proclamation encouraging young men and women to enlist in the Royal Army, to serve their country in this time of unrest.

"There is one more," Didrik said, holding up a sheet he had set aside. "Have you decided on naming Major Mikkelson as acting Marshal?"

Devlin shook his head. "I wish I could, but you were right. He is too new to his rank, and the other commanders will not follow a man who was a mere Ensign only six months before."

The officer corps of the Royal Army had long been a place of political patronage, where family connections and noble ancestors were far more important to advancement than military skill. Devlin was trying to change that, but there was a limit to how swiftly he could shake up the army and still expect it to follow him.

"And I need Mikkelson in Korinth. I am convinced that the invasion this summer was but a test of our readiness. There were too few troops for them seriously to expect to succeed. If a real attack is to occur, it will be in the spring. The Major will have his hands full this winter drilling his soldiers and strengthening the coastal defenses."

"Then who shall it be?"

"Garrison Commander Erild Olvarrson. He has the seniority, and seventeen generations of nobility behind him. The other commanders will follow his lead."

If Erild Olvarrson had a fault, it was his complete lack of initiative. But for that reason he could be counted on to preserve the status quo. He would make no bold moves to strengthen the Kingdom's defenses, but neither would he meddle with the reforms that Devlin had already put in place.

"And his wife is from Ringstadt, so if the invasion comes there, hopefully he will be moved to defend her home and will release the troops from their garrisons," Didrik added.

"There is that," Devlin said. "Though with luck we will be back before the spring."

He had to believe that, for the alternative was to believe that he was deserting the people he had sworn to protect, leaving them undefended in their time of peril.

He vowed that he would find the damn sword and return in time to lead the defense of Jorsk against any that dared to disturb the peace.

Devlin took the order and filled in Erild Olvarrson's name at the top, designating him as acting head of the Royal Army in Devlin's absence. Then he signed the order, folded it in thirds, and stamped it with the wax seal.

"There," he said. "Anything not done is now Olvarrson's headache, not ours."

"Do you need me for anything else?"

"No, you should go now. You have your own preparations to make and good-byes to say."

Didrik rose. "I have left orders with the night sentry to wake us at the second hour before dawn," he said.

"I will see you then," Devlin said.

After Didrik left, Devlin ate a solitary dinner, his thoughts already far from this place. Now that the moment had come, he was impatient to leave. A chamberman cleared away the remnants of the meal, leaving behind a bottle of a rare Myrkan wine, a gift from Lord Rikard. Devlin ignored the wine and instead checked his baggage one last time, to ensure that he had everything he would need for the journey.

He knew his caution was excessive. After all, he was no longer a poor traveler. He had a generous purse for expenses, and as the Chosen One he could requisition whatever he needed. The Royal treasury would be duty-bound to reimburse those who had the dubious honor to receive his requests. But still old habits died hard, and where possible he preferred to be self-sufficient rather than depend on others.

Assured that everything was as it should be, Devlin turned at last to his weapons. He took the great axe from its leather case and inspected it. True to its forging, he found the edge sharp and the metal free from corrosion, so he merely oiled the steel before returning it to the case.

His throwing knives were next, and though he had cleaned them only a week before after practicing, he still inspected each blade before replacing it in the leather roll. The two forearm sheaths were another matter. He put one on his wardrobe, to be donned in the morning. But as to the other ... He turned it over in his hand, wondering if he was deluding himself. He had lost none of his skill with his left hand, but his crippled right hand no longer threw truly. He might never regain the skill in that arm, and it was foolish to drag along something that he did not need. He knew that, and yet he found himself tucking the second sheath in his open saddlebag.

Finally, he turned his attention to the long sword that hung in a place of honor on his wall. This was the sword given to him by Captain Drakken, the sword that had ended the life of the traitorous Duke Gerhard. It had served him well, and yet if he was successful, he would replace it with a blade of more dubious lineage.

He took the sword down from the wall and drew it from its scabbard. Crossing to the workbench, he turned the blade over in the bright lamplight, then ran the fingertips of his left hand over the blade. As he had suspected, there were several nicks in the edge of the steel, reminders of how poorly his last practice bout had gone. Placing the blade so the edge hung over the table, he used his right forearm to hold the blade steady as he ran the sharpening stone along it with his left. The rhythm of the work soothed him, reminding him of a simpler time when his ambition had extended no further than the walls of his smithy.

A knock on the door roused him from his thoughts, and he looked up to see Signy standing at the door.

"Brother Arni begs a moment of your time, sir," she said.

Devlin nodded, putting down the sharpening stone, and rose to his feet.

As Brother Arni appeared in the doorway, Devlin saw that the priest was wearing the elaborate gold-stitched robe that was reserved for the high feast days.

"Enter and be welcome," Devlin said, in formal greeting.

"I know it is late, Chosen One, but I could not retire until I knew your wishes," Brother Arni said, with a nervous jerk of his head. "I have been waiting this day to bless you for your journey. When you did not come, I began to think that maybe you planned to attend the dawn services, but I wished to be certain. I had sent you a message but there was no reply . . ."

"I see." No doubt Brother Arni's missive was among those scrolls he had so callously discarded.

"I thank you for your consideration," Devlin said, choosing his words carefully. This man had helped save his life and he owed him his respect. But he would not lie to him and pretend to a piety he did not feel.

"Then I will see you at the dawn service? I know the people of the palace will be glad to join you in requesting the blessing of the Gods."

Devlin felt his mouth twist; he wanted no part of this. "I will ask for no blessing. Pray for me if you must, but I will not speak to your Gods."

Brother Arni's brow wrinkled in apparent puzzlement. "But they are your Gods, as well. The Gods of both our peoples. You swore your service in the name of Lord Kanjti."

Devlin felt the bitterness well up inside him and he could not remain still. Crossing over to the sideboard, he picked up the bottle of wine and pulled out the stopper.

"Will you take wine?" He did not wait for an answer, but poured two goblets, then carried one over to the priest before taking his own and settling in a chair near the fire.

Brother Arni sat gingerly in the opposite chair and took one sip of his wine before setting the goblet aside.

Devlin took a long draught of his own.

"I bear you no ill-will," Devlin said. "I respect you, and am grateful for the aid you have given me. But I will not beg the Gods for favors. I have had enough of their interference in my life. Do I make myself plain?"

"I do not understand."

Devlin drained his goblet, the fine vintage tasting like so much vinegar water. Then he set the goblet aside and ran his left hand through his hair as he gathered his thoughts.

"Brother, tell me. Do you think the Gods favor your Kingdom above all others? Is there some reason they hold Jorsk in such high regard?"

This was the question that had haunted him since he first beheld that damning portrait and realized that he had known all along where the mythical Sword of Light could be found. The moment he realized the strange trick that destiny had played upon him.

The moment that he had realized that he had been

truly cursed by the Gods, made a mere pawn in their games.

Brother Arni did not hesitate in his response. "The Seven offer their blessings to all those who honor them, and who strive to live just lives. No one country has the exclusive claim to their favor, though there are some that have turned their face from them and suffer accordingly."

"So I once thought," Devlin said. "But you also believe that the Chosen One is sent by the Gods, do you not?"

"Of course. Though there were doubters when you were first called to serve, those of weak faith soon learned the error of doubting the Gods' choices."

The priest beamed happily at this reminder of how his faith in the Gods he served had been proven to all.

"I did not think myself God-touched," Devlin said softly, his gaze on the flickering flames. "I became the Chosen One because I needed the coins, and I wanted to die. It was only later that I came to realize that my life still had purpose, and that there were those I could protect with my service."

"Your heart was always good, even when your mind was confused," Brother Arni said. "The Gods knew this, and this is why they called you."

"Is it? The Gods have no interest in my heart. They did not call me so I could use my strength and wits to protect the innocent. They chose me so I could fetch the damn sword that your people so carelessly lost."

"I do not understand," Brother Arni said.

Of course he did not. The priest saw only the light and missed the dark shadows that it cast. To him being Chosen One was a glorious calling. He had no idea of how the Gods had twisted the lives of Devlin and his family, to bring him to this point.

Angry words trembled on the tip of his tongue, but he swallowed hard and forced them back. This man was not his enemy. Brother Arni was not responsible for what had happened to Devlin. It was not his fault that the Gods he served were undeserving of his faith.

Brother Arni stared searchingly at him for a moment, then sighed. "I will pray for you," he said.

"You will do as you must, and I will do the same."

Five

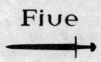

THEY LEFT KINGSHOLM AT DAWN. IN AN ATTEMPT to throw off any watchers, there were no well-wishers, nor ceremony to mark their leaving. Even the guards at the eastern gate had been warned to forgo the formal salute, letting Devlin's party blend with the other travelers hastening to return to their homes before winter set in.

Nils Didrik flexed his hands within their leather riding gloves, trying to keep them warm and limber. He could feel winter's approach as a palpable presence. Gray clouds overhead threatened rain, while the paving stones beneath the horses hooves were rimed with frost. It seemed a poor omen for the start of the journey. All too soon those same clouds would bring snow and ice, and then where would they be?

The frosty weather was matched by the icy silence of their party. Devlin had said scarce a dozen words as they readied themselves for departure, and nothing since. Even the normally cheerful Stephen had forgone his usual chatter in deference to Devlin's grim mood.

By contrast, even at this hour the streets were

crowded and noisy. Farmers called greetings to one another as they pulled handcarts or drove laden wagons carrying the last of their harvest in to sell at the market in Kingsholm. Day laborers who lived outside the city walls chattered among themselves as they made their way to their jobs within the city. Against this tide a small but steady stream of travelers headed east. Traders who planned on wintering in the provinces, bearing goods from the capital. Brightly dressed messengers on fine horses, carrying noble correspondence. Perhaps even a courtier or two, who had tarried overlong in the capital and now sought to return home before the first snows.

Didrik scanned the crowd ahead of him, but could see nothing unusual. He glanced behind, and saw Stephen following a few lengths back, leading their packhorse. Everything seemed just as it should be, and yet he could not shake his feeling of unease.

He took a deep breath and willed himself to calmness. They were still in sight of the outer walls, where safety should be assured. There was no reason for fear.

And yet he could not help but be afraid. Until last spring he had never been farther than a dozen leagues from Kingsholm. Now he was expected to journey across the length of the kingdom to the wilds of Duncaer. A place where the natives spoke their own tongue and held to their own customs, and danger might well come in a guise that he would not recognize until it was too late.

Last spring he'd had a squad of trusted guards with him, along with Ensign Mikkelson and the dubious protection of the Royal Army. There had been two dozen blades to keep the Chosen One safe, and even then they had nearly failed. Now there was just himself.

For while no one could doubt Stephen's courage, at heart he was a minstrel. He lacked the instincts of one trained to detect danger or sense the mood of a hostile crowd. Stephen could hold his own in a fight, but he could be taken off guard by a stealthy attack.

And then there was Devlin. Devlin had the instincts of a warrior and an ingrained caution that had saved his life on more than one occasion. But that was before the duel had left Devlin with a crippled hand. And before the discovery of that cursed painting, which had plunged Devlin into a mood of black despair. Now, if an assassin struck, Devlin might well choose to embrace death again.

It was Didrik's duty to keep Devlin safe, in spite of the Chosen One's inclinations. It was a task he would entrust to no other, and yet at the same time he could not help wishing that he had been permitted to bring just one trusted guard. Someone to watch their backs. Even the greatest of warriors needed to sleep.

"We are being followed," Devlin said, breaking into Didrik's musings. "I count three in their number. One riding before us, and a pair of farmers driving a cart behind."

Devlin reined his horse to a halt, and Didrik drew his horse up alongside. He turned to peer through the crowded streets behind them. He could see the wagon but not the driver, so he stood up in the stirrups. After a moment, the crowd parted, and the driver came into view.

"The rider in front of us is Behra. I recognized his build, and his miserable seat on a horse. But who are the pair behind us? Yours? Or someone else's?" Devlin asked. There was only mild curiosity in his tone, but Didrik knew he was in trouble.

At least there was nothing wrong with Devlin's observational skills.

"They are ours."

Stephen drew up alongside them, and Devlin gestured for him to ride on ahead.

"I ordered that we were to have no escort," Devlin said. "Did I fail to make myself clear? Or have you decided that you need no longer heed my commands?"

Didrik swallowed hard. "They are not an escort. Their orders are to follow us for today, and to try and spot if anyone else is paying undue attention to our passing. If all is well, tomorrow they will return to the capital."

"Whose idea was this?"

"Mine," Didrik said. He knew better than to lie to the Chosen One. "Captain Drakken approved. As a precaution, nothing more."

Devlin shook his head. "If I can spot the watchers, then so can others. And as for the risk, if someone is following us, they will not be so foolish as to strike here, where we are still within sight of Kingsholm's walls."

"They can't attack if they can't find us," Didrik argued. "And the more distance we put between us and Kingsholm, the harder it will be to pick up our trail."

"If they lose our trail, they need only to journey to Duncaer. There are only a few passes that lead into the mountains. If they set watchers on them all, they will find us easily enough. They won't attack while we are in your country."

Would that he shared Devlin's confidence.

"Why not?"

"This expedition is a gift to my enemies, getting me out of their way without their having to shed a single drop of blood. I am far more use to them as a living fool, off on a useless quest. Dead, I could be turned into a martyr. They will not risk killing me. Not while we are still close enough for news to reach the capital."

"And when we reach your homeland?"

"Duncaer is a different matter," Devlin said. His eyes sought out the figure of Stephen, who now rode before them. "As a lore teller, Stephen's life is sacred to the Caerfolk. But you and I will have to be vigilant. Should I regain the sword, then we will face the greatest danger. There will be many of your people and my own who do not wish to see the Sword of Light returned to Jorsk."

It was something he had not considered. Didrik had thought only of getting to Duncaer and finding the lost sword. He knew full well that Devlin had made enemies both within Jorsk and among those countries that sought to conquer her. Now it seemed that Devlin would have enemies in his own land as well.

"Is there anything else you have forgotten to tell me? For if I find you have deceived me—" Devlin began.

"No," Didrik said firmly. "I swear by my oath that there is no deception. I set the watchers to guard our departure, but that is all. The rest you know."

Devlin's eyes searched his, and Didrik forced himself to return the gaze calmly. Then Devlin nodded once, and Didrik knew he had been reprieved.

"Cross my will again, and I will leave you behind," Devlin promised.

"I understand," Didrik said. But he knew better than to promise that he would never disobey one of Devlin's orders. In the end, the Chosen One's safety was his responsibility. It was up to him to protect Devlin—even from himself.

Didrik's fears proved unfounded, for the first day of the journey passed without incident, and the guards were sent back to the capital. He remained alert, but as the days passed, he realized that there was no sign that anyone was following them. Though this did not mean that they were safe from danger. On the contrary, messengers could have been sent ahead to arrange an ambush. Still, the Chosen One was likely correct when he said that any trouble would come once they were far from Kingsholm.

Devlin remained aloof, speaking to Didrik only when the journey required he do so. At first he suspected that Devlin had not forgiven him for ignoring his orders about the escort, but then Didrik noticed that he treated Stephen with the same coldness. Though it was difficult to tell if Stephen minded, for he was invariably cheerful.

Unlike their last journey, Devlin did not insist on pressing on after sunset, or leaving before dawn. But still there was an underlying sense of urgency, and regardless of the weather, they started each day's ride at dawn and seldom stopped before sunset.

The early stages of the journey took them along the great southern highway, a well-traveled road where even the smallest of villages boasted an inn to host travelers. In the larger towns, the innkeepers took Devlin's presence in stride, being used to noble guests. But in the small villages the Chosen One was an unexpected novelty, and the innkeepers strove to offer their very best to such a famous lord. It became Didrik's lot to try to convince them that Devlin appreciated simple fare and an absence of ceremony.

However, on this day driving rain had slowed their progress, and as night fell they made camp in a small clearing a stone's throw from the road. With no moon to see by, it was too dangerous to continue in the dark. Didrik watered the horses at a small stream and set out grain for them while Stephen and Devlin set up the tent. After some struggling Devlin managed to light a small fire at the edge of the tree line and boiled water so they could have hot kava to wash down the dried meat and cheese.

Once the rain had stopped, they sat around the fire as they ate.

Stephen leaned back against a tree, his feet stretched toward the fire. In his right hand he held a chunk of cheese, which he peered at with vague dismay before sighing and taking a bite.

"The inns are making you soft," Didrik said, not bothering to hide his smile. "You've forgotten what it is like to travel rough."

Not that Didrik had been able to muster any enthusiasm for the cold meal, but he had eaten his rations without complaint. As had Devlin. Indeed it struck him that he couldn't recall hearing Devlin complain about food. Ever.

Devlin was known to obsess about ale from Duncaer, and to despise most wines. But if he found Jorskian food as strange as its drink, he had never said so.

"I have traveled in rougher conditions than this," Stephen said. "And last spring, when we journeyed to

Korinth, you did not hear me complaining. I even ate Olga's cooking, which was enough to try any man."

Didrik swallowed reflexively, as he remembered the strange, greasy, half-raw and half-charred meal. The rules of their expedition had said that each member should take their turn at cooking, but Olga was living proof why there should be exceptions to every rule.

"But I see no harm in staying in inns when providence has placed them in our path. Nor in preferring a hot meal over a cold one," Stephen continued.

Devlin spoke for the first time. "Here, at least we have peace. No gawkers come to stare, no hovering inn servants who hang on your every word until one can scarcely think."

"You cannot blame them. How often does a town get to play host to a hero?" Stephen asked.

Didrik winced, knowing how little Devlin wished to be reminded of his heroics.

"And for that I have your brethren to blame," Devlin said. "If I hear one more child singing how Haakon's hand steadied the blade . . ."

"I had nothing to do with that," Stephen said, throwing up his hands. "The song is badly written. The rhyme barely scans, though the tune is catchy enough. If I had written a song about the duel—"

"I've heard your song making," Devlin said, a ghost of a smile on his lips. "What were those words? The heart of a wolf? The courage of a she-lion?"

Stephen flushed and ducked his head. "I have written better."

"And you will write more. But not about me." He turned to Didrik, and asked, "How many leagues do you think we made today? Four?"

"Closer to five," Didrik said. Being a royal highway, the Southern Road was paved stone, which was a boon to travelers. Even rain had not slowed them down too much, for they had planned to journey six leagues today, and managed nearly five. The real test would come ahead, when they left the royal highway for packed-dirt roads. Rain would turn the roads to mud, and a cold snap would freeze the muddy ruts into icy puddles that would require great care on the part of both horse and rider.

But those were worries for another day. For now, his duty was plain.

"I'll turn in now," Didrik said. "Stephen, wake me for second watch?"

"I could take second watch this night. You do not always have to do so," Stephen said.

"I am trained for it," Didrik said. Keeping watch was hard when there were only three members of the party. On a long journey, without resting in daylight, the shortened nights would begin to wear on travelers, making them fatigued and prone to ill judgment. They did not keep watch when they stayed in inns, but Didrik was too much of a city dweller to be comfortable camping outside. There were dangers to be found in the wild places; robbers that preyed upon travelers as well as creatures that bore no love for man. It was only prudent to make sure that they could not be taken by surprise, and Devlin agreed.

Already they had established a routine. Stephen took the first watch, which was generally the easiest. The second watch was the hardest, for the watcher had to make do with a couple hours of sleep, followed by wakefulness, then another short nap before he was expected to rise and travel. Fortunately, Didrik's years in the Guard had made him accustomed to night watches and snatching sleep when and where he could.

And Devlin claimed the last watch, in the dark hours before morning when all was still. He claimed to prefer it, or perhaps he simply enjoyed the solitude, of being awake when all others were at rest.

Didrik ducked into the low tent, sat on his blankets to remove his boots, and placed his sword so it would be close at hand. Then he rolled himself in his blanket, which had already been set out. He heard the ring of metal as two cups clanked together, and someone put the remnants of their meal away.

As he settled himself in to sleep, he heard Stephen's voice.

"Devlin, will you answer a question for me?"

There was a long moment of silence, then the sound of someone settling back down on the ground.

"Ask, and I will see."

"When I was a boy, I learned the history of the conquest of Duncaer, and memorized the songs that had been handed down. I never questioned them. Not until now."

Stephen's voice was soft, almost meditative, and Didrik had to strain his ears.

"And?" Devlin's voice was sharp.

"You tell us this will be a difficult journey, which makes me wonder how Prince Thorvald and Lord Saemund managed to lead an entire army across the border into the mountains without being seriously challenged. And how is it that your people surrendered so quickly? Only Ynnis seems to have fought back. The more I think on it, the less I can make sense of it. You would not have given up so easily."

"You should not judge a people by one man," Devlin replied.

"Perhaps. But the Caerfolk tell a different tale of the conquest. Don't they?"

"Yes."

"Will you tell it to me? Or must I wait till Duncaer to hear it from a stranger?"

There was another long silence, and just as Didrik was convinced that Devlin was not going to answer, he finally spoke.

"We govern ourselves differently than you do. Or rather we did." Devlin's voice was soft and melodic. "The leaders from the high families assembled once every seven years to elect one of their numbers as the ruler overall. In those days, the Queen was Ysobel, she of the white shoulders. Ysobel's family had waited long to see one of their own named as High Queen. They enjoyed their newfound prominence, but Ysobel ruled wisely enough, and at the end of seven years, she was chosen again. This time it seemed to go to her head, and as she flaunted her power, she made many enemies. When the end of her second term approached, all knew that she would not be chosen again."

"And then the invasion happened," Stephen said.

"Then Ysobel invited the army in," Devlin countered. "She called it a peaceful delegation, come to talk about a joint expedition to cross the Endless Mountains and explore the fabled lands beyond. The residents of Alvaren decorated the gates and opened their doors, only to realize too late that they had welcomed in an invading force. Ysobel welcomed her new allies, and ordered the Caerfolk to surrender to their new masters. The lowlands fell swiftly, for the river proved no barrier to the army. The mountain folk resisted longer. Ynnis was in the south and got news of the invaders before they arrived. They resisted, and you know of their fate."

"But surely there was a resistance? What of the people who fled the invaders or journeyed into the mountains? Surely Ynnis wasn't the only city to fight."

"The army had secured the borders, and as their troops poured in to occupy the towns and cities, most surrendered. And as for the resistance, we had far better things to do. The Jorskians may have invaded, but all knew that the true blame lay with Ysobel."

"What happened?"

"She was assassinated less than a week after she welcomed Prince Thorvald into Alvaren. The high families called blood feud on her kin, and chaos ensued. We had no time to fight the Jorskians, for we were too busy murdering each other. It took years, but today there is no one left alive who claims Ysobel as kin."

"No one?" Stephen's voice rose in astonishment.

"Not nearkin, nor farkin, not even unto her cousin's cousin's children. All slain, from the eldest to the least. Many of the high families lost their own kin in the feud. Hundreds killed, on both sides. And now there are six high families instead of seven."

Didrik shivered in his blanket. Such bloody vengeance was beyond anything he had ever imagined. To carry out such a feud over so many years would take implacable hatred and unwavering determination. He shivered again as he realized that Devlin was fully capable of such vengeance. Already Devlin had ruthlessly sacrificed his own hand in order to strike at his enemy.

One such man would be dangerous. A province filled with people who shared Devlin's beliefs would be a nightmare. And yet it was to this place they must go.

He wondered what other surprises Duncaer had in store for him.

Six

Stephen appeared shocked by the story of how Ysobel had met her doom, for he asked no more questions. Devlin finished his kava in silence, then bade him good night. He crawled through the narrow opening into the low tent and wrapped himself in his bedroll, but sleep proved elusive. Instead he listened to the soft sound of Didrik's breathing and the low crackle of the fire as Stephen tended it. It seemed he had only just fallen asleep when he was disturbed by Stephen rousing Didrik to take his watch. And though Stephen fell asleep readily enough, Devlin could not.

He tried to will himself to sleep, but such a feat was impossible, and he gave up in frustration. He sat up, and with slow movements so as not to wake Stephen, he put his boots back on, then his cloak. Picking up his axe with his left hand, he crawled out of the tent.

Didrik's eyes widened as Devlin emerged.

"Your watch isn't for hours," he said. Though the stars were covered by clouds, Didrik's years in the Guard had given him a keen sense of passing time, even when neither sun nor stars could be seen.

"I could not sleep," Devlin said. "No sense in two of us being wakeful, so you should get what rest you can."

Didrik frowned and opened his mouth as if he was about to object, then apparently reconsidered.

"Stephen said the horses were restless earlier. They may have scented a wolf on the wind," Didrik said, his voice carefully neutral. "And a short time ago I heard an animal moving through the brush. A deer, perhaps."

More likely it was nothing more than a brown digger waddling back to its den after an evening of foraging. In the marketplace Didrik could pick a cutpurse out of a crowd with a single glance, but his woods-knowledge left much to be desired. And on a night like tonight, with the gusting breeze swirling the fallen leaves, it would be difficult to pick one sound out of many.

"Wake me if you feel tired," Didrik said mildly.

"I will," Devlin promised, though he knew he would not wake him no matter how tired he became.

He waited until Didrik had settled himself to sleep, then rose and paced the perimeter of the camp. The clearing was small, barely a hundred paces wide, bounded by the road on one side and surrounded by trees on the other three sides. The tent and fire had been set up at the edge of the tree line, where the trees would provide shelter if it rained. The horses had been tethered in the center of the clearing, where they could graze on the stubby grass if so inclined.

All seemed quiet, and though he strained his eyes and ears, he detected nothing amiss. He returned to the fallen log they had placed near the campfire and propped his axe against it. As he sat down, he positioned himself so that he had a view of the road, with his back to the fire. On a night like tonight it would be far too easy to lose himself by gazing into the flickering flames.

An hour passed, then another. When his muscles grew stiff with cold, he rose and repeated his circuit of the camp. It felt wrong to be sitting here idle, and his hands ached to find some task that would occupy him. He reached over to the axe, thinking about checking the blade, then reconsidered. The damp night would do the blade no good, and he could hardly sharpen it by the low firelight.

And his sword was wrapped with the rest of his gear. He continued to carry it, but such was more habit than for protection. For though he practiced at every opportunity, he had yet to regain his old skill. Even in a two-handed grip, his maimed hand could not keep firm hold of the sword, and more often than not it was knocked out of his hands by his sparring partners. With brute force and relentless practice he had regained his mastery of the axe, but such tactics would not work with the sword.

He heard a low whinny and turned to see that the gray gelding had awoken. The packhorse began tugging at the picket line, which woke the other three horses, who stamped their feet and voiced their own displeasure at the disturbance.

"Flames," Devlin cursed. The stable master had sworn the packhorse was a reliable beast, but so far it had proven skittish and prone to starting at shadows. He rose to his feet and walked toward the horses to settle them down.

He stroked the packhorse's neck to reassure him, but the horse tossed his head uneasily, swinging it from side to side.

Devlin fumbled in the pocket of his cloak for the pouch of horse treats he kept within. Just as his fingers found it, the unpredictable breeze died down for a moment, and he heard the unmistakable crunch of leaves underfoot.

"Didrik! Stephen! Awake!" he called, turning to his left, where he could see the shapes of moving figures through the trees on the northern edge of the clearing.

He turned and ran back toward the fire, cursing himself for being so foolish as to leave himself unarmed.

"What is it?" Didrik called.

He had no time to explain, as the attackers abandoned their stealthy approach and rushed into the clearing. The two men headed straight for Devlin.

He grabbed frantically for his axe. His fingers clumsy with haste, he managed to free the axe blade from its covering just as the first attacker reached him, sword extended.

Devlin parried the blow, then retreated a few paces. His two opponents kept pace with him easily, spreading out so they could engage him from either side.

He heard the ring of steel against steel, and saw that Didrik and Stephen had both emerged from the tent and were now engaged with their own foes. The two newcomers must have come in from the opposite side of the clearing. Now it was four against three, but who knew how many more opponents were lurking in the woods?

The tallest of his two foes lunged forward, sword extended. Devlin dodged the blow, then swung his axe in a sweeping arc, forcing the attacker to pull his blade back lest it be shattered. But as swiftly as the first blade retreated, the second fighter parried. He was a left-handed swordsman, and the two alternated their attacks with the well-timed precision of those who had been trained to fight together.

Devlin began to sweat, and his breathing quickened. Never before had he fought two skilled opponents at once. And the axe was no match for the longer reach of the dueling swords that his opponents wielded. Time and time again they forced him to retreat, and yet he could not get under their guard.

He cursed himself again. Even a single throwing knife would be enough to tip the odds in his favor. But fool that he was, he had only the axe and his wits to defend himself.

The left-handed fighter broke off and began to edge to the right, seeking to get behind him. Devlin slashed furiously with his axe, then took three quick steps back, nearly slipping on a patch of slick grass.

He knew he was getting close to the edge of the woods for they had driven him nearly across the clearing. If he was going to escape these two, he needed to do so now. Before they had him pinned against a tree.

He risked a quick glance over his shoulder and saw that Stephen and Didrik were each engaged with the foe. A stinging slash on his right arm brought his attention back to his own peril. He knocked aside the next thrust with the flat side of his axe.

It was a strange fight, for his opponents spoke not a word, neither taunting their enemy nor offering encouragement to their comrades. There was only the occasional grunt as a well-timed thrust was delivered.

Their silence and the skill with which they worked together argued that these were not mere bandits, but rather assassins. And yet, if so, they showed an amazingly poor grasp of tactics. Swords were weapons for duels. Had the attackers possessed a transverse bow, they could have killed Devlin where he sat, heedless of their approach.

Regardless of their tactics, they had skill in plenty and showed no signs of flagging, even as Devlin's own breathing grew labored.

Stephen cried out, and Devlin took two hasty steps back and turned to see Stephen sprawled on the ground near the fire, the body of his opponent under him. Neither were moving.

There was nothing he could do to help his friend. Nor could Didrik lend aid, for he had disappeared into the trees along with his foe, though the sounds of steel striking steel told Devlin that Didrik, at least, was still alive.

It was up to him. Devlin held the axe before him, but let it drop a bit, as if his arms were weary. He swung it in increasingly shallow arcs, and panted heavily.

After a few moments, and one parry which he nearly failed to block, the right-handed swordsman took the bait. He waited until Devlin's attention was focused on his partner, then lunged toward Devlin's exposed right side.

Devlin took his right hand off the axe and flung his right arm outward, tangling the sword blade in the swirling fabric of his cloak. With his left hand he swung the axe downward, and as the heavy steel of the axe met the thin sword blade, it shattered. The axe continued on its murderous arc, biting deep into the assassin's leg. He screamed as he fell to the ground.

Blood spurted into the air as a sharp tug pulled the

axe free. The assassin clutched his wounded leg with both hands, but it was a futile effort, as his lifeblood drained away with each heartbeat.

Now the odds had evened, and Devlin grinned even as he parried the left-handed swordsman's attack. "It will take more than a fancy sword to kill me," he said.

The swordsman did not respond to his taunt, sparing his fallen comrade not a single glance as he came toward Devlin.

"This one's dead," Stephen called out, from somewhere behind him.

Devlin felt the knot inside his chest loosen, even as he battled the increasingly furious blows of the left-handed swordsman.

"Find Didrik," he ordered Stephen.

"No, you stubborn bastard." Didrik's hoarse voice came from the trees to his north. "I can take care of this one."

"I'm here," Stephen said, coming up to stand on Devlin's right. Stephen's sword was bloody, as was the front of his tunic, but if he was injured, he gave no sign.

"Tripped and knocked the wind out of me," Stephen explained. His eyes were bright with manic glee. "Luckily I had someone to cushion my fall, and that of my sword."

Only Stephen would manage to defeat a trained assassin by tripping over a root in the dark. And only a minstrel would have breath to jest about the deed. He wondered if Stephen was indeed uninjured, or if he was merely bluffing for the benefit of their enemies.

Stephen took several quick steps to his right, trying to attract the swordsman's attention so Devlin could circle in behind him. But the swordsman was wise to such a ploy, and he spun to his right so that his back was now to the forest.

Devlin heard a short choking scream, abruptly cut off. He waited for several heartbeats, but there was no cry of victory, and he feared that Didrik was either dead or unconscious.

Stephen lunged toward the assassin, but was beaten back in a swift flurry of blows. Seeing Stephen's strength begin to fail, Devlin darted forward, coming close enough to the assassin to be within sword reach, as he lifted his axe overhead and swung a killing blow.

The assassin dived and rolled, twisting his body like an acrobat as he bounced back to his feet, sword still in hand.

Then Devlin saw a movement in the trees behind the assassin. "Stephen," he called, nodding in the direction where he had seen the movement.

Stephen nodded, showing that he had seen the shadowy figure. And then his eyes widened with relief as Didrik stepped through the trees.

His silence was now explained, for he had managed to creep up on the assassin unaware, and now the swordsman was surrounded.

"Can you use my aid?" Didrik asked, announcing his presence.

"We need him alive," Devlin said, feeling lightheaded with relief.

The assassin gave a quick glance over his shoulder, only to discover that Didrik now stood less than a half dozen paces behind him.

"Surrender and tell us who sent you, and I will spare your life," Devlin said. After all, these assassins were but tools. He needed to know who had hired them.

The assassin raised his sword in salute, then smiled grimly. "Chosen One, you are a worthy foe," he said.

Devlin paused, waiting for the words of surrender.

Instead, the assassin reversed the sword, and plunged it deep into his own belly. Blood spurted from the wound, as the assassin fell to his knees and toppled over on his right side.

Devlin knelt beside his fallen enemy, but it was already too late. A skilled healer might have saved him, but without such a healer the man would be dead within minutes.

"Damn," Devlin cursed.

Captain Drakken handed her sword over to the equerry and straightened her dress tunic. It had taken three days and a series of increasingly undiplomatic requests before King Olafur had finally consented to see her.

A chamberman opened the door to the King's inner chamber. "Your Majesty, Captain Drakken has arrived," he announced.

She took three paces into the room, then stopped, bowing low as if this was a formal court appearance. She held the pose for a dozen heartbeats and straightened to attention. The King might be dressed in a quilted robe more suited for the bedroom than giving audiences, but that did not mean that he would tolerate any informality from her.

"Tell me, Drakken, what message do you have that is so urgent you threaten my steward when he comes to speak in my place?"

She crossed the room until she stood a mere half dozen paces from the King, then stood once more at attention. "A royal messenger came bearing the news that the Chosen One was attacked by assassins."

"I have heard this news as well," King Olafur said. He turned slightly away from her. Reaching into a crystal bowl filled with precious glasshouse fruit, he withdrew a yellow pear, then picked up a small silver knife. "I fail to see why this is a concern of yours. Devlin survived, did he not? Another glorious triumph for the Chosen One, as he defeats a band of petty thieves."

King Olafur carefully began to peel the skin of the pear, seeming far more interested in the fruit than he was in the fate of the Chosen One.

"These were not mere bandits. The report I received described them as skilled swordsmen, at least two of whom spoke with the accent of Kingsholm."

King Olafur shook his head, not even bothering to look up from his task. "Devlin is a foreigner and hardly likely to know one of our accents from another. And as for the skill of the swordsmen, surely he is mistaken there as well. The tale I heard was that the odds were four against three, yet Devlin and his party managed to kill all four attackers without receiving a single blow in return? Surely skilled swordsmen would have been able to draw blood."

"If you had read the report yourself, you would have seen that it came from Lieutenant Didrik. He is an experienced officer, well able to judge the accents and the skill of those who attacked."

From Devlin himself she had heard nothing. She wondered if he even knew that Didrik had sent a report back to the capital. His report had been brief, as if hastily scrawled, but she had the impression that their survival had been as much a matter of luck as of skill.

"This lieutenant is your man, so of course you stand by him. Pity we will have to wait until our wandering servants return before we can question them fully on this matter. As for the present, I see no reason to alarm ourselves unduly."

His lack of concern infuriated her, as did his implied slur upon the competence of her Guard. She wondered if he was deliberately trying to provoke her or distract her from her mission. But she was no novice to be so easily led.

It had taken a fortnight for word of the attack to reach her in Kingsholm, and any help she could send had no chance of catching up to Devlin before he crossed the border over into Duncaer. Instead, she had to hope that Didrik would persuade Devlin to see reason and arrange for soldiers from the border garrison to serve as their escort.

But that did not mean that she was entirely helpless.

"The report from Lieutenant Didrik spoke of four swordsmen who had been trained to work together. These were no common thieves or back-alley murderers. Even in Kingsholm, trained swordsmen are not common. They must have been part of someone's retinue. Armsmen or dueling instructors, perhaps. The disappearance of four such is bound to be noticed. All I need is your permission to question those nobles who remain in the city."

Find out who was missing four swordsmen, and she would find out who was behind the attempt on Devlin's life. Even if Didrik had been wrong about the accents, it did no harm to look here first. At least two of Devlin's most vocal critics had decided to winter over in the capital rather than returning to their own estates. And if inquiries here proved fruitless, she could widen the scope of her investigation, beginning with those whose estates were closest to the capital. For the assassins to have caught up with Devlin on the road, they must have left soon after Devlin himself, or have come from one of the towns that lay along the Southern Road.

"No," King Olafur said.

She rocked back on her heels. "Your pardon, Majesty, but I do not understand."

Did the King already know who had hired the assassins?

"I will not give you permission to badger my nobles," King Olafur replied. He sliced off a chunk of the now-peeled fruit and ate it with two sharp bites. "I will not let you use this attack as an excuse to cast doubt upon those who have opposed Devlin in council."

"But—"

"I have spoken," King Olafur said. "There is to be no investigation. Not until you bring me proof that these men were from Kingsholm."

Any proof had died along with Devlin's attackers, as King Olafur surely knew.

She wondered at his motive for refusing to allow her investigation. As Captain of the City Guard she had broad powers to investigates crimes both high and low, though custom held that she obtain the King's consent before investigating one of his nobles for possible treason. His refusal made no sense. Were he anyone else, she would have suspected that he had something to hide and thus thwarted her investigation.

Yet even as the thought occurred to her, she dismissed it as being absurd. If he truly wished to be rid of the Chosen One, then King Olafur had merely to dismiss Devlin from his post. He had no need to set killers upon Devlin's trail.

The King was simply allowing his dislike for Devlin's politics to color his judgment, and thus dismissed this threat as insignificant. And he saw her role in this as Devlin's ally, driven by partisan politics. Forgotten was the twenty-five years of faithful service that she had given to King Olafur and his father before him. The King had made it plain that he no longer trusted her impartiality.

"I understand, Your Majesty," she said, realizing that he was still waiting her response. "Do you have any further instructions for me?"

"No," King Olafur said. He waved the hand holding the paring knife toward the door. "You may leave, and the next time you feel the urge to disturb me with nonsense, I suggest you think twice."

She swallowed hard. It was clear from his tone that her next misstep might cost her her post.

"Of course, Your Majesty. I regret having troubled you," she said.

She kept her face expressionless as she backed out of the room and accepted her sword from the equerry. She left the King's chambers, speaking to no one as she made her way through the palace, down the long stairs, and then across the courtyard to the Guard Hall. Only when she was in the sanctum of her office, with the door closed behind her, did she allow herself to relax.

"Of all the damn fools. In the name of the Seven, I swear he will lead us all to our deaths," she cursed, giving vent to her anger. Not only had King Olafur once again put his self-interest ahead of the welfare of the Kingdom, he had made it clear that he no longer trusted those who dared disagree with him. She would have to be very careful indeed if she wished to retain her post. And hope that Devlin found the damn sword and returned to Kingsholm before the King lost patience with her.

With the King's approval or no, she had no intention of giving up the search to identify Devlin's attackers. If an open investigation was not possible, then she would investigate in secret, relying upon a handful of her most trusted guards. She would find out the identity of Devlin's enemies, and once she had proof, she would force the King to mete out justice.

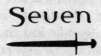

Seven

THE SCENT OF SPILLED BLOOD AND BOWELS WAS
heavy on the air, as the bodies of their attackers had
been dragged over near the fire so they could be examined.

Devlin watched, as Didrik took on the grim task of
searching the bodies of their attackers. The attackers
carried no tokens or badges, not even coins that could
be used to identify the district they came from. Devlin
examined their weapons, which were similarly unre-
vealing. The tapered dueling swords had no household
marks or unit crests on their hilts. Such swords were
commonly used by officers of the Royal Army, and by
those nobles who fancied themselves as duelists.

"I found nothing," Didrik said in disgust, standing
up from the last body and wiping his hands carefully on
a rag. "Their baggage could tell us more, if we could
find the spot where they left their horses."

Devlin, too, had noticed that the attackers wore
finely made riding boots. After discovering Devlin's
campsite, the attackers must have journeyed farther
along the road and hidden their horses, then crept back

through the woods hoping to surprise the sleeping travelers. No doubt this was the source of their earlier disturbance.

He knew their survival was a matter of sheer luck. He did not deserve to be alive, for he had been foolish beyond all reason. First he had chosen a campsite so close to the road that any passerby could see the glow of their fire. And while he had set a watch, he had not truly believed they were in danger. He had been convinced that his enemies preferred a live Chosen One off on a foolish quest to a dead martyr. After all, if Devlin were killed, they would have to deal with a new Chosen One.

So confident had he been that he had ignored the basic cautions which had kept him alive for so long. His throwing knives, which could have made all the difference in the first moments of the fight, had been tucked away in his saddlebags. Worse yet, he had left his axe behind when he went to check on the horses. If the attackers had struck mere moments sooner, he would not have had time to retrieve his axe, and instead would have had to face them with a mere dagger.

After the fight, he had cleaned his weapons and strapped on his throwing knives. For the first time since his injury he strapped on his right-hand knife, adjusting the harness so it did not chafe the ridged scar tissue. His aim with that arm was still chancy, but he reasoned that even a poorly aimed throw could provide a distraction.

"It is too dark now, but we can search the woods in the morning," Stephen said, from his seat on the fallen tent. The blood on his tunic had been his enemy's, not his own, but his ribs had been bruised by the fall, so Devlin had ordered him to rest.

"No," Devlin said. "While we are wasting time searching the woods, others can find us. Our best strategy is to make haste. We will continue our journey, but be on our guard for trouble."

"A moving target is harder to hit," Didrik agreed.

In the days that followed they kept vigilant watch, but saw no sign that they were being followed. The farther they journeyed from Kingsholm, the smaller the towns became, and the more widely spaced. Eynford was a mere speck on the map, but it had the virtue of being the last town of any size before they would reach the Kenwye River and cross over into what had once been the lowlands of Duncaer.

Devlin grimaced. The Jorskians called the territory Saemundsland, but not even in his own mind would he give that much respect to the butcher of Ynnis. Instead, he followed the custom of his people and called them the stolen lands, for the Jorskians had taken the fertile lowlands for their own, turning honest Caer farmers into refugees in their own country. After fifty years the stolen lands were indistinguishable from other provinces of Jorsk, farmed by descendants of the conquering armies who had been given land grants. Only in the mountains did the old Caer ways still hold sway.

It would take them several days to cross the lowlands. Ten days, if the weather held fair. Then another three days to climb the foothills till they reached the town of Kilbaran. And then he would see his people and hear his language spoken for the first time in nearly two years.

It was a journey he had never thought to make. Even in his dreams, when he imagined a life free from the burdens of the Chosen One, he had never pictured himself returning to Duncaer. How could he? There was no place for him there. A man who had neither family nor craft did not exist. He would be as a foreigner in his own country. Worse than a foreigner, for Jorskian traders were granted the courtesy due to outlanders. But for a man who had been declared kinbereft there would be no courtesy, only cold silences and empty gazes that slid over his form rather than acknowledging his presence.

In Jorsk it was easier to pretend that he was still a man. There he had made a place for himself, and found those he called friends. In Kingsholm there were no reminders of all he had lost. But once he crossed the border into Duncaer, he would be surrounded by the reminders of all that he had once been part of, and could never be again.

They had reached the town of Eynford at midday, and paused to exchange their mounts for sturdy ponies that would be better suited to the rugged mountain terrain ahead. Devlin had overseen the purchasing of the new ponies, but had left Didrik in charge of taking the ponies to be shod. He had no wish to set foot in a smithy.

But perhaps that had been a mistake, for it left him alone with his thoughts, which had grown increasingly grim as they journeyed toward his homeland.

Devlin lifted his cup of bitter red wine and drained it dry. Then he set the cup down precisely in the center of the table and leaned back in his chair. He was a pathetic excuse for a man, hiding here in the inn simply because he could not bring himself to greet one who practiced his former craft. This journey would open enough old wounds, and he saw no reason to rub salt in them. It would be hard enough to face Murchadh once they reached Kilbaran.

Stephen had gone off to restock their provisions, leaving Devlin alone, ensconced in the best room of the town's finest inn. Not that it would be given a second glance in Kingsholm, but the place was clean, the wine drinkable, and the staff left him alone, which was what he needed. Traveling with companions eased the burden of the journey, but Devlin had had very little time to himself. And he needed time to prepare himself for what was to come. And time to think. For there was a niggling doubt in the back of his mind. A voice that had grown stronger as the leagues had disappeared beneath their horses' hooves. A voice that said that there was something he had overlooked. Something that he had forgotten, that would place them all in danger.

There was a knock at the door. "Enter," he commanded.

The door swung open, revealing the figure of Jensine, the inn-wife. "If you please, Lord Devlin, there are callers in the common room who beg the favor of your presence."

Devlin sighed. He had been expecting something like this. At every place where he had been recognized, there had been folk eager to meet the Chosen One. Sometimes they simply wished to see him, to say that they had seen the legend in person. Others wished to curry favor, as if he had any to give. But usually it took them more than a few hours to work up the courage to seek him out, and in most cases he and his companions were long gone by then.

"I have no time for idle gossip. Tell them begone."

Jensine shook her head, her double chins quivering

with indignation. "I know better than to trouble a noble guest with idlers. These folk have come seeking the Chosen One to settle a dispute."

There was no point in reminding her that he was not a nobleman. At least she had stopped bowing to him.

"Have you no lawgiver?"

She looked at him blankly, and he tried again. "Why not send for the magistrate? Surely there is one nearby, if you have none of your own."

"They have already seen the magistrate, and sent to the lord for justice. And still the quarrel goes on, and the factions have gone from angry words to exchanging blows. I fear that soon it will come to killing. I would not trouble you elsewise."

He wondered how they expected him to solve their problems when both the magistrate and their lord had been unable to do so. He was no lawgiver, merely a metalsmith turned warrior. He had no words of wisdom to share with these people, and no patience for their quarrels. He was of a mind to refuse, but his sense of duty would not let him. The Chosen One was empowered to dispense both high and low justice. It was part of his task, like it or not. And since he was idle, he could not plead other pressing duties instead.

Devlin rose to his feet. "Lead me to them, and I will do what I may."

As Jensine led the way down the passage, he heard raised voices coming from the common room. It sounded as if half the town had gathered, but when he stepped inside he found that there were only a dozen or so people.

The folk were clearly divided into two factions. On one side there was a tall haughty woman who looked down her sharp features at the man opposite her. The woman yelled, her voice shrill and her words indistinguishable, while the man's reply was an angry growl. Arranged beside and behind each of the two were their supporters, who waved their hands and added their own voices to the din.

"Good people," the inn-wife called. "Sunniva. Klemens."

The quarreling folk paid her no heed. Devlin kicked his heel back, slamming the door shut behind him.

There was a brief gasp and the folk fell silent, turning to stare.

"If you have no time for me, I will leave," Devlin said.

The woman was the first to recover. "My lord Chosen One, forgive our rudeness. We welcome your presence, and your wisdom," she said with a graceful curtsy.

"Will you still call it wisdom when he decides in my favor?" the man asked. Then he turned to Devlin and gave a bow. "My lord."

"Let us discuss this as civilized folk," Devlin said. The crowd parted before him, and he made his way to the front of the room. He took a chair from the head table and turned it so it faced the room. Then he took his seat and watched as the partisans divided themselves behind their supporters.

The man and the woman remained standing. They were both in their midyears. The man was shorter than most, and made up for his thinning hair with a finely combed beard. The woman was tall, and slender, dressed in a simple smock and trousers in the style of a farmer, though no true farmer ever wore such spotless linen. If she smiled, she might have been pretty, but her ill-tempered expression gave her face a sour cast.

"Who can tell me what this is all about?" he asked.

It was a mistake.

"My lord, this woman and her family are conspiring to cheat me—" the man began.

"Cheat? It is you that is the thief. You and your cousin the magistrate—" the woman countered.

One of the man's supporters took offense, and called out "Who was it who tried to bribe the Baron?"

"You tried that first—" another interjected.

"Silence!" Devlin ordered. His head was beginning to ache. "You will remain silent unless I ask you to speak, understood?"

All present nodded.

He motioned to the inn-wife, who stood by the door. "Jensine, do you know the nature of the quarrel?"

"Yes, my lord."

"And are you kin to either of these folk?"

"No, my lord."

"Then tell me what you know."

Jensine wiped her hands on her apron. "Sunniva," she said, indicating the woman with a nod of her head, "was married to Klemens for nearly twenty years. The pair agreed to part last winter. They divided their goods between them, but cannot decide what to do with the land. Klemens says the land is his, because it was before his marriage. But Sunniva wishes to sell the land and divide the proceeds equally."

It seemed strange to him, but so far it was plain enough. And far too simple to be the cause of a bitter quarrel. "And what did the magistrate say?"

"The magistrate sided with Klemens and said the land was his."

"The magistrate is his cousin. Of course she took his

side," Sunniva interjected. "I appealed to Baron Rostik, who said I was in the right."

"If your Baron has already passed judgment, what need have you for me?"

Klemens glared at his former wife. "The Baron made no writ. There is no proof of what he did or did not say. Regardless, it is certain that he was not told the full truth, so the magistrate has refused to allow the sale."

It was unfortunate that Baron Rostik had not seen fit to record his judgment. Such spoke of carelessness on the Baron's part, or outright deception by Sunniva. The simplest course would be to send the former husband and wife off to seek the Baron's judgment in person, and let him settle the affair.

"And this year's crop lies rotting in the orchards because you would not let my workers harvest it," Klemens declared.

"There would have been no need for such if you had behaved in an honest fashion and let me sell the land," Sunniva replied.

"Hold," he said. Surely he had misheard. "You did not harvest this year's crop? You let it rot?"

Klemens nodded. "I would have hired laborers, but Sunniva's family harassed all those who would have come to help."

"Those are my trees," Sunniva said. "My family gave me the seedlings, and it was I who planted them on lands you thought useless. Without me you would have had nothing."

"It was my land," Klemens countered. "And twenty years of my sweat and toil that made the orchards what they are."

"I would rather see them burned to the ground than fall into your hands."

"Spoken like the shrew you are."

"Enough!" How had these folks endured twenty years of marriage if they quarreled so bitterly? He could not comprehend how low they had sunk in their pettiness. To think that they had let healthy fruit rot on the trees rather than cooperate with one another. It was more than stupidity. It was a sin.

But stupidity was not something for which he could punish them.

"And what of your parents? Did you not sign a marriage pact?"

An elderly man rose to his feet. "I am Eyulf, father of Klemens. A deed was signed, that if the marriage was dissolved and there were no children, then the land would stay in my family."

"I am not asking for all of the land. Just for the orchards, where my trees are ten times—no, twenty times—the value of the land they sit upon," Sunniva countered. "Surely you see this is only just, my lord."

"And you, Klemens, what do you feel is just?"

"The land is mine. And as for the orchards, my home sits in the middle of them. You cannot sell one without the other. Sunniva left me, so she has chosen her lot. She has a tidy sum from our years together, far more than she brought as dowry. She will not starve."

"And that is all? No one has claimed harm? There is nothing else that requires judgment?" Devlin asked.

"All else was settled between us. Only this remains."

He schooled his features to blankness, being careful not to let his confusion show. It would not do to let these folk see that he had no sense of their quarrel, or of how to mend it. If he were in Duncaer, he would know what answer to give, but he sensed that in this place matters were handled far differently.

"I will think on this matter, and tell you my decision this evening, after the late meal," Devlin said.

It was not enough that he pass judgment. He must make a decision that they would understand and obey.

"And that is the whole of the matter," Devlin said. He had waited until the evening meal to recount the story of the afternoon's deliberations. "My instinct is to sentence the woman to gaol for letting good fruit go to rot. And the man would have his own cell, for lacking the sense to compromise."

"I gather you did not tell them that," Stephen said, pushing his plate away and tilting his chair back so it balanced on its back legs.

"No, I told them I would pass judgment later tonight."

Didrik used his fork to spear another slice of duck from the platter in the center of the table, then began to cut it into small pieces. All three had done full justice to the food, enjoying the rare chance for an unhurried meal. As the towns had grown farther apart, they had seldom been able to stay in an inn, spending their nights camped along the roadside instead, eating whatever could be hastily assembled by firelight. When they did stay in a village, they usually arrived near nightfall and had to settle for the common fare. But here they had spent nearly an entire day, and the cook had made use of that time to prepare a feast in their honor. The table was covered with empty plates and bowls scraped clean, and Didrik was doing his level best to finish up what food remained.

Didrik swallowed, then asked, "So what are you planning to say?"

"I was waiting till I could ask your advice. I confess, I do not understand this matter at all."

"What is there to understand? Many marriages start out promising but end badly. There are nearly as many songs of unhappy romance as there are love ballads in my repertoire," Stephen said.

"That I know," Devlin said. He was not ignorant. Divorce was a long held custom of both their peoples. And he had lived in Jorsk long enough to know that here it was possible for a man to own a home and farmland, though such ownership still seemed unnatural to him. The ways of his own people made more sense. A woman was the center of the family, and of all kin relationships. Women belonged to the land, and the land belonged to them. Such was the only way to ensure stability.

In his own land, nobles governed territory, men and women alike. A man might own a shop, or the place where he practiced his trade. But land, particularly precious land for growing crops or raising livestock, that belonged to women, because they were made in the image of the Mother Goddess Teá. To live any other way was to invite chaos.

As had happened here.

"It seems the fault lies equally between them," Devlin said. "I see no merit in one claimant over the over."

Left to his own inclinations, he would strip the land from both of them, directing that the harvest and the money from the sale be given to the poor of this county. But such a verdict was hardly likely to be seen as justice. He was only here for a day, but these folk would have to live with his judgment for years to come.

"Whatever you do, it will make someone unhappy. Toss a coin, and leave the ruling up to the will of Kanjti," Stephen said.

Devlin frowned. He had no wish to call upon the luck God, even in such a trifling affair. The Gods had meddled enough in his life as it was.

"Send them both to see the Baron. It is his province, and his problem," Didrik offered. He surveyed the table, then asked hopefully, "Do you think the cook has any more of those honeyed apples?"

Later that evening, after Didrik had eaten another dish of honeyed apples, thus ensuring that he would feel ill during tomorrow's ride, Devlin and his friends returned to the common room. There he found Sunniva, Klemens, and their supporters awaiting his decision.

"Will you both promise to abide by my judgment?"

"If it is wise, then—" Sunniva began.

"There is no if," Devlin interrupted. He caught her gaze in his and let her feel the full force of his will. "You asked for my help, and now you will swear to abide by the word of the Chosen One, upon peril of your lives. Do you so swear?"

Sunniva turned pale, but her voice was steady. "I swear to accept your judgment."

"Klemens?"

Beads of sweat covered the man's face. "I swear as well."

Devlin felt a brief flare of satisfaction at seeing their obvious discomfort. The quarrelsome pair had thought to use the Chosen One for their own gain, but they had not considered just who it was that they had dragged into their petty games. He was no mere country magistrate, but rather the Champion of the Kingdom, anointed in his task by the Gods themselves. Or so these folks professed to believe. And to forswear an oath to him was treason.

Seldom did he invoke the full power of his office, and he knew there were some who might consider his treatment of these folk to be overly harsh. But he felt no sympathy toward these two, who had let their personal quarrels blind them to what was right and just.

"And do your families swear as well? I hold all present here as witnesses to this oath. Will you bind yourself to obey my judgment and to see that it is carried out in full?"

The witnesses shuffled their feet and looked anywhere but at him. But one by one they swore their agreement.

"Then this is my judgment. The land will stay with Klemens," Devlin began. Klemens smirked, and Sunniva looked positively thunderous. But he was not finished. "But for the next seven years, Sunniva will continue to manage the orchard, and to oversee the harvest. Two-thirds of every crop will be hers to do with as she sees fit, and one-third will be payment to Klemens for the use of his land. At the end of the seven years, the agreement is over, and Klemens assumes control of the orchards."

Now Klemens appeared distinctly unhappy, while Sunniva's face bore a calculating look.

Eight

DEVLIN LIFTED HIS HEAD AND PEERED THROUGH the stinging rain that pelted his face. There was nothing to be seen save sodden countryside and the muddy path before them. He blinked and wiped the rain from his eyes with his gloved left hand, but it made no difference.

The sun had been hidden all day, which made it difficult to tell the hour, but he felt in his bones that it was approaching sunset. And there was no shelter in sight.

He glanced toward his two companions. Didrik's face revealed nothing, though his horse stamped its hooves and bobbed its head, impatient with the delay. Stephen, on the other hand, simply looked miserable, huddled within his cloak.

Devlin cursed himself, for he knew this was his fault. It had been his decision to leave the safety of the well-tended trade route and take the old way over the hills. True it was a shorter route, and in fair weather would save nearly four days of travel. But this was not fair weather. Instead it had rained steadily ever since they left the main road—a winter rain that chilled a man till his bones ached and left his skin feeling raw. They had not been truly warm in the past three days. Last night had been spent in the dubious shelter of a ruined cabin. One of the cabin's walls was half-crumbled, but the rest served to block the wind, and the roof had kept the worst of the rain at bay.

Now even such a ruin would be welcome. Kilbaran was still two days away by his reckoning, and from the looks of the sky it would be another two days of misery.

"Do you wish to stop here and try to erect the tent? Or ride on?" Didrik's tone was carefully neutral, offering no opinion either way.

"The wind would tear down any tent," Devlin said.

He looked over at Stephen, wondering at his unusual silence.

Stephen lifted his head and opened his eyes, as if he could feel the weight of Devlin's gaze upon him. "I am fine," he said. A hoarse cough gave lie to his words.

He realized that Stephen was falling ill, unused to the hardships of winter travel. Earlier in their trip they had passed through snowstorms and the minstrel had hardly batted an eye. But the cold rains had sapped his strength.

This was another fault laid at Devlin's door. And it hurt all the more, for his companions spoke not a word in complaint. Better by far that they curse and grumble and question the sanity of a man who scorned civilization in favor of a trek through the unpopulated countryside. But they did not question his need for haste. They thought the Geas drove him to make the journey as swift as possible. He had heard them, murmuring together one night when he was supposed to be asleep.

Devlin had not corrected their assumption. How

could he tell them that it was not the Geas that drove him, but rather his own cowardice? He feared returning to Duncaer. Feared the first time he would see one of his own folk, after nearly two years absence. Dreaded the moment when he would face Murchadh's scorn.

But rather than making him drag his feet, his fear urged him forward. Better to have the confrontation over with and behind him. So he had ignored common sense, and now his companions were paying the price for his weakness.

"We will ride on. We can reach the crest of that hill before dusk. With luck we may find shelter, and if not, the lee side will give us protection from the wind," Devlin said.

As they rode, he kept an eye on Stephen. The minstrel's head remained lowered, his face hidden within the hood of his cloak. His hands were slack on the reins, trusting his pony to have the good sense to remain with his companions. Devlin's concern grew. If Stephen were truly ill, there were no healers to be found between here and Kilbaran.

When they crested the hill, he caught a glimpse of a stone cottage, nestled against the hillside. A tendril of smoke curled upward from the chimney.

"There," Didrik said, lifting his arm and pointing.

"I see it," Devlin replied. He swallowed hard. It was what he had hoped for, and yet dreaded.

At least Stephen would have a warm place to sleep this night. No one of his folk would dare scorn a minstrel, regardless of his race. And if the inhabitants were kind, perhaps they would allow Didrik and himself to take shelter in their barn.

There was only one way to find out.

"Come," he said, turning the pony's head in the direction of the cottage.

The cottage proved a fair-sized dwelling for these parts, two full stories in height, made of stone courses and topped off with a slate roof. A few yards away from the cottage a long, low barn rambled along the curve of the hillside. From the shape of the building and the scents carried on the breeze, he knew the barn was meant for sheep.

Devlin drew his pony to a halt a short distance from the door and dismounted. His companions did the same.

"A warm fire will take the chill from our bones," Didrik said, as he took the reins of Devlin's pony.

Devlin grunted noncommittally. He realized that there was much that he had not told his friends about the customs of his people. And now there was no time. He could only trust that they would follow his lead.

"I will do the speaking," Devlin said. "And we will take whatever they see fit to grant us, even if it is the shelter of the sheep pen."

"But you are the Chosen One. In the King's Name—" Didrik said.

"Here my name is Devlin and the title of Chosen One bears no weight," Devlin interrupted. And mentioning the King's name would be far more likely to provoke hostility than an offer of shelter.

For a moment he wished himself back in Jorsk. There his rank would entitle his party to hospitality from anyone, be they the lowest pig-herder or the highest of nobles. But in Duncaer the old ways held sway, no matter what those of Jorsk believed. He would be lucky if they let him sleep in the barn.

Devlin stepped forward and rapped on the door. After a moment it was opened by a middle-aged woman dressed in a woolen shirt and leather pants. Her black hair was liberally streaked with white, but her blue eyes were sharp.

"I seek the woman of the house," Devlin said. He tossed back the hood of his cloak, revealing his features. The rain began to plaster his hair to his head.

"I am she." She spoke the tradespeech credibly, with a lilting accent.

She glanced at his companions.

"May I have the honor of your name?" he asked. It was a breach of courtesy, but only a minor one.

"I am called Niesha."

It was but half a name, but still a gift to strangers come calling.

"This is Stephen, youngest son of Brynjolf, Baron of Esker, and of the Lady Gemma whose own mother came from far-off Selvarat. Stephen is a singer and a lore-teller," Devlin said, placing his hand on Stephen's arm to draw Niesha's attention to him.

Niesha inclined her head graciously. "Stephen, I bid you welcome to my house."

Stephen bowed credibly, managing not to look half-drowned.

"And this is Nils Didrik, lieutenant of the Guards in Kingsholm. His father Lars and his mother Brenna are bakers in the royal palace."

"Nils," she said. She did not bid him welcome.

"And your name?" she asked.

"My name is Devlin. I can offer you no other, for I am kinless and craft-forsaken. My name holds no power."

She eyed him steadily. "I know who you are. No one else would travel in such company. You are the one they call General, the one who has sworn to defend our oppressors."

He could feel Didrik bristle at the insult.

"Yes," Devlin said. "There they call me Chosen One."

Niesha nodded. Then she extended both her hands outward, palms facing upward. "Nils, Devlin. I bid you welcome to my house."

It took him a moment, certain that he had misheard her. Then he bowed low, humbled by her generosity to one who had no means to repay her. "Your kindness does you honor."

Stephen was warm. Warm and dry, and he luxuriated in the sensation, stretching out his stocking feet toward the low-burning fire. Turf, Devlin had called it, though it looked more like clay bricks than grass. Whatever it was called, it filled the cottage with a cozy warmth. Both his hands were wrapped around a clay mug of hot tea, and he raised it to his lips to take another sip. The taste was bitter, but not unpleasantly so, and he could feel the warmth spreading within him, to match the warmth outside. He sighed with contentment.

It felt almost as if he was dreaming. He remembered riding that day, his fingers and toes going slowly numb from the cold. He had begun to dream about warmth, picturing first his father's house, then a cozy inn—such as were to be found along the trade routes. Then they had found this cottage. His initial relief had turned to disappointment at the thought that they would be turned away. For though Devlin had spoken in the trade tongue, his words had made no sense. It was as if Devlin and this woman Niesha held some quarrel, except clearly they had never met before.

And then, in an instant, the hostility was gone, and the woman was welcoming them into her house. Her brother was sent to help Devlin and Didrik stable their horses, while Stephen was bustled inside, his sodden cloak and boots stripped off. After being wrapped in a blanket and given a mug of tea, he was told to sit by the fire until he had warmed himself.

When Devlin and Didrik came in, they were made welcome as well, though perhaps with a trifle less enthusiasm.

"There is more tea in the kettle if you want it, Minstrel Stephen," Niesha said, seeing that he had drained his mug.

"Thank you, I am fine," Stephen said. "And please, it is just Stephen."

Niesha nodded, and turned her attention back to the chopping board. Her knife rocked rhythmically back and forth, and a stack of white tubers were reduced into thin strips.

Boots clattered on the wooden staircase and her brother Feilim entered the kitchen. "I've made up a pair of pallets in my room for your guests."

"Good," Niesha said. "After dinner, we will put the bed down here. It will be warmer for the lore teller."

Feilim nodded. He was older than his sister, but slighter in build, and clearly he took his orders from her.

Stephen flushed, wondering what he had done to earn such special treatment. Was it because Devlin had named him the son of a Baron? And yet that made no

sense, for plainly anyone could see that Devlin outranked him.

"I do not wish to be a burden—"

"It is an honor to have you in my house," the woman
corrected him. For a moment she sounded like his
mother, and he resisted the urge to reply "Yes, ma'am."

He sank back a bit in his chair, trying to ignore
Didrik's grin.

"I'll want some sausage to fry with these. The lamb,
that we traded for from Seanna's girl Meaghan. It's in
the root cellar," Niesha said.

"I'll fetch it," Feilim said, moving toward the door
and reaching for his dark woolen cloak. "After I feed the
animals. It's nearly nightfall, so they'll be expecting
me."

The door opened, and there was a chill draft that reminded him of how glad he was to be indoors and out
of the rain. And then the door closed.

"So, tell me, what brings you to my door on this foul
day?"

Niesha looked at Stephen, but it was Devlin who
replied.

"We are on our way to Kilbaran," he said. These were
the first words he had spoken since entering the cottage.

Niesha shook her head. "These two are strangers, but
you should have known better. What made you think to
try the old way in such weather?"

"We had need of haste," Devlin said. He shot a warning glance at Stephen, warning him to say no more.

Stephen caught his eye and nodded, but inside he
fumed. Did Devlin think him a child? Stephen knew

better than to blurt out their secrets to any chance-met stranger.

"Lucky for you that I took you in. Else you would have spent a wet night on the heath."

"Your kindness does you honor," Devlin said.

It was the same phrase that he had used before, and Stephen still did not know what it meant. It was almost as if Devlin was trying his hardest not to actually thank Niesha.

"We are grateful for your hospitality," Stephen said. Then he added in the Caer tongue, "I am in your debt."

Niesha chuckled, which was hardly the reaction he expected. "And if I held you to that?"

He wondered what he had actually said. Had his accent been that bad?

"He does not understand," Devlin said swiftly, rising to his feet, putting himself between Stephen and their hostess.

Niesha turned to face the least welcome of her guests. "He is your friend. And a man of honor, is he not?"

"Of course," Devlin said. "But he does not know our ways."

"Then you should teach him. Swiftly. Kilbaran is less than two days journey from my doorstep."

Now it was Devlin's turn to flush red.

Niesha dumped the tubers she had been chopping into a pot, then stepped out of the kitchen on some errand of her own.

"What did I say?" Stephen asked. "I meant to say I was in her debt."

Devlin ran his good hand through his damp hair. "That *is* what you said."

"Then why did she laugh?" He felt as if he had stumbled into some bizarre play, where everyone knew their lines except him. He glanced over at Didrik, relieved to see that the lieutenant seemed equally confused.

"A debt of hospitality must be repaid threefold. And in kind," Devlin explained.

Now this made even less sense. How was he supposed to offer this woman hospitality? She was hardly likely to visit Kingsholm and ask to stay in his rooms over the Singing Fish tavern. Still, what he had, she was welcome to.

"And where is the harm in that?"

"There is no harm done. But any pledge you make binds your family as well. Should one of Niesha's kin wish to travel to Jorsk, they could claim guest right from your father, or your brothers and sisters."

"Or your father's brothers and your mother's sisters, and indeed from any that you claim as nearkin," Niesha added.

He jumped, for he had not heard her reenter the kitchen.

"Not that I will hold you to your rash words," she added.

Stephen swallowed. He imagined trying to explain to his father why it was that a peasant family from Duncaer needed to stay in the baronial manor, and to be treated as honored guests.

Still, a promise was a promise, no matter that he had not understood what it was that he was promising to do. "I stand by my words," he said.

"A good heart. And a man of honor. Hardly the company I expected you to keep," she said to Devlin.

"You are neither kin nor Guild Mistress, to question

the company I keep. I have no quarrel with you, but if you wish me to leave—"

"No, no need to be so prickly," she said. "I did not mean to offend. And if you leave, no doubt your friends will insist on following you, and then where would my manners be? Sit now, and make yourself to home. And perhaps, after dinner, the minstrel can tell us tales of Kingsholm. It is a long time since I heard a storyteller speak, and such kindness would more than repay his debt to me."

"It would be my pleasure," Stephen said. He wished that he had been able to bring his harp with him, but the instrument was too delicate to survive the winter journey. But he could always sing for her. It wouldn't be the first time he had sung for his supper.

And later, he would take Devlin aside and insist that he explain what was going on, and what other customs they might run afoul of. Stephen had already made one mistake, and he did not intend to make another.

Supper was an awkward meal. Feilim did not speak unless addressed by his sister, and there was thinly veiled hostility in his gaze. He made it plain that if it had been up to him, he would never have let Devlin and Didrik cross his doorstep. Fortunately, it was his sister's cottage, and he seemed firmly under her control.

Didrik said little, speaking only to thank Niesha for the meal. But his eyes watched every move carefully, showing how uncomfortable he was in this place.

Devlin had no wish to quarrel, and left Stephen and Niesha to carry the burden of conversation. After the meal, he and Didrik retreated to the front room, unloading their saddlebags and checking their gear to make certain that nothing had been damaged by the rain. Stephen remained in the warmth of the kitchen, entertaining Niesha and Feilim. He sang several of his favorite songs until a fit of coughing overcame him. Devlin heard the sound of someone moving around, then the ringing sound of a glass set hastily down.

No doubt someone had offered Stephen a glass of distilled meadowsweet, and he wondered what the minstrel had thought of the fiery liquid.

He wondered, too, if Stephen realized that it was in his honor that they were being offered the very best that the house had to offer. The best of their food, a glass of the rare meadowsweet. He knew without having to ask that it would be the finest bed in the house that would be moved into the kitchen, so Stephen could be warm on this night.

It had been a long time since Devlin had been privileged to offer such hospitality to another. And an even longer time since he had been the recipient of such a gift. He cast his mind back, trying to remember the last time he had enjoyed the privilege of guest right.

Didrik's low voice broke into his ruminations.

"Niesha seems pleasant enough, but I do not trust her brother. I think we should set a watch tonight."

"A watch?" he repeated.

"In case he decides to try and kill us while we sleep," Didrik elaborated.

"There is no need. Niesha spoke the words of hospitality. We are safe as long as we are under her roof."

Had they met Feilim anywhere else, the man might well have tried to do the harm even if the odds were against him. There had been something in his eyes when he first caught sight of Didrik's uniform. Something that spoke of old memories and a loathing for Jorskians that went far beyond the ordinary.

Feilim had smiled grimly as he recounted how a mere two days before he had seen a crimson hawk flying high over the mountains, against the wind. Niesha had changed the subject, but Feilim's message had been clear. The crimson hawk was part of the old tales, a giant bird whose wingspan was greater than the height of a man. It had not been seen for generations, but legend had it that the return of the hawk would symbolize the end of Jorskian rule in Duncaer.

It was a threat of sorts, and one Devlin understood even if his companions did not. Had they met Feilim along the road, there would have been reason for concern. But for this one night, they need have no fear.

"It is not Niesha I am worried about, but rather her brother," Didrik hissed. He picked up the dagger he had just polished and thrust it into his belt meaningfully. Pointedly he turned his back on Devlin, as he began to repack the saddlebag.

"I said no," Devlin snapped. He was tired of this. Since the start of this journey, Didrik had been watching him, questioning Devlin's judgment, even going against his orders as he had when he arranged the escort. All done in the name of protecting him. More than once Devlin had been tempted to order Didrik back to the capital simply to free himself from the strain.

But each time he had relented, remembering that Didrik's concern was as much for his friend as it was for the man who bore the title of Chosen One. If Didrik was overcautious, it was as much the result of past experience as it was his character. And for that he could not be blamed. Nor could he be blamed for not understanding the ways of the Caerfolk. If he did not understand what an oath of hospitality meant, it was Devlin's fault for not explaining.

Devlin reached over and grasped Didrik's shoulder, forcing him to turn and face him.

"There is no need for your worries," Devlin said. "This is Duncaer, and the oath of hospitality is sacred. Once Niesha named us as guests, she and her brother became responsible for our safety while under their roof. We could be fugitives from justice, or even murderers who had slain their kinfolk, and still they would not raise a hand against us. We have shelter for the night, and the chance to depart unhindered."

Didrik shrugged. "And what of guests? Do they also forswear violence toward their hosts?"

"Of course." The customs of hospitality were among the oldest of their traditions. Only a man with neither heart nor soul would even dream of violating them.

He counted himself lucky that Niesha had welcomed them all. Had he and Didrik been offered the use of the barn, then they might well have needed to sleep with one eye open. As it was, for this night at least, they could rest easy.

He could only hope that their reception in Kilbaran would be half as welcoming.

Nine

KILBARAN WAS SMALLER THAN DEVLIN HAD RE-
membered. The gray stone buildings nestled close to
one another, rarely rising above two stories in height.
There were only a few people on the streets, as was to be
expected in a place that made its living from the summer traders. But even the few folk that he saw made
him uneasy, and Devlin found himself constantly on
edge, searching for some unknown threat. He watched
them carefully, then felt ashamed as he realized the
source of his unease. He was a stranger here, he realized. After nearly two years in exile, he was accustomed
to seeing crowds of pale-skinned Jorskians, with their
long braids of flaxen hair. And his ear was tuned to the
deliberate cadence of their speech. He had forgotten
what it was like to be surrounded by folk who bore his
own dark hair and whose voices rang with a musical
lilt.

It would take time for him to accustom himself to
their ways. And then he wondered when he had started
thinking of the Caerfolk as "them" and not "us."

Fortunately few spared him more than a glance as he

made his way through the streets of Kilbaran. His gray wool cape was similar to those worn by Jorskian messengers, who were a common enough sight in this border town. With luck he would pass unnoticed and leave before any knew he had even been here. For that reason he had sent Didrik to pay their respects to the commander of the city garrison rather than going himself. Were the Chosen One to call upon the commander, it would turn this into an official visit, with all the attendant fuss.

Stephen had been left behind at the inn, with instructions not to wander off. The inn-wife had been more than pleased to fuss over him, since few from Jorsk ventured to Kilbaran during the dead of winter. In fact the three travelers were her only patrons at the present.

Devlin tasted the acid tang in the air that meant he had reached the wool dyers's quarter, which meant that Murchadh's forge was nearby. He had been to Kilbaran only once before, but the memory was burned into his brain. He turned left and followed the lane into a large open square. Used by the wool traders in the summer, it was deserted now, with only the scarred earth and long watering trough built into the northern wall giving any hint as to its purpose. Across the square was a small stable and a stone building whose double doors stood open even on this chill day. Through the open doors the glow of a firebed could be seen, and smoke curled from the chimneys, indicating the smith was hard at his craft.

Devlin paused outside the doorway, gathering his courage. The last time he had seen Murchadh, they had exchanged angry words. Once he and Murchadh had been friends, but this, too, belonged to his past and the man he had been. Now, all he hoped for was civility. And even that was in doubt.

He took a deep breath, then stepped within the forge. He stood for a moment, his eyes adjusting to the darkened interior, feeling the welcoming warmth against his face. Steel rang as the smith hammered at a long bar of bright copper, flattening it until it was nearly double its original length. Then he put down his hammer, and using a pair of tongs, he carefully picked up the bar and placed it back in the firebed. He pumped the leather bellows until the fire turned from sullen red to bright yellow.

Only then did he acknowledge his visitor. Murchadh stepped away from the firebed and wiped his hands on his leather apron.

"You have need of my service? A horse, perhaps, in need of shoeing?" Murchadh asked in the trade tongue.

Devlin tossed back the hood of his cloak and unfastened it against the heat.

"I have need of your counsel," he said.

"And why would a messenger come to a smith for counsel?" Murchadh asked, his head tilted to the side as he studied his visitor. Then his eyes widened with shock. "You."

"Murchadh."

"Stranger," Murchadh declared, showing his anger by refusing to speak Devlin's name. "After all this time, now you dare to show your face? Have your foreign friends tired of you, so you return to lord it over us instead?"

Murchadh's eyes swept over him, as if to catalog the changes that time had wrought. Devlin held himself steady under their regard, though inside he was anything but calm. He tucked the thumb of his crippled hand into his sword belt.

Murchadh drew in a sharp breath. "A sword? You came here bearing weapons, as if to the house of one without honor? Have you no shame? What kind of man are you?"

A very good question. For one who was neither peacekeeper nor soldier, to enter a man's home openly displaying a weapon was tantamount to declaring your host without honor. An insult worthy of challenge.

In his former life Devlin would never have made such a mistake. But since becoming Chosen One, Devlin had grown accustomed to his life being at risk, and the need to carry a weapon at all times. In addition to the sword, he had two throwing knives hidden in forearm sheaths and a dagger tucked in the top of his left boot. The only thing he had left behind at the inn was his great axe.

But he had not worn the weapons because he had a right to them as the General of the Royal Army. He had worn them because it had not occurred to him to do otherwise. It was just another sign of how far he had drifted from the ways of his people.

"I meant no insult. I am a soldier now, as you must have heard."

"Your presence here is an insult," Murchadh said. "And no matter what they call you these days, it does not give you the right to come into my forge."

"For the sake of our past friendship—"

"What friendship? I thought I knew you once, but then you forsook your craft. You left it behind, as if it were nothing, then turned your back on your kin and those who had called you friend." Murchadh's face was flushed with anger, but his voice was cold.

It was the old argument, made a hundred times worse by what had followed. Murchadh had never understood Devlin's decision to give up his promising career as a metalsmith in favor of the life of a homesteader in the New Territories. He had argued passionately against such a move. If only Devlin had listened to him, Cerrie and Lyssa might well be alive.

Or perhaps not. Perhaps it had always been their fate that they would die, to ensure Devlin would be driven to become the Chosen One, a pawn of those forces that would see the Sword of Light returned to Kingsholm. No matter what the cost.

He pushed that thought to the back of his mind. Now was not the time for fruitless speculation.

"I yield all claims of friendship. But, in the name of the debt you still owe me, I need the answer to a question. One question, and then I will leave, and all will be finished between us."

He held his breath. Such a demand was within the code that governed their people, and yet Murchadh was stubborn enough to refuse. And if he did so, Devlin did not know what he would do. As Chosen One, he could compel the obedience of any citizen of Jorsk, including those of conquered Duncaer. Those who refused would face judgment. Murchadh could be fined, or imprisoned if Devlin so chose. But the thought of using this power against one who had been his friend left a bitter taste in his mouth.

"One question. If it is within my power," Murchadh agreed.

"When your uncle Roric died, what happened to the sword he held? The one from Ynnis?"

News of Roric's death had reached Devlin in the New Territories, but there had been no mention of the sword. At the time it had not occurred to him to wonder.

"The sword was left in the guild hall. To be held in trust for you, on the day you should return."

Devlin sighed. He had half hoped that the sword would be here. Murchadh was his uncle's heir, after all. Then it would have been simply a matter of persuading Murchadh to relinquish the sword. He should have known that nothing about this quest would be easy. Now, rather than returning to Kingsholm, he must journey onward into Alvaren, to the place he once called home.

He wondered why Roric had left the sword to him. Had it been a whim of his final days? Had it been his intention all along to leave the sword to his favorite student? Or had there been other influences at work? The same influences that had conspired to turn a onetime farmer into an instrument of justice?

He pushed the thought ruthlessly from his mind. He could not change the past. Nor could he change who he was. Though he loathed the very idea of the sword, in the end what he felt mattered for nothing. He was the Chosen One, and the path to his duty was clear.

"I thank you for your courtesy," he said. "I will leave now and trouble you no more."

Devlin turned and took a step toward the door.

"Wait," Murchadh called.

Devlin turned back as Murchadh approached, waiting until they were only an arm's length apart. Close enough that he could see the beginnings of wrinkles at the corners of Murchadh's eyes, which stared at him with a mixture of bewilderment and suspicion.

"You put claim on past friendship, and now I claim the same right. Last time we met I asked you a question and you did not answer."

Devlin nodded once, already certain he knew what the question was.

"Did you kill them?"

For a moment, he was swept back in time. Nearly two years ago, he had stood in the square outside as Murchadh had given voice to his anger. Then Devlin had simply turned and walked away, for there had been no answer he could give.

There was still no answer, but he owed it to Murchadh to explain what he could.

"I do not know," he said.

The color drained from Murchadh's face. "I do not believe you," he whispered.

Devlin reached for him, then paused, letting his hand drop back to his side. "They did not die at my hands. Nor was I there when they were attacked, though I know Agneta tells a different tale. But am I responsible for their deaths? To that I fear the answer is yes. And for that, you were right to blame me."

With that he turned and walked out of the forge. He had taken but a handful of steps when he heard Murchadh calling his name.

"Devlin! Wait!"

He stiffened his shoulders and kept walking.

"For Egil's sake, wait."

He heard Murchadh's voice, quite near, then a hand

grabbed his left arm. He allowed himself to be spun around, to face his old friend.

"I swore to myself I would not do this. For nigh unto two years I have cursed myself because I let you walk away once. I swore it would not happen again," Murchadh said. "And now, as soon as I saw you, I let my temper get the best of me."

He did not understand. "What do you want of me?"

"I want you to talk to me. As a friend."

"We are no longer friends. You said so yourself."

Murchadh dropped his gaze, but he still held firmly to Devlin's arm. He took a deep breath and looked up. "I was angry. Just as I was that spring. I had thought of you as a brother, and yet suddenly I did not know who you were. We heard of Cerrie's death from strangers. Strangers," he repeated. "Months without word from you, while the tales we heard grew wilder. And then when you finally came here, you would not speak to me."

It had been a dark time for him. After burying his family, Devlin had spent two months tracking down the banecats that killed them, and then weeks recovering from the wounds he had received when he had killed their leader. But destroying the banecats had brought him no peace, and so he had come to Kilbaran, searching for something he could not name. Only to find that even here, folk had already heard news of Devlin's shame. They called him kinslayer, and a part of him agreed with their accusations.

When Murchadh had scorned him, it had been the final straw. Devlin had left Duncaer and set his feet on the path that would bring him to Kingsholm and to his destiny as Chosen One.

Devlin shook his arm free of Murchadh's grasp.

"What did you expect me to say? Did you want me to tell you what their bodies looked like when I found them? How it felt to find my beautiful baby ripped to shreds? To have to tell my brother's wife that she had lost both husband and son? Did you want to know how many nights I spent awake, tormented by the knowledge that if I had been there, I might have saved them?" Devlin's voice broke and he struggled for breath.

"Yes. I would have listened as you shared your grief. Or I would have sat watch with you while you mourned in silence. I should not have let you run away so swiftly. I failed you, and proved myself a poor friend."

The anger drained away as swiftly as it had arisen. What had passed between them was not Murchadh's fault alone. Devlin, too, was to blame. He had done his best to push away any who sought to aid him.

"What was done was done. And you were right when you spoke earlier. I am not the same man that you once called friend."

"Then give me the chance to know this new man. Come to dinner tonight. Alanna will never forgive me if I let you go from here without seeing her," Murchadh said.

Devlin hesitated. A part of him wanted this. Wanted to see if he could reclaim a portion of his friendship with Murchadh. To make peace with a man who was bound up with so much of his past. But another part warned him that this would only bring heartache, reminding him of all that he had once had, that he would never have again.

"Please," Murchadh said.

"I have two friends who journey with me. Stephen, a

minstrel, and Lieutenant Didrik, who serves as my aide." It would not be right to leave them alone.

"Your friends will be welcome," Murchadh assured him. It was a bold promise to make, for only a woman could offer hospitality. But then again Alanna was a generous soul, and Devlin had no doubt that she would treat his friends with all courtesy, regardless of their country of birth.

"Then I gladly accept," Devlin said.

"Good."

Murchadh held out his right hand in the clasp of friendship. Devlin hesitated, then took the smith's hand with his own. He could see from the shock on Murchadh's face the moment he recognized the uneven grip, and the missing fingers.

"In the name of the Seven, what have they done to you?"

Devlin smiled, but it held no mirth. "This I did to myself. Tell Alanna I look forward to seeing her at the evening meal."

Didrik cooled his heels for nearly two hours, sitting in the antechamber outside the commander's office while a steady stream of soldiers and petitioners passed in and out. The delay irked him, and he was tempted to reveal his identity so the commander would see him at once. But Devlin had requested that their mission be kept quiet, and so he held his tongue and waited his turn. He passed the time trying to guess their errands, speculating why none appeared particularly pleased when leaving the commander's office.

At last he was the only one left. The clerk, after conferring with the person behind the closed door, motioned to him.

"Commander Willemson will see you now."

Didrik rose, and reached absently for his sword belt to straighten it, only to remember that he had left his weapons with the door guard. He squared his shoulders and entered the commander's office.

Garrison Commander Willemson was shorter than average, but his stocky build and heavily muscled arms indicated he would be a fierce opponent. He wore the field uniform of dark blue trimmed with crimson, and his tunic jacket was partially unbuttoned. He sat behind a small desk, which was covered with papers and a partially unrolled map.

"What brings a trader here in midwinter, Nils of Denvir? And what do you want from me?" Commander Willemson glanced up briefly, then returned his attention to the duty roster before him.

Didrik shut the door firmly behind him.

"I apologize for the ruse, but what I have to say is for your ears alone."

The commander eyed him, but his gaze was unfriendly.

"If this is about the Children of Ynnis, then your information had better prove reliable or you will meet the same fate as your predecessor. I will not pay coin for stale marketplace gossip."

"I am not here as an informant," Didrik said. He reached into his belt pouch and withdrew the enameled badge that was the seal of his office. "I am Lieutenant Nils Didrik of the Kingsholm Guard—"

"Personal aide to the Chosen One," Commander Willemson finished the sentence.

"Indeed."

Commander Willemson rose to his feet. "And the Chosen One? Is he here?"

"He is in Kilbaran, yes."

"Why? Why here? And why now?"

"May I sit?" Didrik asked.

The commander nodded, then waited as Didrik took his seat before resuming his own.

"What news have you heard from the capital?" Didrik asked. Devlin had warned him not to reveal too much of their mission, but before he could spin a plausible story, he had to know what the commander already knew.

"Only what all others have heard. That the Chosen One revealed Gerhard's treachery and slew the duke in a duel. The King then named him King's councilor and General of the Army."

"That must have come as a surprise."

Commander Willemson snorted. "A shock, more like. When the gossip first reached here, I thought it a jest. It was not till the royal messenger came with the official proclamation that we realized it was true. Half my officers were ready to resign that day."

"Because of their love for the Duke?"

"Because we have dedicated our lives to keeping Duncaer pacified, only to find one of their own set above us. The troops were convinced that it would only be days before the General ordered the garrisons disbanded and control of Duncaer handed over to the rebels. It took all my skill to persuade them to stay at their posts."

"But you knew better."

"General or no, he still answers to the King. And

King Olafur is not going to give up the prize his father won. No matter who leads the army these days."

He supposed it was too much to ask that this man have faith in Devlin. After all, he had never met him. Still, Didrik would not allow Devlin's character to be slighted.

"Devlin would never betray his oath. He is an honorable man, and you should be grateful to serve under him."

The commander did not look convinced.

"So then, why has the Chosen One returned here? His presence can only be taken as a provocation. I have enough to do here, keeping order and catching smugglers."

"Smugglers? These are the Children of Ynnis you mentioned?"

"No, the Children of Ynnis are rebels rumored to be hiding in the mountains, waiting for the moment when they will rise up and lead their people to freedom. But so far we have no proof of their presence, only rumors, and the tales of the mischief they have wrought in Alvaren."

"Then why do you fear them?"

Commander Willemson looked grim. "Five years ago, my predecessor concerned herself with merchants trying to avoid taxes or those bringing in food stores without a license. But these days, when we catch smugglers, it is not food they carry, but weapons. Steel swords, transverse bolts, and the like."

"And for every one that you catch—"

"Another two slip by us," the commander agreed. "I have offered rewards for information on the Children of Ynnis, but not surprisingly the Caerfolk have kept their silence. The damn kin ties mean that everyone is someone's brother or cousin, and no one will inform on their kin."

This was a complication they did not need. Bad enough that they feared enemies might have followed them from Kingsholm. Now they had to worry about Devlin's own countrymen. And to make matters worse, they were heading for Alvaren, the center of the unrest.

It would be too much to hope that they could pass unnoticed.

"Lord Devlin does not come here lightly, nor did he come here to add to your troubles," Didrik said. "I am surprised that you had not heard of his journey."

Commander Willemson shook his head. "I have heard nothing."

"No one asking about the Chosen One? No newly arrived visitors who aroused your suspicions?"

"Nothing," Commander Willemson said. "The trading season is long over, and we keep a firm eye on newcomers who might start trouble. So far there has been nothing unusual. Nothing except the report of three out of season traders arriving last night, staying at the first guesthouse past the gate."

This news should have reassured Didrik, but it did not. Devlin had enemies aplenty in Kingsholm, including whoever had arranged the ambush at the start of their trip. He had expected more trouble, yet there had been no further attempts. Could it be that they thought him no longer a threat, now that he was engaged upon this fool's errand? Or was there something else brewing here?

At least there was one consolation. If Commander Willemson had not heard of Devlin's journey, then presumably the rebels shared his ignorance. With the Gods' own luck, they would be able to slip in and out of Alvaren before the mischief makers had time to react.

"Our visit is unofficial, and we will be gone on the morrow. We hope to leave before Devlin is recognized, which is why he did not come here himself."

This was but a half-truth. Devlin had refused to meet with the commander, and indeed had not wanted to reveal their presence in the city. Didrik had argued long against the decision, pointing out that the commander would be insulted by Devlin's refusal to meet with him. And they needed the commander's help, for he would be in the best position to know if anyone was looking for Devlin or his party. In the end, Devlin had relented and allowed Didrik to be his emissary.

Devlin's refusal to see reason was uncharacteristic of him. But he had been acting strange on this trip, and the closer they had come to Duncaer, the more he had drawn into himself. Not for the first time, Didrik wondered what Devlin had felt when he saw the soldiers guarding the gates into Kilbaran. Did he see them as troops under his command, obeying the orders of their commander and the King? Or did he see them through Caer eyes, as the representatives of those who had conquered his people?

"One would think the Chosen One had better things to do with his time than to jaunt about the countryside," Willemson observed.

"This is no pleasure trip. Devlin returned because he was bidden to do so, to search for the Sword of Light."

"Of all the damn fool ideas. The sword has been lost for fifty years, and now he thinks to find it? Will he spend the next decade digging up the ruins of Ynnis?"

"This was not his choice. And as for finding the sword, Devlin does not intend to tarry long. He will be needed back in Kingsholm by the summer, for he fears invasion is not far off."

It was the only reassurance he could give. Devlin had forbidden him to explain to the commander, or indeed to anyone, that they already knew that the sword had not been lost in Ynnis.

"What does he wish of me?"

"Simply to ask that you and your troops keep an eye out for those who show an interest in the Chosen One and his destination. We will have to pass through Kilbaran upon our return, and would not wish any unpleasant surprises."

"Of course. And I will send a squad of my best with you as escort to Ynnis."

"Thank you, but no," Didrik said. He had no reason to distrust the commander, but neither was there any reason to reveal that Ynnis was not their destination.

Commander Willemson frowned. "I hope you have enough troops to keep him safe."

Didrik murmured in agreement. He was not about to reveal that Devlin's bodyguard consisted of a mere two people.

"If he will not accept my soldiers, then the least I can do is to give him advice. Tell the Chosen One to be careful whom he trusts. The rebels may wish to use him as a figurehead for their revolution—or to kill him as a traitor."

Ten

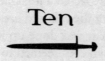

MURCHADH LIFTED A FORKFUL OF MEAT TO HIS mouth. He chewed and swallowed with full deliberation, though the food had no taste. Indeed he was not even certain if the brown meat was mutton or pork. Instead his attention was fixed upon the strange collection of folk that had sat down to this meal.

At the head of the table sat his wife Alanna, presiding over the gathering with the graciousness that was her nature, making certain the guests received the best of everything and that the children were well behaved. Murchadh sat at the foot of the table opposite her. To his right sat their three children, Declan, the oldest at eight, then Ailill, and finally their baby Suisan, who had just turned five. On his left sat Devlin, then next to him the soldier Didrik, and finally the young minstrel Stephen.

Never had he imagined the day when they would welcome two Jorskians as guests in their home. Sharing their food, dining off their best plate. Though they seemed pleasant enough. Stephen had surprised Alanna by greeting her in the Caer tongue. He seemed a friendly sort, and even shy Suisan had warmed to him. It was hard to believe that his father was a noble lord.

On the other hand, Lieutenant Didrik was exactly what Murchadh expected a Jorskian to be. Slender, but well muscled, with the callused hands of a swordsman. His long blond hair was done up in a warrior's braid, and his cold brown eyes seemed to take in everything, as if preparing to pass judgment. Not that he had said or done anything to offend. On the contrary, he had been well taught, for he had offered up his sword before entering the house. Though Murchadh would wager that there was at least one knife hidden on his person.

Didrik, at least, had been grateful that all of Murchadh's family spoke his own tongue. From an early age all children were taught the tradespeech. Such was only prudent in a town where most earned their living by trading with those from Jorsk. Weavers and wool-dyers like Alanna made cloth that was sold in markets from Tamarack to Selvarat. Murchadh himself often dealt with Jorskian traders, shoeing their horses and the like. He knew Jorskians. But he did not understand them. Their ways were not his ways. It was the same all over Duncaer, wherever the two races had cause to mix. Both sides knew this, and understood that there was a line that one did not cross.

Not until tonight. Not until Devlin.

His eyes narrowed as he looked over at Devlin. His friend held a knife in his left hand and the fork in his right, eating with no signs of clumsiness. One had to look closely to see that he was maimed. Devlin's hair was streaked with white, and there was a pale red scar around his neck. And there were changes of the soul as well. Devlin's expression was guarded and his eyes hard.

It was impossible to tell what he was thinking. He, who had once worn his emotions on his face for all to see.

Murchadh stared, trying to find some trace of the boy he had once known, the man who had been his friend. They had known each other for nearly twenty years. Apprenticed at the same forge, they had worked side by side for nearly a decade. Once they had been as close as brothers. Now he struggled to reconcile his knowledge of who Devlin had been with the reality of what he had become.

When the first messenger had arrived from Jorsk, bearing three golden disks, Murchadh had been astounded. And afraid, wondering how Devlin had come into such a fortune, since the messenger refused to say. The second messenger was equally tight-lipped. But the third messenger who had brought the final three golden disks, also brought the news that a foreigner named Devlin had been named Chosen One, champion of Jorsk.

It had seemed absurd. A jest. Devlin barely knew one end of a sword from another, and he had no love for their conquerors. And yet the nine golden disks, a fortune by any reckoning, said otherwise.

And then the tales began. The late-season traders told of the foreign champion who destroyed a lake monster, though few knew the name of this man, calling him only the Chosen One. Murchadh had spent a few sleepless nights worrying about his friend, only to scoff at his foolishness as he realized that these tales could not be about Devlin. There must be some other champion they spoke of. Then this past summer, they heard that the Chosen One had defeated the King's champion in a duel, exposing his treachery. In reward for his service he was named General of the Royal Army. Marketplace gossip was swiftly followed by an official royal decree. Now all in Kilbaran knew the story of the metalsmith turned champion, Jorskian and Caerfolk alike.

Gossip painted Devlin as a fearless warrior who had faced countless dangers in his pursuit of justice. Murchadh had dismissed these tales as exaggerations. But now, seeing Devlin's face, he wondered how many of them were true.

"More winter ale?" Alanna asked, lifting the enameled pitcher.

"If you would be so kind," Stephen replied. He took the pitcher from her and filled his cup, then passed the pitcher to Didrik on his left.

Stephen lifted his cup, turning it in his hand to study the carved bowl and enameled base that turned an ordinary copper cup into something worthy of a King's table. "This is a beautiful piece of craftsmanship. I've seen enameled brooches but never have I seen it on such a scale, or done so well."

"Each cup and plate match, yet no two are alike, are they?" Didrik asked.

The soldier had a keen eye.

"There are fourteen in all," Alanna explained. "One for each of the twelve months, and one each in honor of the Heavenly Pair. See, Stephen, yours has the salmon of knowledge, and Nils, yours shows the flowers of early springtime. They were a wedding gift—"

"They were made for us by one of the greatest smiths Alvaren has ever seen," Murchadh interrupted, ignoring Alanna's frown. "Each piece has no less than a half dozen colors, and even after nine years, the colors are as clear today as they were when they were first fired."

"A true craftsman indeed," Didrik said.

Murchadh turned his gaze toward Devlin. "He was the youngest to be named Master Smith in living memory. All knew he was destined to create works of great beauty. In time he would have become Guild Master. Instead he threw it all away, turning his back on his craft to become a farmer."

There was a low exclamation and a hiss of indrawn breath, but Murchadh had no eyes for anyone except his friend.

Devlin set down his cutlery with slow deliberate movements. "I did not leave Alvaren lightly. But when the time came, I chose family over craft. You would have done the same."

"No." Of this he was certain. Murchadh would have given his soul for one-tenth the talent that Devlin had possessed. He could not imagine anyone turning their back on such a gift.

"Alanna's craft brought her here, and you followed, did you not? Why should my life be any different?"

"Because that was different. You were different. I could be a smith anywhere, it did not matter. Plain work such as mine does better in the outlands than it did in the capital. But you had the true gift."

"It was not to be," Devlin said, with a shrug.

"But you've come back now, so you're going to be a smith again. You can share the forge with my father," Declan said.

Devlin winced, a flash of pain so brief that he almost missed it. "My days as a smith are long over. Now I have a new task, and a new oath."

"You could still teach," Murchadh said stubbornly. "Even with a crippled hand, there is much you could do."

"I do teach," Devlin said. "But these days it is Cerrie's craft I teach."

Impossible. He had once been called Gentle Heart, Devlin of the Gifted Hands. It was impossible to think of him as a warrior. Soldiers were common but artists were all too rare and precious.

"You have your destiny—"

"Not as a metalsmith. Not anymore," Devlin said. Then he turned to face Alanna, deliberately giving Murchadh a view of his stiff neck and back. "Tell me, is your sister Mari still in Alvaren?"

Alanna did not blink at the abrupt turn in the conversation, instead replying, "No, she finished her apprenticeship two years ago, and is now a trader in her own right. She planned to winter over in Darrow, last that we'd heard."

"I am sure she is a skilled trader," Devlin said.

Not wishing to quarrel in front of his children and the foreign guests, Murchadh held his tongue as the conversation turned to lighter topics, and Alanna told Devlin the news of their mutual acquaintances. There would be time later for him to speak with Devlin alone.

After dinner, the children begged until Stephen agreed to sing for them. Though he had no instrument, his voice was fine, and he sang "The Mountain Rose" as if he had been born speaking the Caer tongue. Then he switched to his own language, and began a silly song about a little boy who wished to be a dragon. The children were delighted, clapping their hands along with the refrain. Murchadh rose from his seat and left the parlor to visit the necessary. When he returned, he found the soldier standing in the hallway. Waiting for him.

"A word with you, if you would," the soldier said.

Murchadh nodded. "Come, there is no one in the kitchen." He led the way down the hall, then opened the door to the kitchen and walked in. The soldier followed, his eyes sweeping the kitchen seemingly by habit, as if confirming that they were indeed alone before shutting the door firmly behind them.

"You are Devlin's friend, are you not?" Didrik asked.

"Yes." Or rather he had been, and wished to be still. But he could not help wondering how Devlin would answer the question.

"Then why do you torment him?"

"What?" He had not meant to raise his voice, and looked toward the door, hoping that the sound of the music had covered his outburst.

"You know he can never be a metalsmith again, so why do you throw that in his face? Why are you punishing him?" The soldier drew himself up to his full height, his body radiating tension. The fingers of his right hand drummed restlessly on his belt, where the scabbard of his sword had hung.

He should have known that one sworn to follow the sword would not understand. Only another craftsman could understand.

"A gift like Devlin's does not die merely because his hand is maimed. The great works may be beyond him, but he seems to have enough control of that hand for ordinary tasks. And he can still teach others. It is time for him to give up this folly and to return home to his people."

Two years ago, Murchadh had turned Devlin away, at the moment his friendship was needed most. This time he was determined not to fail his friend. He would save Devlin, even from himself.

Didrik's gaze searched his face. "You do not know, do you?"

"I know my friend."

Didrik's hand dropped away from his belt, and the deadly tension in his frame drained away.

Murchadh released a breath he had not been aware of holding.

"Devlin swore an oath as Chosen One."

"He swore an oath to his guild," he countered.

Didrik shook his head. "The oath of Chosen One is for life. Devlin is bound to serve until his death, or until King Olafur releases him from service. He can more easily cut off his left hand than he could forswear that oath."

The room grew suddenly chill, despite the blazing fire on the cooking hearth.

"Bound," Murchadh repeated.

"Bound," the soldier affirmed. "Bound by oath and by spell. He will be Chosen One until the day he meets his death."

Spellbound? Such a thing was an abomination. From the sympathy on Didrik's face, Murchadh knew his own horror was plain to see.

"My task is to keep him safe," Didrik said. "And to do that, he must be focused on his duty. This journey is already hard enough, bringing back dark memories. If you are truly his friend, do not add to his burden."

Devlin watched in silence, forgotten by the children as they persuaded Stephen to sing one song after another. When the minstrel's throat tired, he was given a cup of honeyed tea, and pestered with questions about what it was like to live in what they fondly imagined to be the frozen northlands. Someone who was both a minstrel and a foreigner was far more interesting than the grim-faced man who had once been their father's friend. No matter that he had once taught Declan how to roll a hoop, or that he and Cerrie had spent sleepless nights pacing the floor with their friends when Ailill had nearly died from the winter fever. All that was in the past. It had been more than four years since he had seen them, an eternity to a child.

Murchadh left the room, then a few moments later Didrik followed, no doubt visiting the necessary. When they returned, they brought a fresh pitcher of ale, and a plate of sweets the children shared with Stephen. He noticed they were careful not to get too close to Didrik, making sure that their mother or father was between them and the lieutenant at all times. And their caution was understandable, for Didrik was in uniform.

He took slow sips of the dark brown ale as he considered the tableau before him. There, on the one side, was his old life, represented by Murchadh and Alanna. Their friendship connected him to his past. He had stood witness at their wedding, and they had been honored guests on the day when Cerrie had finally claimed him as her own. And on the other side were Stephen and Didrik, who represented the new friendships he had made, and the new responsibilities he bore. Both sides seemed to find pleasure in each other's company.

It was tempting to believe that his old life and his

new could so easily be reconciled, but Devlin knew that for an illusion. Murchadh had set aside old grudges for the sake of past friendship, but he would never claim a Jorskian as friend. Nor would he understand the new claims that now held sway over Devlin's loyalties.

Perhaps it was for the best that there was no opportunity for private conversation with Murchadh. With these others as witnesses, there was no danger that they would quarrel. Instead they would part on civil terms, and Devlin would be able to look back on this evening with pleasure.

It was late when Alanna finally declared it time for Declan to go to bed. His sisters Ailill and Suisan had already fallen asleep, lying stretched out on cushions before the fire. Alanna shook them both awake, then lifted Suisan in her arms. The children said yawning good nights to their guests and were led upstairs.

"When Alanna returns we must make our farewells. It is time for us to seek our own beds," Devlin said.

"A word with you, if you please," Murchadh said.

He glanced over at Didrik. Didrik nodded, then took Stephen by the arm and they exited the room, leaving Devlin and Murchadh alone.

"I had hoped we would have a chance to talk, to clear up past misunderstandings, but the evening slipped away from us. Will you come back on the morrow?"

Devlin shook his head. "No. We leave at dawn for Alvaren."

"Surely you can spare a day. It will take you three weeks to get to Alvaren, and one more day will not matter."

"My duty is to retrieve the sword without delay. With hard travel we can be in Alvaren in a fortnight, no more. Then we must return with all haste to Kingsholm."

It would be full winter during their return journey, which would slow them down. But with luck they would be back in Kingsholm before spring, in time for the annual gathering of the court.

"Duty," Murchadh repeated, his mouth twisted as if he tasted something bitter. "Is this part of what it means to be Chosen One?"

"Yes." There was no need to elaborate. No need to tell him of the Geas that commanded Devlin's obedience whether he willed it or nay. He did not want Murchadh's sympathy.

"Why the sword? What is so important about it?"

He hesitated a moment, then decided Murchadh deserved the truth. "I tell you this in strictest confidence. The sword that Roric brought from Ynnis was not an ordinary sword. It was the sword of Saemund. The Chosen One, killed in the siege."

The blood drained from Murchadh's face and Devlin felt a grim flicker of satisfaction.

"In the name of the Seven, how? And why?"

"Those are the wrong questions. Ask rather why was I called to become Chosen One? What strange fate led me to Jorsk, the one man who could tell them how to retrieve their lost heirloom?"

"You cannot do this," Murchadh declared. "Your parents' nearkin were all killed in Ynnis, perhaps by the very sword you now seek. How can you even think of touching it? Let alone returning it to the land of our conquerors?"

"I have no choice. It is not just a sword, it is a symbol. Made for the first Chosen One by a son of Egil, or so they say. Without it I am simply a man who serves at the King's whim. With the sword in my hand, none can deny my authority. I will be able to face down the royal court and lead the army in preparing to defend Jorsk against the attack that all know is coming."

Murchadh was silent, as Devlin's words put an end to any illusion that he was still the man who had been his friend. There was no room in Murchadh's life for a man who was marked by the Gods for some fate even Devlin could not imagine.

"I have imposed upon your kindness long enough," Devlin began.

"No."

"No?"

Murchadh wiped one hand across his eyes, then shook his head as if to banish some dark thought. "You will not leave yet. Not until you have heard me out. Two years ago, I let my anger blind me, and when I had come to my senses you had disappeared. I will not wait another two years to have my say."

Devlin braced himself for his friend's anger.

"I do not understand what you have become. Nor do I know what it means that you are Chosen One. Though the lieutenant took me to task for my ignorance."

He wondered what Didrik had told Murchadh.

"Your road has twisted since you left Alvaren and your forge behind. I have no wish to walk it, but I will not deny you your path. At heart, you are the same man you have always been. I put my trust and my friendship in that man. And I ask that you forgive an old friend for being too hasty in his judgment and too slow to understand."

It took a moment for Murchadh's words to sink in. Devlin took a deep breath, feeling a tightness in his chest ease.

"There is nothing to forgive," Devlin said.

"I know that Agneta has cast you out, and what farkin you had left have denied you at her urging. But know now that you are not kinless. Alanna and I claimed you, on the day we learned of Cerrie's and Cormack's deaths."

Devlin swallowed hard. "You cannot mean that."

"I would not have said it elsewise. Come now, you stand second father to our children. How could we not claim you as kin?" Murchadh reached over and squeezed Devlin's shoulder with his right hand. "Even in my anger, it was the anger of the elder brother to a younger brother who has gone off on his own path. We did not mean you to be alone."

The temptation was dizzying. With a few sentences, Murchadh had restored to Devlin all he had lost before. For among their people, a man without kin was not a man at all. He was utterly cut off from all society. Thus the word for kinbereft was the same as for an exile, for one with no kin was forced to leave his homeland and become a rootless wanderer.

It was a truly generous act, and had Devlin known of this two years ago, he might never have left Duncaer. But two years had changed him greatly.

"Your kindness overwhelms me, but I cannot accept. Your kin might claim a farmer or a smith, but do you truly wish to call the General of the Royal Army your brother? To know that the garrisons in Duncaer go and stay at my command? Not to mention that my debts are no longer my own. My duty as Chosen One must come before kin ties."

"The kinweb is strong enough to bear the burden."

There were a dozen reasons, no, a hundred reasons why he should refuse. But instead Devlin found himself saying "Then I accept. And I pledge that I will do my best to protect our kin, and bring honor to our name."

Eleven

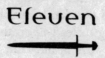

THE NEXT DAY THEY LEFT KILBARAN BEFORE THE sun had even risen. The two soldiers at the southern gate eyed the three travelers curiously, then turned to Devlin and gave him the formal hand over heart salute due a senior officer.

"Lord General," the corporal said.

Devlin glanced around, and was grateful to see that there were none of his own folk close enough to witness this folly. He had accepted his role as Chosen One, but the title of General was still new enough to make him uneasy. Especially here, where the Royal Army played the role of conqueror.

Devlin inclined his head, in acknowledgment of the salute. "Corporal. My respects to your commander, and inform him that I will see him upon my return."

"Yes, sir," the corporal replied. He gestured, and the second soldier swung open the outer gate.

Devlin was the first to ride through the gate, eager to resume the journey. Seeing his friends had stirred up old feelings within him. It had been hard to be faced with living reminders of what he had once been, and all he had lost. Such regrets had no place in his life, and so he was eager to focus instead on the task before him.

The road from Kilbaran to Alvaren was well maintained, with inns spaced at regular intervals to serve the needs of Jorskian travelers. Caerfolk would never stay at an inn, relying instead upon the elaborate web of hospitality owed to kin and craft brothers. With the blessing of Murchadh's name, Devlin could have claimed guest right for himself and his friends, but such favor was not to be squandered lightly, so instead they stayed at Jorskian inns, where hospitality could be bought with coin.

The innkeepers were glad enough to welcome them. Winter travelers were rare, so much so that the government paid an allowance to the innkeepers in order to ensure the inns stayed open year-round. And travelers brought news from home, which was nearly as welcome as the coins that supplemented the winter allowance.

Best of all, the innkeepers knew enough to respect his privacy. They asked no questions, and unlike in Jorsk, their stays were not disturbed by curiosity seekers come to see the legendary Chosen One.

As they journeyed into the mountains, the steep terrain took its toll on both men and horses. Fortunately, the weather turned fair, and Devlin set a pace that was swift but not brutal. Unlike his other journeys, the Geas did not urge him to reckless haste. Instead, for the most part, it left him alone—though sometimes he heard its voice whispering in his mind like the distant hum of far-off conversation. He felt it as much as heard it, often at the end of a hard day's travel when they had journeyed till they were nearly asleep in their saddles. And once he had woken in the still hours of the night to hear the same hum of voices. But he could never make out the words, nor was there any sense of compulsion, as there had been before.

He wondered if the power of the Geas grew weaker the farther he journeyed from Kingsholm. Perhaps if he journeyed far enough, he would be free from its influence altogether. But such a thought was perilously close to oath breaking, and he banished it from his mind.

On the ninth day after leaving Kilbaran they arrived at the village of Bengore, just after dusk. The inn was easy to spot, for as was the custom, it was set on the northern edge of the village, separated from its neighbors to the south by a rocky field.

The stableboy was nowhere to be found. The lone occupant, an elderly mare, snorted her disapproval as they proceeded to untack their horses and rub them down. Stephen pitched clean straw into three empty stalls, while Didrik pumped fresh water into the buckets, and Devlin filled their mangers with grain from the feed room. After settling the horses in the stalls, they picked up their saddlebags and made their way to the inn proper.

The windows were ablaze with light, and the door swung open at their touch. As they entered, they found themselves in a large open room, with a half-dozen trestle tables on each side and twin hearths that burned brightly. In the back of the room was a hallway.

"Glad tidings and welcome to you," a disembodied voice called.

Devlin heard slow steps and a scraping sound, as if someone was dragging a heavy load. A man stepped from the hallway. As he came toward them, Devlin could see that the man's left leg was crippled, for it dragged behind him with each step.

"I apologize for not being here to greet you, but with the hour so late, I did not expect any guests to arrive. Not on Midwinter's Eve. Do you have a carriage or horses that need stabling? My daughter Edyth usually takes care of that, but she is in the kitchen now, helping with the feast."

"We have already seen to our own horses," Didrik said. He normally took the lead in dealings with the innkeepers, since most responded better to a fellow countryman. "But we'll need a pair of rooms for the night, and a hot meal, if you can manage."

The innkeeper drew himself up to his full height. "We can manage better than a mere meal. You must join my family for the winter feast. It will be our pleasure to have guests on this evening—a touch of home as it were. The heathens here are a dour lot, and have no sense that tonight is one to make merry."

Didrik coughed, and Stephen shuffled his feet.

Devlin came forward and threw back the hood of his cloak, revealing his features.

The innkeeper's face paled. "Sir, I meant no disrespect, of course," he said. "I did not know—"

"No matter," Devlin said. "I am sure my friends will be glad to join you and your family at their revels. As for me, I have no taste for such things and will retire early."

He had his own plans for this night and they did not include a celebration. But he would not begrudge Stephen and Didrik their fun.

In a short time they were settled in their rooms, Devlin in one large chamber, Didrik and Stephen sharing the room across the hall. The innkeeper's daughter Edyth had brought hot water for washing up and Didrik had seemed quite taken with her.

The innkeeper, who bore the name Wendell, personally brought up a dinner tray to Devlin's room. The food was excellent, but Devlin ate only sparingly and soon pushed the tray aside.

There was a knock at his door.

"Enter," he called.

The door swung open, and Didrik came inside, followed by Stephen. Both had exchanged their dusty travel clothes for cleaner garb.

"Will you not join us? Midwinter's Eve is best spent with friends, and our hosts would be honored at your presence."

Devlin shook his head. "I have no mood for merrymaking. And this is your holiday, not mine. I will be well content on my own."

"I do not feel right leaving you here alone," Didrik said.

"I do not need a nursemaid. Go, enjoy your holiday, and smile at Edyth's sallies. Just be careful how much you drink, for, aching heads or no, we leave tomorrow at first light."

Didrik grinned. "It will be as you command."

"Will you stay indoors tonight? Or do you plan on marking the Day of Remembrance?" Stephen asked.

This was not the first time Stephen had surprised him with his knowledge of Caer customs. Stephen had known little of the Caerfolk when they first met, but since then he had apparently studied the matter at some length, even taking time to learn the language. Whatever scrolls he had consulted had apparently included a discussion of Caer beliefs, though strangely they had omitted the fundamental truths that were taught in childhood, such as the sacred obligation of hospitality and the ties between women and the land.

Devlin knew he should be flattered but instead he felt vaguely uneasy. He did not like being understood so well.

"I will mark this night," he said, conscious of Didrik's curious stare.

"Then may I join you? I would keep vigil, as a friend."

He hesitated. A part of him wondered at the reason for Stephen's request. Was he asking as a friend? Or was he asking as a minstrel, as one ever curious for bits of arcane lore that could be added to the legend of the Chosen One?

The silence stretched between them, until it grew uncomfortable. Stephen opened his mouth to speak, but Devlin forestalled him. "At moonrise. If you wish, you may join me then."

Stephen watched, his eyes bright with curiosity, as Devlin placed the copper bowl on the ground before him. The firelight flickered over the hammered metal surface, glinting it with gold. He shivered a bit, for the ground was cold underneath him.

"Haakon, Lord of the Sunset Realm, I, Devlin, son of Kameron and Talaith, now called Devlin the Chosen One, greet my dead. May the burdens they carry be lighter for my remembrance."

He took the dagger from his belt and pricked the

thumb of his left hand, holding it over the bowl and squeezing until several drops had fallen.

Then he replaced the dagger on his belt and picked up the flask of distilled meadowsweet. Uncorking the flask, he poured a small measure into the bowl, watching as the blood turned the clear liquid red. Then he took a healthy swig for himself.

He extended the flask to Stephen, who sat on his right side. "Drink," he urged.

"Is this part of the ritual?" Stephen asked.

"No. But it is cold tonight, and a drink will warm your blood."

Stephen nodded and took a long draught. He had yet to develop a taste for the sharp liquor but he swallowed manfully before handing the flask back to Devlin.

"What happens now?" Stephen asked, his voice roughened by the whiskey.

Devlin shrugged. "Now we wait."

He would not voice his hopes aloud. They were so fragile that to speak them might destroy them. Instead, he turned his gaze from the fire to their surrounds. The waning moon provided only enough light to see the vague outline of shapes. Behind them, the rock wall that separated this field from the inn provided shelter for their backs. A short distance to his left, a pair of young oak trees raised slender branches to the sky. And in the distance, he saw the glow of a bonfire, where the villagers held their own ritual.

Devlin could have joined them, but had chosen not to disrupt their remembrances with his controversial presence. At least he had Stephen to bear him company this year, reminding him that he now had friends and craft to sustain him.

And this year's vigil was quite different from last year's. Then he had performed the full ritual, pledging the soul price for his murdered family. This year he had neither kin nor friends to ease on their final journey. Instead he came merely to pay his respects, and to listen to whatever wisdom the dead might choose to share.

They sat in silence as the moon rose above them. Stephen kept a careful eye on the fire, and from time to time they took sips of meadowsweet from the flask.

Devlin gazed into the flames, lost in reverie, as one by one he silently recalled each of his dead. Once that count had included family and treasured friends, but now he added enemies to their number. Soon after becoming Chosen One he had learned what it was to kill in cold blood, to order the execution of those whose crimes deserved the ultimate punishment.

More than one soul had met their end at Devlin's hand, and his soul already bore the burden of these killings—justified though they may have been. And if Jorsk did go to war, he would bear the burden of many more deaths as he led the army against the enemy.

A gasp from Stephen brought him back to the present.

"Look," Stephen said, his arm pointing to the distant field.

Devlin raised his eyes from the fire and blinked as he peered into the darkness. A silver mist drifted toward them. As the mist drew closer, it solidified until he could no longer see through it.

Devlin rose to his feet, and Stephen did the same. The mist paused on the far side of the fire, and then a woman stepped out. She was tall, taller than Devlin, with dark curly hair cropped close to her head, and green eyes that held a spark of mischief. She wore dark green leggings and a matching tunic. A sword hung from her waist, and around her left arm was an engraved copper armband.

Devlin drank in the sight of her, joy and grief mixing within him as he realized that he had forgotten just how beautiful she had been. For a moment, time stood still. Then a branch shifted on the fire, sending sparks into the sky, and the spell was broken.

"Honored husband," the apparition said.

"Beloved wife," he replied.

Stephen made some exclamation, but all of Devlin's attention was focused on Cerrie. The fire was between them, so he took several steps around it, only to stop as Cerrie mirrored his movements.

"Gentle Heart," Cerrie said. "You have changed, but still I would know you anywhere."

He swallowed against a throat gone tight with emotion. "Would you?"

"I never thought to see you a soldier, but you have done well. But there is a different kind of danger around you now, and I begged Lord Haakon to let me journey here, to warn you of your peril."

"Haakon," Devlin said, the name bitter in his mouth. "The Gods have already meddled enough in our lives. And now he sends you to do their bidding?"

Cerrie stretched one hand across the fire. "Listen to me, for there is very little time. There is danger, from where you least suspect," she said.

To be Chosen One was to live with danger every day. He had become accustomed to it. And yet Cerrie's urgency infected him with a sense of unease. She had never been one to worry over trifles.

"What kind of danger? From whom?"

She shrugged. "I can see the shape of the peril but not its creator."

"How dare Haakon use you in this way? Is he trying to torment us both?" Devlin was furious. The ceremonies of remembrance were supposed to ease the dead into the next life. Instead Cerrie's hard-won peace had been disturbed. She had been gifted with a glimpse of Devlin's peril, then denied the chance to offer him the knowledge that might help him defeat it. And he knew full well how it felt to be helpless, unable to save a loved one.

It was monstrous to think that she could be used in such a way. It only confirmed his belief that the Lord of the Dread Realm had purposely chosen to torment Devlin. At first he had withheld death, refusing to take Devlin's soul when every fiber of Devlin's being craved release. Now that Devlin had once again found the will to live, Haakon discovered a new way to ensure his misery, condemning him to a hell on earth.

"Tell Haakon I will not be his pawn," Devlin declared. "And when the day comes that he finally decides to face me, I will demand a reckoning."

Cerrie had died because of him. She, Lyssa, Cormack, and Bevan. All killed because the Gods had decreed that he would be the Chosen One and would return the lost sword to Jorsk. The familiar anger and guilt rose up within him. He could feel it pounding in his veins, and a dark haze clouded his vision.

He shook his head and blinked as Cerrie's ghostly form dissolved and a new figure stood in her place. The figure wore a dark cloak, the hood pulled over his head. His features were obscured, and there were two glowing points of light instead of eyes. In his right hand the figure held a staff that glowed silver.

"Long have I waited for the chance to speak with you." The voice was soft but low, with a rumbling underneath, as if a stone had decided to speak.

This was Haakon himself, the Lord of the Dread Realm. Devlin had felt his presence before, when illness or injury brought him to the brink of death. But each time Haakon had refused to take him.

"I am not afraid of you," Devlin lied. He did not fear death, but there were other torments that Haakon could inflict. He could well deny Devlin's spirit entrance to the Sunset Realm, forcing him to wander endlessly in the twilight realms, forever cut off from the spirits of those he had known and loved. Condemned to an eternity spent alone in darkness.

Haakon laughed, and despite his brave words Devlin felt a chill run up his spine. "If you knew me, you would fear me. Soon your soul will be mine."

"Why now?" This made no sense. If fate had decreed that Devlin was to die, then why would Haakon allow Cerrie to warn him of his peril?

"Because I wish it," Haakon said. He took one step forward, then another, and the flames parted around him, for they had no power to touch him. Haakon came to stand directly before Devlin.

Devlin took half a step backward before he could stop himself. But he could not outrun a God, nor would he give Haakon the satisfaction of seeing his fear.

Haakon stretched out his hand and placed it on Devlin's head. "You will be mine," he whispered.

Burning pain filled him, and to his horror he heard

Haakon's words repeated, this time within his own mind. "You will be mine."

Devlin could not move, could not even scream—a prisoner in his own body as the fire consumed him from within. "I do not belong to you. I am Devlin, Devlin of Duncaer," he chanted, holding on to the shards of his identity. Cerrie's face rose before him, shouting a warning. And then the blackness overwhelmed him, and he knew no more.

Twelve

THE FIRST RAYS OF DAWN CAST A PITILESS LIGHT over Kingsholm, though few people were awake to witness the start of this New Year. Most revelers had long ago sought their beds, or staggered off in a drunken stupor to sleep where they fell. Only those with urgent duties were still awake and sober at this hour.

Captain Drakken was one. As was her custom, she had taken personal command of the Guard last night, supervising those whose job it was to ensure that the holiday revelries remained peaceful. There had been the usual troubles last night. A band of drunken youths had been discovered smashing windows in the merchants' quarter. They were taken into custody until their parents could pay their fines. The guard had been summoned to break up a handful of tavern brawls, though there were no serious injuries. And patrols had found at least a dozen fools passed out drunk in the streets. All but one had been rescued before they had frozen to death.

Compared to the celebrations of past years, it had been a quiet night, in part because few truly felt like celebrating, given the uncertain state of the Kingdom. And in part because of the extra patrols she had ordered, and the vigilance of her guards. She had already thanked the guards who had taken last night's watch and dismissed them to seek their beds. She, too, would welcome sleep, but she had one thing more to do.

She paused on the steps that led into the Royal Chapel, knocking her boots against the stone to dislodge the snow that clung to them. Then she climbed the half dozen steps and pushed open the door.

Sunlight streamed through the skylights, illuminating the stone altar. In contrast the rest of the temple was dim, for only one in four of the oil lamps that ringed the walls had been lit. Brother Arni was nowhere to be seen. Presumably he had gone to his own bed after performing the midnight observances. She wondered if he had found any faithful to lead in prayer, or if once again he had prayed alone.

As she drew even with the altar, she bowed respectfully and gave it a wide berth. To the left of the altar was an alcove, and she paused in front of the map wall. Here a delicately crafted stone mosaic depicted the entire Kingdom in intricate detail. Provinces, cities, rivers, roads, all laid out with astonishing accuracy.

One stone differed from the rest, for it protruded from the map, glowing with a ruby light. Her fingers hovered over the soul stone, though she knew better than to touch it. She knelt and looked at the stone, which was in the far southwestern corner of the map. This section was not as well marked as the central provinces, but she could see that the stone was on the road that led from Kilbaran to Alvaren.

For a moment the red light within the stone seemed

to fade. Her heart froze and she blinked her eyes. When she opened them the light again shone with a steady glow. Captain Drakken sighed with relief. Her eyes had been playing tricks on her. Too little sleep could do that, even to the Captain of the Guard.

Devlin was safe, and making steady progress in his quest. He would reach Alvaren in a few days. And then, if the Gods were kind, he would find the sword and begin his journey back to Kingsholm.

With luck, he would be back before the spring solstice, ready to take his place on the King's Council at the official opening of the court. Not that politics were in abeyance for the winter. On the contrary, this winter a greater number of courtiers and nobles than usual had chosen to winter in Kingsholm, rather than returning to their own provinces. And while the court was not in session, there was nothing to prevent them from gathering informally, furthering their own schemes.

The wind was shifting. Alliances were being formed, and even she could see that Devlin's allies were being shut out. Border nobles such as Lord Rikard and Lady Vendela were invited to fewer and fewer social occasions. In response the progressives held their own parties, and when they could not find enough nobles to fill their guest lists, they began turning to the wealthy merchants to fill the empty seats at their tables. This tactic outraged the conservative courtiers, who held that merchants had no business interfering in the Kingdom's politics.

And she herself was being closely watched, since the day when she had confronted the King and demanded that he allow her to search for whoever had set the assassins on Devlin's trail. So far her private inquiries had turned up no clue as to the identities of the four swordsmen, much to her frustration. A public search with the full weight of the Guard behind it might well have succeeded where she had failed.

But she had to be careful these days. As Captain of the Guard, her position demanded neutrality. She might urge the King's Council to authorize additional guards, or to strengthen their defenses, but she could not openly back one faction of the court against another. Not if she hoped to retain her post.

Six months ago her position had been secure. She had earned it on her own merits and proven herself worthy of trust through years of faithful service to the King. But then she had backed Devlin in his challenge against Duke Gerhard.

It had been the right thing to do. Gerhard had been exposed as a traitor, who threatened her kingdom and the King she had vowed to protect. King Olafur had rewarded Devlin for his service, naming him King's councilor and General of the Army. And her own position had seemed untouchable, backed by Devlin's patronage.

But these days the Chosen One's name held little power. Even those who were favorably inclined toward his policies had been dismayed by Devlin's abandoning Kingsholm to quest after the lost sword. Should Devlin return swiftly in triumph, all would be forgiven. But if not . . .

"I hoped I would find you here," Lord Rikard's voice interrupted her solitary musings.

Captain Drakken rose to her feet and turned. Underneath his fur cloak, she could see the hint of silken robes, which meant the Thane of Myrka had come here directly from the evening's festivities.

It was no longer safe for them to be seen together in public. Lord Rikard was too closely associated with Devlin's policies. Should the King's Council be called into session, Rikard had been appointed to take the seat that Devlin would normally occupy.

She could not consult with him openly, but in casual conversation with Solveig of Esker, she had let fall the news that she visited the Royal Chapel each morning at dawn. It was a custom she had begun not out of an excess of piety, but rather so she could keep watch over Devlin's travels.

It was foolish, she knew. Though the soul stone would reveal if Devlin were in trouble, there was nothing that could be done from here. Any help she could send would reach him far too late. Still, it was comforting to watch his steady progress and to know that he was yet unharmed.

Besides, her visits to the Royal Temple served another purpose. Brother Arni was discreet, and few others ventured here. Especially not at dawn, when most courtiers were asleep. It was a perfect place for a seemingly casual encounter.

"Has he found the sword?" Lord Rikard asked.

"No, for he continues to journey deeper into Duncaer, toward Alvaren."

"I was hoping that by now—"

"There is time," she said. "The spring council does not begin for three months. He will return by then."

Rikard peered at the map. "Duncaer is larger than I thought. How can he hope to find a single sword in that wild place?"

"The Chosen One is resourceful. He has triumphed against far greater odds. You must do your part and trust that he will be successful."

"Of course," Lord Rikard said, but his brow was furrowed in doubt.

She could not blame his misgivings. Devlin had not told Lord Rikard the full truth of the quest for the sword. He trusted Lord Rikard's motives, but the young thane had a hot temper and in the heat of debate might well blurt out what ought to be kept hidden. Thus Rikard, along with the rest of Devlin's friends and supporters, had nothing to rely upon but their faith in the Chosen One. And their belief in his destiny.

Captain Drakken bit back a yawn, rubbing the sleep from her tired eyes as her body reminded her that she had seen more than forty winters and it was past time that she sought her bed.

"You wished to speak with me?" she prompted.

"Were you at the royal celebrations last night?" Rikard asked.

"I made a courtesy visit, but did not stay. I saw that you had been placed at the King's own table."

Eighteen courtiers had been chosen to dine with the King and Princess Ragenilda. It was a rare mark of favor that Rikard had been chosen to join their ranks.

"The King was civil, but I suspect the invitation had more to do with my palate than my politics."

"I beg your pardon?" He was talking in riddles, and she was too tired to play these games.

"After the feast, I mingled with the other guests during the entertainment. Several of them complained that the wine they had been served was inferior. I took a cup for myself, and found they were right. The King's table was served the Myrkan reserve from five summers ago. A good year. But the rest of the guests had an inferior wine from Grimstadt."

"So they did not like the wine. That is hardly news to keep us from our beds."

She liked wine, but would hardly call herself a connoisseur. She drank red Myrkan wine by preference, though ordinary vintages, not the reserve that was meant for the King's court. Still, she did not see what difference it made if the wine had come from Grimstadt. They, too, made good wines—though as Thane of Myrka, Lord Rikard would no doubt disagree.

"Every year, Myrka sends a shipment of its best wines to Kingsholm, as part of our taxes. These shipments are sent by sea to the port of Bezek, and then brought upriver to Kingsholm. Shipping the wine by the water route preserves the flavor and ensures that only the best reaches the King's table."

She hazarded a guess. "The wines from Grimstadt come by land?"

"Precisely," Lord Rikard said.

"I still do not see why this matters. Perhaps they simply ran out of Myrkan wine and had to make do with the other instead. Such things happen."

"They shouldn't," Lord Rikard said. His features were grave, telling her that there was far more at stake than the Royal Steward's choice of wine to serve at a banquet. "I questioned the servers, and they insisted that the wine was from Myrka. But it wasn't. Which means the royal cellars are running empty."

"There are far more courtiers in Kingsholm this winter than in the past. That may have strained the King's resources. And his cellars."

"Or is it because the last three shipments of wine never arrived? The pirates have taken a far greater toll on our shipping than most realize. And it is not just Myrkan wine that the King is running short of. Ships carrying taxes from the other coastal provinces have also been attacked, their gold and goods seized. If matters do not improve, soon the King will have to borrow from the moneylenders in order to pay the army."

"It may not come to that. We still have the taxes from the interior provinces," Drakken said.

"And it is no coincidence that those are the provinces who have the King's ear these days," Lord Rikard replied.

"So what will you do?"

"Watch and see if other shortages are being reported. I ask that you do the same. Try to find out if the merchants are hoarding goods."

"I appreciate your warning."

Kingsholm had experienced shortages before, when poor weather led to crop failures. She still had scars to show from the sugar riots, when angry mobs had attacked those merchants they suspected of hoarding sugar to drive up the prices. She hoped fervently that matters were not as bad as Lord Rikard feared. Jorsk needed to prepare itself for war, and defend itself against outside threats. Civil unrest would simply play into their enemies' hands.

"I will leave you to seek your well-earned rest," Lord Rikard said. "I bid you fair greetings and wishes that this year brings peace and prosperity to you."

"May it bring peace and prosperity to us all," she replied, giving the ritual answer, though she knew neither was likely. Not unless the Chosen One returned swiftly, to save the Kingdom before it dissolved into utter chaos.

Lord Rikard's words had planted the seed of doubt, and it was not long before Captain Drakken was able to confirm at least some of what he feared. Under the guise of a surprise inspection, she had visited the King's treasury and noticed that while the shelves were filled with the requisite number of locked chests, more than a few of them sounded distressingly hollow when tapped. The King's storerooms, too, were emptier than one would expect given that it was only midwinter.

In the marketplace, the wine sellers complained that Myrkan wine was in short supply, but blamed the shortage on the courtiers who had decided to winter in the city. No other shortages were reported, and prices remained steady, easing her fears of riots. But spring was still months away, and much could happen in that time.

It was with mixed emotions that she sought out Solveig, to see what she knew of the matter. Like Lord Rikard, Solveig was closely associated with Devlin's supporters. But she had an advantage in that her grandmother had been from Selvarat, and the family still had ties to that empire. She had sources of information that others did not.

A few days after she had met with Lord Rikard, Captain Drakken went to the old wing of the palace and began speaking to courtiers there about several instances of petty thievery that had recently occurred. Most claimed no knowledge of any thefts, but two of them were more than happy to provide a detailed list of all they had lost. Which was interesting, since to her knowledge there was no thief operating in the palace. This was merely a pretext, allowing her to move freely among the nobles. Still, she dutifully recorded all that was said, and after two hours of such conversations, she arrived at the apartments assigned to Solveig.

She rapped on the door, and as Solveig opened it, Captain Drakken repeated her rehearsed speech. "My apologies for disturbing you. I am investigating reports that a thief has broken into several chambers in this wing and taken small objects of value. Have you missed anything recently? Or seen someone lurking about who should not be here?"

"Not that I have noticed, but I do not count my jewelry daily," Solveig replied. "If you would come in, I would be pleased to check and see if anything is missing."

"That would be helpful," Captain Drakken said.

She entered, and Solveig swung the door shut behind them.

"Should I assume there is no thief?" Solveig asked.

Captain Drakken smiled. "Not that I know of, though Lady Vendela believes that she lost an emerald brooch, and Councilor Arnulf is certain that he lost a jade chess set, along with a pair of jeweled drinking cups."

"The chess set I am not sure of, but I'd heard he lost the drinking cups while gambling with his cronies."

Falsely reporting a crime was a grave offense, but even if Captain Drakken could find proof that the cups had been gambled away and not stolen, Councilor Arnulf could simply claim that he had made a mistake, having been too drunk to remember the wager.

"No doubt he hopes the King will recompense him for his losses," Solveig added.

"Then he has not seen the state of the King's treasury recently," Captain Drakken replied.

"I see you have spoken with Lord Rikard."

"Yes. And I have inspected the treasury room myself. The full complement of chests is there, but more than half of them are empty. As for the rest, I could not tell if they contain gold, silver, or mere brass."

She fervently hoped that the remaining chests held gold, or silver latts at the very least. But there was no way to be certain, for the Royal Treasurer reported directly to the King. The King's Council could demand a full accounting, if it were in session. But it would not meet until the spring.

"There is one bit of good news. Devlin has nearly reached Alvaren. With luck it will not be long before he reclaims the sword," Captain Drakken said.

"The journey back will be more difficult," Solveig said. "Once it is known he is returning, his enemies may seek to prevent him from reaching Kingsholm."

"It is possible," Drakken admitted. "If we knew the roads he was to travel, we could send an escort."

But as long as they did not know which roads Devlin would take, neither did his enemies. And there were advantages to being a small, swiftly moving party.

"Devlin must return bearing the sword. Nothing less will sway the mood of the court. Only he can persuade the King and council to shore up the border defenses and release the army from its interior garrisons," Captain Drakken said.

"Then you think there will be war. Sooner, rather than later."

"Yes."

"Why? Up until now, our enemy has remained unseen, content to stir up troubles along the borders and try to weaken us from within," Solveig said.

"True. Even the failed invasion of Korinth was more a feint than a true attempt," Captain Drakken agreed.

"Then why attack now?"

"Because the King named Devlin as the General of the Army. Already, they have seen Devlin act to strengthen our defenses, dispatching Major Mikkelson to guard the northern coast and sending armsmen from the interior provinces to the Nerikaat border. When Devlin returns, he will continue his work, and the Kingdom will grow stronger. Thus the moment to strike is now, before Devlin has a chance to build up the border defenses. If our enemy is planning an invasion, then they will attack this spring. Of that I am certain."

And if Devlin did not return, command of the army would be left in the hands of the newly named Marshal Erild Olvarrson. The Marshal would do whatever the King and council advised. Which, in the case of war, might well lead to disaster.

"You know that Count Magaharan remained in Kingsholm after the court adjourned," Solveig said. "He said he enjoys the informality that exists when the court is not in session, and I had several private dinners with him."

Indeed, many had been surprised that the Selvarat ambassador had chosen to linger in Jorsk, rather than returning to his own country for consultation with his emperor. Still, there had been a constant stream of messengers going back and forth, and no doubt the Count was well versed on what was happening in his homeland.

"Before he left the Count gave me assurances that Selvarat intends to honor their treaty with us. In the spring, they will send an emissary to the King with a formal offer of troops, to help defend our borders against attack. If war comes, we will not stand alone."

This was good news indeed. Over a hundred years ago, Selvarat and Jorsk had ended their long-standing hostilities and signed a treaty promising mutual assistance against third parties. Till now, the treaty terms had never been invoked—though there were many who grumbled that at the very least Selvarat ought to take action against Nerikaat, to punish it for its incursions against Jorsk.

"Did he inform the King?"

"He told me this in strict confidence. I believe he has hinted as much to the King as well, but there will be no public discussion until he returns with the formal offer."

Such were the games of diplomacy, where hints and innuendo were substituted for honest discussion. And none were better masters of the game than those of Selvarat, whose own courtly intrigues made the schemes of the Jorskian court seem mere child's play.

Now they had two reasons to hope for the coming of spring. Devlin's return, and the promise of well-trained troops to help defend their borders.

All she had to do was ensure that the city remained peaceful until that help arrived.

Thirteen

THE HAMLET HAD BURNED DAYS AGO, BUT THE scent of smoke lingered in the air and tasted bitter upon the tongue. Devlin swallowed hard as he stood on what had been the threshold of the largest of the four cottages. His eyes picked out a chunk of roof timber and piles of burned thatch, but the rest of the debris was unrecognizable. Even the stone walls were scorched.

It had been only three days since they had left Bengore. Three days since the Day of Remembrance, where Devlin had faced his own worst nightmare. Yet nothing could have prepared him for what he found here. For even as Haakon had been tormenting Devlin, the last of these folks had been burned alive.

"Have you seen enough?" Niamh asked. She had been the one to meet them when they entered the hamlet, and though she had tried to dissuade him, he had insisted on seeing the destruction for himself.

"The fire was deliberately set. It destroyed everything, as they meant it to," he observed. A part of him was amazed at how calm his voice sounded, for inside he felt like screaming.

"There were two bodies found in here, near the door, which had been barricaded shut, but as for their babe, we found no sign. Perhaps her body is elsewhere, or it may have been consumed utterly in the fire," Niamh replied.

He wondered how old the child had been and whether she had any inkling as to what was happening. Surely her parents would have tried to save her, and yet the fire had been set from the inside. . . .

And this was but one of the litany of horrors that Niamh had recounted, in her flat nasal tones. Stephen had turned white as she began the tale, and he had not protested when Devlin suggested that Stephen wait with the horses. Didrik, who had seen his own share of horrors while serving with the Guard, had listened impassively to Niamh's tale, then gone to the field where her husband was erecting cairns over the bodies. Ostensibly he was there to lend assistance, but also to find out if the husband's story was the same as the one that Niamh had recounted.

Devlin felt the need to see the ruins with his own eyes, and so he had insisted that Niamh take him through the hamlet and show him the ruins. Now he wished he had been content with mere words, for he knew the image of the missing babe and the burned-out shell of the cottage would haunt his nights.

"What of the others?" Devlin asked, gesturing to the remaining cottages.

"We searched them as well, but they were empty when they burned. Perhaps it was the madness, or perhaps one of those not yet sick thought to purge the infection."

"Tell me again what happened." He turned on his heel and began to walk away from the burned cottage, wishing he could put the memory behind him as easily.

Niamh fell into step beside him, pulling her shawl tightly around her shoulders, as if to protect herself from more than the chill of day.

"My husband Duald is kin to those who live here. Lived here," she corrected herself. "It is scarcely the time of year for visiting, but two days ago he got it in his head to look in on his father's brother. Felt that there was something wrong, so he walked across the mountain. But he arrived to find them already dead."

"All of them?"

"From Gavin the ancient down to the littlest babe. All dead, some for days."

So she had told him before, but he still could not quite believe it. Yet the large patch of freshly turned earth at the eastern end of the hamlet was all too convincing. If this woman was to be believed, under the covering of dirt and stones was a mass grave containing the remains of more than two dozen folk.

"When Duald did not return by nightfall, I knew something was wrong, and so the next day my brother and I came after him. Duald had searched for survivors but there were none to be found. It took nearly a full day for us to gather up the dead and bury them properly."

"And you think this was grain madness?"

"What else could it be? One man was hacked into a dozen pieces, while others had their bellies slashed open. Two sisters were found hanging in the barn, their dead children at their feet. Some folk were found naked and frozen to death on the road, having torn off all their clothes. Those are the acts of folk gone mad."

He was forced to agree with her. Duncaer was not like Jorsk. Its folk had no need to fear either bandits or foreign raiders. Whatever had harmed these people had come from within.

"There have been outbreaks of the grain madness before," he said. "But never have I heard of everyone being killed."

Niamh's gaze turned inward. "I assure you, it can be nothing else. These were good people. They did not deserve to die in this way," she said.

If this had been a larger village or a town, then the signs of the madness might have been recognized sooner. Those still uninfected could have taken steps to isolate the sick and prevent them from coming to harm. But in such a small place, if even a quarter of them fell ill at the same time, it must have spelled doom for the rest of them.

Many of those who had died had been children. They must have been terrified as the adults around them went mad and began killing one another. He could only hope that the children had not been made to witness the worst of the horrors.

"Are there other places in this district where the grain madness has struck?"

"Do you take us for fools?" she asked, her voice dripping with scorn. "If we had heard aught of this, we would have burned the cursed grain ourselves before letting a single mouthful pass our lips. My brother has already left to warn the other villages in this area."

"My apologies. I did not mean to offend you," he

said. It had been a foolish question. No one would eat grain that they knew might be tainted.

Rye grain came from the stolen lands, now farmed by those of Jorsk. Two generations ago rye had been unknown in Duncaer, but now the cheap grain was a staple of the winter diet. Yet the grain was both a blessing and a curse. It was less expensive than golden wheat, but from time to time it would spoil, and grain sickness was the result. Few of those infected with such madness had ever recovered. And those who had lived through the experience often killed themselves later, unable to live with the memories of the horrors they had committed.

It had been more than a dozen years since the last outbreak of grain sickness. Now it had returned, and with winter fast approaching, this hamlet was just the first of many that would suffer.

"Who else bought grain from the same trader as these folk?" he asked.

"Each year the folk from roundabouts send two of our own into Alvaren, to trade fleece for grain and other necessities. My people live across the valley, and then there are the folk to the south who live by the creek."

The taint might have been confined to this village's share, but it was a chance that they could not afford to take.

"You will have to burn your grain. And get me the name of the trader who sold it to you, so I can send warning to his other customers."

"We do not need you to tell us what to do," Niamh said. "We can take care of our own."

"Of course," he said, and he felt his cheeks heat with

a blush. He had given orders instinctively, as he would in Jorsk, where folk great and small looked to the Chosen One to lead them.

In Duncaer kin took care of each other in good times and in bad, but surely this was the worst of all possible circumstances. Devlin could hardly bring himself to think about the horrors that had occurred here, and these folk were strangers to him. It must have been unbearable for those who called them kin.

Yet bear with it they had, honoring the dead as best they could, and still taking time to warn others of their peril. And if Niamh and Duald resented the strangers who had interrupted their grieving, who could blame them? Indeed, he was lucky to have found someone here who could tell him the tale, Niamh and her husband having stayed behind to finish piling stones on the graves, while others herded the abandoned sheep down the valley.

"Your kin are your own concern, but the trader is mine. Give me his name, and I will see to it that no one else suffers this same fate."

Niamh nodded.

"And one more thing." Devlin pulled his coin pouch from his belt and held it out to her.

Niamh took a step back, refusal written in the stiff lines of her body.

He tossed the pouch so it landed at her feet with a jingling clang.

"The winter has only just begun. You will need new grain to replace what you have lost. Take the coins. This time buy golden wheat, to ease your stomachs and your hearts."

"You can keep your Jorksian coins. We do not need the charity of strangers."

Her stubbornness reminded him of himself. But there was more at stake than mere pride. The shepherds who lived in these isolated valleys used their land for grazing sheep, not growing grain. They depended on the sale of the fleece to buy provisions for themselves. Now they had neither fleece to sell, nor grain that they could trust. At best they would be forced to sell their sheep, which would deprive them of their livelihoods.

"I speak as Devlin, brother to Alanna the weaver. Alanna has three fair children of her own, and would not want to see your children go hungry. In her name, take the coins."

"I do not know this Alanna—" Niamh said.

"You can find her kin in Alvaren, when you go to buy the wheat. Give your thanks to them, for the gift made in the name of her children."

Niamh glanced down at the coin pouch, while Devlin held his breath. If she still refused the coin, then he would have to find some other way to help them. Perhaps he could buy grain at the next town and arrange for it to be brought here. Surely they would not scorn a wagon load of wheat, no matter who had sent it.

At last Niamh nodded, and he released the breath he had been holding.

"I will give Alanna my thanks when I see her, and as soon as may be, we will repay this debt."

"I will leave you to your mourning," Devlin said. "May the Earth Mother watch over you and yours."

They left behind the ruined hamlet, but even after it disappeared from sight, it remained foremost in their minds. They rode in silence, for there was nothing that could be said about such a senseless tragedy. He was the Chosen One, and yet he could not defend his people against a plague, nor could he alter the poverty that caused them to rely upon such a chancy food source. And mixed with his anger over his helplessness was the fear that they might encounter more such tragedies as they continued their journey.

Devlin guided his horse ahead of the others, in part driven by a wish for solitude, and in part because he wished to spare them his foul mood. He knew it was unfair, yet when he saw Stephen and Didrik, a voice within him whispered to him that these were Jorskians, born of the same race that oppressed his people, and were responsible for their plight.

"You are wise not to trust them," a deep voice said.

It was a voice he had come to know well in these past few days. But this time it had taken visible form, as a dark cloaked rider on a coal black steed. The rider swung his head toward Devlin, but his face was featureless except for two glowing eyes.

"I see this morning's finds disturbed you," Haakon continued. "Can you imagine how those people felt, as they saw husband turn on wife, and mothers killing their own children? Do you think they realized they were going mad? Or did they cheerfully embrace the horrors, enjoying the suffering of those they slew?"

Devlin shook his head and began to hum softly. He would not give Haakon the satisfaction of reacting to his taunts.

But no matter what he tried, the voice seemed to burn itself into his brain.

Haakon laughed. "Of course you don't have to wonder what they felt. You feel it, too. You are going mad, after all. How much longer do you think it will be before you turn on your friends?"

"Never," Devlin said. He kneed his horse to a trot, but the spectral horse matched his own, stride for stride.

"Of course you will. You bring death to all those around you. It is your gift, for you are my creature. I could end your life in a heartbeat, but why should I bother, when you are so entertaining? I wonder how much longer you will persist in this foolish struggle before you beg me to take your life? Will it be when you have led your friends to their deaths? Or will you wait until you have witnessed the slaughter of your own people at the hands of those to whom you have sworn your allegiance?"

"Never," Devlin repeated. He would hold true to himself. He would not let the seeds of doubt that Haakon planted destroy him.

"Kinslayer," Haakon said softly. "Why should Cerrie wait for you alone? Think of all those souls you have sent to join her and all those whose deaths you will carry. Stephen. Didrik. Murchadh, Alanna, and, of course their children. This will be your doom—I will never take your soul, and you will be left alive to grieve, long after those you loved have perished. All those still living will call you kinslayer and shun your presence, but you will not be able to escape into death. Instead your soul will remain on earth, even as your body rots and crumbles around you. Or perhaps if you beg me—"

"No!" Devlin shouted. It took but a split second to release the throwing knife on his left arm and throw it toward his tormentor. Just as the knife pierced the edge of the cloak, both horse and rider disappeared.

"Devlin!" Stephen cried.

He came to himself as he saw Didrik bent over his saddle, having ducked to avoid the knife which flew over his head and landed harmlessly in the grass beside the road. Had Didrik's reflexes been any slower, the knife would have struck him.

Devlin yanked the reins, bringing his horse to an abrupt stop. The horse whinnied in protest, and bucked halfheartedly before subsiding.

Devlin began to shake, and he balled his hands into fists to control them. He had come so close. If he had been a second slower on his throw, or if Didrik had not seen him in time . . .

Haakon was right. Devlin was a danger to himself. And to his friends.

Fourteen

"HE IS GETTING WORSE," DIDRIK SAID.

"I know," Stephen replied, his voice pitched low. His eyes sought out Devlin, who rode a few hundred yards ahead, seemingly oblivious to his companions' worries.

It was the fourth day since they had left Bengore. Four days since Devlin's collapse on Midwinter's Eve. Four days since he had witnessed the impossible. Four days of watching and fretting as Devlin's behavior grew more and more strange.

Didrik bit his lip, as he often did when uncertain.

"It has been a long journey and hard enough on those of us who are ordinary men. Devlin has endured the pull of the Geas for nearly two months now, and what we saw yesterday at that village shook him. It is no wonder he is showing signs of the strain."

Didrik's words held the sound of a man trying to convince himself.

"It is not merely the journey," Stephen said. "Devlin could have killed you yesterday."

"That was as much my fault as his. We are all on edge

after what we have seen, and I startled him," Didrik said loyally. "Next time I will be more careful."

"Devlin has been under strain before, but never has he raised his hand against a friend. This is not the Geas. Or not the Geas alone," Stephen said. "On the journey to Esker the Geas drove him nearly past reason, but he was not as he is now. And since that time, Master Dreng has shown him how to discipline its power."

The Geas could drive Devlin to fulfill his duty with fanatic dedication, heedless of danger or of consequence. Under its influence Devlin the man could be consumed by Devlin the Chosen Champion of the Gods. It was a form of madness, and both Stephen and Didrik had witnessed its influence. But never before had they seen Devlin start at shadows, or hold one-sided conversations with someone who was not there.

"Could it be a spell of some sort? Though we have seen no one I recognized as a mage, perhaps in Kilbaran there might have been someone..." Didrik's voice trailed off into silence.

"It is not a spell," Stephen said. "The Geas serves to protect Devlin from mind-spells. That is why the mind-sorcerer sent a creature of darkness to attack us, rather than striking at Devlin directly."

Didrik stared at him. "And you know this how?"

"I was curious about the creature, so I asked Master Dreng."

Master Dreng had initially been reluctant to discuss either Devlin or the Geas spell, but after sharing three bottles of wine his tongue loosened and he spoke freely. Sadly, the fourth bottle had put him to sleep before he could answer all of Stephen's questions.

"I would give ten years of my life for an hour of

Master Dreng's counsel. Only he knows the Geas spell and how this might be cured," Didrik said. His hands closed into tight fists around the reins. "Or if not Dreng, then Captain Drakken. Anyone who could counsel us, and whose advice he might heed."

Stephen sympathized with Didrik's frustration, but he could not shake the feeling that Didrik was looking in the wrong place for answers. "What if this is not the Geas? What if it is something else? The strangeness began on Midwinter's Eve."

"And now we are back to your story. Were it anyone else, I would say they had drunk too much and imagined the whole thing."

"I know what I saw," Stephen insisted. "I saw her. Devlin's murdered wife, Cerrie."

Even days later, the memory of her made his pulse thrum, his heart quicken with wonder. He had thought the Caer tales of wandering spirits to be mere legends, and their annual rite of remembrance simply a memorial to those who had passed on. His offer to join Devlin had been made out of friendship. He had never even considered that there might be truth to the old tales. Not until the mist had risen and taken shape before his very eyes.

"She was beautiful," Stephen said. Tall, and wellbuilt, with the muscled arms and shoulders of a swordwielder. At first glance her features were plain, and then she had smiled and the merely ordinary became transfigured.

"What did she say?"

"She warned Devlin that he was in danger, from a source unsuspected to all."

"Our long-sought traitor at the court. We never did

find Duke Gerhard's allies. Nor his paymaster," Didrik interrupted.

That was true. But those were dangers they already knew of, even if they did not know the name of their enemy. Stephen could not shake the feeling that Cerrie had been trying to warn them of something else entirely.

"Cerrie mentioned the Dread Lord's name, and Devlin grew angry. She continued to speak to him, but it was as if he did not hear her. He spoke, but his words made no sense. And then he fell to the ground unconscious. When I looked up again, Cerrie had vanished."

The wonder of Cerrie's appearance had been offset by the horror of Devlin's collapse. It had taken Stephen several long moments to rouse his friend. When he did awaken, Devlin had muttered one word. Haakon. The Lord of the Dread Realm.

But then he had seemed to come back to himself. As Stephen had helped Devlin to his feet, Devlin had shaken off his friend's concern, blaming his fainting on his weariness, coupled with the traditional fast. Stephen had allowed himself to be reassured. His concern for his friend had offset his eagerness to discuss what he had just seen, and he had allowed Devlin to seek his rest undisturbed.

The next morning, he heard Devlin speaking to someone, only to walk into the common room and find Devlin alone. At first he assumed that the other party had just left the room. But Devlin's manner had been odd, and he had gruffly brushed off Stephen's attempts to discuss the events of the night before.

Didrik, at least, had listened to Stephen's tale. But he, too, had dismissed Stephen's concerns, until they had both witnessed Devlin conversing with the empty air. Not once, not twice, but thrice.

And then, after they had left the ruined hamlet, Devlin had fallen into a deep reverie. When Didrik tried to rouse him from it, without warning Devlin had drawn steel and thrown a knife that barely missed striking Didrik. Rather than being horrified by his actions, Devlin had appeared angry. He blamed Didrik for startling him, and Didrik had agreed.

Later, when Didrik had asked Devlin if all were well, he had been firmly set in his place. There was a coldness about the eyes of the Chosen One that warned them not to push any further. They were all too well aware that they traveled with Devlin at his sufferance. Should they anger him, he could easily order them to leave. Not that they would obey such an order. But in any confrontation with Devlin, they were bound to lose. Should they refuse to obey his orders, he could easily have them imprisoned.

Such action should have been unthinkable. Devlin was their friend, and they had pledged their loyalty to him. But Stephen was no longer certain that Devlin was in control of his actions. There was no predicting what he might do.

"So what should we do now?" Stephen asked.

"Watch. Wait. This mood may pass as swiftly as it sprang up. Or perhaps he will come to himself once he holds the sword in his hands."

"And if he does not?"

"Then I do not know," Didrik replied. "We must put our trust in Devlin. And in the Gods. They have led him thus far; surely they will not abandon him now."

Stephen had already prayed to the Gods, but that

had brought little comfort. He thought again of the long leagues that separated them from his homeland, and from those who might aid Devlin. It would take nearly two months to make their return. And in this foreign place, he did not know whom he could trust to help them. He would have to trust to fate and luck to see them through.

"He is getting worse."

A stray breeze brought Didrik's words to his ears. Devlin shifted in the saddle but kept his posture relaxed, giving no sign that he knew he was the topic of Stephen and Didrik's whispered conversation. He listened a moment longer, but either the wind had shifted or his friends had grown more cautious, for he heard no more.

They know. The voice echoed within his head. *Even your friends can see that you are already mine.*

"No," Devlin said. He spoke the word aloud, not caring that his companions might take this as another sign of the strangeness that had infected him.

You should not trust them. They will try to stop you. Already they whisper between themselves, trying to change what cannot be changed, simply because they do not understand. They will thwart your efforts. You must leave them, or your mission will fail.

The voice was insidious, giving voice to the seeds of doubt that lingered deep within Devlin's soul. The Geas did not understand friendship, but surely it understood that a solitary traveler was far more vulnerable than a small group? Alone he could fall victim to any number of hazards. Illness. Rockslides. An attack by creatures that walked on four legs or two.

And while his companions were concerned, they knew of the Geas that drove him. Though they did not fully understand, that was not from lack of trying. No man could truly understand the force of the Geas unless his own will had been spellbound. Already it had driven him to do things that no sane man would attempt.

And now a new element had been added to the mix, for Haakon had added his own taunts to the relentless murmuring of the Geas. The strain of this new burden was tearing at the fabric of his mind, and the shreds of his control, with potentially deadly results.

Yesterday he had lashed out without thinking, and Didrik had nearly died because of his mistake. Only the lieutenant's swift reflexes had enabled him to avoid the knife as it flew through the air at a target that only Devlin could see. If it had been Stephen riding there instead, he might well be dead.

And there was no explanation he could offer, for who would believe his story? They would think him mad, and he would not blame them.

It might be safer for them all if he sent Stephen and Didrik away from him. But he did not know if he could bear to be alone. Surely if he exerted all his will upon the task, he could prevent another deadly lapse of concentration.

He balled his left hand into a fist, feeling the warm metal encircling his second finger. He knew if he were to strip off his glove, he would find the stone within the ring was flickering with a dull red glow. And this, too, was new. Never before had the ring come to life without his bidding. He wondered if the ring sensed that they were nearing Alvaren, and the long lost Sword of Light.

Was the ring somehow linked to the sword? Master Dreng had never mentioned such a thing, but then again the sword had been lost for decades. Much of what had once been known was now the province of legend.

Stephen, of course, knew all the legends of the Chosen One. But any discussion of the ring would give Stephen a chance to question him about the Day of Remembrance, and Devlin had spent the past four days avoiding that discussion. He knew Stephen had seen Cerrie and heard her words of warning. But Stephen had not seen Haakon. The God's message had been for Devlin alone, and Devlin saw no reason to reveal what he had seen.

Or what he thought he had seen. For while a part of him believed that he was indeed haunted by Haakon, another part of him whispered that the Lord of the Dread Realm would never condescend to speak with a mere mortal. That what Devlin had seen and heard had not been the God at all, but merely the symptoms of a growing madness.

There were two kinds of folk who heard voices when all others heard silence. Those who were touched by the Gods and those who had been driven to madness. And time alone would reveal the source of Devlin's affliction.

When they reached the next inn, Devlin called a halt for the day, despite the fact that it was only the middle of the afternoon. Didrik and Stephen exchanged glances, but made no comment. After handing over his laundry to the inn-wife, Devlin went through his packs, carefully examining each piece of equipment. As always he saved his greatest care for his weapons. The assassins' attack had reminded him he could not afford to take his safety for granted. The throwing knives were inspected and oiled before being replaced in their sheaths. The steel bolts for his transverse bow were counted and checked for signs of rust.

The simple routine of the tasks comforted him, for they spoke to a danger that was familiar. He could do nothing to defend himself against the spirit that taunted him. But opponents who were mere flesh could be brought down by sharp steel and a strong arm.

They were fortunate that their journey so far had been marred only by the one attempt on their lives. Constant vigilance since then had revealed no sign of their enemies. No shadowy figures following their trail, no ambushes in the deserted countryside. Perhaps they had outrun their pursuers. Perhaps they had chosen to ride ahead and lay in wait at Alvaren instead, rather than trying to determine which roads the travelers had chosen.

Or perhaps their enemies had realized that there was no point in trying to harm Devlin. They had no need to kill him, for he was already doomed. He would fail, as the voice within him whispered in moments of despair.

No, he vowed to himself. He would not fail. He would find the cursed sword and take it back to Jorsk. What matter whether he had chosen this path or it had been chosen for him? He had sworn a sacred oath, to serve as Chosen One and protect the people of Jorsk with every last ounce of his strength. Neither fickle Fates nor treacherous Gods would make him forswear that.

That evening, after they had dined, Devlin invited Stephen and Didrik to join him in his room. In a peace-making gesture he asked the inn-wife to provide a pitcher of wine. Stephen poured the dark red liquid into three goblets and handed them around. Devlin took a sip for politeness sake, then set his aside. His mind was restless enough, without befuddling it with drink.

"Tomorrow we will reach Alvaren," Devlin said.

Didrik nodded. "So the inn-wife informed me."

"Are you expecting trouble? Is that why you had us inspect our gear?" Stephen asked.

"A precaution, no more. But we must be on our guard. Through the years my people have learned to live in peace with the army and the Royal Governor. But I do not know how they will react when they hear the Chosen One is in their midst. At best they may scorn me as a traitor."

"Or the Children of Ynnis may try to assassinate you, in hopes of sparking a rebellion," Didrik said dryly.

It was possible, but Devlin doubted that the Children of Ynnis were organized enough to form a true rebellion. Such groups had risen and fallen with regularity in the years since Jorsk had conquered Duncaer. Usually they were composed of young men and women who gathered in taverns to drink and lament the lost glories of Duncaer. Rarely did they rouse themselves to more than the occasional act of mischief.

And when they did take it in their heads to commit violence, the consequences were swift and brutal. So the stalemate in Alvaren endured, and while the folk were not happy, both sides knew better than to risk the consequences of all-out warfare.

He doubted that anything had changed in the time he had been gone.

"With luck we should be in Alvaren only long enough to retrieve the sword and reprovision ourselves for the journey back to Kingsholm."

"And you are certain this is the sword we seek," Didrik said. It was not quite a question.

"It can be no other. Murchadh knew it as well as I, and told me that Master Roric had left the sword in trust for me at the guild hall. It is my inheritance." The knowledge left a bitter taste in his mouth that no wine could erase.

Didrik rubbed his chin thoughtfully, while Stephen appeared fascinated by the contents of his goblet. Neither of them could meet his gaze, and who could blame them? Each man liked to believe that he carved his own path in this world, yet the sword was evidence that Devlin's fate had been sealed long ago.

"You said your people have no love for us. What if they refuse to give you the sword? What will you do then?"

Trust Stephen to give voice to Devlin's most secret fear.

"By custom and law it is mine. They have no choice."

"And if they refuse?" Stephen persisted.

"Then I will take it. By force if needed. That is why our first destination will be to call upon the governor. Out of courtesy to let him know that I am in his territory and to arrange the use of soldiers should I need them."

Lord Kollinar, the Earl of Tiernach, was the Royal Governor of Duncaer and the commander of the occupying troops. As governor he took orders from the King. But as a Marshal he took orders from Devlin, in his role as General of the Royal Army. Dealing with Lord Kollinar would be tricky, especially given Devlin's origin.

Lord Kollinar had governed Duncaer for the past dozen years. Early in his tenure he had gained a reputation for being hard but fair, enforcing Jorskian decrees but abstaining from cruelty. He had been widely praised for his efforts to open up the New Territories and offer those lands not to Jorskian settlers but rather to the land-starved Caerfolk. But the ill-fated settlements had cost the governor much of the goodwill his earlier acts had gained.

Devlin knew Lord Kollinar only by reputation. Court gossip held that the conservative faction had considered Lord Kollinar a political threat, and thus had banished him to the relative obscurity of Duncaer. But simply being one of Duke Gerhard's enemies did not make him Devlin's ally. He would have to make his own judgment and decide just how much he could tell Kollinar and what he could not.

He shook his head, trying to dispel the dark mood.

"You have told us little of Alvaren," Stephen said. "What is the city like? Are there great buildings? What kind of people will we find there?"

Devlin accepted the change of subject gratefully, and began to describe Alvaren. It was more than three years since he had walked the streets of the place where he had been born, and there was a hunger inside him to see it once again, even if only for a few short days. He pushed aside his dark imaginings as he told of those places he had once known so well. There would be time enough to face his troubles on the morrow.

Fifteen

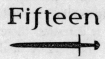

"WERE IT NOT FOR THE MESSENGER BIRD FROM Commander Willemson, you would have caught me wholly by surprise," Lord Kollinar said. "You should have sent word ahead, and I could have prepared for your arrival."

As they entered Alvaren they had been met by a squad of soldiers who had insisted on escorting Devlin and his companions to see the Royal Governor. Since such had fit in with his own wishes, Devlin had not disagreed.

In his memories the governor had been a larger-than-life figure, the embodiment of all the ills that afflicted Duncaer. But in person Lord Kollinar was simply a man in his middle years somewhat shorter than Devlin. He had a round face, and though he wore his graying hair in a warrior's braid, his body had gone soft from years of easy living.

"What preparations were needed?" Devlin kept his tone mild, but he remained standing, so Lord Kollinar remained standing as well. It was a petty trick, but he did not want this man to feel comfortable in his presence.

"You should have an escort at the very least. I do not know what Commander Willemson was thinking—"

"He was obeying orders. I needed no escort."

"The countryside is restless these days, and no safe place for Jorskian travelers. A small party like yours would have made an easy target."

"Your reports to the King have mentioned nothing of these troubles."

"One tells the King what he wishes to hear. The King does not wish to hear of the difficulties of his most unruly province, and so I do not burden him with my problems."

"One tells the King the truth, regardless of how unpleasant it is."

Lord Kollinar studied Devlin for a moment as if to gauge his seriousness, then grinned. "And I'll wager that is exactly what you do. It is no wonder Gerhard hated you. You must have driven them all crazy."

Devlin fought the urge to smile in return. He did not want to feel a kinship with this man. He needed his respect and cooperation, but that was all. His loyalties were already divided enough without making a friend of one who symbolized the conquest of his folk.

"Winter is always a bad time in the city, and I do not know how your presence will be received. If you had asked, I would have advised against making this journey."

It was true that tempers tended to flare as the months of winter rains and gray skies stretched on with no end in sight. But it was only midwinter. The worst of the troubles would not happen till later. In the past the riots had come at the end of winter, when the food supplies ran short or winter fevers ravaged the population. Devlin and his friends should be safe. For a little while.

"I know all about Alvaren. I lived here myself for most of my life, as you surely must know."

Lord Kollinar flushed. "Of course, my lord."

"And as for my presence causing difficulty, perhaps you should have thought of that before you assigned a squad of soldiers to escort me through the city streets as if I were a conquering general on parade. There is no way to keep my presence secret, but it would have been better to keep my presence unofficial rather than linking me so publicly to the army."

"I did what I thought best to ensure your safety. And when you leave, I will insist on providing a suitable escort."

"You will do as you are ordered, or find yourself on the road back to Kingsholm," Devlin said. He locked eyes with Kollinar, letting him feel the weight of his will until Kollinar gave in and looked away.

When he spoke again, his tone was mild. "May I know the reason for your visit? It can be no light thing that brings the Chosen One to travel so far from Kingsholm in the dead of winter."

Devlin hesitated, then realized there was no reason not to tell him the truth. After all, he might well need the help of Kollinar and his soldiers to complete his errand.

"I have come for the sword," he said.

"The sword?"

"The Sword of Light."

Kollinar gave him another searching look and

walked over to the window of his office, which looked out onto a courtyard where soldiers were drilling.

"Men have searched for the sword for decades, braving Ynnis's crumbling ruins and restless dead. And now you think you can succeed where so many have failed?"

"Yes," Devlin said.

Kollinar shook his head. "This is a fool's errand. Your duty lies in Kingsholm and yet you have abandoned your responsibilities to waste your time poking among ruins? I had heard you were a man of honor but apparently I heard wrong."

It was a deadly insult. Devlin's right hand fell to his sword belt, but he did not draw it. He knew Kollinar was baiting him deliberately, hoping that in his anger Devlin would let slip what otherwise he would hold in confidence. Two years before Devlin might have fallen for such a trick. But now he was the veteran of dozens of council debates, and had faced down far more devious souls than Kollinar.

Instead he took a deep breath. "I need no man to lecture me on my duty. And as for the sword, the reason the others failed is simple. The sword is not in Ynnis. It is here. In Alvaren."

"Are you certain?"

"I saw it myself, not more than five years ago. Though this knowledge goes no further than this room—and should you tell another I will see you tried for treason."

"I understand," Lord Kollinar said, though from the look on his face it was clear he did not. "What can I do?"

"For now, I need quarters for myself and my companions. And provisions need to be assembled so we can leave as soon as we have accomplished our task. I must be back in Kingsholm before the spring council."

"Of course," Kollinar replied. But Devlin doubted that he could truly comprehend how important the upcoming spring council would be. How could he? Kollinar had spent most of the last twelve years here in Duncaer. Were he to rely only upon official reports, the governor would be hard-pressed to imagine the true state of the kingdom, where the border provinces trembled on the edge of disaster. Even at court, the thin veneer of normality could barely disguise the growing panic underneath.

War was coming. Devlin felt it in his bones. And when it came his place would be in Jorsk, to lead the army against their enemies. He could not afford to be delayed.

As Devlin emerged from the governor's residence, Didrik drew himself to attention and thumped his right fist on his left shoulder in formal salute. From his packs Didrik had unearthed his dress green uniform, with the silver shoulder cords that marked him as the Chosen One's personal aide. Next to Didrik were the half dozen soldiers who had escorted them into the city, led by a young woman wearing the uniform of an army Ensign. As Devlin caught her eye, she placed her hand over her heart and inclined her head. Beside her, the soldiers stood at rigid attention, their eyes fixed in the middle distance.

Devlin inclined his head in acknowledgment. After speaking with Lord Kollinar and accepting his offer of hospitality, Devlin had paused at the governor's residence only long enough to change into his court uniform. Though normally he hated the stiff garb, today he wore it as a sign of respect to the guild members who had once been his equals. And as a warning, to remind all who saw him just who it was that they dealt with.

As Devlin descended the stone steps to the street below, he glanced up at the sky. It would be dark soon, but there was still time to visit the metalsmiths before the Guild Master sought out his own home and hearth.

"Chosen One," Didrik greeted him, using the formal title as was his custom when they were in the presence of strangers.

"You understand what I need of you?" Devlin asked.

"Yes. The Ensign and I will accompany you to your destination. She and her troops will wait outside while we go within. Should assistance be needed, I will summon them," Didrik said. His face was a blank mask, giving no sign if he were offended at being asked to repeat such simple instructions.

"And you, Ensign Annasdatter. You understand that your presence is a precaution only? If you are summoned within, you are to look imposing but that is all. You will not draw your weapons unless I so order. Understood?"

"I hear and obey," the Ensign replied. She looked absurdly young to be an Ensign, her wheat-colored hair barely long enough to be tied back into a warrior's braid. She was a child, and he briefly considered requesting that someone more senior take charge.

But there was no time. And with luck he might not need her aid. The troops were there as a precaution, nothing more. Should the Guild Master balk at turning over Devlin's inheritance, the troops would be there to make him see the wisdom of obeying the law.

Not that such a gesture was likely to endear him to his people. On the contrary, it went against custom to involve the Jorskian army in such an affair. By long-held agreement, the peacekeepers were responsible for civil affairs within Alvaren and for enforcing Caer laws. But in this case Devlin could hardly turn to the peace-keepers, for who knew where their loyalties would lie?

"Come, then. Let us be done with this."

Devlin led the way through the narrow twisting streets, Didrik at his side, while the Ensign and her soldiers followed behind. At this hour of the day there were few folk on the streets, but those they did see stepped aside and whispered as they passed. The back of his neck felt chill, for their gazes were not friendly. And more than once he heard a muttered curse, or the word *fearnym*, which in the tongue of his people meant traitor.

It took a scarce quarter hour for them to arrive at the Square of the Artisans, where the metalsmiths had their guild hall, flanked on one side by the glassblower's guild, and across the square from the potter's hall. By Jorskian standards the square was too small to merit such a name, merely being a wide spot where two great streets met. Were he to cross the square and continue down the Street of Egil, a hundred paces would take him to the forge where he had labored from the time he was a boy. First as an apprentice, then a journeyman, and finally as a master in his own right.

The square was empty save for a rushing apprentice carrying a bundle in his arms. It was as he had hoped. Devlin had kept their destination secret from all but

Didrik, lest word leak out. Given time to reflect on his plans, no doubt troublemakers could stir up a crowd or even a small riot, and such would lead to senseless bloodshed. Far better to move swiftly and in secret, so the deed would be done before any had a chance to stop him.

"Wait here and remember your orders," Devlin said.

"Yes, sir." Ensign Annasdatter gestured, and four of the soldiers took up positions in the street, while the remaining two flanked the great door that led into the guild hall. She took her own position to the right of the great door.

Devlin swallowed hard and steeled himself for what was to come. Then he reached forward with his right hand. So perfectly balanced was the massive heartwood door that at his mere touch it swung open on silent hinges.

He stepped through and into the entranceway. Like most buildings in Alvaren, space was at a premium, and the entranceway was small in size. But what it lacked in size it made up for in sheer grandeur, with walls of black marble lit by cunningly fashioned lamps. The left wall was covered by an intricate carving depicting Egil's gift of fire. On the right wall, three hundred years of the guild's greatest smiths were honored, the names of the Grand Masters carved into the stone and filled in with copper so they glistened in the lamp light. It was considered an honor for an apprentice to be assigned the task of polishing those names, and in his youth Devlin had spent hours carefully burnishing the metal and dreaming of the glory that would one day be his.

Pain lanced through him as he saw that the wall was marred, for the second name from the bottom of the list was gone, the name scraped from the stone until only a blank spot remained. The fingers of his good hand traced the roughened surface, and he felt the faintest of indentations where once his name had been. His heartache swiftly turned to anger. Not for the insult, but for their heedless destruction. What lesson did it teach future apprentices to see the masters so heedless of their heritage and of what it meant to be a craftsman? Whatever Devlin had since done, he had once been acclaimed Grand Master in all honor. Regardless of what these fools thought, they could not deny his past.

Nor could they deny who he was now, as Didrik's gentle cough recalled him to the present. Turning his back on the ruined wall, he led the way through the archway opposite, into the main hall.

Here all was as he remembered. At the front of the room, a handful of clerks labored at their desks, scribing the records of the guild. The center of the room was open to allow for the guild members to meet in assembly. Around the edges of the room were pedestals and display cases showing off the finest works of the guild. An enameled torc that he had made as a journeyman had once been displayed in the third cabinet on the left, but he knew better than to suppose it still held a place of honor. He felt a brief pang as he wondered what they had done with it. Had it been destroyed? Or had they sold it off or simply hidden it away?

At the back of the room there was an alcove where the Guild Master and his friends were most often found. Master Jarlath had his own office on the second story, but in his declining years he seldom bothered to climb the stairs. And he was even less likely to be found in his forge. Devlin could not remember the last time he had seen Master Jarlath at his craft. Nor had he taken an apprentice for at least a dozen years. Despite this, Master Jarlath ruled the guild with an iron fist.

He heard the sound of laughter, then all fell silent as Devlin's boots rang out on the stone floor. Not since his days as a new apprentice had he been as conscious of the size of the hall, or of the feeling that all eyes were focused on him.

Devlin drew to a halt a half dozen paces away from where Master Jarlath sat.

"Grand Master Jarlath," he said, greeting him in their own tongue, and giving the short bow due to an equal in craft or degree. As Chosen One, it was a great courtesy for him to greet a mere craftmaster in such a fashion. But as one who had once been a guild member, such a bow might be seen as an insult.

From the narrowing of Jarlath's eyes, he knew it had been taken as an insult.

"What brings you to my hall?" Jarlath asked in the tradespeech, as if Devlin were a foreigner. In a pointed lack of courtesy he did not rise, nor did he offer Devlin any of his titles.

"I have come for my inheritance, given into your keeping by Master Roric, to hold until my return," Devlin said. Following Jarlath's lead, he, too, spoke in the trade tongue.

A woman laughed, and Devlin recognized Amalia the weapons maker. On her right hand she wore the silver ring that indicated she had finally made master—though the rank of Grand Master was far beyond her talent.

"You gave up all claim on the guild years ago, when

you forsook your craft. There is nothing here for you now," she declared. The venom in her words surprised him, for to his knowledge he had never wronged her. Still, perhaps it was enough that he had once had what she never could, and that he had turned his back on the honors that she had long sought.

"Is Amalia now Guild Master? Should I treat with her instead?" Devlin asked mildly.

"I am Guild Master," Jarlath said.

"Then act the part. Send one of your lackeys here to fetch that which is mine and I will take my leave and trouble you no longer."

"You were always trouble," Jarlath said. "And what need has our most famous traitor for whatever trinket Roric left behind?"

Didrik hissed as the word traitor was uttered. There was a faint rasp, and Devlin did not have to turn around to know that Didrik had loosened his sword within its scabbard, making sure it could be drawn in an instant.

"Enough." He had no patience for Jarlath's baiting, nor for reigning in Didrik's anger at the slight to his commander. It was time to put an end to such foolish theatrics.

Devlin braced his feet apart and hooked both hands in his own sword belt. "Jarlath, Grand Master, Leader of the Metalsmiths' guild, husband of the much-mourned Leila of Bright Waters, in the name of Egil and in the presence of these witnesses I call upon you to honor your sworn word. Give over to me what is rightfully mine or bear the name of oathbreaker to the end of your days."

There was a moment of silence, and Devlin feared

that he would be forced to summon the soldiers after all. But then Jarlath crooked one finger, and an apprentice stepped from his post by the fire. "Cathan, the box I want is in the storage room, where we keep the copper bars. It is a long, narrow case, with Roric's name inscribed on the top. Fetch that to me."

The apprentice scurried off, out the back of the hall and down the steep stairs that led to the basement storerooms. Devlin stood there, his gaze carefully fixed on the wall above Jarlath's head. He schooled his features to blankness, but inside him he felt a churning excitement mixed with dread. He had spent two months and traveled over two hundred leagues to come to this place. In a few moments he would once again behold the Sword of Light, the object he both craved and feared.

The fingers of his right hand began to tremble, and he gripped the sword belt tightly to hide their shaking. It took far too long, but finally the apprentice returned, bearing a box that was nearly as long as he was tall. After a glance at Master Jarlath for confirmation, the apprentice approached Devlin and handed him the box.

It was a plain box, made out of smoothed oaken boards, with brass hinges and a bright red wax seal on the hasp. On the top of the box was inscribed Roric's name and underneath Devlin's had been added in a second hand. The box had been well stored, for there was not a trace of dust to be found on it.

"Satisfied?" Master Jarlath asked.

"Almost," Devlin replied. He turned to Didrik, who held out his arms, and Devlin laid the box level on them. Then, taking his dagger from his belt, Devlin sliced through the wax seal. It broke easily, revealing traces of a different-colored wax underneath. He replaced the dagger in its sheath, then drew a deep breath. He looked into Didrik's face and saw his own anticipation mirrored within his friend's eyes.

Stephen was going to be angry that he had missed this moment, Devlin realized, and he felt a smile forming on his lips. Then he turned the hasp and lifted the lid of the sword case.

He blinked for a moment, unable to believe what he was seeing. Dark laughter echoed in his mind, as Haakon chose to make his presence felt.

"My lord? Devlin?" Didrik's voice was strained, and Devlin realized that the partly raised lid prevented Didrik from seeing what lay inside the box.

Devlin withdrew the scroll, and closed the lid of the sword case. It took him two tries to untie the ribbon with fingers that seemed suddenly stiff and clumsy.

"The Children of Ynnis send their greetings," he whispered to Didrik. Then he turned to Jarlath. "You have failed at your duty. The sword entrusted to you has been stolen."

Sixteen

"YOUR FRIEND MURCHADH BETRAYED YOU." DIDRIK'S tone was flat, but there was sympathy in his dark eyes.

Murchadh betrayed you, echoed the voice within his mind. *See how your friends turn against you.*

"No," Devlin replied, his hand slashing through the air in a gesture of negation. As his restless pacing brought him to the window, he spun on his heel to face the room.

They were in the governor's private receiving room, which Devlin had appropriated to his own use. The hour was long past midnight, but he felt no urge to seek his bed. Sleep was impossible for him now.

Stephen was sprawled out on one couch, his stocking feet tucked under him. Didrik had chosen to perch on top of the governor's desk, which put him closer to Devlin's eye level. As for Devlin, he could not sit, could not stay still. The churning of his mind was matched by the restlessness of his body as he tried to understand what had happened and what he needed to do next.

"It is the only explanation that makes sense," Didrik continued. "Who else knew that the sword your old master held was the lost sword of the Chosen One? Everyone believed the sword lost in Ynnis. Only the three of us, Captain Drakken, Solveig, and your friend Murchadh knew the truth."

"No," Devlin insisted, though the words were like acid in his mouth.

"But—"

"No," he shouted. Then he lowered his voice. "If it were you or Stephen so accused, should I be so quick to judge? Murchadh is not here to defend himself, so as friend and adopted brother I must do so for him. I hold him innocent until proven otherwise. There must be another explanation."

Murchadh could not have betrayed him. It was not possible. Yet even as he denied the accusations, he felt the seed of doubt form within him. Perhaps the betrayal had not been deliberate? Perhaps Murchadh had simply spoken out of turn, entrusting the secret to one who had ties to the rebels? Yet even this was cold comfort, for a true friend would never have betrayed Devlin's confidence by sharing it with another.

Devlin ran the fingers of his good hand through his hair as he tried to order his thoughts. Even if Murchadh had been the one to reveal the secret, such was little help to him. Any answers that Murchadh possessed were a fortnight away. Devlin needed knowledge now. Who had taken the sword? What had they done with it? Was it still here in the city or had it been spirited far away?

Ensign Annasdatter and her soldiers had supervised the guild apprentices as they searched each square inch of the storeroom, then they searched the rest of the guild hall. They had found a surprising number of swords, far more than the guild hall should have any reason to own. But none were the sword he sought.

Devlin had given orders that Jarlath's personal residence was to be searched as well, but that, too, had turned up nothing. Not that he really suspected Jarlath. The Guild Master had been genuinely outraged by the theft of an object under his care. Such an incident was unknown in the history of the guild. He angrily denied any link between the guild and the outlaws, even when confronted by the cache of swords.

A messenger had been sent to Lord Kollinar, instructing him to round up suspected members of the Children of Ynnis for questioning. There was no point in trying to keep this quiet. By morning the entire city would know what it was that he sought.

Devlin wondered when the rebels had grown so bold, and well organized. The weapons cache spoke of planning, and he wondered just how many other such stockpiles were hidden around the city, or in the surrounding countryside. He had lived in Alvaren most of his life, yet never suspected that the Children of Ynnis were more than a small handful of malcontents. Had things really changed so much in the three years he had been gone? Or was he only now seeing the truth?

"What is it these rebels want?" Stephen asked.

"They want to undo the events of the past sixty years. They want the invasion never to have happened. They want the garrisons emptied of soldiers, the granaries unlocked, and the clan leaders to elect a new queen to the throne. In short they want the impossible."

"And what do they expect of the Chosen One?" Didrik asked.

"The scroll did not say, only that they awaited the

chance to meet me. No doubt they will send a further message, telling me when and where this is to take place."

He felt helpless, for there was nothing he could do. Not until he either heard from the rebels or the soldiers brought news as to where the sword might be hidden.

So much depended on the Children of Ynnis, and of what they wanted from him. Did they have any understanding of the value of the sword? Or of what it meant to be Chosen One? Did they think him sympathetic to their cause?

If so, they were in for a nasty shock. To be Chosen One was to bear a terrible burden, for it meant he could not leave this place until he had recovered the sword or convinced himself that it was destroyed. Theft of the sword could be considered treason, and Devlin would be well within his rights to order retribution against the folk of Alvaren. He could impose fines, seize property, or take hostages. He could even order the executions of those suspected of aiding the rebels. It would be as if the dark days of conquest had come all over again.

Or perhaps that was what they wanted. Perhaps they hoped to provoke him into acts of oppression that would enable them to unite the people in rebellion. They would not accept that such a rebellion would ultimately be doomed. The Jorskian army was too entrenched to be dislodged.

He wondered if this is what Haakon had meant when he had told Devlin that he would lead his people to their deaths.

"I wonder if the rebels know just what it is they have done. By furthering their cause, they place the entire Kingdom in jeopardy, trapping you here to search for the sword as the enemies of Jorsk wreak havoc on our borders." Stephen's face bore a troubled frown and Devlin knew he was thinking of his home province of Esker, which was far too close to the border with Nerikaat for comfort.

"It will not come to that," Devlin said, trying to project a sense of optimism that he did not feel. "We will find the sword, then make all haste back to Kingsholm. And once there, I will convince the King to release the army from its garrisons. Esker will not be left to fend for itself, that I promise."

Yet even as he spoke the comforting words, a voice inside him whispered that they were a lie. *You are doomed to fail,* the voice whispered. *And in defeat you will be mine.*

The long night passed with no further news on who had taken the sword or where it might be. At dawn the servants brought fresh kava, and hard on their heels was Lord Kollinar. He, too, had spent a sleepless night, and it showed in his unshaven face and the dark circles under his eyes. But his voice was calm as he described how he had carried out Devlin's orders. Searches of homes of senior guild members had turned up nothing. And as instructed, they had rounded up and questioned two dozen folk suspected of sympathizing with the Children of Ynnis. Apprentices and students for the most part, though whether they were guilty of anything more than singing seditious songs on the feast days was a matter for debate. If the army had any real proof of their treason, they would have been imprisoned, and not merely on a list of potential troublemakers.

Lord Kollinar suggested that stronger forms of questioning might reveal the truth that was sought, but Devlin wanted no part of torture. Instead he directed that those rounded up be questioned again, to see if a night in gaol had freed up their tongues. And then they were to be released.

"Arrange with the peacekeepers to have them followed. Should there be any among them with a guilty conscience, they may seek to leave the city, or lead us to their friends," Devlin said. The chances of such were slim, but he was ready to grasp at any straw.

"It will be as you say. I have already spoken with Chief Mychal, the commander of the peacekeepers, and he assures me that they are willing to do whatever they can to catch the thieves," Lord Kollinar said. He lifted his mug to his lips and swallowed the remains of his kava in two quick gulps. Then he rose to his feet. "I must return to the garrison. Do you wish to accompany me and supervise the final questioning personally?"

"No. With your permission I will send Lieutenant Didrik as my representative." He could trust Didrik to ensure that those in custody were treated fairly. "As for myself, I have other inquiries I wish to make."

"There is a squad of soldiers outside who will accompany you wherever you wish to go."

"I need no such coddling."

"I disagree. It is not safe for you to wander the streets alone. Especially not now. The Children of Ynnis have achieved one success. This may embolden them to even more rash actions. And I have no wish to be known as the officer who let the Chosen One get murdered on his watch."

How often had he heard the same speech from Captain Drakken? Strange to think that he had traveled all this distance only to find that nothing had changed.

"You may find it useful to have an escort, should you need to search somewhere," Didrik pointed out. "And you can always use them as runners, to keep in touch with us at the garrison."

"I will consider it," Devlin said, knowing he had been outmaneuvered. "If you do not hear from me before then, I will plan on meeting up with you here, at the hour of sunset, so we can share what we have learned."

"Yes, General." Lord Kollinar gave a short bow, then he and Didrik took their leaves.

Stephen rose to his feet and raised his arms over his head, stretching to relieve muscles grown stiff with inactivity. Then he picked up his mug and crossed to the table, where he refilled it. After a glance at Devlin he brought the pitcher over and refilled his mug as well.

Devlin took a sip. The kava was now barely lukewarm, and bitter on his tongue. Still he welcomed the harsh bite and the energy that surged through his veins. Sleep was a luxury he could not afford, and he would need all his wits about him today.

"So what errand do you have for us?" Stephen asked. "What inquiries do you have to make? Someone or somewhere you don't wish the good governor to know about?"

"We are going nowhere. I must consult the peacekeepers, and they will talk more freely if I am alone," Devlin said. Though whether they would help him he did not know. Mychal he knew of old, for he had been chief in Cerrie's time. Mychal held little love for

Jorskians, but even less for those who disturbed the order of his city. If he could convince Mychal that the Children of Ynnis were a threat to that order, then he would have the full weight of the peacekeepers behind him.

"As for you, I have something different in mind. The folk of the city got a good look at Didrik and I yesterday, especially with the fracas at the guild hall, but you may have been overlooked. I want you to go to the taverns and see what gossip you can pick up."

Stephen lifted his left hand and tugged at his long brown hair. "I can hardly pass as one of your people. They will know I am a foreigner."

"And that is exactly what you shall be. A wandering minstrel, come to Alvaren and anxious to collect new songs for your repertoire. There is enough truth in it that you should have no trouble playing the part. Steer the conversation as you will. Ask for news of recent events, or turn the talk to the old days and the songs of the time before the conquest. Whatever you think will work," Devlin said with a shrug. "Just watch how much you drink, and if you think you are in any danger, make a hasty exit and summon help."

"The taverns will not open for hours yet."

"Then you should seek your bed. If you are going to spend the day drinking, you should not be sleepless as well. Just be careful."

"And you as well," Stephen said. "Remember, without the right man to wield it, the sword is nothing more than a lump of metal. Jorsk needs you. Alive."

"I will do my best," Devlin replied.

Yesterday the crowds had whispered as he passed. Now the braver among them called out *fearnym,* or turned and spit as he passed. Had he still been wholly of Duncaer, such insults would be sufficient to provoke an honor challenge. Now they were simply part of the price he paid for having sworn allegiance to their conquerors. He searched his memory but could not recall Lord Kollinar ever inspiring such ill treatment. Then again, the governor was of Jorsk. He, at least, was not a traitor to his own people.

Either the squad of soldiers at his back or their own native caution prevented the crowds from offering anything more than mere taunts. Still the threat of violence was ever-present, and Devlin could not help scanning the faces of those that watched him pass, wondering who among them concealed a throwing knife or a small bow under their cloaks.

He wondered if any of the voices that shouted insults at him belonged to someone he had once called friend.

The peacekeepers' compound was located at the southern end of the city, where the steep hillside briefly leveled off to provide an open training ground. As he approached, he saw that the field was occupied, with a group of peacekeepers practicing staff drills under the watchful eye of a senior sergeant. He counted twenty in all—a double band in peacekeeper terms. His attention was caught by a tall, slender woman, whose dark curls bounced as she spun around, then thrust her staff forward and disarmed her opponent. She grinned, and to show there were no hard feelings bent down to pick up the staff and handed it back.

Devlin's heart twisted in his chest, and his voice was rough as he turned to his escort. "Wait here," he told them. Then he began picking his way around the edges of the muddy field. A few halted their bouts to stare at him until they were swiftly recalled to their duty by the shouts of their instructor. As he reached the far side of the field, one of the sergeants who had been observing the practice came to meet him.

"I am here to see your chief," Devlin said.

The sergeant nodded, but did not speak. His features were familiar, and Devlin remembered meeting him before. Eoin or perhaps Sean was his name, and he had been one of the veteran trainers in Cerrie's day. But if he recognized Devlin, he made no sign of it. Instead, he turned and led the way, past the stable and storehouses into the main building. They walked past the entrance to the mess hall, up a flight of stairs, then down the corridor until they reached a partially opened door. The sergeant knocked once, then pushed the door open.

Devlin entered, and shut the door behind him.

Chief Mychal was much as he remembered. His once black hair was now totally white, but his blue eyes were sharp, and his muscled arms had lost none of their power.

"Devlin. General. Your noble pomposity, or whatever they call you these days. You cost me a month's salary, I'll have you know."

Devlin paused, and rocked back on his heels at the unexpectedness of the greeting.

"How so?"

Mychal smiled, but there was no mirth in it. "When the news came that a man of Duncaer calling himself Devlin Stonehand had been named Champion of Jorsk, a few swore it was you, but I told them they were fools. The Devlin I knew could hardly hold a sword. He was not a man to slay monsters or banish demons. I insisted it must be some other misguided soul. Imagine my surprise when the royal decree arrived, naming you General of the Royal Army, and listing your parentage. Saskia treated her entire band to a three-day drinking spree on what she won off me."

He remembered Saskia, who had been of an age with Cerrie and the first to join her band when Cerrie had made sergeant. She had been a good friend to Cerrie, and thus had known Devlin well, in the days when he had been a metalsmith, renowned for his skill in creating objects of beauty. He wondered what Saskia had seen in him then that convinced her he was the man mentioned in the strange stories emanating out of Jorsk.

"So tell me, did you really do all they say?" Mychal asked.

Devlin took a seat opposite his host, not waiting to be invited. "Probably not. Not if you have been listening to tavern ballads."

"And still they named you General?"

Devlin took a deep breath, reminding himself that he needed this man's good will, not his enmity. "Yes, I slew a lake monster in the province of Esker. Yes, with the help of a friend I destroyed a hellborn creature of magic. Yes, I led troops as they fought forest bandits. And yes, I challenged Duke Gerhard, the General of the Army and the King's Personal Champion to a duel to the death, and yes, I prevailed and proved him traitor. Is that what you wish to know?"

Mychal shook his head thoughtfully. "It is hard to believe. I remember the day when Cerrie had you join her novices at their training. You did not know one end of a sword from the other, and were more a danger to yourself than to anyone else."

"Then I had no need for sword skills. Now many things have changed."

"True. But plainly those who taught you had no skill of their own to share. If they had, you would still be whole and not crippled," Mychal said, proving that his eyes were as sharp as ever.

"Their training served me well. And as for this," Devlin flexed the remaining fingers of his right hand. "This was about winning, regardless of the cost."

"If Cerrie could see you now—"

"Enough," Devlin said. He had not come here to open up old wounds. "The past is gone, and cannot be changed. If Cerrie were here, alive, then I would still be a metalsmith, the missing sword just one more relic of Ynnis."

But Mychal was not willing to let the matter rest. "I warned you. I warned you both," he said. "The New Territories were dangerous. Risky. You had no place there, and no business dragging Cerrie along with you."

"You tell me nothing I do not already know," Devlin said.

The New Territories had been a risk. But they had also offered opportunity. For the first time in over fifty years, Caerfolk were offered the chance to buy land that could be cleared for farming. Against such potential riches, few had paid heed to the old legends surrounding the forest that bordered the endless mountains. Instead, families who had endured exile in the cities for two generations had joined together to raise the necessary coin to allow their most favored daughters to take advantage of this opportunity.

Agneta had been one such, born with a craving in her blood for land that she could farm and pass down to her children. She and Cormack had been among the first to purchase one of the Earl's land grants. Devlin and Cerrie had been among the last. They had no burning desire to start life over again as farmers. But Devlin had been grief-stricken at the prospect of separation from his brother, the only living member of his family. And Cerrie, generous soul that she was, had taken pity on him. Having no close kin ties of her own, and an adventurous spirit, she had declared herself ready for the challenge of settling a new land. They had left Alvaren with high hopes, little guessing the grief that lay ahead.

"Enough of what once was. Tell me what I need to know now. What do you know of the Children of Ynnis? Who are they, and what do they want with me?"

"Things have changed in these past years. Once the Children of Ynnis were mere malcontents and hotheaded youths. From time to time they'd pull off some prank, like the time they painted 'Death to the Usurpers' on the wall of the governor's residence. We'd haul the ringleaders into gaol, fine them or sentence them to a few months of labor, and that would be all."

Such matched Devlin's memories. The Children of Ynnis had been simply a nuisance, more of a jest than a threat. It did not seem possible that they could be responsible for the planning and execution that the theft of the sword would have required.

"And now?" he prompted.

"About two, maybe three years ago now we noticed a change. The petty mischief stopped, and at first I breathed a sigh of relief. Then a royal messenger disappeared on the road from Kilbaran. The commander sent out search parties, looking for bandits, but found nothing. A fortnight later, his dismembered corpse was found in a ditch outside the main gate."

"Did you ever find his killers?"

"A note pinned to his body claimed the Children of Ynnis had executed him, to send a message that no Jorskian should feel safe. We never did find out who had actually committed the deed."

"Have there been other killings?"

"A few. Two more of yours and some of our own, suspected members of the Children of Ynnis who had their tongues cut out perhaps as a warning to others. I've come to believe that the killings are the work of a new group, hiding within the Children of Ynnis to throw us off the scent. From time to time we hear whispers of their doings and rumors that they are arming themselves for rebellion. But so far we've not been able to find their leaders, and the weapons you found last night were the first proof that they are indeed arming for war. They must be getting help from somewhere."

"You think they have outside help?"

"The weapons you found were steel. Unlicensed imports. That takes gold and connections in Jorsk. A traitor on your side."

"Or someone else stirring up trouble," Devlin mused. Jorsk had its own enemies, who had already shown their willingness to use gold to fund unrest. Devlin had defeated their efforts in Korinth province, but who was to say that was the only scheme they had? A rebellion in Duncaer would be equally distracting, tying up troops and diverting attention from the real enemy.

"What of Jarlath, the Guild Master? Do you think he is involved?" Mychal asked.

"No, he seemed as outraged as any." Once Jarlath had been known as a great craftsman, but as his eyes grew weak and the skill left his hands, he had turned instead to politics. For nearly twenty years he had prided himself on his control of the Metalsmiths' Guild. Now his stewardship was called into question, for not only had he lost an object entrusted to him, but his own hall had been used to store illegal weapons. Devlin was not the only one who would be asking questions about whether Jarlath was still fit to lead.

But that was a matter for another day.

"The sword must be found," Devlin said. "Whatever it takes."

Mychal's gaze searched his, then dropped down to Devlin's crippled hand, as if reminding himself just how ruthless Devlin had become.

"Why? You will still be their General even without the sword."

Devlin bit back the oath that rose to his lips. They did not understand. The General of the Royal Army was a reasonable man, one who would hesitate before lifting a hand against his own people. It was not the General they needed to fear, but rather the Chosen One. The Chosen One acknowledged nothing save duty. And as Chosen One, he would tear this city apart stone by stone, if that was what it took to find the sword.

"If you have not guessed already, you should know that the sword Roric brought out of Ynnis was no ordinary sword. It was the Sword of the Chosen One, handed down from one to another until Lord Saemund lost it in battle. This is the sword that Roric left to me, knowing nothing save that he wanted to leave it to his most favored student."

Mychal blinked, his eyes wide with amazement. "But how can this be? How did he know? Roric was in his grave long before we had word that you had been named Champion."

"Not Champion. Chosen One. And as for Roric, perhaps he, too, was touched by the Gods. You may ask them, when next you see them. As for me, that sword is destined for my hand. I will find it, and I will wield it in battle when I lead the army against the enemies of Jorsk. Any who stand in my way will be counted as traitors and dealt with according to the laws which govern both our peoples. Is that understood?"

Mychal shook his head, his shaggy hair falling into his eyes. "I do not understand any of this. I want no part of this strange madness that you have brought with you. But I will do everything I can to help you find that sword and send you on your way."

Seventeen

STEPHEN LIFTED THE GLASS OF ALE TO HIS LIPS and tried not to grimace as he took a sip. He had never developed a taste for the bitter drink, and here the brewers had outdone themselves, producing a gritty, grain-filled beverage that practically demanded he chew it before swallowing. He set the glass firmly down on the table before him, trying not to shudder. And to think this was the finest this place had to offer.

At least there was one consolation. He had no fear of becoming so drunk that he forgot himself.

He leaned back on his stool and surveyed the room. Like the previous four taverns he had visited, this one was smaller than he was accustomed to, with a low ceiling that made it feel even more cramped. There were no private booths, but rather two long tables in the center of the room, where perhaps two dozen could sit elbow to elbow. A narrow shelf ran around three sides of the room, just wide enough to hold a glass or a tankard. Stools were lined up underneath the shelves, and Stephen had appropriated one of these for his use.

Three men and two women sat at one of the tables,

eating a late midday meal, or perhaps an early supper. They were far more intent on their food than on conversation, and when they did speak, it was of ordinary things. One complained that his new boots had blistered his feet. Another complained of their taskmaster and his habit of making them labor in the rain when anyone could see that such was wasted effort. The taskmaster was soundly disparaged by all, and then one woman began to describe the difficulties she was having with her new husband.

Ordinary conversation by ordinary folk. Not a single whisper of the Children of Ynnis, or of Devlin's return to his homeland. Nothing that was of any value.

Stephen surveyed the handful of other drinkers who occupied stools around the room, but they were all solitary souls, far too intent on their drinking to pay any mind to a stranger. And he had learned from his first two tavern visits that a stranger did not try to introduce himself. Behavior that was considered courteous in Jorsk had gotten him ejected twice, with the polite but firm request that he not return.

At the third place he had visited, the problem had been the opposite. The servingwoman had suggested that she could teach him the ballad of the Crimson Hawk, an offer which made the other patrons laugh. But the laughter had an ugly ring to it, and there had been a cold glint in her eye, that belied her jesting words, so he had quickly taken his leave.

He was beginning to suspect that Devlin had sent him on a fool's errand. Devlin must have known how insular these taverns were and how slight the chance was that any would talk to a stranger. As for overhearing incriminating conversations, he could hardly do so when the taverns were practically deserted. Perhaps later, after the sun had set, he might be able to mingle with the crowds unobserved. But for now, this was wasted effort.

And while he sat and tried to choke down bitter ale, who knew what Devlin was up to? He could have helped him, but once again Devlin had chosen to distance himself from Stephen. Ever since Midwinter's Eve, in fact, he had been cold and aloof. Yesterday he had refused to let Stephen accompany him when he went to retrieve the sword and had given no reason for his actions. It hurt that he had taken Didrik with him instead. Didrik, who knew nothing of the lore of the great sword and had no true understanding of its history. Stephen had tried to console himself with the knowledge that Devlin was merely showing prudence in taking along a bodyguard.

But while this was the most obvious explanation, it was not necessarily the true one. Didrik was Devlin's friend, but first and foremost he was a lieutenant of the guard, accustomed to obeying his commander, even when he disagreed. Didrik seemed to have forgotten that Devlin had nearly killed him, but Stephen could not. And while Didrik expressed concern over Devlin's growing strangeness, in the end Didrik would do as he was told.

Stephen was a different matter, for he was not under Devlin's command. Stephen would put his friendship with Devlin over the success of the quest, going against Devlin's wishes if it meant helping his friend. He had done it before. And Devlin knew this—which perhaps explained why he was keeping Stephen at arm's length these days.

Not that there was anything he could do. If the Geas was weighing heavily on Devlin's spirit, there was little he could do save offer his friendship. And even that was denied.

He sighed.

"The porter is not to your liking? If it is sweet wine you want, there are taverns near the garrison that cater to the tastes of northern soldiers."

Stephen flinched at the unexpected voice. He had been so lost in thought that he had not noticed the tavern servant's approach. "The porter is fine," he lied, speaking in the Caer tongue. "But I will admit I am disappointed. I am no soldier, but rather a minstrel come to learn new songs. But if no one will speak with me, how can I hope to learn anything?"

"If you are a minstrel, where is your harp?" the man asked.

"The journey was too arduous to risk either lap harp or lute, so I left my instruments behind," Stephen said. It had pained him not to bring his lute, but Devlin had insisted that they pack only the bare essentials. For a winter journey, an extra woolen cloak or sack of grain was far more valuable than a mere lute. Though if he was to continue this ruse, he might need to find a lute he could purchase to bolster his story.

Wood scraped against stone as the diners pushed their benches back, then rose to their feet. As they left, they called out farewells to the servant, whose name was apparently Teomas.

Teomas left Stephen's side and disappeared through a curtain that led to a back room. He emerged carrying a tray, which he set on the table, and began to fill it with the empty plates and glasses.

"You still have your voice, do you not? A song would make the work go faster," Teomas called over his shoulder.

It was less an invitation than a challenge, but Stephen had sung before far more hostile audiences.

"It would be my pleasure," he said. He thought a moment, then launched into the first verse of "Cold Hearts," a song about two feuding lovers trapped by a blizzard.

In Jorsk it was an old song, but here he wagered it was new, and the subject would be novel to a people that seldom saw more than a few flakes of snow in the sky. As the verses unfolded, Teomas's movements slowed, and finally he gave up even the pretense of wiping down the trestle table. The song ended with springtime, and the discovery of the bodies of the two lovers, frozen in their final embrace. There had been nights when he made men and women weep with a rendition of "Cold Hearts," but now, as the last notes faded away, there was silence.

Stephen felt vaguely foolish. An old woman banged her glass against the shelf. He thought it might be a sign of approval, but Teomas picked up his tray and brought the dishes to the back room, then returned carrying a pitcher of ale, which he used to fill the old woman's glass. Then he proceeded around the room to check on the other drinkers before returning to Stephen's side. He filled Stephen's glass back up to the top, then poured a glass for himself.

This time he pulled out a stool and sat beside him. "Whatever else you may be, you have the singer's gift," Teomas said.

"Thank you."

The servant took a long draught of his ale. "After-noons are quiet, but come evening you will find singers and lore tellers in most places. Some have the true gift and others just entertain their friends. Ordinarily I'd invite you to come back here tonight and trade songs. But not this night, nor any night this week."

"Why not?"

"Because the *fearnym* has come to stir up trouble."

"The what?" Stephen's grasp of Caer speech was improving, but this word he did not recognize.

"Him that turned his back on his people and went to serve your kind." Teomas made a gesture with his right hand that was probably intended to be insulting.

"The Chosen One?"

"Whatever he calls himself. He came here where he had no right and is making trouble. First he used some pretext to harass the metalsmiths because they banished him from their ranks. Now he is using the soldiers to harass honest folk, settling old scores."

A protest rose to Stephen's lips, but he swiftly bit it back. Defending Devlin was hardly likely to endear him to this man, nor would it help him find out what he needed to know.

"I heard he was searching for rebels. The Children of somewhere or another."

"The Children of Ynnis are a myth, made up to give the army an excuse to do what it pleases," Teomas said loudly.

"Hear, hear," one of the drinkers agreed, raising his glass in salute.

"There is no threat here, just a power-mad man come to take his revenge. The metalsmiths banished him from their ranks, and his own kin disowned him.

An honest man would accept their judgment, but this Devlin is a different breed. He curried favor with your kind and is now using his power to crush those who once stood against him. And what defense do we have? None. His master the King cares not what happens in Duncaer. He can do as he likes to us."

"The Chosen One is a man of honor," Stephen said, unable to keep silent any longer. "He acts only to punish wrongdoers or to defend the Kingdom."

"Maybe that is the way of it in Jorsk," Teomas said. "But here in Duncaer it is a different story. Until he leaves there will be no peace for any of us, and neither will we welcome any minstrel who may be a spy. If you're still here after the Chosen One leaves, then we can talk again. But for now, my patrons and I would find it a kindness if you would return to your own people."

At the end of the day they met back at the governor's residence, with nothing to show for their troubles save aching feet and a growing sense of frustration. Devlin's head throbbed, and his eyes burned from lack of sleep as he listened to the others recount their lack of progress.

And every time his thoughts wandered, he heard the Dread Lord whispering to him, telling Devlin that his quest was doomed to fail.

"We must start at the beginning, with who could have taken the sword and why? Who knew of the sword's existence? And how did the rebels know you were coming to retrieve it?" Lord Kollinar ticked off each question on his fingers.

"More importantly, when was it taken?" Didrik

asked, not to be outdone. "For all we know this could have been done months ago, when they first heard of Devlin's appointment as Chosen One. The note refers to the 'Sword of the Chosen One,' but that does not mean that they know it is the sacred sword. They could have taken it as an act of retribution, simply because it belonged to Devlin and they now consider him a traitor."

Lord Kollinar nodded slowly. "You may be correct. In which case the culprits may have vanished months ago, taking the sword with them."

"Or destroyed it. Thus they could punish the Chosen One and eliminate the one thing that could tie them to the crime," Didrik said.

"No," Stephen protested. "The sword was forged by a son of Egil. I do not believe it could simply be melted down or broken. Not without a great working of magic, which surely would have attracted the attention of the guards."

"Here they are peacekeepers," Devlin corrected him. "But I agree with you that the sword is probably intact. They may have preserved it as a bargaining tool. Or simply kept it as a weapon, for even a fool can see that it is an uncommonly fine sword."

"Then we must begin again with the metalsmiths," Didrik said. "A stranger could not wander into the storeroom and find the sword. Not without help. Someone in that guild helped them find the sword. Perhaps the same person who is responsible for the weapons cache."

"We have already questioned Jarlath and the senior guild members. And searched their homes," Devlin said.

"Then we question them again. And we question the junior members, down to the lowliest apprentice. Anyone who might have knowledge of the sword or of suspicious goings-on."

"I agree with the lieutenant," Kollinar said. Like Didrik, he seemed to put his faith in discipline and regulations. Good qualities to have in an administrator. Any search he conducted would be painstakingly thorough. "We need to start with those who had access to the sword. Someone in that guild hall knows the truth, and when we find that person, they will lead us to it."

It was not that simple. Maybe in Jorsk it could be done that way, but this was Duncaer. His people had decades of practice in keeping secrets from their conquerors. And the web of kin and craft ties would ensure that no one would step forward on their own, for to break the code of silence was to risk ostracism, the ultimate punishment in a society where mutual interdependence was a way of life.

Not to mention that regardless of what happened, they would hate him for this.

"General? Will you give the order or shall I?" Lord Kollinar prompted.

"I will sign the order," Devlin said. Because, in the end, he had no choice. Retrieving the sword was the only thing that truly mattered. And if there was even the smallest chance that someone in the metalsmiths guild could be persuaded to break their silence, then he had to act.

He thought for a moment, then continued. "I will not insult them by offering a reward. But we should let it be known that if the sword is returned within the next two days that no questions will be asked of the bearer and no reprisals made. And the questioning should be done by the peacekeepers. You may send one of yours to observe, but Chief Mychal's people will be in charge."

"If you insist—"

"I do." Devlin said. The peacekeepers would be fair, and would ensure that the questioning did not get out of hand. This situation was bad enough. He did not need to worry about an overzealous soldier deciding that a judicious bit of torture would be more likely to inspire the truth from his reluctant witnesses.

He tried very hard not to think about the fact that these were not faceless enemies that would be questioned. These were the men and women who had taught him his craft. Friends who had sweated with him as they labored at the forge, then fidgeted at their desks in the great hall as the masters lectured from their books. Even his own two former apprentices would be dragged in for questioning.

They would hate him for involving the Jorskians in guild affairs. For the humiliation of being treated like criminals, for ordering their homes searched and their families questioned. And yet he knew there was nothing he could do or say that would make them understand. How could he? Three years ago he would not have understood it himself.

He felt an ache in his soul. This hurt far more than seeing the blank spot on the wall where once his name had been engraved. That he could blame on guild politics and the envy of a few senior masters. But what he was about to do now would ensure that the entire guild turned its back on him, as word of what had happened here spread throughout Duncaer.

His name would be reviled, along with that of Saemund and the treacherous Ysobel. And there was nothing he could do to stop it.

A soft voice broke into his musings.

"Devlin?"

"Yes?" Devlin blinked, surprised to find himself the focus of three pairs of eyes. Kollinar's face was that of a politician, with no expression that could be read. But Didrik and Stephen looked worried.

He wondered how many times Stephen had called his name before he had finally responded.

"It has been a long day. For all of us," Didrik said diplomatically. "Let me scribe the order for you to sign, then I think we should dine and seek our beds."

Devlin did not know how he could be expected to sleep. But there was nothing else he could do. As much as it irked him, he would have to rely upon others to lead the hunt for the sword.

Lord Kollinar summoned his servants and instructed them to set out a simple repast in the dining room. While they were doing so, Devlin dictated the order and Didrik made three copies. The first was given to Lord Kollinar, while the second was sent by runner to Chief Mychal. The third was kept by Didrik, for the Royal Archives.

Now there was nothing to do except wait and see what news the morning brought.

Eighteen

TWO DAYS AFTER THE MISSING SWORD HAD BEEN discovered, a scroll addressed to Devlin was found on the garrison steps. Apparently it had been left there overnight, though the soldiers who had sentry duty swore that they had seen nothing. The message was simple enough, that the sword would be returned to Devlin only after the army garrisons were emptied and the last Jorskian soldier had departed Duncaer. The letter was signed in the name of the Children of Ynnis.

Their demands were absurd. Only the King himself could order the withdrawal of the occupying army, and that he would never do. King Olafur clung too tightly to Duncaer as the symbol of his father's greatness, a reminder of the days when Jorsk had been a military power to be feared. Other pieces of his empire might be crumbling, but Duncaer, at least, was still firmly within his grasp, and so it would remain.

Didrik was of the opinion that the scroll was a hoax, since the writer offered no proof that they were the ones who had taken the sword. Without a sketch of the hilt, or even a mere description of the sword, there was no way to tell if these were the people who held the sword. Not that it really mattered. Devlin could not meet their demands, and they had given him no means to contact the Children of Ynnis and open negotiations. He would have to wait until they chose to send another message, and hope in the meanwhile that the teams scouring the city found some trace of the missing sword.

That night a servant awoke Devlin shortly after midnight, with the news that Chief Mychal had arrived and wished to speak with both Devlin and Kollinar. He wondered what was so urgent that they must be roused in the middle of the night. Had the peacekeepers found the missing sword?

"Shall I wake your aide?" the chamberman asked, handing Devlin a robe which he belted over his nightshirt. He did not bother with socks, but forced his feet into boots.

"No. If I need him, I will send for him later," Devlin said. It had been late when they sought their beds, and they had not slept at all the night before.

"Chief Mychal is waiting in the governor's study," the chamberman said.

"Thank you." He took the offered lamp and made his way swiftly through the corridor and down the stairs. He entered the study to find that Governor Kollinar was already there, looking remarkably alert considering the hour and his own lack of rest.

One look at Chief Mychal's face told him that he was not the bearer of good news.

"What has happened?" Devlin asked.

It was Kollinar who responded. "Ensign Annasdatter failed to report for duty this evening, not unheard of, but unusual in one so conscientious. I sent a patrol to check the taverns, and asked the peacekeepers to keep a watch for her."

"We found her body a short while ago, in a street not far from the Metalsmiths' Guild's hall. The cord used to strangle her was still wrapped around her neck, and the sign of a bird had been carved into her forehead," Chief Mychal said.

"A bird," Devlin repeated stupidly. He rubbed the back of his neck with his good hand, as he tried to force his sleep-addled wits to respond.

"The shape of a hawk. A crimson hawk."

Chief Mychal's voice was curiously flat as he elaborated, drawing the conclusion that should have been obvious. His people used birds as symbols in many ways, but always as part of a larger motif. A solitary bird could have only one interpretation.

"This means something to you," Kollinar said.

"Yes," Devlin replied.

He remembered Ensign Annasdatter. He had met her two days ago, when she had taken charge of the patrol that accompanied him to the Metalsmiths' Guild. At the time he had thought her a mere child, one too young for her rank. Now she would never grow older.

A chill swept over him, and he crossed the room, taking a seat on the bench closest to the hearth. A part of him wondered when the servants had had time to build up the fire. Had it taken them that long to summon him? Or did they not bank the fire at night, keeping the room warm in case of late night callers?

Even as he mused, he realized the absurdity of his thoughts. Whether they were bright flames or sullen embers, it did not matter. No fire could dispel the chill on his soul as he realized that this was another death that he had caused, however indirectly.

Deathbringer, the mind-voice whispered, and Devlin was forced to agree.

"Chosen One?" Lord Kollinar prompted.

He came back to himself with a start, realizing that his companions had taken their own seats and were waiting for him to explain.

"In our oldest tales, the crimson hawk is the guardian spirit that led our ancestors to settle in these mountains. Legend says that it will return to guide us in times of great need. Of late, some tales say that the return of the crimson hawk will signal the end of Jorskian rule," Devlin explained.

"The Children of Ynnis have not used this symbol in the past, but this may be a sign that there is new leadership at work within the rebel groups. Is there any reason why they would have singled out this Ensign?" Mychal asked.

"She was in charge of the detail assigned to me, and she supervised the search of the Metalsmiths' Guild," Devlin said.

Another death added to his tally. The choice of Annasdatter had not been random. They had not chosen just any army officer, but one with a direct link to Devlin. The Children of Ynnis were sending him a message that they were to be taken seriously.

But it did not matter if they killed one soldier or a hundred. He could not give them what they wanted. And without a means to contact them, he had no means of negotiating.

"My people questioned everyone they could find, but no one witnessed the Ensign's killing, or saw who dumped the body," Chief Mychal said. "I doubt very much we will catch the killers. We don't even know if they are connected to those who took the sword."

Kollinar nodded. "But we cannot let this go unpunished. My men will select the hostages in the morning."

"Hostages?" Devlin asked.

"Three hostages, chosen at random from the city," the governor explained. "We will choose them at dawn, and then give the true murderers a chance to win their freedom by confessing. If the killers do not come forward, then we will execute the hostages on the following day."

"No," Devlin said. He understood Kollinar's anger. Ensign Annasdatter had been one of his own. Her death must be avenged. But the killing of innocents was not justice, it was murder.

"No?" Kollinar repeated. "Shall I let the city degenerate into chaos? Already I have enough troubles. Just this past week I have received half a dozen reports of new outbreaks of the grain sickness, including the first report from the southern districts. We must replace the bad grain with city stores, which leaves us dangerously low, and yet to let the people starve would be an even surer way to incite rebellion. And your presence here has stirred up decades of resentment. It would take very little to provoke the people to violence. Now, of all times, we cannot afford to appear weak."

"Bad enough that they have made us all look foolish by stealing the sword," Chief Mychal said. "The search of the city is turning even ordinary folk against you. If we do not act swiftly, there will be more killings."

"And can you guarantee me that peace is to be bought at the cost of three innocent lives?" He could not believe that Mychal was arguing in support of Kollinar's plan.

"It is the law, when one of theirs is killed," Mychal replied. "Three of our lives for each one of theirs."

It may have been the law, but it had not been enforced in Devlin's lifetime. Not since the first years after the conquest, when, exhausted by the years of blood feuds, the surviving Caerfolk had settled into an uneasy peace with their conquerors.

"It may be the law, but it is not right. It is not just," Devlin argued.

"Fine," Kollinar snapped, throwing up his hands. "Then tell me, how do you plan to control this city? They tested us once by taking the sword. A second time by killing Annasdatter. The next step may well be armed riots in the streets, which will lead to dozens of innocents being killed. Who will find justice for them?"

Devlin ground his teeth in frustration, for a part of him knew that Kollinar was right. To appear weak or indecisive was to incite further violence. As Chosen One it was his duty to preserve the peace and to uphold the law. Never had he hated his duty more than he did at this moment.

"Very well, you may take your hostages," Devlin said. "But I will not rest until we have found the sword and seen the true killers brought to justice."

"Then we must hope that the true killers surrender themselves. Only cowards would let others die in their place," Kollinar replied.

"Of course," Devlin said, but in his heart he feared that it would not be that simple. The rebels might well decide that three innocent lives were a fair price to pay, if it helped rouse the ordinary folk of Alvaren against the occupying soldiers. And then more killings would follow, as the cycle of murder and retaliation escalated, with neither side sparing a thought for the innocent lives that were being destroyed.

The next morning, two men and a woman were taken as hostages. As he had feared, no one came forward to take their place, so they were executed the next day. Devlin knew his presence would only incite the crowd, so he sent Didrik as his witness. Didrik reported that those gathered had cursed the Chosen One and Governor Kollinar, rather than placing the blame on the rebels. It was an ominous sign.

He dismissed Didrik curtly and went to the governor's study, leaving orders that he was not to be disturbed. The long worktable was covered with stacks of bound scrolls, containing the records of the peacekeepers for the past seven years. Didrik and Chief Mychal's people had already combed through the reports once, but now Devlin wanted to read them for himself, looking for any patterns that might emerge. Surely the new Children of Ynnis had not sprung into being overnight. Their activities would have been noticed over the years, perhaps written off as small mischiefs or isolated incidents, but still there would be some record of them in these journals.

There was no one else who could take on the task. The peacekeepers were unlikely to find what they had already overlooked, and Didrik did not know the Caerfolk well enough to know what was significant and what was not. So it was left to Devlin to comb through the watch reports, listings of those arrested for drunkenness, public brawling, the occasional petty theft, or the rare acts of violence. His eyes began to burn, but he saw no great patterns or signs of hidden conspiracies. Just the tedium of everyday life, laid bare in dry prose. He came across mention of a murdered Jorskian trader, but the man's lover had confessed to the deed, her hands still red with his blood when the peacekeepers arrested her. It was unlikely that she had killed the trader as part of a rebel plot, but Devlin made a note that her family was to be questioned. Just in case.

Yet even as he squinted at the faded writing, his thoughts kept turning to the hostages who had been executed that morning. Now that it was too late, he wished that he had been present to bear witness to their deaths. It seemed somehow wrong that he knew their names and not their faces. In a sense, they, too, had died for him. Died because the Chosen One had come to their city.

Their families curse your name.

Devlin raised his head from the reports to see a dark figure seated opposite him. It was the mere shape of a man, with no true features to be seen, save for the glittering eyes.

Devlin closed his eyes and shook his head. But when he opened his eyes, the figure was still there.

"Deathbringer." This time he heard the voice with his ears, instead of in his mind. "I am pleased with how well you have used my gift. The young Ensign is a fine addition to my realm, as are the three followers you sent to join her."

Devlin shivered, the blight of Haakon's presence leeching every scrap of warmth from the room. He swallowed against the bitter taste of fear, striving to project a calm he did not feel.

"I will find those who murdered Ensign Annasdatter and see them punished," he said. He was proud that his voice did not shake, though he knew a god would not be fooled by his show of calm.

"The Ensign was only the first. Remember my promise? You will bring death to all those around you. Even those you call friends are not safe, for they will betray you and you will be forced to kill them."

"No." Devlin pushed his chair back and rose to his feet. "My friends will not betray me," he insisted.

Haakon gave a mirthless chuckle. "Already they think you half-mad. What would they say if they saw you now, talking to a shadow that no one else can see? They would try to lock you away. For your own good, of course."

Devlin's stomach lurched. With the cruelty that was intrinsic to his nature, Haakon had given voice to Devlin's greatest fear.

Stephen and Didrik already suspected that something was amiss with Devlin. He had heard their whispered conversations and seen the wary glances cast his way. It would not take much more to convince them that he was mad. And then they would act. The Geas would not let him desert his duty. He would be forced to resist, drawing steel against his companions. Then Haakon's prophecy might well come true, as Devlin killed his companions.

Or, if they managed to overpower him, his fate would be no better. It did not matter if they chose to imprison him here under the eyes of the healers, or take him back to Jorsk under guard. Any action they took would have the very result they feared, for if he were unable to fulfill his duty, then the Geas would drive Devlin mad.

"If I am imprisoned, then you have lost your sport," Devlin replied.

"Your suffering will be ample repayment for my labors on your behalf," Haakon said. "And do not sell yourself cheaply. Even your mere presence, witless or no, will be enough to set this city ablaze."

The Death God's words held the ring of truth. Chief Mychal and Governor Kollinar had both warned him as much, in their own ways. The longer the search for the sword continued, the more disturbances there would be. The cycle of violence that had begun with Annasdatter's death would continue and grow, until no one could stop it.

"What do you want of me?" Devlin shouted.

"Death," Haakon replied. Then, as Devlin watched, the figure slowly dissolved into nothingness, and he was once again alone.

"My lord?" a woman's voice called.

Devlin turned to see a servingwoman standing in the open door to the study.

"Did you want something?" she asked.

He wondered how long she had been standing there, watching him converse with empty air. Or had she come at his shout?

It did not matter. Nothing mattered. He turned his back on the table and the useless reports.

"Ale," he said.

She shook her head and bit her lip, plainly afraid of displeasing him. "We keep false ale for our own folk, but the governor drinks no ale himself. Wine we have in plenty, both red and the straw-colored."

"Then bring me wine. The red from Myrka." Myrkan wine had always reminded him of the color of blood. It was a fitting drink for one such as he.

"Bring it to my chambers," he added. "And this time pass the word that when I am not to be disturbed, it means that no one is to bother me. For anything."

"Of course, my lord," she said, bobbing a nervous curtsy. She could not leave his presence fast enough.

Devlin woke the next morning to a pounding head and a foul taste in his mouth. Sitting up proved his undoing, for the room swayed and his stomach rebelled. He barely made it to the basin before heaving his guts up, a dark bile that told the tale of too much drink on an empty stomach. After a few moments the spasms subsided, and he was able to raise his head.

This time the room stayed level, though his head continued to pound. He poured water from the pitcher into a cup and rinsed the taste from his mouth, then splashed water on his face to clear the grime of sleep.

He found it hard to believe his idiocy. How could he, of all men, have drunk himself into a stupor? What if he had been needed during the night? What would the others have thought if they sought the Chosen One, only to find a drunken lout in his place?

Never mind that he had been provoked beyond all measure, driven by Haakon's ghastly prophecy. There were no answers to be found in drink. He had learned this lesson before. The last time he had drunk himself to the point of unconsciousness he had taken it in his head to serve as Chosen One. He was lucky that he had not committed some equal foolishness this past night.

Only when the wash water turned gray did he realize that his hands were filthy, covered with black dirt of some sort. He scrubbed until the worst of the stains were gone, wondering what had happened during those missing hours. Try as he could, he could remember nothing after he had begun drinking the second bottle of Myrka red. Had he sunk so low that he had crawled on the floor to find his bed? He looked around his chamber, and saw that his pale gray traveling cloak was thrown carelessly on the floor. He picked it up, noticing that the sleeves of the cloak were filthy, and he smelled the unmistakable odor of soot.

The room was chill, and the small fire in the grate had burned itself out. Devlin had been too drunk to tend to it, and the servants, following his orders, had left him alone. Perhaps he had tried to relight the fire, but when that failed had donned his cloak against the chill. He was fortunate that he hadn't set himself on fire.

There was a soft rap at the door. Devlin opened it, to find a chamberman bearing a tray on which sat a mug of kava and a bowl of porridge. Typical morning fare, but now the very smell of it threatened to make him ill once more.

"No," Devlin said, shaking his head and taking a step backward.

"But, my lord, you did not join the others, so the minstrel asked me—"

"My thanks but not today," Devlin said, raising one hand to fend off the offending object. "Are Lord Kollinar and my companions awake?"

"Yes, and already broken their fast. Chief Mychal is with them, and they wait upon your presence."

Devlin grimaced. So he had added oversleeping to his sins.

"I will join them in the governor's study. And see to it that I am brought sweet tea."

"Yes, my lord." The chamberman nodded.

Devlin finished dressing and joined the others in the governor's study. It was not as late as he feared, merely a half hour past the time he had appointed for their meeting. They were too polite to mention his tardiness, though Kollinar's lips were thin as he bade Devlin good day. As Devlin took his seat at the table, he wondered who had taken the time to tidy the bound reports, which he had left in such disarray the day before.

He noticed that Stephen had chosen the very seat where Haakon had appeared, and he took a sip of the sweet tea to cover his unease.

"Governor Kollinar, is there any progress to report?" Devlin asked.

"No," Kollinar said. "Our informants claim no knowledge of these doings. I was thinking of offering a reward—"

"And I told you that would be folly," Chief Mychal interrupted.

"What harm can it do? Surely there is one of these scum who is willing to trade their honor for gold. Someone who can lead us to Annasdatter's killer. Or don't you want them to be found?"

Chief Mychal braced both arms on the table and leaned forward. "I want justice. Can you say the same?"

"Peace," Devlin said. "Bickering among ourselves is useless."

"Of course," Chief Mychal said, sitting back in his chair.

Kollinar merely nodded.

"Chief Mychal, have the peacekeepers found anything of interest?"

"We are continuing to question members of the Metalsmiths' Guild, as well as the nearkin of those members who had keys to the storeroom where the sword was kept. But we have turned up nothing yet."

It was as he had expected. If Chief Mychal had found any evidence that linked a guild member to the theft of the sword, he would have informed Devlin at once rather than waiting for this status meeting.

"Lord Kollinar's aide is working with my deputy to compare our lists of suspected members of the Children of Ynnis. Most of the names are the same; but the army has a few suspects that I had not spotted, so they are being included in the round up for questioning."

"How many?" Devlin asked.

"Fifty so far, with perhaps another dozen or so that we need to hunt down. Tobias has the list, I'll see that you get a copy of it."

"Sixty? Sixty rebels that you let walk the streets in freedom until now? How can this be?" Didrik could scarcely contain his astonishment.

Chief Mychal shook his head. "Sixty folk who may have done no more than sing a forbidden song or been caught spitting at the governor when he passed. Doing those things makes them foolish, but does not make them criminals."

The act of spitting at someone's footsteps was a profound insult in the Caer culture, but merely considered rude by the Jorskians. As such it was a time-honored form of expressing contempt for the conquerors, one which did not involve true risk.

"Anyone we judged a serious threat has already been imprisoned or executed," Kollinar declared.

"You missed those who were stockpiling weapons under your very noses," Didrik pointed out. "Those who took the sword are still out there, as is the person who killed Annasdatter. What will you do if they are not found on one of your lists?"

"We will keep looking," Chief Mychal answered. "But in the meantime we had best be on our guard, lest they seek to cause more harm. You heard of the tavern that burned last night?"

Kollinar nodded. "I heard it was an accident."

Devlin's heart quickened. "A tavern burned? Where? When?"

"The Golden Crown, a tavern near the main barracks. It is frequented mostly by soldiers and travelers from Jorsk. No one was harmed. The tavern was already closed when the night-watch reported the fire. It may have been the result of carelessness, but these days I am suspicious of any misfortune that befalls one of Jorsk."

Devlin let loose the breath he had been holding, as he realized that no one had been injured. He knew the narrow twisting alley where the Golden Crown could be found, and could picture in his mind the gilded sign that hung above the door.

He remembered his blackened hands, and the sooty cloak. He felt unclean, and rubbed his left hand against his thigh, trying to remove a taint that could not be seen with the naked eye.

Had he been at the tavern last night? Had he witnessed the fire?

He looked toward Stephen, but it was not the minstrel he saw. Instead he saw the dark figure of the Death

God, as he promised that Devlin would set the city ablaze. Was this what Haakon had meant? Had Devlin set the fire himself, driven by some mad impulse?

If so, why couldn't he remember? The entire night was a gaping hole in his memory. Two bottles of wine should not have been enough to cause such memory lapse. A half dozen bottles of wine would not have been enough.

He could not shake the sense that the Death God was toying with him. If Devlin had set a fire at Haakon's bidding, then surely he would have chosen a place that was filled with people, sending new souls to join the Dread Lord's realm. Burning down an empty tavern made no sense.

Unless the burning was an accident. Maybe Devlin had left his quarters last night, and ventured into the city in search of information. He might have seen something or found someone with knowledge of the sword. Perhaps the fire had been set not to destroy the tavern, but rather to destroy the evidence that it had held. Evidence that might have led him to the Children of Ynnis. Knowledge that might have helped him stop the escalating spiral of violence before more of his people paid with their lives.

He ground his teeth in frustration, as he realized that Haakon had found yet another way to torture him. Whatever had happened last night, his memories of it were gone, and the uncertainty would continue to plague Devlin like an open sore.

"Chosen One?" Kollinar's voice was sharp-edged, and Devlin realized that he had missed whatever question had been asked.

"I agree with Lord Kollinar that more patrols are in

order, particularly around the barracks and the New Quarter where most of the Jorskians live," Didrik chimed in, covering for Devlin's lapse. "Though I know it will stretch your people thin, Chief Mychal."

Thin indeed. It would be hard for the peacekeepers to search for the sword, if they had to expend all of their manpower patrolling the city. "Do what you can Mychal, and I will give you gold to offer bonuses to those who take on extra duties. And if you think it will not stir up more trouble, the soldiers can join your folk patrolling the New Quarter, or take over the patrol entirely," Devlin said.

"I will consider your offer," Mychal said. It was as much as Devlin had hoped for. The lines of responsibility between the peacekeepers and the Royal Army had blurred over the past days since Devlin's arrival, and Chief Mychal was naturally wary of anything that would further erode his authority.

"And as for the tavern owner, the Chosen One will pay for his losses," Devlin said.

He did not believe the fire was an accident. Even if his fears were groundless, and he had not been near the tavern last night, there was still truth in Haakon's words. It was Devlin's presence in the city that had stirred the population to unrest. And he knew the violence would not stop with a simple tavern fire. There would be more violence and more killings. If he did not find the Sword of Light soon, he might well destroy Duncaer in his quest to save Jorsk.

Nineteen

STEPHEN FELT HELPLESS. HE MIGHT AS WELL HAVE stayed in Kingsholm. Devlin had no more use for a minstrel than he did for a trained bear. Anyone else would have been a better choice than he. Captain Drakken. Major Mikkelson. Even the rawest Guard recruit would have been of more help than Stephen could possibly be.

Stephen could fight by Devlin's side, but he was not trained as a Guard. He did not know how to search a city for contraband or how to find traitors and thieves. In Kingsholm there would have been no limit to the amount of useful gossip a minstrel could pick up, but here in Duncaer his brown hair marked him as an outsider, and no one would confide in him.

The only thing he had to offer Devlin was his friendship, but even this was not welcome. Devlin had made it clear that he did not want or need his companionship. Since Ensign Annasdatter's murder, Devlin had gone out of his way to avoid both Stephen and Didrik, eating solitary meals in his room and seeing them only when duty required. It was as if a stranger had taken his place.

Not that Didrik was much better. Indeed, the lieutenant was in his element, trotting back and forth between the peacekeepers' compound and army garrison as he monitored the status of the search and relayed Devlin's orders. The city might be foreign to him, but the task of searching for criminals was one Didrik knew well, and he threw himself into it wholeheartedly. He had no time to spare for Stephen. And if he shared Stephen's concerns over Devlin's growing strangeness, he refused to speak of it.

At least Didrik had the comfort of duty and a task that required all of his energy. Stephen had no such distraction, so instead his mind was filled with dire imaginings. He tallied every incident over and over again. The times when he had observed Devlin talking to an empty room. The reveries that Devlin would fall into, unaware of his surroundings or companions. Devlin's increasingly common flashes of anger. Not to mention the thrown knife that had nearly taken Didrik's life.

Taken alone, any one of these incidents was explainable. Understandable even. Taken together they indicated that something was gravely wrong. Even Didrik had admitted as much, though now he seemed to have forgotten his earlier fears. But what could Stephen do? If this was the power of the Geas, then the only thing that would help would be to find the sword. Once Devlin had completed his task, the demands of the Geas would ease.

Which brought Stephen back to the source of his frustration. It was imperative that they find the sword, but there seemed nothing Stephen could do to help.

"Flames," Stephen cursed. He would drive himself mad if he stayed here, dwelling on everything that could go wrong and had.

He left the study Devlin had taken as his office and returned to his room, where he selected the native cloak of faded blue wool that he had borrowed from one of the governor's servants. With the hood up, he would not be immediately recognized as an outsider. Prudence dictated that he arm himself, but carrying a long sword would declare his origins as surely as if he wore the tabard of a royal messenger. Instead he compromised by thrusting a dagger through his belt.

Misty rain was falling as he left the governor's mansion. He turned right, down the hill and toward the center of the city. A few minutes of walking took him out of the New Quarter, with its population of transplanted Jorskians, and he became just another of the faceless mass, intent upon their errands.

He was lost, of course, but it did not bother him. Kollinar had offered one of his servants as a guide, but Stephen had refused. He could hardly play the part of traveling minstrel if he had one of the governor's servants dogging his footsteps. And though the city was crowded with narrow twisting streets that met at bizarre angles, he had but to glance up to see the garrison that dominated the city from its lofty perch on the highest of the many hills that made up Alvaren. He could always find his way to the garrison, and from there he could find his way back to the governor's mansion.

After a time he reached the central market, which was curved like a crescent moon, wide in the middle and tapering to the width of a single stall at either end.

Here the folk of the city went about their business as if the weather were fine, despite the steady light rain. In Jorsk such open-air markets were a thing of the summer months, but here the elaborately crafted wood stalls showed signs of permanence, with waxed linen canopies protecting the goods from the ever-present rain.

Stephen wandered idly among the stalls. There were woven goods, of course, from yarn to bolts of finely dyed wool to garments that the seller swore had had only one previous owner. Household goods were for sale as well, pots and utensils made out of copper or brass. There were even trinkets to be found, and while he passed over the cheap jewelry he could not resist buying a bone flute that had a surprisingly sweet tone, yet was small enough to fit in his pack.

He noticed that a few stalls sold common food stuffs, tubers and the like. But there were no spices, and no meat of any kind.

The streets surrounding the crescent were filled with small shops, whose stone walls protected the more expensive goods. Conspicuously absent were the Jorskian traders, who had their own enclave in the New Quarter. Unlike other cities where like congregated with like, here the merchants were segregated by their country of origin. A wine merchant might be flanked by a tailor on one side and an herbalist on the other.

It was an unusual arrangement. But nothing about this city seemed normal to him. Even the landscape was oppressive. Accustomed to the flat plains around Kingsholm and the forests of his own father's barony, Stephen was uncomfortably aware of the surrounding mountains that loomed over the city, hemming them in. It gave him the feeling of being trapped, a feeling reinforced by the twisting streets that made the city seem a stone maze. Even the very buildings, with their dull stone and lack of ornamentation seemed unfriendly, rejecting his very presence.

Never before had he felt so unwelcome. Though Kilbaran had more than its share of Jorskian inhabitants, the residents of the border trading town managed to live side by side in peace. But here in Alvaren the air was thick with tension. It was as if it were a city under siege, an impression reinforced by the omnipresent patrols. Soldiers strutted by in their red-trimmed tunics, never in groups of less than four, and always with their hands firmly on their sword hilts. When they approached the crowds gave way, then muttered after they had passed.

He wondered if the city was always like this, the residents grown accustomed to the threat of unrest that simmered below the surface. Or was he seeing the city at its worst, its normal rhythms disturbed by the presence of the Chosen One and the search for the missing sword?

A display of woolen goods caught his eye, and he spent some time lingering over a basket of knitted socks. When he picked one up, he was surprised by its weight, for the sock was several times thicker than he was accustomed to.

The young woman standing behind the stall offered him a practiced smile. "Keep your feet warm even when soaking wet," she said.

"Truly?"

"You won't find none better, not if you searched the whole of the market thrice over. A man who had a pair of these could stand all day in a stream and not feel the chill," she said.

He doubted that very much. Still, they were substantial and would be better than the army issue that Didrik had requisitioned to replace those items worn out during their journey.

"How much?" he asked.

Her eyes swept over him carefully, assessing the worn state of his cloak and boots against the features that marked him as one of their foreign overlords.

"For you? Two coppers. New style."

He had already learned that new style meant coins from Jorsk rather than the smaller native coins that dated from the time of the last Duncaer Queen. The price was less than he would have paid in Kingsholm, but he suspected that if he had been one of her folk he would have been offered an even better bargain.

"I will give you five coppers, in return for three pairs."

"Done," she said, so swiftly that he knew he had paid too much. Still it was well within his means. He handed over the coins and selected three pairs of unbleached wool, which he rolled up and stuffed inside his belt pouch. If he were to make any more purchases, he would need to buy something to carry them in.

As he turned to leave, he found his way blocked by a small knot of people who were deep in earnest conversation.

"I swear it is true. My wife has farkin in Tirlaght. Or rather she had, for we learned just this morning that nigh unto all of them are dead," declared the man whose back was to Stephen.

"Mother Teá defend us," a woman prayed. "How

many does this make? Seven villages taken by the madness?"

Stephen edged closer, straining his ears to listen. Could they be talking about the grain sickness?

"More like thrice seven," another woman responded. "And not in just one region either. It started in the north, then the south lands, but now it is has spread to the west."

Could this be true? Even now Stephen's nightmares were haunted by images of the ruined hamlet and those who had perished there. Were the same acts of mindless violence being played out across the province of Duncaer? Governor Kollinar had mentioned that there had been other cases of the grain madness, but Stephen had thought the situation well in control, the blighted grain replaced by new stores. Surely rumor lied. It was not possible that the plague had been allowed to spread unchecked to dozens of villages.

"It is not right. It is not natural," the man declared.

Another man said something Stephen could not make out, but which caused those gathered to nod their heads vigorously in agreement.

"They will kill us all if we let them," the man closest to Stephen said, his voice dark with hate.

Another voice demurred.

"And what will you feed your children this night? Or tomorrow and the day after?" the strident man asked.

His listeners shrugged or shook their heads.

"Be sheep if you must," the man said, turning his head and spitting on the ground to express his contempt. "But I will not wait tamely for my death."

With that the man strode off, and the knot of people drifted apart. Stephen waited a moment, then followed the strident man as he made his way through the market. Twice more the man stopped to talk with folks he apparently knew, but neither time could Stephen get close enough to listen. The sound of shouted insults caught his ear, and the minstrel turned his head as an army patrol came into view. When he looked back, the man had vanished.

He hurried over to the spot where he had last seen the man, but though he looked in all directions, he could not see a trace of his quarry. Indeed he would be hard pressed to identify the man's features, having had a better view of his back than his face. At the time he had been too worried that the man would recognize Stephen as a foreigner, but now his precautions were for naught. He could not even give a description of the man to the peacekeepers. A man of average height, stocky build, with a deep baritone voice, wearing a faded blue cloak that had been patched many times over. There must be a dozen men in this market right now who fit that description.

It was no consolation that he had no real grounds for suspecting the man of being anything other than an angry citizen, enraged by the death of his wife's kin. The man's words had been intemperate but not treasonous. And Stephen could hardly blame him for his distrust of those who had supplied the tainted grain.

And yet there was a part of him that felt a failure. Didrik would not have allowed himself to become distracted. Didrik would never have lost the man in the crowd. He would have followed him, and watched until it could be certain whether or not the man was a member of the Children of Ynnis.

The taunts grew louder as the army patrol drew near

where Stephen stood. Even as he watched, the lead sergeant flinched, and the steady cadence of their boot steps faltered. Almost before Stephen could react, a second stone flew through the air and hit a soldier in the cheek, drawing blood.

The patrol halted, the two in the rear pivoting swiftly so they stood back to back with their comrades, facing the crowd.

"Killers," a voice called.

"Murderous lackeys," said another.

The soldiers drew their swords.

The crowd shifted, as some sought to leave the area, while still others pressed closer, calling insults. There was no way to determine who had thrown the stone, or indeed if more than one person had been involved. But the soldiers did not hesitate. As a youth was pushed within arm's reach by the crowd behind him, the nearest soldier struck him down with the flat of his blade.

Stephen was stunned by the casual cruelty of the act. He watched frozen in horror as the youth fell to the ground. There was no way to determine if he was dead or merely insensible.

More objects were hurled at the soldiers, as those taunting them stayed just out of arm's reach. He heard shrill whistles over their cries and those around Stephen began to melt away.

A woman standing next to him tugged at his cloak. "Fly, you fool, unless you want the peacekeepers to haul you off for questioning."

Apparently she had mistaken him for a fellow countryman. With one last muttered curse at those who could not mind their own affairs, she took her own advice, climbing over a display of woven mats as she made her escape.

Stephen told himself he had nothing to fear. He had done nothing wrong. He was an innocent here, one whose character would be vouched for by the governor himself, if it came to such. But such reassurances rang hollow as he saw that there were now several bodies lying on the ground around the soldiers. A running man carrying a child in his arms barreled into him, nearly knocking Stephen off his feet, before taking off again. The whistles grew closer, and from close by he heard a scream that was suddenly cut off. Stephen took one last look, then he turned and ran.

Twenty

THE SEARCH FOR THE REBELS HAD TAKEN ON NEW
urgency with Annasdatter's death, but as their first
week in Alvaren came to an end, they were still no
closer to finding the sword than they had been on the
day they entered the city.

Questioning the members of the Metalsmiths' Guild
had yielded no useful information. They had uncovered several minor infractions of the law, along with evidence that Amalia had been diverting money from the
guild treasury to pay off her creditors after she had lost
money investing in a trading scheme. But there was
nothing that could be used to link any member of the
guild to either the Children of Ynnis or the theft of the
sword.

On his own initiative, Lord Kollinar offered a reward
for information about the Children of Ynnis and the
murder of Ensign Annasdatter. When there was no response, he doubled it—without any effect.

Devlin had half expected the Children of Ynnis to
use the sword as bait to convince him to meet with

them. Yet there were no further messages. It was as if they had disappeared into the mist.

That was not to say the city was quiet. On the contrary, each day there were more reports of disturbances. Stephen had nearly found himself caught up in a street riot, provoked by news of the latest outbreak of grain madness. Stephen had made good his escape, but two soldiers and nearly a dozen Caerfolk had not been as lucky. Fortunately, their injuries were no more serious than cuts and broken bones, but he knew it was only a matter of time before the violence escalated into more deaths.

And there was nothing he could do to calm the city. Indeed, every action he took seemed to make matters worse. Faced with his impotence, Devlin's temper grew shorter each day. The governor's servants steered a wide berth around him, and the soldiers of the garrison grew pale whenever they caught sight of him. Yet no one, not even his friends, called him to task. Even his most outrageous outbursts brought him only blank faces or looks of sympathy.

He knew their forbearance was a measure of how deeply concerned they were about him—concerned that the fruitless search was wearing him down and that the Geas was weighing on his mind. He could see it, in the way Stephen and Didrik exchanged worried glances when they thought he was unaware, or how they would fall silent when he entered a room.

Haakon did not appear to him again, but he continued to taunt Devlin, feeding upon Devlin's own self-doubts and fears. Even his dreams were no longer a haven, and Devlin felt himself beginning to slip deeper and deeper into madness.

More than once, he had found himself somewhere with no recollection on how he had gotten there, or why. And once he had found himself in the middle of a conversation with Didrik, with no idea what they were discussing, or even how long Didrik had been in the room. He had covered his lapse as best he could, but he knew that Didrik had not been fooled.

He wondered what it was like for his friends, sworn followers of a man they suspected was going mad? He could offer no reassurances. Even he did not know what would happen if the search continued to drag on.

Would the Geas release him? Would he be allowed to return to Kingsholm empty-handed? Already he felt pulled in two directions. One part of him needed to find the sword, no matter how long it took. The other part of him reckoned troop strengths and fortifications, worried about how swiftly the spring thaws would come, and whether the coastal regions had enough trained armsmen to repel an invasion force. Could Solveig and Lord Rikard keep the conservative council members in check? If he were delayed in his return, would Olvarrson lead the army into the field? Or would he do what Devlin most feared, abandoning the borderlands and retreating to the secure fortifications?

It was his duty to be in Jorsk. To do whatever it took to ensure that the Kingdom was prepared to meet her enemies.

But he knew it was also his duty to recover the sword, the symbol of his office. The one talisman that no one could deny. With the sword in hand, he could force the councilors to accept his authority and forever silence the nay-sayers who questioned his worthiness.

And if he returned now, having tried to find the sword and failed, it would all be for nothing. His enemies would seize on his failure as evidence that the Gods had not truly chosen Devlin as their champion. He would be stripped of his titles, and with them would vanish any hope of leading Jorsk in her own defense.

In the end it all came back to the blasted sword. He had to find it. For the sake of the Kingdom and for the sake of what was left of his soul.

Throwing off his dark musings, he left his private chamber and sought out the receiving room, which had been turned into the headquarters of the operation. Someone could usually be found there at any hour of the day and night. As he approached he heard the sound of voices, and he entered to find Didrik, Stephen, and Kollinar all gathered around the desk, on which they had unrolled a map of the city.

"It is an old neighborhood, but respectable," Kollinar was saying. His back was to Devlin, so he did not see him approach. "Neither rich nor poor. Unremarkable, really, which I suppose makes it a perfect place for him to hide in plain sight."

"For whom to hide?" Devlin asked.

Kollinar abruptly straightened and turned to face him. "We may have a lead," he said.

"Tell me."

"An informant told one of my soldier that the leader of the rebels is a man calling himself Peredur Trucha, who lives on Green Alley off the Old One's Way."

"And can this informant be trusted?"

"The informant ran off as the soldier tried to take her into custody. He gave chase, but lost her in the crowded marketplace. On its own it is hardly convincing evidence—"

"But I also heard the name Peredur Trucha," Stephen said. "I was at a tavern tonight, near the traders' quarter, when I overheard three apprentices praising Peredur's cunning and how he had humiliated the great champion of Jorsk."

"I am surprised they spoke so freely," Devlin said. Despite his misgivings, he had allowed Stephen to continue to seek out information in the taverns, more as a means to keep Stephen out from underfoot than from any real expectation that he would overhear anything useful. "Did they know you were there?"

Stephen shrugged. "I do not think so. The tavern was crowded and dimly lit. And it was just a brief snatch of conversation. They left as soon as they finished their drinks. I was going to try and follow them to find out where they lived, but all three split up as soon as they left. Rather than choose which to follow, I came here to report instead."

"Wisely done." Stephen had courage in plenty, but lacked the training and instincts of a professional. If those apprentices had been members of the Children of Ynnis, Stephen could easily have found himself in a trap. And his friends would know nothing of his peril until they found his bloody corpse.

"We should not wait. Stephen may have been recognized or the informant may repent and try to warn this Peredur," Didrik said.

"Agreed." Devlin felt his spirits lift at the prospect of being able to take action, any action, after these long days of waiting. It would be too much to hope that this Peredur did indeed hold the sword in his possession, but he could lead them to those who did. "Have you sent a runner to Chief Mychal?"

Lord Kollinar cleared his throat. "I would advise against that, Chosen One."

"Why?"

"Because the last two homes we searched, the residents had already fled before we arrived. Someone is warning them. I have no reason to doubt the loyalty of my soldiers, but as for the peacekeepers . . ." Kollinar's voice trailed off in silence.

"Mychal is an honorable man," Devlin insisted.

"Can you swear the same for the peacekeepers? For all of them?" Kollinar insisted.

Devlin opened his mouth, then closed it as he realized he could not. There were nearly a hundred folk who wore the peacekeeper uniform or served those who did. Many of their faces were new in the years since he and Cerrie had left Kingsholm, and even those he had once known were strangers to him now. There could be rebels among them. Or it could even be as simple as one person speaking out of turn because they had kin-ties to one of those who had fallen under suspicion.

"We will try this your way," Devlin said. "Bring a handful of your best soldiers. And make sure they understand that there is to be no bloodshed. We need this Peredur alive so he can talk to us."

"Of course," Lord Kollinar said. "If we move swiftly, we can have him in the garrison before anyone realizes he has been taken. And then, Chosen One, you will get the answers you need."

Devlin hoped it would be that easy. It was time for their luck to turn.

Didrik cursed as he paced back and forth in the hallway outside Lord Kollinar's office. The door was closed, but he could hear the faint murmur of voices from within. No doubt Devlin was apologizing. Again.

It had gone wrong from the start. Peredur Trucha had proven to be a wizened old man, startled to be awoken from his sleep by armed soldiers in his bedroom. But he displayed admirable composure, requesting that he be allowed to dress himself. Even fully clothed he was a mere shadow of a man, his limbs so frail that it seemed he would crumble at the slightest touch. But there was nothing wrong with his brain or his tongue.

Rather than being intimidated, he had scolded Didrik as if he were a foolish child. He insisted that his record scrolls be brought as evidence, and gave a list of seven people who could attest to his good character.

Chief Mychal's name topped the list. It could have been a bluff, but in his gut Didrik had known that a mistake had been made. Still, they had to see this through, and a litter was summoned to take Peredur to the garrison, the old man being too frail to risk on the icy cobblestones.

When Peredur was brought before Devlin, the Chosen One's eyes had widened in disbelief. Didrik and Lord Kollinar bore witness as Devlin patiently questioned the old man. To no one's surprise, the man denied all knowledge of the Children of Ynnis. Peredur Trucha, it seemed, was what the Caerfolk called a lawgiver. A judge, in other words. A highly respected one at that.

When he arrived, Chief Mychal had confirmed his

story. As did the other witnesses summoned. The record scrolls held no devious plots but rather years of Peredur's judgments, including several examples where he had ordered stern punishments for those who disturbed the peace by inciting revolt or attacking Jorskian traders.

They had been played for fools. The so-called informant. The drunken apprentices. All part of a plot to make the Chosen One look foolish and to rouse further the anger of the people against their Jorskian rulers.

Didrik's professional soul was outraged. This was no way to run an investigation. If they had stopped to consult with Chief Mychal they could have avoided the embarrassment. But their enemies had cleverly capitalized on the tension that existed between the soldiers and the peacekeepers.

Now they were no better off than they had been a week ago. Worse, in falsely arresting Peredur, they had further offended the city's residents, putting an end to any hope of voluntary cooperation. Gloom sank over him as he realized that they might never find the sword.

Devlin had tried to warn them that it would be difficult, that methods that worked in Jorsk would not work here, where the web of family ties meant that not even the most wretched of the poor would consider turning informant. Here, it seemed, everyone was related to everyone else. Already three of the governor's servants had resigned their posts in protest because they were somehow related to members of the Metalsmiths' Guild.

The execution of three hostages in retaliation for Ensign Annasdatter's death had been necessary, but it had only served to increase the people's anger and make them even less willing to cooperate.

All this in a city that was impossibly crowded, with a maze of twisting, narrow streets that made it difficult to patrol, let alone try to follow a suspect or carry out any kind of organized search. Especially if you were a foreigner.

The peacekeepers had their own ways of dealing with lawbreakers and their own network of family and acquaintances that helped them discover evildoers. From what he'd heard, the system worked well enough for ordinary matters of justice. Certainly Alvaren was a well-ordered city, in spite of the overcrowding and number of impoverished residents. But in this instance, neither law-abiding citizen nor lawless denizen of the back alleys was prepared to betray one of his own to their Jorskian overlords.

"This is my fault," Stephen said in a low voice.

Didrik looked up, surprised at Stephen's presence. Devlin was keeping the minstrel at arm's length these days. He allowed Stephen's voice in their private councils, but had not permitted him to witness any of the interrogations, nor to accompany the soldiers on their searches. He wondered where Stephen had spent these last hours, and how long he had been cooling his heels waiting for news.

"I should have known it was too good to be true. Why should I be the one to find what everyone else had missed? But I didn't stop to think."

"The same could have happened to any of us," Didrik said. Though that was not strictly true. Stephen had been the only one of them to go off on his own, hoping to pick up gossip. No doubt he had been spotted once too often, and the rebels had decided to make use of him. "Kollinar's soldier was duped as well. If you had not been in the tavern, they would have found another way to pass this rumor on to us. We knew the information might prove false, but still we could not ignore it."

They should have consulted with Commander Mychal. But it was always easier to make correct judgments after the fact. Knowing what he knew then, excluding the peacekeepers had been an act of prudence. "We know better now. We will not make the same mistake the next time."

"If there is a next time. How much longer do you think Devlin can endure? Each day that passes saps the strength from him."

There was truth in Stephen's words, but it was a truth Didrik did not want to hear. "Devlin will endure as he must. As will we."

"We have to find the sword. We must," Stephen muttered.

"And we will," Didrik said. "We will find the sword and be back in Kingsholm in time for the first council of spring."

This he had to believe. He would not let himself be defeated by doubts. Devlin had triumphed over far greater challenges. With or without the sword he was still the Chosen One, the man picked by the Gods to defend Jorsk in this time of crisis. He would prevail. He had to.

Didrik folded his arms and leaned his back against the corridor wall, a sloppy pose that would have earned him a tongue lashing from Captain Drakken had she seen him. But he could not bring himself to care. He was not on guard duty, and as the morning wore on his body reminded him that it had been a full day and night since he had last slept. After a moment's consideration, Stephen mirrored his stance, leaning on the opposite wall of the corridor.

Didrik let his mind drift. Some time later, the door to Lord Kollinar's office opened, and he straightened abruptly as Peredur Trucha emerged, leaning on the arm of his escort. Two soldiers followed, carrying the chests of documents. He watched as the procession disappeared down the corridor, toward the main door.

There was no sign of Devlin, so after a moment he walked over to the still-open door and looked inside. Lord Kollinar sat at his desk, scribbling on parchment. Devlin stood at the window, staring out at the city revealed below.

Didrik cleared his throat. Kollinar looked up, but Devlin remained oblivious.

"Chosen One?" There was no response. He wondered if Devlin had fallen into another one of his strange fits. "Devlin?" He called in a louder voice.

Lord Kollinar's eyebrows went up at the familiarity of the address, but Devlin's head turned.

Didrik was shocked by what the daylight revealed. Devlin appeared to have aged years in mere hours, and his eyes were sunken into his face.

"What are your orders?" Didrik asked.

"We have caused enough harm for one day," Devlin said. "Chief Mychal is furious at our blunder, but he has agreed to meet with us this evening to discuss our next course of action."

"Why not now?" If he truly wished to help them, why make Devlin wait for his advice? Was this simply

Mychal's way of showing his displeasure for not having been consulted earlier?

"Because he must first undo the damage we have done," Devlin said, a bitter twist to his expression. "He fears restlessness in the poorer quarters and has gone to organize extra patrols."

"Does he think there will be trouble?" Reason said that the Caerfolk should understand that a mistake had been made, but that Peredur had been treated with all courtesy and released unharmed. But reason and the Caerfolk seemed to have little to do with one another, and who knew what might provoke these strange people to riot?

"A precaution, no more," Devlin said. "This time, at least, I thought it best to heed his advice."

Didrik felt the sting of the rebuke, though he knew Devlin held no one but himself to blame.

Lord Kollinar chose to remain behind, saying that he wished to comb through the reports from his troops one more time in the hope of uncovering something they had missed.

A small crowd had gathered outside the garrison, and they jeered as Devlin came through the gate, followed by Didrik and Stephen. His eyes swept the crowd, looking for any threat, but there were no signs of weapons, and the people seemed content merely to hurl insults instead of objects. *Fearnym* was among their favorites. He had learned from Stephen that it meant traitor.

Two soldiers led the way, and four followed behind, keeping Devlin in a protective square. Didrik kept his own hand on his sword and wished that he had thought to warn Stephen to bring a weapon. The minstrel had worn a sword during their journey, but once they reached Alvaren he had set it aside, to play the part of innocent traveler. But his guise had already been penetrated, and now that he had been seen with Devlin, he could no longer hope for the safety of anonymity. Didrik would have to warn Stephen that he could no longer wander the streets of Alvaren unarmed.

They turned a corner and began the steep climb that led to the governor's residence. Like the garrison, it was situated on top of one of the many hills that made up the city. As the residence came into view, Didrik allowed himself a sigh of relief. Except for the crowd outside the garrison, the streets had been unusually quiet, and he was glad to see that his worries had proven unfounded.

The last stretch was the steepest, and he felt the familiar burn in his calves. Coming down the street toward them was a woman pushing a handcart, which was half-filled with winter roots packed in straw. No doubt she had just completed her delivery to the residence, and he felt a moment's sympathy for the labor required to push a heavy load up the steep hill. The cart rattled and bounced on the cobblestones, and it seemed all she could do to hold it in check.

She smiled at the soldiers, and wished them a cheerful good day. Then she caught sight of the Chosen One and stumbled. Trying to catch her balance, she leaned heavily on the cart handles, and the cart tipped on its side, spilling its burden into the street.

The soldiers in the lead scattered, trying to avoid the rolling roots. Devlin picked his way among them and went over to her.

"What have I done?" she exclaimed. Her eyes swept

over the street, watching as some of the roots wobbled to a halt in the gutter while the rest continued to bounce and roll down the street.

Behind him, he heard one of their escort laugh at the woman's predicament.

The vegetable woman tucked her arms under her cloak as if she were cold.

"An accident," Devlin said. He stepped in front of her and reached down, putting his hands on the sides of the cart, preparing to lift it upright.

Didrik glanced around, but all seemed calm. Stephen was gathering some of the fallen vegetables, collecting them into his cloak. The sole female soldier was helping him, while her counterparts watched as if they were at a play.

As he turned back to face Devlin, he caught a glimpse of silver in the woman's hand. Time seemed to freeze in that instant.

"Devlin! Knife," he shouted, even as he leapt forward.

Devlin began to turn, slowly, as if there were all the time in the world. The woman's dagger slashed at his side, tangling in his cloak. As Devlin turned to face her, she drew her arm back for another blow.

From the corner of his eyes Didrik saw a soldier drawing his sword, but the man was too far away to reach the woman before she struck again. As he rushed toward them, he waited for Devlin to draw his own weapon, or for the flick of a wrist that would place a throwing knife in his hand. But to his horror, Devlin made no move to arm himself. He did not even try to evade the woman's blade. Instead he stood there, his arms hanging at his sides, his face strangely peaceful as he waited for the killing blow.

Didrik launched himself into the air, crashing into the woman's left side and knocking her to the ground. There was a sharp crack and she screamed as her right arm took the brunt of their fall. The dagger tumbled from her grasp and lay on the street, the once silver blade now covered in bright blood.

He feared he had been too late.

"General! Are you injured?" the Ensign called.

Didrik looked up, and saw that Devlin was still standing. He appeared oblivious to the blood running down his left arm. His eyes still held that blank gaze, as if he saw something the others did not. He waited for Devlin to take charge of the situation, but the Chosen One was either trapped in some private hell or his injuries were worse than first appeared. Either possibility was enough to make his blood run cold.

"You. Come here," Didrik caught the eye of the nearest soldier. "Take charge of this prisoner."

Didrik rose to his feet, then the soldier helped the attacker up. Her face was sullen and her eyes dark with hate as she spat in Devlin's direction.

"Show some respect," the soldier said, cuffing her head with the back of his sword. The woman reeled.

"Enough," Didrik said. "We need her alive to be questioned. Take her inside and confine her to the servants' quarters. Keep watch on her so she does not injure herself. We will send the healer to tend her after he has seen to the Chosen One."

"Yes, sir." The ensign saluted, seemingly grateful that someone had taken charge.

Didrik was angry as he realized that he did not even

know the ensign's name. And yet he had entrusted Devlin's life to these soldiers without bothering to learn either their names or their skills. In Kingsholm this never would have happened. Those who guarded Devlin had been personally hand-picked by either himself or Captain Drakken. But he had grown careless, and Devlin had nearly paid the ultimate price.

Shame swept over him as he watched Stephen fold his cloak and press it against Devlin's side. "Devlin, you need to leave the street. It is only a scratch, but you need to get this bound up. And we do not know if the woman was acting alone." Stephen's voice was soft and reassuring, though his hand shook slightly as he looked down at the bloody wound.

Devlin shook his head, then seemed to come to himself. His eyes lost their glazed stare as he took in the scene with the fallen cart, the bloody dagger, and the prisoner whose eyes spit hate.

"Of course," he said. Then he allowed Stephen to guide him up the street. Two of the soldiers held the prisoner between them, while the remaining four formed a wall of living flesh around Devlin, as they should have done from the start. Didrik followed, with drawn sword in hand. He would not fail Devlin a second time.

Twenty-one

DEVLIN'S WOUNDS PROVED LESS SERIOUS THAN
Didrik had feared. There was a long shallow slash on
his left arm, which had bled messily but caused no lasting damage. And a stab wound on his left side, which
looked nasty, but—the healer assured him—the dagger
had merely glanced off a rib rather than penetrating a
vital organ—well within the skill of the novice healer
who was assigned to Lord Kollinar's household. It took
only a few minutes for the healer to clean Devlin's
wounds and stitch them closed. And then he was sent to
tend their prisoner.

They had been lucky. Very lucky. Not even a healer of
the first rank could save a man who had been knifed
through the heart. And the woman had had two
chances to strike at Devlin unopposed. Her first thrust
had gone wide, but if her second blow had been just a
finger's-breadth higher . . .

It did not bear thinking about. And yet he must.

Didrik waited until the healer had left, then dismissed the chamberman and shut the door behind
him.

Devlin lay in his bed, propped up by pillows in a half-reclining position. He appeared diminished, dwarfed by the enormous bed, his habitual energy replaced by a terrifying stillness. His eyes were dull, and his normally ruddy complexion was now nearly a match for the bleached-linen sheets. It was as if his life force had drained out of him, and Didrik fought the urge to send for the healer to return.

"What happened?" Didrik asked.

"I was taken by surprise," Devlin replied. He closed his eyes and leaned back against the pillows as if preparing to rest.

But Didrik was not about to be brushed off. For too long he had followed orders and let Devlin go his own way. Now he was going to demand answers. "What happened out there? Why didn't you defend yourself?"

Devlin sighed and opened his eyes. "I was helping her, not expecting an attack. And what need have I to worry when I had my own personal guard?"

A guard that had failed him. The soldiers had been negligent, but it was on Didrik's shoulders that the true blame fell. He was the one who had sworn to defend Devlin with his life. The woman should never have gotten close enough to strike even a single blow.

If Captain Drakken ever heard of this debacle, he would be stripped of his rank in a heartbeat.

"It was my fault—" Didrik began.

"No," Stephen said firmly.

Both men turned to face Stephen. "There is blame enough to go around. And shame on my head, for walking at your side without a blade of my own. But we will not let you turn the talk to our failings in order to distract us."

So Stephen had seen what Didrik had not. Devlin had been trying to focus Didrik's thoughts on his own failures and away from Devlin's own inexplicable behavior. A tactic that had nearly worked.

"You heard my warning, but made no attempt to draw your sword. Nor even one of your knives," Didrik pointed out.

That worried him most of all. True the woman had been so close that there might not have been time for Devlin to draw his sword and use it effectively—especially since his back had been to the fallen cart, blocking off any chance of a tactical retreat. At the time, he had thought Devlin might not have had his knives with him, but when Devlin's shirt had been removed, they had seen that he wore the familiar throwing knives strapped to his forearms. On his left arm, the harness was bloody and two of the straps had been sliced through by his attacker's blade. But there was no reason why he could not have used the other one. Even with his crippled hand, Devlin could still release the blade and let it fly with a speed that most envied, as Didrik knew all too well. And though the knife blade was not as long as a dagger, it would have been better than no blade at all.

"You did not even try to defend yourself," he repeated.

Devlin turned his head so that he did not have to meet his friends' eyes, but he said nothing.

Didrik clenched his fists as he felt the frustration rise within him. He fought the urge to try and shake some sense into this stubborn man.

"You were going to stand there and let her kill you.

Do you want to die that badly?" Stephen's voice trembled with anger. Or fear.

"When did it ever matter what I wanted?" Devlin asked softly.

Didrik opened his mouth but Stephen silenced him with a gesture and they waited for Devlin to elaborate.

Devlin's voice was soft, almost as if he were speaking to himself. "I heard the Dread Lord calling my name. There was no sense in fighting his summons. You cannot outrun your fate." He ran the fingers of his maimed hand along the bandage that covered the wound on his chest. "I do not understand why Haakon changed his mind. He must be furious that his servant failed at her task, but I have no doubt that he will send another."

Didrik shivered. What did one say to a man who thought the Death God had summoned him? If it were any other man, he would curse him as a superstitious fool. But this was the Chosen One, who had been God-touched when he was called to their service. Anything was possible.

"When did Haakon speak to you?" Stephen asked.

"He has been whispering to me for weeks now."

"Since Remembrance Day," Stephen said.

"I saw him then. He came to me, taunted me, saying that soon I would be his. I thought to fight him, but now I realize such resistance is futile."

"I do not believe this," Didrik said.

"Nor do I," Stephen added.

Devlin opened his eyes wide and leaned on one elbow, pushing himself upright. "You believe in the Gods when it suits your purposes," he said, with a flash of anger. "You tell me that the Gods called me to serve as Chosen One. That the son of the Forge God crafted this cursed sword that I now seek. That Kanjti, the God of luck, has blessed my service. But now that Haakon calls my name, now you no longer believe in the Gods?"

Devlin's right arm began to shake with the strain of supporting his body.

"It is not that, but—" Stephen began.

"But nothing," Devlin said, collapsing back on the pillows. The energy that had briefly animated him was gone. "Believe me mad instead, if that comforts you. Just go, and leave me in peace."

Even as they watched, Devlin's eyes closed, and his breathing grew shallow as sleep finally claimed him.

Stephen's eyes met his, and Didrik wondered if his own shock was as easy to read.

"If Haakon is truly calling Devlin's name—"

"No," Didrik said. It was not true. Devlin's tired mind had played tricks on him. Or if not a trick, it was merely another challenge for them to face. A test of their courage, or of their commitment to serve the Chosen One.

"We will talk of this later," he said. "For now, I want to find out what our prisoner knows. Maybe if we find out who is behind the attack, we can prove to Devlin that he was wrong."

And if Devlin was right—

No. Not even in his own mind would he complete that sentence. For no man could stand against one of the Gods.

The prisoner's arm was splinted by the healer, then she was interrogated, first by Didrik, then by two army officers, and finally by Chief Mychal himself. Hours of questioning yielded little of value. She refused to name her accomplices, or indeed to answer any of their questions. Instead the prisoner kept repeating that though she was a member of the Children of Ynnis, she had acted alone in attacking Devlin, feeling it her duty to strike down one who had betrayed her people. Her one regret was that she had not managed to kill him.

Didrik had attempted to reason with her, pointing out that though the attack on the Chosen One was treason and punishable by death, the sentence could be commuted by the Chosen One if she were to cooperate. The woman had laughed in his face, claiming that she looked forward to her martyrdom.

When questioned about Ensign Annasdatter's death, she had denied any knowledge, though she expressed admiration for whoever had committed the crime. There was no reasoning with such blind fanaticism. Didrik had turned over the interrogation to others, but they were no more successful than he had been. In the end, he gave orders that she was to be taken to the army garrison and locked in one of their cells, with only her thoughts to keep her company.

So far they had observed the letter of the law, but as the woman's defiance continued, Didrik found himself wondering if she would be quite so brave when faced with the possibility of torture. There was a dark part of him that very much wanted to see her bleed, and to punish her for everything that had gone wrong since they entered this cursed land.

As the day grew to a close, he returned to Devlin's chambers to report their lack of success. Devlin acknowledged the report with a grunt. He did not ask to see the prisoner himself, nor did he give any orders for her treatment. And though his wounds were not life-threatening, Devlin claimed he was too weary to attend the council that he himself had called for that night.

Didrik reported this fact to the others, who took the excuse at face value. But then, neither Lord Kollinar nor Chief Mychal truly knew Devlin. The Devlin he knew would never have shirked his duties in this way. This past summer, grievously wounded during his duel with Duke Gerhard, Devlin had remained on his feet through sheer force of will, demanding justice from the King. He had stood there as his lifeblood drained onto the sands, refusing to show any sign of weakness. Only after he was assured that the traitors would be punished did Devlin finally give in to his wounds and collapse.

It was hard to believe that the same man now let a mere scratch confine him to his bedchamber. That he showed no interest in either the search for the sword or in finding out who was behind the attack upon him.

Only he and Stephen knew the truth. Only they knew how out of character Devlin's behavior was. And only they had heard the hopelessness in Devlin's voice as he confessed that the Death God was calling his name.

And that was a secret Didrik was not willing to share with the others. He trusted them, but only to a point. Instead, as Devlin's aide, he listened to their reports on the search for the missing sword and those who had stolen it. Neither had yielded fruit so far, but their approaches seemed sound, and he could think of nothing else to suggest.

Though they did have one self-proclaimed rebel in their custody. To his surprise, it was Chief Mychal who suggested that a more strenuous form of interrogation might yield the answers they sought. Didrik demurred, saying that for now the Chosen One's orders stood. They could question the woman again in the morning, but she was not to be harmed.

They talked of the possibility of another attack, on Devlin or on those in his party, and he approved the increased security measures suggested by Chief Mychal.

It was long past sunset when they finally agreed that there was nothing more to discuss and nothing else to be done until the next day. As he rose to his feet, Didrik felt the bruises he had taken earlier make their presence known and put his hand over his mouth to smother a yawn. A glance showed that his three companions seemed equally weary.

Lord Kollinar rubbed the back of his neck with one hand. "You're probably right about the woman. Bruises, you know," he said.

"I beg your pardon?"

"Traitors are always executed publicly. It will stir up enough trouble if she appears hale. But if she were to be seen bruised or injured—"

Didrik nodded. This much he understood. "Trouble," Didrik agreed. He had seen a city caught up in a riot. Once. He had no wish to repeat the experience.

"Trouble for all of us," Chief Mychal said. "But nothing my peacekeepers can't handle, if we get fair warning."

It seemed Chief Mychal had no intention of letting them forget the mistake they had made by not informing him of their plans to arrest Peredur. So be it. Had Didrik been in his place, he would have done the same.

———

Stephen wondered at Didrik's composure. How could he sit there calmly discussing search grids and lists of witnesses to be questioned? Had he not heard Devlin's words? Didn't he realize the enormity of what they were faced with? Their enemy was not to be found in a house to house search, nor in the systematic examination of all those who had access to the storeroom in the Metalsmiths' Guild.

Then again Didrik had always been one for rules and regulations, for the discipline of service. He understood order and what it took to uphold the law. He was not a man capable of great imagination. No doubt it comforted him to pretend that Devlin was simply the commander to whom he owed his allegiance and whom he had sworn to protect with his life. Far easier to close his eyes and ignore what it meant that Devlin had been summoned by the Gods to their service, and that even now the Gods continued to touch his life and the lives of those around him.

Though Didrik might find comfort in routine tasks, Stephen had no such luxury. He would not will himself to blindness. Devlin was in trouble, and if none could see it except Stephen, then so be it. He had saved his friend once before when all seemed hopeless. He would do so again.

But he needed help, and so he sat patiently through their councils until Didrik called an end to the debate.

As Chief Mychal donned his cloak and prepared to leave, Stephen followed him into the hall.

"A moment of your time, if you would be so kind," Stephen said.

Chief Mychal looked at Stephen, then back into the

brightly lit receiving room, where Didrik and Lord Kollinar lingered, still talking over the day's events.

"Walk with me," Chief Mychal said.

Stephen led the way down the staircase, nodding as they passed two servants about their errands. When they reached the main corridor, rather than turning left toward the main door, he turned right and opened the door into a small room that held but two chairs and a fireplace. He supposed it was normally used to house unexpected visitors until the chief of the house could determine whether or not they were welcome. For the moment it was as private a place as he could find, away from curious eyes and ears.

Chief Mychal followed him in the room, but made no move to sit down. Now that the moment had come, Stephen's doubts began to assail him. Was he doing the right thing? How did he know if this man could truly be trusted? Perhaps it would be better to wait and discuss this with Didrik first. After all, he had no proof of his suspicions, only a dreadful gnawing fear that there was indeed something very wrong with Devlin.

"Now, then, boy, what is it that you had to say to me that you could not say in front of your countrymen?" Chief Mychal asked.

"I am no boy," Stephen snapped, angry at being dismissed so easily.

"Then prove it. Either talk with me or let me take my leave. It has been a long day, and I have no time to waste on fools."

Stephen was tempted simply to spin on his heel and walk out. Instead, he took a deep breath and held on to the shreds of his temper. *Devlin trusts this man,* he reminded himself.

"I need your help," he said.

"So I gathered," Mychal replied.

"Devlin is . . ." Stephen hesitated, wondering how to explain. "Devlin is not himself."

"He is not the man I knew four years ago. Were Cerrie to return, even she would not recognize what he has become." Mychal shook his head from side to side, as if in sorrow. "He has become hard. Bitter. A stranger to us."

"That is not what I meant." Though he knew there was truth in what the chief said. There were only glimpses now of the man that Devlin had once been, the gentle artist whom his friends mourned. The man Stephen knew had been shaped by tragedy, the softer parts of him burned away in white-hot grief and rage. He had finally found a reason to live, in his desire to save others, to protect them as he had not been able to protect his own family.

Though his new calling was not one that his people would understand. They would never understand why Devlin had chosen to serve their conquerors. And Devlin was too proud, too stubborn to explain himself.

"I saw Cerrie's spirit," Stephen said musingly. "On Midwinter's Eve she came to Devlin and warned him of danger."

Mychal smiled. "She was a little thing, but fierce. And her long black hair was her pride."

He wondered what kind of fool Mychal thought him. Did he think he had so little honor that he would lie about something the Caerfolk held sacred? "Her hair was indeed black, but short and curling. And she was taller even than Devlin himself."

Mychal drew in a deep breath, then slowly exhaled.

"Perhaps you did see her," he conceded. "But what does that have to do with me?"

"Cerrie warned Devlin of danger. An unexpected enemy."

"The Children of Ynnis."

"No. We already knew of them, from Commander Willemson in Kilbaran. And as for today, assassins have tried to kill Devlin before now, and never before have the Gods seen fit to warn him."

"So what do you think it is?"

His mouth was dry, and he swallowed. "I think there is more going on than meets the eye. I think there is something wrong with the Geas spell. I need to find a mage who can examine Devlin and tell me the truth."

Chief Mychal took two steps backward until he was as far from Stephen as the tiny room would allow. "A spell?"

Stephen nodded. "I think the Geas spell has gone wrong. Maybe the spell deteriorates over time. The legends do not say, but few of those bespelled have survived as long as Devlin. Maybe Master Dreng lacked the power to cast a lasting spell. Or it simply may be weakening because we are so far from Kingsholm. Or—"

Chief Mychal broke into his musings. "Are you saying Devlin is ensorceled? That his wits are not his own?" Mychal's cheeks were flushed with anger.

Stephen stopped in midsentence. It was such a relief to speak his fears aloud, he had forgotten how little the Caerfolk knew of what it meant to be Chosen One.

"When a candidate comes to be chosen, he swears an oath to the Gods, and a binding spell is placed upon him to ensure faithful service," Stephen explained. "We call it the Geas spell."

"And Devlin consented to this abomination?"

"Yes," Stephen said.

Chief Mychal turned his head away, and spat on the floor in a deliberate gesture of disrespect. "I will never understand him," he said.

"He does not need your understanding. He needs your help. I need to find a trustworthy mage, one who can tell me if the spell has gone awry."

"We have no mages as you call them," Mychal said. "No one of our people would put such a spell on another."

The cold words dashed Stephen's hopes. He had been so certain that a mage would be able to help Devlin. He had no idea what he should do now.

"But there is a woman I know," Chief Mychal said slowly, as if the words were being dragged out of him. "A wizard, named Ismenia. Her powers are far different than what you describe, but she is wise and may be able to help Devlin."

"And do you trust her?"

"With my life," Mychal said. "I knew her from before, you see. The gift came to her late, and even though she renounced her family as was proper, she continues to live here in Alvaren."

"Then I beg you, summon her swiftly," Stephen said.

"I will call on her tomorrow and see if she will come. But I make no promises," Mychal said.

"Just bring her here, and I will do the rest," Stephen said. One way or another, if there was the slightest possibility that this woman could help Devlin, he would make certain that she had that chance. No matter what Didrik, Kollinar, or even Devlin himself had to say.

Twenty-two

THE MORNING AFTER BEING ATTACKED, DEVLIN awoke to find that the mind-whispers that had plagued him had gone mercifully silent. It was a relief to have the peace of his own thoughts, though he knew better than to suppose that the Death God had forgotten about him.

He rose from his bed and examined his injuries dispassionately. The dressings would need to be changed, but neither showed any signs of wound sickness. He knew that some would call him lucky. If the woman's aim had been a bit better, or if she had been able to strike a third blow, she might well have killed him. As it was, his injuries were merely inconvenient.

Dressing himself was a slow affair, for his injured arm was stiff and the wound in his side made it difficult for him to bend or turn. But with effort, and more than a few muttered curses, he managed to don his uniform.

He made his way to the ground floor and asked a servant to bring his breakfast. Stephen joined him as he ate, reporting that Lord Kollinar had already left for the garrison, and that Didrik was with the peacekeepers, supervising the latest attempt to wring information from his attacker. Devlin made noncommittal noises at the appropriate moments, feigning interest.

Surprisingly, Stephen made no reference to Devlin's assertion that the Death God was stalking him. It was as if the conversation had never happened. He wondered at the reason for the minstrel's behavior. Was Stephen holding his tongue out of concern for Devlin's injuries, waiting until Devlin had regained his strength? Or was Stephen hoping that given time Devlin would come to his senses?

Whatever the reason, he was grateful for the reprieve. Even as the words had left his lips, he regretted his confession. It was hard enough for any man to accept that he was doomed and that the Death God had chosen him as a plaything. Even faced with this grim knowledge, Devlin still must strive to obey his sworn oath and to fulfill his duty. Balancing the two compulsions took all of his strength. He did not think he could bear to accept his friends' solicitude. Their help, while well-meaning, could shatter the fragile balance that he had managed to achieve.

Though not truly hungry, Devlin ate the food that had been brought, knowing he needed to rebuild his strength. Afterward, he went to Lord Kollinar's office, where the latest reports awaited his attention. Stephen accompanied him, a silent yet watchful presence. Devlin methodically made his way through the stack of scrolls. The peacekeepers and army seemed determined to outdo each other in the sheer number of reports that were written. But in the end, they all bore the same message. They could find no trace of the stolen sword or of those who had taken it. Nor was there even the slightest whisper as to who was responsible for the death of Ensign Annasdatter, or even if the two events were linked. The circle of the investigation spread wider and wider as the number of those questioned steadily climbed. But so far, they had nothing to show for their efforts except a steadily growing sentiment against the Jorskian occupiers and the traitor who had joined their ranks.

He might as well take up the inquiries himself, going from house to house, shop to shop, until he had questioned each of Alvaren's residents personally. He had exhausted all other possible courses of action.

Or had he? He reached for his mug of kava and took a hasty gulp. There was one avenue of inquiry he had not pursued.

He had agreed with the others when they suggested that the sword might have been stolen simply because it belonged to him. Yet his instincts told him otherwise. The thieves had covered their tracks far too carefully. They knew what the sword was and precisely how valuable it was. And there was only one person who could have given them that knowledge. Murchadh. The man who had taken his hand in the clasp of friendship and claimed him as kin only weeks before. Had that all been a lie? Had Murchadh's smiling face concealed a treacherous heart?

Or had Murchadh offered friendship in good faith, only to reconsider once Devlin had left Kilbaran? Had reason taken the place of emotion as others reminded him that Devlin was no longer truly of Duncaer? Had they convinced him to betray Devlin's quest or had he simply let the information slip? There was one way to find out. A messenger bird could be sent to Commander

Willemson, ordering that Murchadh be arrested and interrogated. Once they found out whom Murchadh had told of the sword, they could then trace that person's contacts and find his allies in Alvaren.

Simple logic demanded that he consider all possible suspects, no matter the ties of past friendship. A dozen times Devlin had been on the verge of scribing the letter that would order Murchadh's arrest and interrogation. Each time he had resisted, hoping against hope that there would be some other way to find the information he needed. But he had run out of both time and choices.

With sinking heart he picked up the pen and began to write. He had gotten no further than the formal salutation when the study door swung open and Commander Mychal entered, followed by a woman. Grateful for the interruption, Devlin set down his pen and rose to his feet, stepping out from behind the desk to meet his visitors.

"Devlin, son of Kameron and Talaith, husband of Cerrie who once wore the colors of the peacekeepers, this is Ismenia of Windgap, whom I have long called friend," Mychal said.

He wondered why Mychal felt the need for a formal introduction in the Caer style. Ismenia was an ordinary-looking woman, past her first youth, but there was not a strand of gray to be seen in the black hair that was braided and coiled around her head. She was dressed in a plain gray tunic and dark leggings, her only concession to vanity a silver torc worn around her neck.

"I am honored to meet one whom Mychal calls friend, and bid you welcome," Devlin said, inclining his head in a show of respect. "This is Stephen, son of Lord Brynjolf of Esker, a singer and lore teller."

Stephen bowed, but Ismenia ignored him, choosing instead to stare at Devlin. She squinted and tilted her head to one side as if he were a strange beast she had encountered at the menagerie. Then she abruptly straightened and turned so her attention was divided between Mychal and Devlin.

"I apologize for doubting you," she said to Mychal. "This is worse than you described. There is not one spell here, but at least three workings of magic."

"Who are you?" Devlin demanded.

"A student of the unseen realm," Ismenia replied.

A wizard, in other words. He did not know what surprised him more, that Mychal knew such a person or that he had thought to bring her here. What madness had possessed him to involve a wizard in Devlin's affairs?

"I have no need for such." There were too many already who knew of the Geas spell and the burden he bore. "Mychal, you and this woman must leave. Now."

Mychal looked over at Stephen, whose fair complexion darkened.

"No," Stephen said, moving to stand between Devlin and their visitors. "I am the one who asked Commander Mychal to bring her here."

"Then I will leave, and you three may talk to your hearts' content," Devlin said. His instincts screamed at him to run, to leave. He knew all too well the dangers of involving a magic user in his affairs.

He strode toward the door, but Commander Mychal blocked his way just as Stephen grabbed his shoulder from behind. Angrily, he spun around, his right hand raised in a fist.

"Release me. I will not warn you again," Devlin said. He locked his gaze with Stephen, but his friend showed no signs of backing down. For a long moment they stood there, frozen, and Devlin wondered what would happen if he were to strike the minstrel.

"Enough of this foolishness," Ismenia said.

Devlin turned to face her, glad to have another target for his anger. "I do not want you or your help. Begone."

"And I have no wish to force myself on the unwilling," Ismenia said. "But neither can I leave you here, ignorant of your peril. You have been bespelled."

Devlin took a deep breath, reminding himself of the laws of hospitality. He had welcomed this woman as a guest, albeit under false pretenses. Yet having said the words, he could not harm her. Not while she was under this roof. All he could do was to hope to be rid of her swiftly. "You tell me nothing I do not already know. Commander Mychal has wasted your time."

His calm words must have reassured Stephen, for he relinquished his grip on Devlin's shoulder and came to stand beside him instead. But a quick glance showed that Mychal still blocked the door. To get past him, Devlin would have to fight. And he was not ready to do that. Not yet.

Ismenia came toward him, and Devlin fought the urge to back away. Magic of any kind made him profoundly uncomfortable, as did those who practiced it. She stopped just one pace away, and stretched out her arm, so that her hand nearly touched his chest.

"You wear an object of power under your shirt," she said.

Devlin nodded.

"May I see it?"

"Why?"

"Indulge me. A moment of your time and I will leave you in peace. If you still wish me to do so."

He hesitated, but reasoned what harm could it do? He would show her the ring, then trust that she was honorable enough to leave him in peace as she had promised.

And then he would take Stephen to task for his part in arranging this bit of foolishness.

The fingers of his crippled hand fumbled with the button of his collar, then reached inside to grasp the leather cord. He tugged on it, until the ring of the Chosen One was revealed.

The ring dangled on the cord, the dark stone glowing with dull red fire, as it had for the past weeks. As he had drawn nearer to the sword, the ring had begun to glow, and had grown warm to the touch. Such portents made him uneasy, so he no longer wore it on his finger.

"How long have you hidden the ring away, ignoring its message of peril?" Ismenia asked.

"What message?" Stephen asked.

"That ring is bound to you," Ismenia said. She reached for it, but he drew it back swiftly. "It was meant to act as a symbol of your power and to warn you of danger."

Devlin struggled to recall what Master Dreng had told him of the ring. At the time he had paid little heed to the mage's words once he realized that the magic that fueled the Geas spell was far beyond Dreng's understanding.

"The mage who crafted it put a spell on it to warn

me of poison," he said. It had been Dreng's attempt at an apology of sorts, for failing to safeguard the soul stone.

"Not poison," Ismenia declared. She frowned, her gaze unfocused as if she could see right through him. "Tell me, Chosen One. Have you ever angered a mind-sorcerer?"

Devlin took a hasty step back. "A mind-sorcerer?" His voice cracked on the last word, but for once he did not care if others sensed his fear.

"You have been thrice bespelled," Ismenia said. "The first was a mind spell, done with your consent. The second is a minor working, bound to the ring you wear. But the third spell is a thing of evil, meant to warp the fabric of your thoughts."

"No. That cannot be." Dreng had sworn to him that he was protected from any such attack. Yet even as Devlin denied it, some part of him knew that she spoke the truth.

Chief Mychal cleared his throat. "This is a private matter, and so I will leave you," he said. He gave a brief nod and left the room, unable to conceal his haste. His friendship with Ismenia was apparently not enough to overcome his distaste for the practice of magic.

"Shall I leave as well?" Stephen asked.

"No," Devlin said. He did not want to be alone with this woman and her dark tidings.

"Shall I send a servant to bring food or drink?" Devlin asked, abruptly recalling his duties as host. Anything to delay whatever she would say next.

"Thank you but no," Ismenia said.

He waited until Ismenia had taken her seat, then

Devlin took the chair opposite hers. Stephen dragged a stool over so he sat at Devlin's right side.

"Have you ever met a mind-sorcerer?" Ismenia asked.

"Not that I know of," Devlin said. Though if there were a mind-sorcerer in Kingsholm, he would hardly be likely to advertise his presence. "But this is not the first time one has set a spell against me."

"Devlin and I were attacked by an elemental creature of darkness during our return from Esker," Stephen explained. "Master Dreng, the royal mage, said it could have been the work of a mind-sorcerer."

Ismenia frowned. "Did this mage see the elemental?"

"No. We encountered it some distance from the city."

"Then it may not have been an elemental after all. It could have been any sort of magical creature. A working of power, but not one requiring the talents of a mind-sorcerer," Ismenia said.

What difference did it make whether the being had been an elemental or some other breed of magical being? What mattered was that the creature had been sent to kill him, and only through luck had he and Stephen been able to destroy it.

"Master Dreng seemed convinced that it was an elemental," Stephen said. "And there is more. The elemental was able to find us because a spell had been set on Devlin's soul stone."

"I have not heard of these soul stones," Ismenia said.

"One gem, split in two," Devlin explained, with a grim twist to his lips. "Half is set in this ring, and the other half is kept in the Royal Chapel in Kingsholm. The stone is tied to my soul, so it glows or fades according to my strength."

The soul stone could also be used to track his progress, when placed on a mosaic map of the Kingdom.

He had thought the soul stone an abomination. No man's private struggles should be set out for strangers to gawk at. It had only served to confirm his view that magic was not to be trusted.

But now he had discovered a far greater horror, as Ismenia's next words confirmed.

"I cannot say whether it is the work of the same person, but you have indeed been touched by mindsorcery. How long has it been since you first noticed that something was wrong? Strange dreams or perhaps an apparition that you could not explain?"

"It began Midwinter's night," Devlin said. "A figure appeared to me, during the ritual of remembrance. I thought it was Lord Haakon, come to mock me."

Foolish man, you waste your time, bleating your pain to these ignorant fools. They cannot help you. No one can.

Devlin bit his lip, tasting the sharp copper of blood, and using the pain to distract him from the renewed whispers in his mind.

"So that is how it was done," Ismenia murmured, almost to herself. She closed her eyes, and pressed the palms of her two hands together.

She was still for several moments, and then she opened her eyes.

"You must understand that what I know of mindsorcery I have learned from books or from speaking with others who study the unseen realm. I can conjecture, but I cannot know for certain."

"I understand," Devlin said.

"Even an untrained mind has natural barriers

against magic. To break down these barriers, a mind-sorcerer must normally be in close contact with his subject. That may be why he sent an elemental creature to attack you physically, rather than trying to cast a soul spell."

Stephen appeared fascinated by these details. No doubt Master Dreng would have been equally fascinated had he been here. But Devlin did not want theories. He wanted answers.

"So what happened on Midwinter's Eve?" he asked.

"During the ritual, you lower the barriers of your mind so you can make contact with those who have passed into the Dread Lord's realm. The mind-sorcerer merely had to wait until you had started the ritual, then he attacked. Once he was able to touch your mind, he forged a link. He can hear your thoughts, and the voices you have been hearing are almost certainly thoughts he has been sending."

He broke into a cold sweat and fought the urge to vomit. A stranger had touched his mind, feeling what Devlin was feeling, sharing his pain, his hopes, his very thoughts. It was the most horrific violation he could imagine. A rape of his soul.

Devlin swallowed convulsively. He felt Stephen's touch on his arm and took comfort from his friend's presence.

"Are you certain of this?" Stephen asked.

"As certain as I can be," Ismenia said. "There are others who know more than I, though none who live in the city. I could send for them to consult with if you like."

"No," Devlin said. Chief Mychal had vouched for this Ismenia, but that did not mean he was prepared to trust other magic users. Any one of them could be his enemy.

"Could it have been one of our people who set the spell? The only foreigners I saw were the innkeeper and his daughter, and they were too busy to be up to mischief. And only one of our people would know when the ritual could be performed and that it would leave me open to attack."

"Mind-sorcery draws its power from others, and is thus against the tenets of wizardry. I have never heard of one of our folk who became a mind-sorcerer. And if the sorcerer were powerful enough, he could have set the spell on you from a great distance. He could have been many leagues away from you."

"The ritual of remembrance may not be common knowledge, but it is not secret either," Stephen said. "I knew of it even before I met you."

It was strange, but he felt relieved to know that his attacker was most likely not one of the Caerfolk. Easier to blame his descent into madness on his faceless enemies rather than to wonder if someone he had once known had decided to seek revenge on him through this spell.

"I will know more, once I break the spell," Ismenia said.

"When?" Devlin asked.

"I need to prepare, but we can make the attempt tonight."

"What of the risks?" Stephen asked. "Can you be certain that destroying the spell will not harm Devlin's mind?"

Devlin had not thought of the risks, only of freeing

himself from the invader who had taken residence in his mind.

Ismenia's eyes flashed, and Devlin was reminded why the Caerfolk were so careful to give a wide berth to wizards and magic users. It made Chief Mychal's apparent friendship with her all the more strange, but perhaps they had known each other as children, before she felt the call to wizardry.

Or perhaps they had been more than friends. There was a certain resemblance in the set of their eyes and the way they tilted their heads to one side when pondering.

"I will do my best, but I make no promises," Ismenia said. "The risk to your friend is far greater if the spell is not broken."

"I agree," Devlin said.

Already the mind-whispers had driven him till he stood on the edge of madness. He could not endure such torment for much longer and still hope to retain ownership of his soul. He would gamble that Ismenia's skills would be equal to the task.

"One more word of caution. You hear the voice, even now?"

"Yes," Devlin admitted. From the corner of his eye he could see Stephen staring at him in concern.

"The sorcerer can hear your thoughts. He knows we are planning to break his link, and he will try his utmost to prevent you from going through with the ceremony. Between now and the next time we meet, you must be vigilant. Do not relax your guard, even for a moment."

"I will watch over him," Stephen promised.

"See that you do. Remember, he is not himself. Tie him up if you must. Do whatever is required."

"We will," Stephen said.

It was comforting to know that, though Devlin's own strength might flag under the weight of his burden, his friends would protect him. Even from himself, if need be. With their help, he would be ready for whatever Ismenia had planned.

Twenty-three

———+———

ONCE THE ROYAL PALACE OF THE CAER RULERS, the army garrison was the largest structure in Alvaren, with twin towers that loomed over the city. But even here space was at a premium. Four hundred soldiers called the garrison home, along with officers' families and servants. The garrison complex included stables for horses, a fully stocked armory, enclosed practice fields, and one of the three granaries that kept the city fed.

Underneath the central keep were a dozen cells where prisoners could be held. Unlike the gaols Didrik was familiar with, these cells were clearly meant to hold a different class of criminals. No consideration was made for their comfort, and most of the prisoners' time was spent in darkness. They were fed once a day, and at that time a single candle stub that lasted for a half hour was provided. After that, the prisoners were plunged back into a darkness interrupted only by random inspections by their keepers.

Each cell had thick stone walls and a heavy wooden door. The individual cells were separated by storerooms or offices, making it nearly impossible for one prisoner to communicate with another. The sense of utter isolation was meant to break down the prisoners' wills.

And if the isolation and harsh treatment were not enough to break a prisoner's spirit, Didrik had no doubt that there were other places in the keep he had not been shown, places where more stringent forms of questioning could be employed.

Yesterday's interrogation session had been fruitless, but the prisoner had been left in her cell for a full day and night to reflect upon her predicament. As per his orders, she had been awoken every half hour to ensure that she had no chance to sleep. Now it was time to see if his strategy would bear fruit.

The door to the interrogation room swung open and the prisoner stumbled into the room, propelled by a shove to her back. She raised her chained hands to cover her face, blinking in the bright light. Two privates followed her inside.

Ensign Ranvygga gestured to the heavy wooden chair in the center of the room. "Secure her," she said.

Didrik and Ranvygga watched as the prisoner was guided into the chair. Her hands were pulled roughly from her face and secured to the arms of the chair. One private stood behind her, keeping watch, while the other knelt to secure her legs. He received a swift kick for his troubles, and his companion cuffed her in the back of her head.

"Enough," Ranvygga ordered, before Didrik could make his own objection.

His gaze swept over the prisoner, noticing that she had a fresh bruise on one cheek. Apart from the kick, she had made no serious attempt to break free from their custody. Not that she would get far in a place filled with soldiers who would know her on sight as an escaped prisoner. Still, the fact that she did not even try to escape was a sign that the conditions were beginning to take their toll on her.

Indeed, the restraints were not truly needed. There was no real risk that she would escape, and any attack on himself or Ranvygga would fail before it was over. The chains were simply props, stage dressing to remind her of how helpless she was. Just as the interrogation room had been purposefully designed; a large open space with walls that rose to three times a man's height, dwarfing the occupants. The prisoner was placed in the center of the room, the focus of the bright lamps that hung overhead. Against one wall there was a long mahogany table. Ranvygga sat on one side of the table and Didrik on the other, ensuring that the prisoner could only see one of them at a time.

At Didrik's left elbow was a pitcher with cool cider, a plate of cooked meat and a basket of freshly baked bread. The scent of the food filled the room, and he saw the prisoner lick her lips.

Slowly, deliberately, he lifted the pitcher of cider and filled a pewter tankard. He took a noisy gulp, then a second. Then he set the tankard back down on the table.

"Strange how it is the small things that we miss most. Things we take for granted. A hot meal, cool drink, a warm place to sleep." Didrik's voice was soft, as if musing aloud.

Ensign Ranvygga was silent, as they had agreed. Yesterday she had led the interrogation. Now it was his turn to see if he could succeed where she had failed.

"I can make things easier for you," he said. He rose to his feet, still holding the tankard of cider in his hand, and took a few paces toward the prisoner. "A simple exchange to start. This tankard of cider, in exchange for your name."

"I will never fall for your tricks," she spat.

"Are you that ashamed of what you have done?" Didrik asked.

"I am proud of what I tried to do. My only regret is that I failed, and the traitor yet lives."

"Then what harm is there in telling me your name?"

He took a few steps closer, so that she could see the tankard. This close he could see that her complexion was nearly gray with exhaustion, and there were deep purple circles under her eyes. But any sympathy he might have felt for her was vanquished by the memory of her attack upon Devlin.

Her eyes searched his face, then she returned to staring at the tankard. He waited a dozen heartbeats and shrugged, turning away. "If you don't want it—"

"Muireann."

At the quiet whisper, he paused, then turned back.

"What did you say?"

"Muireann," she repeated.

It was but half a name, giving no indication of her family or where she had been born. Still, it was a start.

Her mouth opened as he approached, and he lifted the tankard to her lips. She swallowed greedily, three times, before he pulled the tankard away.

"More," she demanded.

Didrik shook his head and stepped back, holding the tankard firmly out of reach. "Muireann is only half a name. What of your family or your craft?"

"The Children of Ynnis are my family," she said.

"Then tell us their names," Ensign Ranvygga said. "Tell us who sent you to attack the Chosen One, and you can have all the cider you can drink. Tell us who ordered the Ensign's death and you may eat your fill."

Didrik strove to keep his face calm, though inside he was furious at the interruption. He had begun to establish a connection with the prisoner, but at Ranvygga's words, he could see Muireann visibly withdrawing.

"Never," she said, lifting her chin and meeting his gaze defiantly. "You can beat me, starve me, throw me in a cell and leave me to rot. But I will never betray the cause of freedom. The Children of Ynnis will not rest until we have reclaimed our lands and the soldiers of Jorsk lay rotting in their graves."

The moment was lost, and though Didrik spent the next hour trying every trick he knew, Muireann withstood his efforts and refused to speak another word. Finally, he conceded defeat and summoned the soldiers to return the prisoner to her cell.

He waited until Muireann had been escorted from the room before turning his wrath on Ensign Ranvygga.

"You sabotaged my efforts!"

"I was trying to help."

"If I had wanted your help, I would have asked for it."

He stared at the now cold food. Wasted. Just as this opportunity had been wasted, and his stomach turned in disgust.

"She was talking to me," he said. "I got her to answer a question, which is more than any of you have done.

And then you had to interrupt and the moment was lost."

"I judged the moment as I saw fit," Ensign Ranvygga replied. "I have experience interrogating Caer rebels."

"But have you had any success? Or do you simply torture them until they tell you what you wish to hear?" Didrik asked.

"These things take time. Give her another day without food or rest, and we will try again this evening."

Time was one thing they did not have. Their spirits sagged lower with each day that passed without their discovering any trace of the lost sword. Muireann was their one tangible link to the Children of Ynnis, but even if she did decide to break her silence, she might well be ignorant of its whereabouts. The best they could hope for was that she could lead them to others, who in turn would lead them to those who had taken the sword.

"Wait six hours, then see that the prisoner gets her daily rations," Didrik instructed. Mild hunger might serve as an encouragement, but she needed to be fit to talk. "And remind her watchers that the Chosen One has ordered that she be held in accordance with the law. She is not to be tortured."

He remembered the fresh bruise on the prisoner's face and wondered if her clothing had concealed other bruises, inflicted during his absence.

"I take my orders from Lord Kollinar," Ranvygga said.

"You are a soldier, and take your orders from Marshal Kollinar. And he takes his orders from the Chosen One, as General of the Army. The Chosen One has empowered me to speak with his voice. Shall I summon the governor here to confirm this?"

She shook her head. "There is no need."

He wondered. "Remember, you will be held responsible for the prisoner's condition. And she is not to be questioned unless Lord Kollinar, myself, or Chief Mychal is present."

He had tried to be fair, but he did not like this Ranvygga. His feelings ran deeper than the customary dislike that members of the Guard had for those in the Royal Army. He did not trust her. He half suspected that she had deliberately sabotaged his interrogation. Not out of treachery, but out of ambition, a desire that she and she alone receive the credit for whatever information they could pry out of the prisoner. It was telling that she was an Ensign, and yet the name Ranvygga indicated that she was not from one of the noble families. It was rare to find a commoner in the officers' ranks, and no doubt her humble origins had earned her this obscure post rather than a more prestigious assignment. Perhaps she saw this as her opportunity to distinguish herself, and earn a long-sought promotion.

Or perhaps he was starting at shadows. He was beginning to see plots everywhere. It was the fault of this cursed place, with its strange people. The sooner they found the sword and were able to leave, the better it would be. For all their sakes.

As he left Ensign Ranvygga, he could not shake his feeling of uneasiness, so he sought out Lord Kollinar. He knew Ranvygga would make her own report to her commander and wanted to make certain he saw Kollinar before Ranvygga had a chance to influence him.

The governor was not in his office. His aide suggested that he might be in the officers' dining hall, partaking of the midday meal. Didrik was surprised to find that it was midday already, but when he sought out the officers' dining hall, Kollinar was nowhere to be found. Helpful officers pointed him in the direction of the training yard, but Kollinar was not there either. An earnest young Ensign suggested he try the armory, which meant that he had to cross the length of the garrison and climb into the north tower. Something about the Ensign's expression niggled at the back of Didrik's mind. When he finally arrived at the armory, his suspicions were confirmed, for the sergeant in charge appeared quite startled at the idea that Lord Kollinar would want to visit.

He had been played for a fool. No doubt the army officers were laughing among themselves at how easy it had been to dupe one of the Kingsholm Guard. He was angry at himself for falling into their trap and disgusted with those who called themselves soldiers yet played childish pranks.

He wondered if they would have been so quick to play their games had they known the true stakes that were being fought for. Did it mean nothing to them that the Chosen One had nearly been assassinated in their city?

Didrik had a very good memory for faces, as did most of the Guard. A part of him was tempted to hunt down the helpful soldiers and use his fists to teach them the error of their ways. But he had no time to waste in avenging personal slights. The soldiers might forget their duty, but he would not.

He returned to Lord Kollinar's office and was not

surprised to find that Lord Kollinar was seated at his desk, a tray with the remains of a meal at his left elbow.

"Lieutenant Didrik, I had been hoping to see you before you left," Lord Kollinar said.

"I was hoping to speak with you as well," Didrik said. He fixed his gaze on Kollinar's aide. "Strange that you were nowhere to be found. Though several of your officers were quick to direct me to places where you were not."

The aide flushed red and tugged at his collar with one finger. "Err, I—"

"Your directions to the officers' dining hall placed it two floors lower than where I found it," Didrik said. "But for true inventiveness I must salute your comrade who sent me from the stables all the way to the armory."

Kollinar leaned back in his chair, and under his gaze his hapless aide seemed to shrink steadily.

"It was a mistake," the Ensign muttered.

"A mistake," Kollinar repeated. "Perhaps the true mistake was in giving you a position of responsibility to begin with."

He let the Ensign sweat for a moment, then dismissed him. "Leave us. You can spend your free time thinking of reasons why I should not reassign you to lead a border patrol."

"Yes, sir." The Ensign saluted and left.

Suddenly weary, Didrik sat down in the chair nearest the fire.

"I apologize if you were inconvenienced," Lord Kollinar said. "Those involved will be disciplined, I assure you. I will see to it personally."

"There are other matters that concern me more,"

Didrik said. He had made his point about the lack of discipline among Kollinar's troops. Now it was time to hammer that point home. "The prisoner's interrogation did not go well. She was beginning to cooperate, but then Ensign Ranvygga broke in, in defiance of my instructions."

Lord Kollinar picked up a pen in his right hand and began slowly turning it, as if it were an object of great fascination. "Ensign Ranvygga is a dedicated officer and has successfully interrogated suspected rebels before."

"And this time she botched it," Didrik said. "I am no garrison soldier, but a leader of the Kingsholm Guard, with long experience of my own in questioning prisoners. I saw more prisoners as a novice guard than Ranvygga will see in a lifetime serving in the army of occupation."

"Getting information from a cutpurse is hardly the same as questioning a rebel fanatic."

"I have questioned my share of hardened criminals. And would-be assassins. Ranvygga had her chance yesterday, and she learned nothing. I was making progress today, and Ranvygga interfered. She was either malicious or ignorant, and neither is something we can afford."

"And what did you find out?"

"A name." Little enough to show for days of questioning.

Kollinar's hands stilled and he deliberately set the pen down on the desk. "Muireann of Tannersly, a vegetable grower by trade," he said.

"You knew her name and kept it from me?"

"Peace," Kollinar said, holding his right hand, palm outward. "The peacekeepers identified her earlier this morning. When you came to see me earlier, I was still meeting with Tobias, Chief Mychal's second-in-command. Apparently this woman arrived in the city a few weeks before the attack. She was lodging with a distant cousin, who claims no knowledge of what she had planned to do. The dwelling where she lived was also home to the mother of one of the peacekeepers, and that is how he was able to recognize the prisoner."

"And the other residents are being questioned?"

"The peacekeepers are handling the matter," Kollinar said. "From what I've heard she kept to herself, and had no suspicious visitors. If she made contact with other rebels, it was done somewhere else in the city."

And so they were back to where they had started. Without Muireann's cooperation, they were no closer to finding the Children of Ynnis than they had been before.

"I want someone other than Ranvygga in charge of the prisoner," Didrik said. He was too tired to phrase it as a polite request. As a matter of protocol, Kollinar outranked him. He was noble born, and both governor of the province and Marshal in command of the occupying troops. But Didrik was the aide to the Chosen One, who in pursuit of his office outranked anyone in the Kingdom, with the exception of King Olafur himself. And it was Devlin's wishes that he needed to see carried out.

"You blame her for the failure of this morning's interrogation," Lord Kollinar said.

"For that. As well as for the bruises on the prisoner's face and the stiffness in her posture. The Chosen One gave strict orders about how the prisoner was to be treated, and it is incumbent upon us to see that they are obeyed."

Kollinar nodded. "Of course," he said. "I will assign my most trusted officer to be in charge of the prisoner's security and ensure that my orders are understood."

From somewhere deep inside himself, Didrik managed to dredge up words of thanks.

Kollinar continued studying him for a long moment, then looked away. "It must be difficult for you," he said.

Didrik made a noncommittal noise.

"With your years of experience, it must be difficult to serve someone who was not trained in the arts of war. Someone who has not seen what we have seen. Someone who may be too softhearted to make the choices that need to be made." Lord Kollinar let his words sink in. "I will wager that if you were in sole charge of the interrogation that you would not be so hasty as to rule out all possible means of wringing the truth from this prisoner."

A part of Didrik agreed with the governor. The same part that had wanted to strangle the prisoner with his bare hands for having dared to attack his friend. But once his blood had cooled he had reconsidered. Torture was forbidden by law, and with good reason. It was too hard to separate out truth from lies, for those undergoing torture would say anything, even invent stories, just to appease their tormentors.

"I would do many things differently," Didrik said. "No doubt that is why I am still a lieutenant in the Kingsholm Guard, and Devlin is the one the Gods called to their service."

"Point taken," Kollinar said, with a faint smile.

Didrik wondered if this had been a test of his loyalty. Or perhaps simply of his intelligence, for only a fool would cast doubt on the judgment of the man he served.

Or more ominously, had Kollinar truly hoped to win Didrik to his side, seeking to divide his loyalties? He decided that Kollinar would bear close watching.

"I will go to the peacekeepers and hear for myself if they have any more information on this Muireann and who her friends may be. Send word to me there, or at your residence, if you have news."

"At once," Lord Kollinar said. "And I trust you will do the same."

"Of course," Didrik said. "We are allies in this."

Yet even as he spoke the words, he wondered just how far he could trust Kollinar. At best, the conduct he had witnessed showed a troubling laxness in command. The governor might be well-equipped to handle the normal duties of his post, but it still remained to be seen if he could rise to the demands of this situation. And he would have to warn Devlin to be wary as well.

After conferring with the peacekeepers, Didrik returned to the governor's residence. But while he had little progress to report, it seemed his companions had had a far more enlightening morning.

They had gathered in Devlin's chambers, knowing that it was the one place where they could be assured of privacy. Even Lord Kollinar would not enter unless invited. And they most assuredly had secrets they wished to keep from the governor.

For all his skill as a minstrel, Stephen had been

nearly incoherent as he described why he had asked Commander Mychal to find a trustworthy mage, and how she had revealed that Devlin was the subject of a magical attack. Clearly Stephen was pleased that his gamble had paid off. And relieved to discover that the Death God was not truly summoning his friend.

Didrik shared his relief. His fears for Devlin had weighed heavily on his mind, knowing that if Devlin had been marked for death that there was nothing anyone could do to save him. No mortal man could stand against a God. But a sorcerer was another matter. A sorcerer, after all, was but a man—and such a creature could be defeated.

Devlin did not seem to share their excitement. He lay half-reclining on a sofa, his face pale from fatigue and the strain of the past weeks.

"It may be the same sorcerer that tried to kill Devlin once before," Stephen said.

"That was over a year ago," Didrik countered. "Why haven't we heard from him before now?"

"Master Dreng thought he might have been injured when we destroyed his creature," Stephen said. "It may have taken him these long months to gather the strength for another attack."

Devlin opened his eyes and pushed himself up till he was in a seated position. He cradled his right hand in his left, massaging the scarred palm with his left thumb. It was something he did when he was most weary, or when the memories of the past threatened to overwhelm him.

"I betrayed myself," Devlin said softly. "If Ismenia is to be believed, the sorcerer knows what I am thinking.

He plucked the knowledge of the sword from my brain."

His words cast a different light on the matter. "Do you think he is allied with the Children of Ynnis? That somehow they learned of the sword from him?"

Devlin nodded. "We know the traitor Gerhard was not above using magic for his own ends. Someone in Kingsholm set a spell on the soul stone and used it to find me. The creature that attacked Stephen and myself was surely a great working of magic."

"Gerhard's allies also had gold, enough to pay for the mercenaries who sought to capture Korinth," Didrik said. In his mind he could see a pattern forming, and it made him uneasy. "And here in Duncaer, we find that after years of obscurity, the Children of Ynnis now have gold coins to buy weapons, as well as impeccable information."

This was mere speculation on his part. There was no proof of any grand conspiracy. No evidence to tie the rebel group to the enemies who sought to conquer Jorsk. Yet there were too many coincidences to dismiss the matter out of hand. For years their unseen enemy had preferred to attack by stealth, working to destabilize the Kingdom. An uprising in Duncaer would ultimately be doomed, but it would require large numbers of troops to put it down and serve as an effective diversion should there be an invasion elsewhere.

It was a cunning scheme, made all the more brilliant by its simplicity. Even if they managed to keep the peace in Duncaer, their enemy had risked nothing except his gold. They still had no idea who was behind these attacks. All they knew was that their enemy was clever, patient, and powerful enough to employ at least one mind-sorcerer. And yet this person could pass him on the street and he would be none the wiser.

Didrik forced his mind back to the matter at hand. "And this mage thinks she can undo the spell?"

"Ismenia thinks she can break the link. She has gone to make her preparations and will meet me at the second hour past sunset to make the attempt."

Devlin winced, then shook his head from side to side.

"What's wrong?" Stephen asked.

"My uninvited guest is telling me that Ismenia will betray me and that to serve my oath I must flee," Devlin said. Beads of sweat had formed on his brow, and his dark eyes were anguished. "Tell me again that Mychal is an honorable man, and that he trusts this woman."

"Mychal swears by his name that Ismenia is a trustworthy soul who will bring no harm to you," Stephen said softly. "Put your trust in your friends."

They left the governor's residence after sunset, slipping out the servants' door and taking no escort. Wearing the long cloaks Stephen had purchased in the marketplace, with the hoods pulled up to conceal their features, they could have been any three men taking advantage of a free evening.

The cloaks were long enough to conceal the swords that both Stephen and Didrik wore. Devlin wore no sword, nor did he have even one of his throwing knives. For the first time in years he was completely unarmed, and it was an uncomfortable feeling. The back of his neck prickled, and he could not stop searching the shadows, looking for hidden dangers.

This is a trap, the mind-voice told him. *Ismenia is in leaque with the Children of Ynnis. She will betray you. You must flee.*

"No," Devlin muttered. He would not listen to his tormentor. It was the voice of a liar, trying desperately to confuse him. The sorcerer knew Ismenia could break the spell and was afraid of losing his power over Devlin.

And yet, the voice fed into his own doubts. Even if Ismenia was trustworthy, he knew nothing of her skill. Any spell she tried might do more harm than good. What if in trying to break the link she accidentally strengthened it? Or, worse, tampered with the Geas spell? Could he really take that risk? He had lived with the mind-voice for weeks now, and it had done him no harm. Surely it was wiser not to place his safety in the hands of a stranger.

His doubts fed the power of the Geas. It did not care whether Devlin were hale or ill, sane or driven mad by a mind-sorcerer's tricks. The Geas understood nothing except duty. It would not let Devlin imperil himself needlessly.

He came back to himself with a start, to find that he had stopped walking and Stephen's hand was on his arm, urging him forward.

"Come," Stephen said.

It was frightening to realize how easily he had been distracted. Left to his own devices he would never be able to meet with Ismenia and undergo the ritual. Even a momentary lapse in concentration was enough for the mind-sorcerer to use his fears against him. It was for this reason that he went unarmed, for he did not trust himself. He must trust in his friends.

Devlin cleared his mind and focused his will on what

he knew to be the truth. The mind-sorcerer was his enemy and sought to destroy him. Only a magic user could break the spell. Only then would he be free to serve as Chosen One.

He felt the awful pressure of the Geas begin to ease as he repeated the silent litany.

"Come," Stephen repeated.

Devlin took one step forward, then another. He would do this. He must.

It took nearly an hour to make their way through the city streets, until they reached Draighean Naas, where Ismenia was to meet them. A haven of green in the center of the crowded stone city, the grove was the place where rituals were held, including those of remembrance.

As they passed through the double row of blackthorn trees that guarded the entrance, Devlin felt himself begin to sweat despite the chill of the night. All his fears of magic, and his distrust for putting his life in another's hands, rose up within him and demanded that he run from this place. But his will was stronger than his fears, and he continued to move forward.

The guardian trees gave way to a open field, and the frost-kissed grass crackled under their feet as they walked toward the ring of yew trees that formed the heart of the grove. On Midwinter's Eve the space would have been crowded, filled with those who had lost friends and kin in the past year. Their ritual fires would have dotted the field like stars in a night sky. But tonight it was pitch-black, the moon hidden behind thick clouds. The lanterns they carried provided only enough illumination to find their footing.

Devlin saw a speck of light that could be another

lantern. As they approached the speck grew in size, until he could see that it was a ritual fire. Formed of seven oak branches, none longer than his forearm, it would burn hot and swiftly.

Ismenia stood beside the fire, dressed in an unbelted robe of unbleached wool. Her hair was unbound, reaching down nearly to her knees. In one hand she held a long copper staff with a serpent's head on the top.

"Wise one," Devlin said, bowing his head in greeting.

"You are late. The moon is nearly overhead," Ismenia said.

He wondered how she could tell on this cloudy night, then decided he did not want to know.

"What must I do?"

"I have given this much thought, and I believe that the sorcerer was able to touch your mind because you had left it open during the ritual of Remembrance. If you had properly finished the ritual on that night, the link would have been broken. But you did not, and the link has grown stronger as time passes."

"And?"

"To break the link, we will have to finish what you started. I will lend my power to you, and we will use the power of this place, which has been strengthened by all those who have come before us."

"And this will free Devlin?" Stephen asked.

"If the Gods are willing, yes," Ismenia said.

If not, he would be no worse off than he was now.

"Let us begin," Devlin said.

With a low-voiced incantation, Ismenia thrust her staff into the center of the fire, and the copper began to glow from the heat. At her gesture, Devlin took a seat on the ground, in front of the fire.

"Stephen, you were present on that night?" Ismenia asked.

Stephen nodded.

"Then you must help as well. Sit at the right-hand side of your friend, while I take my place to the left. The soldier may watch, but he is not part of the circle and must not interfere."

Didrik took a few steps to the side, positioning himself where he could watch both the ritual and the path by which they had come. He set the lantern on the ground beside him and placed one hand on his sword belt, though it was unlikely that they would encounter any peril that could be defeated by mere steel.

Ismenia handed Devlin a shallow copper bowl, with runes carved around the rim. On top of the bowl was balanced a small dagger, again made of copper.

He unfastened his cloak and withdrew his left arm, knowing instinctively that a true offering was needed. His left sleeve had already been slashed to accommodate the bandages, so it was a simple matter to push up the sleeve and bare the flesh of his upper arm.

Four straight scars already decorated his arm. Now he drew a fifth bloody line beneath them, holding the bowl to catch the blood as it dripped from his arm.

"Haakon, Lord of the Sunset Realm, I, Devlin, son of Kameron and Talaith, now called the Chosen One, greet thee," he said. He waited for twenty-one heartbeats, then placed the bowl in front of Stephen, and handed him the dagger.

The flickering firelight made Stephen's face seem

even paler than usual, but his face was calm as he uncovered his own arm. Unlike Devlin's, his skin was unmarked. His hand shook only slightly as he drew the knife blade across his flesh.

"Haakon, Lord of the Sunset Realm, I, Stephen, a minstrel, son of Lady Gemma and Brynjolf, Baron of Esker, greet you on this night," Stephen said. The cut had been deep, and his wound bled freely as he caught the blood in the bowl.

At Ismenia's nod, he placed the partially filled bowl in front of her and passed her the bloody dagger.

Devlin handed him a strip of linen, which he used to bind up his arm.

Ismenia repeated the ritual, mingling her blood with theirs. Then she thrust the bloody dagger in the heart of the fire so that it touched her staff.

She held out her arms, and the three joined hands so they formed a circle around the fire.

Devlin's gaze was drawn to the copper staff, which glowed with a white light. Reason told him the fire was too small to have such an effect, meaning that some other force was at work. His gaze traveled to the top of the staff, and he saw the snake-head turning in slow circles, though the rest of the staff remained motionless.

He swallowed, his mouth gone suddenly dry.

"I call upon the Seven to bear witness. We three have gathered on sacred ground, under open sky, in the shelter of the trees of wisdom. We have made offerings of blood and fire to the sacred forces that govern all living creatures. Hear us now, as we ask that you punish the one who perverted our sacred rite to his own ends. Cast out the evil spirit that seeks to force Devlin to do his bidding. Unbind his soul so that he may seek his own destiny."

There was a long moment of silence, and then Ismenia squeezed his hand before releasing it. From within her robe she withdrew a small flask and poured a clear liquid into the bowl. Then she raised the sacred bowl up to the heavens and began to name each of the Seven Gods, asking for their blessing.

Devlin's nerves were stretched taut, and it was all he could do to remain still.

Finally there was only one God left to name.

"Haakon, in your name was the deceit committed, and it is your power that the deceiver mocked. Hear us now, and with the sword of justice, cut the ties that chain this man," Ismenia said.

She raised the bowl to the heavens once more, and, with a twist of her wrists, poured the contents on the fire.

Bright sparks flew in all directions. He could hear someone exclaim as the flames suddenly rose up to the height of a man before subsiding just as swiftly. Before he could draw a breath, the flames sputtered and died, leaving only gray ashes where moments before there had been burning branches.

Devlin blinked, his eyes unaccustomed to the sudden darkness.

"Is it over?" Didrik asked, coming toward them.

Ismenia rose to her feet and reached in to withdraw her staff.

"Wait, you'll burn yourself," Stephen protested.

The wizard paid him no heed, and as her bare hand closed over her staff, it was clear she felt no pain.

Devlin placed his hand in the ashes of the fire, not surprised to find that they were cold.

Devlin rose to his feet, and Stephen did the same.

Holding her staff in her left hand, Ismenia placed her right hand over Devlin's heart. She held it there for a long moment, then placed her hand on the crown of his head.

"The link is broken," she said.

Devlin's knees nearly buckled with relief.

"Are you certain?" Didrik asked.

"Yes."

"And the Geas?" Devlin asked. Ismenia had asked the Gods to free him from the chains that bound him, and the Geas was surely one such chain.

There was sympathy in Ismenia's eyes, and he knew his brief hope had been for naught.

"The compulsion spell is beyond my power," she said. "Unlike the linkage, you consented to the Geas being placed upon you, and now it is bound up with your soul. Even the mage who placed the spell upon you might not be able to remove it."

Devlin tried to conceal his disappointment. He already knew that removing the spell was beyond Master Dreng's powers. Perhaps only those who had first crafted the spell knew if it could ever be undone, and they had been in their graves for many years now. Still, the removal of the link to the mind-sorcerer had been a great thing, and with that he must be content.

"I will be forever grateful for your aid," Devlin said. "The debt can never be repaid, but if there is a service I can do for you, you have but to ask."

Ismenia shook her head. "You owe me no debt. As a student of the unseen realm, it is my duty to help those who have been afflicted by those who follow the dark arts."

As a wizard, Ismenia existed outside the normal Caer structure of kin and craft ties. Her allegiance to her art was paramount, which was one of the reasons why his people respected wizards, but feared them as well. Mychal called her friend, but if she had once been kin to him, it was a connection that neither could ever acknowledge. In a way, her calling cut her off from their people as surely as his own oath as Chosen One had isolated him.

"If you will not accept my debt pledge, then you must accept my friendship," Devlin said. "Though I warn you there are few folk in Duncaer who would openly claim the friendship of the Chosen One."

"One can never be too rich in friends," Ismenia said.

"Did you learn anything of the mind-sorcerer in your ritual? A glimpse of where he is, or perhaps even his name?" Didrik asked.

"No. I could sense that he was far away, but that is all."

"How far? As far as the lowlands? As far as Kingsholm? As Nerikaat?" Devlin asked.

"Far," Ismenia repeated. "He was not from any land that once belonged to the Caerfolk. I sensed great distance, but I know not these other realms and so do not know where he may have been."

So once again their enemy had eluded them.

"I can tell you he had great power, in order to forge a link over such distance and to maintain it. As a friend, I must warn you. If you ever come face-to-face with this sorcerer, you will be in grave danger," Ismenia said.

"I will heed your words," Devlin said. Though he did

not know how he could hope to hide from a faceless, nameless enemy.

"What will you do now?" she asked.

"Now I will do what I came for," Devlin said. "Now I will retrieve the Sword of the Chosen One."

Twenty-four

AFTER RETURNING FROM THE GROVE, DEVLIN EN-
joyed his first restful sleep in weeks. He awoke with the
dawn, and despite having slept for only a few hours, he
felt energized, for he realized what he must do.

All along he'd had the means to find the Children of
Ynnis. It was so obvious that he should have seen it before. But he had been distracted, his mind caught between the pull of the Geas and the whispering voice
that he had believed to be the Lord of Death. Now that
his mind was clear, he could see his mistake. He had
forgotten who he was. He had let the title of Chosen
One consume him, relying upon others to search for
the sword.

It did not matter that others had made the same mistake. Even Didrik and Stephen, whose counsel he relied
upon most, had seen nothing wrong with having the
army conduct methodical searches of the homes of
likely suspects, or of using the peacekeepers to seek out
members of the Children of Ynnis. Were they still in
Jorsk, such tactics would be logical.

Devlin should have known better. He was in Duncaer.

More than that, he was of Duncaer, though for a time he had lost sight of that fact. It was time to cast off his blinders and to reason as one of the Caerfolk.

And to see if he had the strength to do what must be done. Regardless of the cost.

Rising and dressing hastily, he rang for a servant and asked him to bring fresh kava and to fetch Lord Kollinar. The servant protested that Lord Kollinar was still in his bed. But when Devlin offered to wake the governor personally, the servant hastily volunteered to do so.

He was drinking his second mug of kava and contemplating fetching Lord Kollinar himself when the governor finally made his appearance.

"What is so urgent that you must see me now?" Lord Kollinar asked. He had not dressed, but wore a belted robe of silk over woolen nightclothes, the elegance of his attire marred by worn leather slippers. His face was puffy from lack of sleep.

Devlin rose and crossed to the table on which a tray of food had been laid out. He filled an empty mug with kava and handed it to Lord Kollinar.

"I want the prisoner Muireann taken from your gaol and turned over to the peacekeepers," Devlin said.

"Why?" Lord Kollinar took a sip of the kava and set the mug firmly aside.

"There is nothing more to be gained from having the army interrogate her. I need her to be in the care of the peacekeepers."

Devlin resumed his seat on the sofa, cradling his mug in his hands. Kollinar continued to stand.

"It is too much of a security risk. For all we know there might well be rebel sympathizers among the peacekeepers. Someone might try to help her escape, or to kill her before she has a chance to talk. Chief Mychal has already questioned her twice, with no results. He is welcome to try as often as he wishes, as long as the prisoner remains under my control."

"No."

"No?" Kollinar's voice rose in disbelief.

"The prisoner is to be transferred to the control of the peacekeepers. There she will be subject to Caer justice, according to the laws of our people."

"She committed treason. By the laws of the Kingdom she must be executed for her crime. After we have learned from her all we can."

And so Muireann believed as well. Which was a mistake she would come to regret.

"Sit," Devlin said, tired of craning his neck. He waited as Kollinar settled in one of the high-backed chairs, located on the opposite side of the antechamber from the sofa where Devlin sat.

"Why do you think Muireann refuses to answer our questions? It is because she has nothing to gain. She knows that regardless of what she tells you, she will still be executed," Devlin said.

Kollinar shook his head. "You cannot be thinking of pardoning her. I will not have it. Think of the precedent that would set. What of the next person who decides to attack one of my soldiers or a royal messenger? Or even dares raise a blade against me? Shall they, too, be offered pardons in exchange for crumbs of information?"

"Muireann does not want a pardon. She is not afraid of death. But I know what she fears far more than mere death, and that is what I will use against her."

Kollinar's brow wrinkled in doubt. "And what is

more frightening than death? The peacekeepers do not practice torture."

He might be an able administrator, but Kollinar was a man of little imagination. Worse, his questions revealed how little he truly understood the people he governed. Whether they dwelled in the crowded cities or the most isolated shepherd's hut, all Caerfolk held the same thing sacred. And all knew that there were worse things to fear than one's own death.

Even a child understood what Kollinar did not. There were horrors not to be found in the Jorskian code of laws, nor even deep within the torture cells that did not officially exist. Horrors that Devlin could unleash on Muireann if he was willing to place himself at risk.

He could try to explain, but it would be a waste of breath. Kollinar had spent a decade in Duncaer and was still ignorant. No words of Devlin's were likely to change his mind, and Devlin had better uses for his time.

"When the time comes, you will see for yourself," Devlin said.

"You will not explain. And I don't suppose you will explain to me either why you slipped out of here last night without word to anyone, taking no escort except your aide and the harp player?"

"The harp player is Stephen, son of Lord Brynjolf, a fact you would do well to remind yourself of. And as for explanations, I owe you none."

Lord Kollinar flinched at Devlin's icy tone, finally realizing that he had gone too far.

"I am responsible for all that goes on in this province. Including your safety."

"And I am responsible for the Kingdom."

Devlin waited a dozen heartbeats until he was certain that Kollinar understood his message.

"Have the prisoner transferred this morning. I will send word to Chief Mychal to expect her. When I am ready to pass judgment on her, I will send word to you, so you may bear witness."

"Is that all, my lord Chosen One?"

"That is all I require. For the present," Devlin said.

Kollinar rose and placed his hand over his heart, bowing in the formal salute of an officer to his commander. His smile was bitter, but Devlin trusted that Kollinar would do as he was told. As the governor left the room, Devlin rose. The prisoner's transfer was only the first step. Now he had to line up the other players in this drama and ensure that they knew the parts they must play.

Didrik was surprised to be awoken shortly after dawn with news that Devlin wished to see him as soon as he had dressed. Hastily he washed his face, rubbing the sleep from his eyes. On his way to Devlin's rooms, he detoured through the kitchen, grabbing a bowl of porridge and a hasty mug of tea, hoping the food would help clear the fuzziness from his head. By his calculation he had had no more than three hours of sleep. It had been quite late when they had returned, but despite the hour, he had difficulty in falling asleep. The ritual had unnerved him—nearly as much as had the realization that a mind-sorcerer had somehow found a way to tap into Devlin's thoughts.

But now Devlin was free. And far too bright-eyed

and cheerful for a man who had scant rest and was still recovering from his injuries.

"Have you eaten?" Devlin asked.

"Yes," Didrik said.

"Good. Come now, we have a busy day ahead of us."

"What of Stephen?" Didrik asked.

"Let him sleep," Devlin replied.

Didrik spared a brief moment of envy for the slumbering Stephen.

"Do you plan to question the prisoner?" If Kollinar had kept to his schedule, the prisoner would have been questioned again last evening. Presumably by an officer more skilled than Ensign Ranvygga had been. Didrik had planned on questioning her again this morning, hoping he might succeed where the others had failed.

"Not today," Devlin replied. "I sent Kollinar to arrange to have her transferred over to the peace-keepers."

Didrik wondered at the reason for the transfer. Did Devlin share his misgivings regarding the way the army was treating the prisoner? Or was there something else going on? Whatever the reason, he knew Lord Kollinar and his officers would be furious over the implied slight.

"So we are going to the peacekeepers' compound?"

"Eventually. But first we must see Peredur Trucha. It will take some time to walk to his residence, so we had better be off to try to catch him before he leaves for the day's errands."

Devlin offered no further explanation, and Didrik did not press him. They donned their winter boots and cloaks and set off for Peredur's residence, accompanied by an honor guard of a half dozen soldiers. After the previous attack, their escort had been handpicked by Lord Kollinar, then personally inspected by Didrik. He knew each of them by name, and nodded in greeting to their leader, Ensign Hrolfsson.

The lawgiver Peredur was indeed awake, although startled to see them. He invited them in, offering kava and freshly baked biscuits that his apprentice's sister had sent over. Devlin accepted, and they sat around a small table in Peredur's kitchen. They made small talk until the biscuits had disappeared, and then Devlin began to speak to Peredur in the Caer tongue. Peredur, his apprentice, and Devlin engaged in a brief but animated discussion.

Stephen, at least, would have known what was being said, which was why Devlin had chosen to leave him behind. Didrik was being kept in the dark. And he did not like it. It showed a lack of trust, and that was an insult to one whom Devlin called friend. But more than mere friendship was at stake. Didrik was the aide to the Chosen One, charged by Captain Drakken herself with keeping him safe. How could he serve Devlin if Devlin insisted on keeping him ignorant of his intentions? How could he protect him if he did not know the shape of the danger he faced? If Devlin was planning something, Didrik needed to know.

At last they seemed to reach some agreement. Heads nodded, then ritual farewells were said, first in the Caer tongue, then in the trade tongue for Didrik's benefit.

Devlin paused on the doorstep and touched Didrik's arm. "We were not trying to hide things from you," he said, responding to Didrik's unspoken anger. "I needed to discuss a point of Caer law with Peredur, and there are some concepts that do not translate into the trade tongue."

The words took the sharp edge off his anger, but he vowed he would have the full story from Devlin. Later, in private, where a quarrel would not draw attention.

"And did Peredur give you the answer you needed?" he asked.

Devlin nodded, a grim smile on his face. "Yes. And he has agreed to bear witness when I pass judgment on Muireann."

He supposed it would be useful to have one of her own present, to see that all was done in accordance with the law. Though it was not as if the judgment was in any doubt. Muireann had attacked the Chosen One with the clear intent of killing him. There was no question of her guilt. Nor of her sentence. Death by hanging, her body left to rot on the gibbet as a warning to other potential traitors.

From Peredur's home they made their way to the peacekeepers' compound. Naturally it was located on the other side of the city and required climbing and descending several steep hills. But though his own calves ached, and he began to suspect that the Caerfolk were part goat, Didrik was pleased to see that the escort showed no signs of flagging, and even in the most narrow and crowded streets, they kept a tight formation around Devlin, ensuring that no one had the opportunity to try another attack.

They found Chief Mychal in the training yard, watching as one of the peacekeepers used a stuffed leather dummy to demonstrate the proper use of a wooden cudgel against an enemy. As she spoke, her words were punctuated by sharp blows, and the trainees watched with rapt attention.

Here the peacekeepers carried cudgels rather than swords, yet the training methods were much the same, and Didrik felt an unexpected wave of homesickness. It seemed a lifetime ago since he had stood in a similar practice yard, hoping for nothing more than to beat some sense into the heads of green recruits. And far longer since the days when he had nothing more to worry about than learning the sword drills and hoping to avoid his sergeant's wrath.

Devlin caught his eye and jerked his head in the direction of their escort, and Didrik instructed Ensign Hrolfsson to wait at the edge of the field.

Chief Mychal came over to them. "All went well?" His gaze surveyed Devlin from head to foot as if he expected to see some physical sign of the magic that had been performed.

"Ismenia was successful," Devlin said. "I am in her debt. And yours."

"No," Mychal said, with a hasty gesture of his right hand, meant to avert ill luck. "What is between you and Ismenia is wizardly business and I want no part of that."

"Fair enough. But I need your help in another matter. Kollinar is sending the prisoner Muireann over, to be held by you until I pass judgment."

"Indeed?" Chief Mychal's bushy eyebrows seemed likely to crawl into his scalp.

"There is more. I need everything you have found on Muireann of Tannersly. Including her family and kin."

Chief Mychal gave one short nod. "We should talk. In private."

"Agreed."

They spoke in the trade tongue, but there were undercurrents to their words that Didrik did not understand. He realized that Devlin was indeed plotting something. Something he had not seen fit to share with Didrik.

It was no comfort to realize that Stephen and even Lord Kollinar were most likely just as much in the dark as Didrik was. It troubled him to see Devlin turning to these strangers for advice rather than trusting in those who had proven their loyalty to him time and time again.

"Nils Didrik is my shield arm, and a lieutenant of the Guard in Kingsholm. Perhaps you could have someone show him around while we finish our discussion," Devlin said.

It was a public dismissal, and Didrik had had enough. He would not be treated in this fashion, and he no longer cared that there were witnesses to their disagreement. "Devlin, I will not—"

"Later," Devlin said. "Explanations now will take too long, and I do not want to waste Chief Mychal's time."

Didrik clenched his right hand into a fist, channeling his anger. "You will tell me everything you are planning."

"I will explain to you and Stephen both. Later."

Chief Mychal called over to the woman who had been leading the training drill. One of the students took her place, and she trotted across the field to where they were standing.

She came to a halt in front of Chief Mychal, drew herself to attention, then stamped one booted foot in what he supposed was a kind of salute. She was tall for a woman, perhaps an inch taller than Didrik, and solidly built. Her dark hair was cut very short and stuck up in spikes as if she were some kind of wild creature. She took a quick look at the visitors, then focused her attention on her commander, as was proper.

"Saskia, this is Lieutenant Didrik, who Devlin tells me is a peacekeeper in his own country. I ask that you treat him as a guest while Devlin and I confer."

"Of course," Saskia said, with a nod. But her attention was on Devlin as she added, "Gentle heart, it has been too many years."

Devlin flushed under her scrutiny. "Much has changed since I saw you last."

"When the news came we held vigil for her. The entire band," Saskia said.

"She would have liked that," Devlin said, and only one who was watching him closely could see him wince. Didrik was not surprised when Devlin caught Chief Mychal's eye, and without further ceremony the two began walking away.

Saskia watched them for a moment, then turned her attention to Didrik, eyeing him as if he were a potential suspect in a series of crimes.

"You are a long way from home. Tell me, do your Peacekeepers have weapons like this?" She twirled the cudgel in one hand, as if it were a mere toy rather than a lethal instrument.

"Cudgels are known, but not common," Didrik said. He would not insult her by telling her that in his land only the poorest criminals used wooden cudgels. "We carry the short sword on patrol and train with a shield for riots. The spear is used for ceremonial guard duty."

"And your most uncomfortable uniforms, no doubt.

Here we are lucky, for the army provides ceremonial guards for the governor. Our duty is merely to keep the peace within the city and bring lawbreakers to judgment."

"A worthy task." Especially considering their small numbers. Including novices, there were fewer than a hundred peacekeepers, responsible for keeping order in a city where ten thousand people crowded into a space meant to hold only half that number. Even with twice as many peacekeepers, they would be hard-pressed.

Were Didrik in charge, he would not feel comfortable until he had at least two hundred fully trained peacekeepers to depend on. As well as assurances that the army garrison could be placed under his command in times of civil unrest.

"It is too cold to stand here idly, and I would not have it said that I shirked my duty. Come, and let me show you how we do things here. If Devlin ever tires of your service, perhaps I can persuade you to join us instead," Saskia said with a grin. "After all, you took one of our own, so it is only fair that Jorsk sends us a sword arm in return."

She led him across the muddy training field where the novices were now being led in strengthening exercises, their breaths steaming in the frosty air. Showing either thorough dedication to her duty or a strange sense of humor, Saskia insisted on showing him everything, from the weapons storeroom to the sleeping quarters where the novices were housed. Even the washroom came in for consideration.

Didrik made the appropriate comments, but his mind was elsewhere. His companion appeared not to notice his lack of enthusiasm and took him from the washroom to the kitchen, which was housed in a separate building because of the risk of fire. He wondered what was keeping Devlin. Were he and Chief Mychal discussing Devlin's mysterious scheme? Or had the prisoner arrived and were they questioning her?

"A sound practice, don't you agree?"

Didrik blinked and realized that he had lost the thread of Saskia's narration.

"Of course," Didrik said.

Saskia laughed. "I just told you that we butcher our failed trainees and serve them to the others, as a means of encouraging success."

Didrik returned her smile. "My sergeant told me never to waste anything. But I don't think that is quite what he meant."

He was fortunate that rather than being offended, Saskia had chosen to be amused by his lapse.

"Have you seen enough?"

"Yes. I apologize for my inattention. Under different circumstances I would indeed be interested in comparing our two forces—"

"But now you are thinking about Devlin, and whatever it is that he and Mychal are plotting between them," Saskia said.

He had not known he was that obvious.

Saskia spoke briefly to the cook, who disappeared into an adjacent room and came back and handed Saskia a cloth-wrapped bundle that smelled like freshly baked bread.

"The seniors have their own room in the main building," Saskia said. "From there we will have a clear view of the corridor leading to Chief Mychal's office, so we will know when they are finished."

"Let us go."

She had already shown him the peacekeepers' headquarters, but this time she led him to a small room that held two square tables and a dozen wooden chairs pushed up against the wall. Saskia set the cloth bundle on the table and hung their cloaks on pegs. Didrik brought over two chairs and positioned them so that both would have an unobstructed view of the door, while Saskia walked over to a wooden cabinet and came back with two tall glasses and a ceramic jug. Removing the stopper from the jug, she filled a glass with dark liquid.

"Thank you but no," Didrik said, as she began to push the glass in his direction. "I do not drink while I am on duty."

"Neither do I," Saskia said. "This is false ale. Sweet, but not intoxicating."

Didrik took a careful sip. It was indeed sweet, and lacked the gritty texture that he associated with Caer ale. He took another sip, and decided it was a fair enough drink for those who had never heard of citrine.

Saskia poured herself a glass, then unwrapped the cloth bundle, revealing two flattened round loaves of dark wheat. These he recognized, for they were usually filled with sausage and cheese and made a good meal for those who were too busy to stop for proper food.

He accepted the roll she handed him and bit into it eagerly. His years in the Guard had taught him never to refuse a meal for you never knew when duty would call you away.

As he ate, his eyes wandered around the room. It was a cozy place, with a small fireplace and two windows high up in one wall that let in a surprising amount of sunlight. The wooden chairs showed signs of hard use, for more than one had newer wood where a leg or back had been mended. The oak tabletop was marred with rings from the glasses, as well as a dark stain that looked like someone had once turned over an inkwell.

His gaze kept returning to the door, and he noticed that the wooden frame around the entryway was curiously marked. The wood appeared pockmarked in some places and nearly rotted through in others.

Recognition dawned and he nodded. "Knives," he said.

Saskia followed his gaze. "The throwing knives. We used to hold contests here, till Ullmer got drunk and missed the target. His knife went into the hall, and clipped the ear of a messenger."

He winced, and his right hand went up to touch his ear, without conscious volition. "The messenger?"

"The messenger kept his ear, but Mychal forbid us to play in here. Now we must hold our contests in the barracks, or in the taverns."

"We had trouble as well with our younger guards," Didrik said. "Fortunately Devlin intervened before there were serious injuries."

"He was a rare one for the game. He could hit a target the size of a bird's eye from twenty paces," Saskia mused. "Not even Cerrie could match him."

"What was Cerrie like?" It was something he had long wondered about, for Devlin almost never mentioned his wife.

"She was bold, brash. Hot-tempered, but a loyal friend. Proud, too. She could have had any man she wanted, and when Devlin began to court her, none thought it would last. He was a jeweler of all things. He seemed too soft, too gentle, to be a match for her. I wagered she'd be bored with him in a month. But he surprised us all, and within a year I was holding her sword at their wedding."

Soft? Gentle? It did not seem possible that she was describing the same man he had come to know. Not that Devlin was a cruel man, but there was a core of steel inside him that none who met him could mistake. Devlin could be ruthless when the occasion required. But he asked no sacrifices of others that he was not willing to make himself.

"It must have come as a shock when you heard he was the Chosen One," Didrik said.

Saskia looked at her hands, seeming surprised to find that only crumbs remained from the sausage loaf.

"He may carry a sword these days, but he is still no warrior," Saskia said. "Not like us."

"What do you mean?"

"You and I, we take our chances. We understand that life is short, and that death may find us at any time. Cerrie understood that as well. She knew the risks. She was in a wild place, where no one had lived for nearly two centuries. And yet she went outdoors, unarmed. She was careless, and it cost her her life."

For Devlin's sake, he felt obliged to defend Cerrie. "Even if she had had a sword, or a bow, it might have made no difference. Others perished on that day, and surely some of them had weapons."

"But none of them had her training. If anyone could have slain the creatures, it was Cerrie," Saskia insisted. "You never knew her, but she was a fierce fighter. Deadly skill wedded to a great heart."

"And what of Devlin? In the end, he was the one who killed the banecats."

"If he had been there on that day, he would have perished trying to protect his family. He only became dangerous when he had nothing to lose. He was a berserker. Not a warrior."

"Once that may have been true," Didrik admitted. Even when Devlin had first been named as Chosen One, he had behaved more like a berserker than a calculating warrior. But since then Devlin had grown into his role and proven his fitness to lead. "I can only speak of the man I know. The Chosen One has proven himself as a warrior and as a leader. I will gladly follow him against our enemies, regardless of the odds."

"And do these enemies go by the name of the Children of Ynnis?"

Would that matters were so simple. "We did not come here looking for a quarrel with the Children of Ynnis. They are the ones who provoked us—first by stealing the sword, then by trying to assassinate Devlin. Once we retrieve the sword we will leave. Devlin's true duties lie back in Jorsk."

"How can one sword be so important?"

Didrik shrugged. "That is not my story to tell."

"If Devlin needs a new sword, why doesn't he simply forge a new one? He is a master at his craft. Look."

Saskia withdrew the dagger from her belt and handed it to him. He turned it over in his hands, noting that the dagger had a decorative swirling pattern etched down the center of the blade. Testing the edge with his thumb revealed that it was extremely sharp, and there were neither nicks nor flaws to be seen.

"True steel," Saskia said.

Her words reminded him that imported steel was rare here, and nearly as precious as gold.

"When Cerrie was named sergeant, Devlin made these for her band. Each one unique, the hilt fitted to the owner's grip, our names etched on one side of the blade, and the name of our unit on the other."

He looked more closely at the blade and saw that the curving swirls did indeed resemble the few pieces of Caer script he had seen.

"Fine work," Didrik said, handing the dagger back to her. "But we need the sword that was lost. Not a copy."

There was no reason to tell her that Devlin would never again create such deadly beauty. Even if he had the inclination to resume his former craft, his crippled right hand meant that he was no longer able to do such intricate work.

There was no telling what great works Devlin would have created, had he stayed in Alvaren and remained a metalsmith. Duncaer's loss was Jorsk's gain, for in losing a jeweler, they had gained a champion.

A smith could make the swords, but it took a General to lead those swords into battle and ensure that they were used wisely.

Twenty-five

IT TOOK AN ENTIRE DAY FOR DEVLIN TO MAKE the necessary arrangements, but by the second morning after the ritual he was ready to meet with the woman who had attacked him.

He paused at the gate that led to the peacekeepers' compound and turned to Lord Kollinar. "Our escort will wait here," he said.

"I do not like this," Kollinar muttered, but then he gave the necessary orders.

Devlin waited until the soldiers had taken up their positions under the watchful eyes of the two peacekeepers who guarded the gates to their compound. As Kollinar returned to his side, he gestured for him to come closer.

"A final word with you," he said. Kollinar's temper did not worry him, but he must have the governor's obedience. Any sign of dissension would ruin the scheme.

As the governor came to stand at his right side, Stephen and Didrik took a few steps back, out of courtesy. Though the minstrel, at least, was still within earshot.

"I will have your pledge that no matter what I say or do, you will obey whatever orders I give. Without question or sign of hesitation. Do you understand?"

"I am the King's representative in this place. I will act according to my duties, as I see fit," Kollinar replied.

It was not enough. He needed the governor's cooperation to make his plan work. Even Stephen and Didrik had seemed skeptical when he had outlined his intentions to them. But they at least trusted his judgment and his knowledge of his people. They would back him, despite their misgivings.

The governor was a different matter. He still thought as a Jorskian, despite his long years in Duncaer. There was no time to make him understand. But Devlin would settle for blind obedience if that was what it took to succeed.

"You will obey me, or I will strip you of your rank and send you home to Jorsk in disgrace."

"You cannot do that. King Olafur appointed me—"

"And the Gods named me Chosen One and gave me the power to speak in the King's name. Only he can countermand one of my orders. If you disobey me, I promise that you will regret it to the end of your days. Am I understood?"

Kollinar seemed to shrink before his eyes. "I will obey. But I pray to all the Gods that you know what you are doing."

Devlin began walking toward the gate, and after a moment Kollinar fell in step beside him, with Stephen and Didrik following behind.

As he led them into the peacekeepers' barracks, he

noticed Lord Kollinar glancing around with curiosity. He realized this might be the first time the governor had ever set foot in the building.

Tobias, who stood second in rank to Commander Mychal, was waiting in the hall outside the peacekeepers' assembly room. As Devlin approached, he drew himself to attention and stamped his right foot in salute. It was a sign of respect, and Devlin wondered if the salute was for him or in recognition of the governor's presence.

"General, those you requested are within," Tobias said.

"Good," Devlin said. He squared his shoulders and took a deep breath.

The dining tables had been pushed back to one side and the assembly room arranged as a hall of justice, with a single long table in the center of the room. At one end of the table sat the prisoner Muireann, with two peacekeepers standing watch beside her. On the left-hand side sat the elderly lawgiver Peredur, the book of justice lying open on the table before him. Next to Peredur was his apprentice Jasper. Commander Mychal sat next to the assistant, and there was an open seat for Tobias.

On the right side of the table were three empty seats for Devlin's witnesses, and the empty space at the foot of the table was for Devlin himself.

Devlin paused at the entryway to the room and waited till he was the center of all eyes. Then he removed his cloak, revealing that he wore not the uniform of the Chosen One but rather simple trousers and a tunic shirt, in the same style he had worn as a metalsmith. He waited as the others stripped off their own cloaks before waving them to their places.

By custom Devlin did not sit, but rather stood in his place. After some prodding by her gaolers, Muireann rose to her feet as well.

"Honored Magistrate, I thank you and your apprentice for coming here to witness justice being served," he said.

Peredur pursed his thin lips, giving his face a skeletal appearance.

"My rulings have no standing in Jorskian courts," he said. The reminder was for form's sake, for all present understood that the laws of Jorsk took precedence.

"That I well know," Devlin said. "By the laws of Jorsk the Chosen One may pass justice both High and Low, and I will do so here today."

Peredur's eyes widened in comprehension. After their conversation yesterday, he, at least, must have an inkling as to what Devlin had planned. Though the news that Devlin was a lawgiver in the eyes of the Jorskian courts was likely a surprise.

"I am not afraid of you, nor of your justice, Cursed One," Muireann said. Her week in captivity had done nothing to improve her manners or to blunt the edge of her defiance.

"It is not the Chosen One's justice you need fear," Devlin said. "As Chosen One, I relinquish all claims for justice against this woman. I declare her innocent of treason."

Lord Kollinar hissed, and opened his mouth to speak. Didrik elbowed him sharply in the ribs, and with a furious glare, Lord Kollinar subsided.

"This is a trick," Muireann said.

"No trick. I call on Governor Kollinar, as the King's representative in Duncaer, to witness my judgment. I will scribe the orders myself."

"But she tried to kill you—" Commander Mychal broke in. "We have witnesses."

"Indeed. The Chosen One has declared her innocent of treason. But Devlin of Duncaer accuses her of attempted murder."

Peredur nodded, but his apprentice's jaw dropped, the pen falling from his slack fingers and rolling across the table until caught by Stephen. With a sympathetic glance, Stephen rose to his feet and handed the pen back to the stunned Jasper.

"You cannot do this," Muireann said. "You are nothing. You are no one."

But there she was wrong, and it would prove her undoing. Indeed it had taken Devlin himself far too long to see the truth. For weeks now he had struggled with what it meant to have returned to Duncaer as the Chosen One and the General of the Royal Army. When in fact, the answer to his dilemma was far simpler.

But merely because it was simple did not make it easy. Indeed, the scheme that Devlin proposed was a high-stakes gamble. If he lost, he would forfeit more than the sword.

"Alanna, a weaver of Kilbaran, wife of Murchadh the smith, daughter of Mari, claims me as her brother. In the name of our kin, I call for justice."

Devlin of Duncaer could do what the Chosen One could not. He could invoke the full weight of Caer justice, bringing down on Muireann's head the one thing she feared more than mere death.

And to think that in his madness he had nearly

thrown away the gift that Alanna had given him when she called him brother. He had gone so far as to begin writing the orders that would have ordered Murchadh seized for questioning. Were it not for the interruption by the wizard Ismenia, he might well have done the unthinkable.

Muireann turned to face Peredur, tugging on the lawgiver's robes. "This cannot be true. He is kinbereft."

Peredur pulled his sleeve free from her grasp. "Two years ago, Alanna claimed this man as kin, and so it is recorded in the book of her family. I have spoken with the sister of her brother's wife, who lives here in Alvaren, and she has confirmed his claim."

Devlin had spent hours wrestling with this plan, wondering how Alanna would react when she learned how he had used the gift of kinship that she had bestowed upon him. Was it too much to hope that she would understand why he was doing this? Or would she be so horrified by his actions that she would renounce him, making him kinless once again?

In the end he had realized that he must place his trust in his friends. The strength of a man was not solely within himself. It rested in those whom he claimed as kin and friends. He had placed his trust in Didrik and Stephen, and they had helped him break free of the mind-sorcerer's spell. Now he would place his trust in the kinweb.

"But—" she began.

"Muireann of Tannersly, you attacked me without warning, without invoking the rituals of protection or notifying kin or judge," Devlin said. "In doing this you have dishonored yourself, and I invoke the right of blood feud."

"He cannot do this," Muireann protested.

"It is his right," Mychal said calmly. Then again, he had had a full day to accustom himself to the idea.

Didrik and Stephen exchanged glances. Lord Kollinar's earlier anger had given way to a thoughtful expression as he witnessed Caer justice in action.

Peredur nudged his assistant, who dipped the pen in the inkwell and handed it to him.

Devlin licked his lips, which were suddenly dry, and said the ritual words. "I, Devlin of Duncaer, brother of Alanna, call for justice. May each drop of blood you shed be repaid a hundredfold upon your kin. This I swear in the name of Haakon."

"You cannot do this," Muireann said. Her eyes darted around the room, as if seeking escape, but there was none to be found. She had dug this trap with her own actions, and now she must live with the consequences.

"Think of those who call you kin," she pleaded. "Would you really do this to them? Is this Alanna ready to see her children slaughtered?"

Devlin knew he would never forgive himself if any harm came to Alanna or Murchadh. And yet the declaration of blood feud could not be a bluff. Muireann must believe that he was fully prepared to invoke the feud and accept the consequences.

"You know as well as I that children are exempt from blood feud," Devlin countered. Though in truth this was scant comfort. Blood feuds were so rare because the outcomes could be horrific. A blood feud could rage for years, as one act of violence begat another. Declan was only eight now, but in six years he would be fourteen, and no longer a child in the eyes of the law.

And should the feud continue even longer, then

Devlin's brother's children could be sacrificed as well. For when he had instructed the peacekeepers to discover Muireann's lineage, he had made a troubling discovery. Muireann's mother was near cousin to Agneta's mother, and thus she counted Cormack and Agneta's children as kin. Farkin perhaps, but close enough that they would one day be targets in a feud.

He wondered what tales she might have heard from Agneta and whether those had played any part in her decision to attack him.

But now was not the time for fruitless speculation, or dwelling on the past. It was the time to clear his mind of all distractions and focus his will on the matter at hand. He could not let Muireann see any chinks in his armor.

"I, Devlin of Duncaer, brother of Alanna, call for justice. May each drop of blood you shed be repaid a hundredfold upon your kin. This I swear in the name of Haakon," he said, repeating the ritual invocation.

Once he said the words for the third time, there would be no going back. Blood would be shed, until one clan or the other was destroyed.

"I beg you, do not do this," Muireann said, wringing her hands. All traces of her earlier defiance had fled.

"Restore to me the sword that is mine and I will forswear vengeance."

"I cannot do that."

"Then think well on Ysobel's fate. Is there one man or woman alive who bears a drop of her blood in their veins?"

As he named the treacherous last Queen of Duncaer, the peacekeepers made the hand sign to avert ill luck. Ysobel's lust for power had precipitated the events that led to the Jorskian invasion, and none would wish to suffer her fate.

"I do not have the sword," Muireann insisted.

"Then you can take a message to those that do," Devlin said. This had been his goal all along. "Arrange for them to meet me, under truce."

"I do not know who took the sword. When I attacked you, I acted alone. No one gave me orders."

For a moment he hesitated. What if she was telling the truth? The threat of blood feud was meant to make her reveal those who held the sword. But if Devlin invoked blood feud only to discover that she truly was ignorant, he would have condemned countless innocents to their deaths.

"You told me that the Children of Ynnis were your family," Didrik said. "Surely one knows the names of those you call kin."

Her own words had condemned her.

"The choice is yours," Devlin said. "You will agree to arrange a meeting with the Children of Ynnis. Or I will invoke my rights, under our laws."

"I will not betray my friends," Muireann said.

"Then by your words and deeds you have betrayed your kin." He nodded to Peredur, who took pen in hand, preparing to record the declaration of blood feud. His pulse pounded in his ears, so loud he could scarcely think. But he forced himself to begin the third ritual declaration that would seal all their fates. "I, Devlin—"

"Wait!" she shouted. Her shoulders sagged and she braced her arms on the table, leaning on them to keep her upright. "I will do as you say."

He felt nearly dizzy with relief.

"You have until sunset tomorrow to arrange for me to meet with those who hold the sword that is rightfully mine. I will meet them before midnight, in a place of their choosing. They will prove their good faith by swearing an oath of hospitality and bringing the sword with them."

"And then you and your soldiers will swoop down on them and seize the sword."

The idea held merit, but the Children of Ynnis would never agree to meet with him if they suspected treachery. Instead he would have to hold to his oath and hope they held to theirs.

"I will pledge to abide by the laws of our people. No harm will come to those who meet with me if they act with honor."

"And as for me?"

"If you do not return to me with news of this meeting by sunset tomorrow, I will finish the blood oath. If you betray me in any way, Peredur will see that news of your treachery reaches my kin, and they will finish what I have begun here on this day. But if you act in honor, once I have met with the Children of Ynnis, Devlin of Duncaer will set aside his grievance with you."

"Do you understand what Devlin has proposed?" Peredur asked.

"Yes."

"And do you agree to his terms?"

Muireann nodded.

"Then so shall it be written," Peredur said.

"You are free to leave," Devlin said.

She shook her head as if to clear it, then straightened herself to her full height and shot Devlin a look filled with venom. Stepping carefully around the peacekeepers who had been her captors, she made her way from the room without a backwards glance.

Suddenly weary, Devlin abruptly sat down. He could feel his legs trembling, not from fatigue but from sheer relief. He had never expected that he would have to issue the second invocation, but Muireann had proven herself made of stern stuff indeed.

There was a moment of silence, broken only by the faint scratching of pen across parchment as Peredur recorded the agreement.

Lord Kollinar was the first to speak.

"Is that it? She just walks out of here, free?" Lord Kollinar turned to Commander Mychal, as if looking for confirmation. "Tell me that you have men following her, at least."

"No followers," Devlin said. "She has parole until sunset tomorrow."

"But why? What makes you think she will return rather than simply fleeing the city?" Kollinar asked.

"Because if she does not return, Devlin will invoke blood feud. And that will mean death for her brother, sisters, parents, and cousins," Chief Mychal explained.

And that was only the beginning. Blood feuds once started were nearly impossible to stop—for both sides must agree to call an end to the feud. Yet once the killing had started, each side would have their own tally of dead and grievously wounded, whose souls would demand revenge. If a feud was not stopped in the early days, the voices of the dead would outweigh any counsel of reason, and the feud would continue until one side or the other was destroyed.

"And anyone can invoke such a claim? Surely there

must be laws against the killing of innocents," Stephen said.

"Blood feud is rare," explained Peredur. "I myself have witnessed only two in my lifetime. But it is within the provision of the law when one person attacks another without warning."

And therein lay Muireann's mistake. She had seen Devlin as belonging to Jorsk and had struck at him without ceremony. By Jorskian law, she had earned herself a traitor's death, though surely she had seen herself as a martyr. If Devlin had truly been kinbereft, he would have had no recourse under the law of his people.

Muireann would never have been so careless as to attack one of their own without warning. Even if he was suspected of being a traitor, he still deserved the ritual warning. Or she would have taken the precaution of disowning her kin and protecting them from possible retribution. But in her arrogance she had done neither, thereby leaving herself open to the full weight of his vengeance.

Stephen turned his attention to Devlin. "I know you. It is not within you to harm the innocent along with the guilty. You knew that she would give in, rather than let you invoke the feud."

Stephen's words were comforting, but they were false. Even now, Devlin did not know if he would have had the strength to say the words that would have completed the third and final invocation of justice. Would he really have sacrificed his newfound kin in order to win back the sword of the Chosen One? If the feud had been declared, he could have sent a messenger to Commander Willemson, ordering him to take Murchadh's family under protection. But it would have been impossible for him to protect every member of Alanna's kin. Some would have been slain, just as he would have been forced to kill members of Muireann's kin.

Already his hands were stained with innocent blood, from those he had failed to protect as Chosen One. How many more deaths would be charged to his soul?

But for now he had done all he could do. Muireann, at least, believed that he was ready to invoke the awful weight of the blood feud. What happened next was up to her. Either she would lead him to those who held the sword, or she would betray her promise and force him to finish what he had begun.

Twenty-six

THE LEGENDARY SWORD OF LIGHT WAS PROPPED up carelessly against the far wall, half-hidden by linen wrappings. From the moment he had stepped inside the room, Devlin had felt the sword as if it were a living presence. Even before the sword had been unwrapped, he had known that it was what he had sought. His right hand had ached to touch it, a ghostly pain that reminded him of the fingers he had lost.

But the Children of Ynnis had withdrawn the sword before he could lay hands on it, and now it was out of his reach as he attempted to reason with these rebels.

A tavern had been chosen as neutral ground, and the owner paid a silver latt to make herself scarce. Peredur had agreed to act as host, and it was to him that they made their pledges.

The Children of Ynnis had pledged to respect the safety of Devlin and his companions, and in return he had promised that there would be no attempt made to arrest the Children of Ynnis. He merely wished proof that they held the sword, and a chance to negotiate personally for its return.

A part of him hoped that those who held the sword were not the same folk who had killed Ensign Annasdatter. It was one thing to ransom a sword, but another thing entirely to let killers walk free. Especially since the killer bore the responsibility for four deaths—if one counted the three innocent Caerfolk who had been executed in retaliation for Annasdatter's murder.

The sword was the only weapon visible, both parties having agreed to come unarmed. Devlin had left his sword with the tavern keeper, and his throwing knives had been left behind in his chambers. Didrik was unarmed, as Stephen appeared to be, though he had noticed that Stephen had found several excuses to touch his right boot and had begun to suspect that Stephen had hidden a dagger within.

As for the Children of Ynnis, three of them wore hooded cloaks and leather masks that covered the top halves of their faces, obscuring their features. Anything could be hidden within their voluminous cloaks. Muireann, alone, wore no mask, and her tunic and trousers had no obvious place for a concealed weapon.

The meeting had begun with the Children of Ynnis giving a rambling denouncement of the Jorskian occupation and condemning Devlin as a traitor for having sworn allegiance to the oppressors of his people. He had let them have their say, and then attempted to reason with them. But after nearly an hour, he had begun to despair.

"The sword belongs to our people. It is a trophy of war," Fist declared. Despite the fierce name, he was a slightly built man with a deep bass voice that rightly belonged to someone with a much larger frame. His cheeks and chin were scraped red, as if he had recently shaved off a beard.

"The sword is mine, by right of inheritance," Devlin countered. "By the law and custom of our people, it belongs to me, and those who took it are no more than thieves."

"You are no longer one of our people," Heart said. She had done most of the speaking so far. A young woman, perhaps Stephen's age, she accompanied her tirades with extravagant hand gestures. He had noticed that both hands bore small white scars, and her left arm had a long dark red line from a recent burn. The marks of a metalsmith, which meant she was likely the one who had taken the sword. It also showed that she was unused to conspiracy, for a cunning person would have worn gloves to cover the identifying marks.

"Devlin has been claimed as kin," Peredur commented.

The young woman tossed her head, a nervous gesture made ridiculous by the hood she wore. "He may have kin ties, but in his heart he is no longer one of us."

This was getting him nowhere. He turned his attention to the third member of the Children of Ynnis, the one who had been named as Memory. So far he had spoken little, yet from their postures the others seemed to defer to him. At a guess he was older, nearer Devlin's own age than the other two, who showed the hot-headed impetuousness of youth.

It was possible that Memory was indeed the leader of the Children of Ynnis, or if not their leader, then certainly someone in a position of power. Mychal had described the Children of Ynnis as being a collection of loosely connected bands rather than a cohesive organization. But their recent actions indicated new leadership had taken over. And while it was unlikely that they would allow their ultimate leaders to take the risk of meeting with Devlin, at least one of those present had to be in the position to negotiate on behalf of the Children of Ynnis. His guess was that Memory was that person, and it was he whom Devlin hoped to convince.

"I ask you, as a man of honor, to return to me what is mine," Devlin said, focusing his attention on Memory. "I will pay two gold disks as ransom price, and grant amnesty for the attack upon me."

"And we have told you, we have no use for your gold. Nor for your pardons," Fist said.

"It is you who should beg pardon of us," Heart proclaimed. "Your sins are many, but you may yet be redeemed. Renounce your traitorous allegiance and join with us in overthrowing our oppressors."

He could not believe the foolishness of the woman, in urging him to betray his allegiance while in the presence of his friends. Either she thought them both ignorant of the Caer tongue, or she was arrogant beyond all measure.

"Join? With you?" It would have been humorous, did he not sense that she was deadly serious in her delusion. "You'd be dead in a week. A fortnight at the most," he told her flatly.

"The Children of Ynnis are not without resources, and there are many who sympathize with our cause. If you joined us, others would surely follow," Memory said.

"I will not lead my people to their deaths."

"Have you so little faith in the people that bore you?

We have steel weapons and the skill to use them," Fist said.

"And we are not afraid to die," Heart added.

Devlin flexed his right hand to relieve the ache. "Weapons you have, I will grant you that. But only someone who has never fought for her life could speak so casually of death."

"With your help or without—" Fist began.

"With or without me you will die. And thousands of others will perish as well, paying the price for your foolishness." Devlin leaned forward, fixing the full weight of his gaze on young Fist. "Tell me, when you were spending your foreign gold, how much food did you buy?"

Fist blinked. "Food?"

"Grain. Roots. Dried fish. How much food do you have?"

Fist shook his head in apparent confusion.

"Who holds the granaries?" Devlin asked.

"The soldiers of Jorsk," Fist said slowly.

"And where does the grain come from that fills them? The wheat for bread? The barley for ale? It comes from the lowlands. From the lands farmed by those of Jorsk."

"What of it? We are talking of our people's freedom, not of crops," Heart scoffed.

"In the old days, we grew enough to feed ourselves. But then the soldiers seized the lowlands and drove the people into the mountains. Many who live in Alvaren once lived elsewhere. Muireann's kin once held a farm on the Kenwye River, isn't that right?"

"Three sisters and their families lived there, growing oats, barley, and flax for linen. The land ran down to the riverbank, and was so fertile that it took all hands working for more than a week to bring the harvest in." Muireann's voice had a cadence that suggested this was a fragment of an oft-told tale.

"What we lost, we will one day regain," Memory said.

"Not by taking up arms. At the first sign of rebellion, the soldiers have orders to set fire to the granaries. The garrisons will seal the passes that lead into the mountains. And then, without the imported grain on which we depend, they can simply starve us out."

Stephen turned his gaze from the rebels to stare at Devlin in shock. Didrik, at least, would have understood, but Stephen seemed horrified at the brutal facts underlying Jorsk's control of Duncaer.

"They would never—" Heart protested.

"They will," Devlin said. "The city folk will be the first to suffer. The sick and the aged will die first. The children will get the best of the food for as long as it lasts. Those who flee the city will roam the hills, slaughtering the sheep meant for wool. The mountain dwellers grow enough to feed themselves, but have little to spare. Faced with the burden of their city kin, they, too, will begin to starve. In six months, those still alive will be begging the Jorskians to return."

Devlin remembered all too well the last time hunger had swept through the city, in the terrible winter nearly twenty years before. Winter had come far earlier than expected, before the granaries had been filled. Food had been scarce, and fevers swept through the city, claiming numerous victims—among them his own parents. By the time spring came, those residents of Alvaren left alive were hollow-eyed shadows of themselves.

Now these fools wished to unleash a horror that would be a hundredfold worse.

"You are lying," Heart declared.

"He speaks the truth," Peredur said. "The governor's standing orders are well-known."

Devlin was surprised at Peredur's interruption, for by tradition a lawgiver remained silent unless asked for his judgment. It was a sign that even Peredur had lost his patience with these fools.

"Playing at rebellion is a child's game," Devlin said. "You may throw away your own life if you choose, but you have no right to drag innocents to their deaths."

Heart bit her lip and turned to look at the senior member of her party.

Devlin pressed home his point. "Those that gave you gold may call themselves friends of freedom, but they care nothing for our people. Their only interest is in causing strife, and in forcing King Olafur to send his troops south, leaving the northern borders undefended. In the end, the rebellion will be crushed, and the deaths will be for nothing."

"There are other ways," Memory said. "I am told you speak in the King's name. You could change the garrison's orders, giving control of the granaries to us. Or you could even order the soldiers to leave Duncaer and return to Jorsk."

"I cannot betray the oath that I have sworn. All I can give you is what I offered. Gold. Amnesty. And a promise that when I return to the King's court I will use what influence I have to try and persuade King Olafur to end the occupation. But before I can do that, you must hand over to me the sword which was bequeathed to me by Master Roric."

"No." Memory's voice was soft, but it was clearly an ultimatum.

Devlin bit back a curse. He had failed. There was to be no peaceful resolution. He had hoped to appeal to their sense of honor, to their desire to avoid bloodshed and the hardships that the search for the sword had already brought to the city. But there was no reasoning with fanatics. Neither Devlin's lawful right to the sword nor the promise of gold had swayed them from their folly.

The sword drew his gaze and he felt again the burning need to touch it. To hold it in his hands. He could take it. The odds were nearly even, four against three, and Didrik was skilled in unarmed combat. Even if one of the rebels had a weapon concealed beneath their robes, it would take time for them to draw it. If he moved swiftly, Devlin could seize the sword before they could stop him.

Such an act would dishonor him, and the pledge he had given. It would be seen as confirmation of all that the Children of Ynnis said about him, that he had indeed forgotten the ways of his people and was unworthy of those who claimed him as kin.

Or he could keep his own hands clean and let another perform the deed. He glanced over at the door where Didrik stood watch, his gaze switching back and forth between Devlin and the rebels. Though Didrik did not speak the Caer tongue, from the tone of their voices he must have understood that the negotiations were not going well. Devlin had but to give the order, and Didrik would give his life to seize the object of their quest.

No matter that Devlin had taken the pledge on behalf of his friends. If he were not the one to seize the sword, he could let the Jorskians take the blame, saying that they had misunderstood the terms of the pledge. And since the sword was Devlin's by right, once in his possession there was no law or custom of either people that would require him to give it up.

It was what the Chosen One would do. Take the sword, regardless of consequences. His friends would understand. They would blame the Geas for forcing him to act against his inclinations. It would be easy.

But it would be wrong. He was more than the Chosen One. More than a puppet of fate or of the hell-born spell. He had reclaimed his soul and his honor, and he would not relinquish them. Not even for the sake of the sword.

"I speak to you now as Devlin of Duncaer, and I ask you one last time to return to me what is mine. The next time we meet, you will meet me as the Chosen One of Jorsk, and I will treat you according to their laws."

"So be it," Fist said, as the others nodded approvingly.

Devlin rose to his feet. He had not won, but the meeting had not been entirely wasted. He now knew for certain that the Sword of the Chosen was still within the city. And Heart, at least, he would recognize again. He could find her through the metalsmiths guild, and once he knew her true name, he would let Jorskian justice take its course.

Devlin turned to Peredur and inclined his head. "Peredur of the lawgivers, I thank you for your hospitality," he said.

"May you journey from here in peace," Peredur said.

"And you as well."

Memory pushed his seat back, and stood as the others followed his lead. Heart went to stand by the sword, resting one hand lightly on the double-barred hilt.

Memory walked around the table, until he stood next to the elderly lawgiver. "Peredur, I thank you for your hospitality," he said.

He reached down and grasped Peredur's arm, helping him rise to his feet. Peredur swayed on his feet, joints protesting his long inactivity, and Memory kept hold of his arm to steady him.

It was a respectful gesture, but something about Memory's proprietary air made Devlin uneasy, and he took a few steps closer to Peredur.

"War is inevitable, you know. It only needs the right spark." The conviction in Memory's voice was chilling, as was the light of fanaticism in his eyes. So much for Devlin's earlier belief that Memory was the most reasonable one of the three.

Abruptly Memory released Peredur, and as the lawgiver faltered, Devlin reached out to steady him. He glanced around, looking for Peredur's staff.

"Devlin! Beware!"

At Didrik's shout he turned, and caught a glimpse of steel as Memory lunged toward him, sword in hand.

Hastily he shoved Peredur to one side and dove to the left as the sword sliced the air where he had stood only a split second before. But the oaken table blocked his retreat, and he found himself trapped. Memory recovered quickly from his lunge, and turned so his sword was pointed straight at Devlin's chest.

The trap had been perfectly executed. By going to Peredur's side, Devlin had placed the Children of Ynnis between himself and his friends. Didrik had exploded into motion as soon as he called his warning, but Fist had moved to intercept him, and he was forced to deal with him. Stephen, his hidden dagger now revealed, was similarly occupied with Muireann. He had no doubt that his friends would triumph, but that would take time. Time he did not have.

Memory came toward him, and as he advanced, Devlin began edging left, along the length of the table. His opponent held his sword as if he knew how to use it. No doubt he expected Devlin to try to flee. If Devlin were to charge instead, he might catch him off guard, and be able to disarm him.

It was a slender hope, but better than none at all.

"Wait," Heart declared, coming to stand at the foot of the table and cutting off his only escape route. In her hand she held the Sword of Light. "True justice calls that he die by his own sword."

She took the sword in her right hand.

He heard a low cry, followed by the thud of a body hitting the floor, but did not know if it were friend or foe who had fallen. All of his attention was focused on his own peril, and he cursed himself for being too honorable to bring a weapon to this gathering. Even a single throwing knife would have tipped the odds in his favor.

Heart's face glowed with excitement as she raised the Sword of Light high over her head, preparing to strike a killing blow. But she was dangerously overbalanced, and he lowered one shoulder, preparing to charge her.

"Die, traitor," she proclaimed.

Then, just as he launched himself at her, she screamed. Her arm jerked as the Sword of Light began

to glow with a strange white light. She was still screaming as his shoulder impacted her midsection, knocking
her against the wall and forcing the air from her lungs.
The sword fell from her hand and Devlin let his mo-
mentum carry him to the floor, grabbing the sword and
rolling under the table to avoid Memory's furious attack. Once clear of the table, he regained his feet, and
stood, the sword in hand.

The Sword of Light lived up to its name, for it continued to glow as if it were white-hot from the forge.
And yet it was cool to his touch, the grip fitting within
his hand as if it had been made for him and him alone.
He traced a pattern in the air, feeling the sword respond
to his command as if he had never been crippled.

Memory glared at him from the other side of the
table as Didrik came to stand at his side, Peredur's now
bloody staff held in his hand. Both Fist and Muireann
lay on the floor, either dead or knocked senseless. Heart
had sunk to the floor, sobbing from the pain of her
burned hands.

Stephen helped Peredur to his feet. The lawgiver
seemed unharmed by his ordeal.

"The sword knows its master," Peredur said, blinking
against the radiance that lit the room as if it were the
noon sun.

"You have proven yourself an oathbreaker and a traitor to the ways of our people," Devlin said. "Surrender
now, and I will leave you to their judgment."

Memory smiled grimly. "You think you have won,
but you have not." He lowered the sword, as if preparing to relinquish it, then suddenly turned it until the
point was resting against his stomach. "I die a hero's
death," he said.

He thrust the sword deep within himself, grunting as the blade sliced into his stomach. He caught and held Devlin's gaze as dark blood began to stain his robe. Then he folded in on himself and collapsed on the ground.

Didrik advanced cautiously, and as he reached Memory, he pulled out the man's sword. Bright red blood gushed from the wound.

"He is still alive," Didrik reported. "But not for long."

Twenty-seven

➤

THE MAN WHO CALLED HIMSELF MEMORY DIED before a healer could be summoned, cursing Devlin with his last breath. His body was taken to the peace-keepers' compound, and once stripped of his conceal-ing mask it did not take long to identify him as Daffyd, son of Jemel, a lore teller who lodged above a tavern in the oldest section of the city. A search of his rooms re-vealed numerous weapons, precisely detailed maps of the city, and a small fortune in gold and silver coins. Even more ominously, a locked chest contained three glass globes of varying sizes, several small bags of herbs, and candlesticks with runes carved along their length. All objects needed to perform ritual magic, much to the disgust of the peacekeepers who discovered them.

As the news spread even those who sympathized with the Children of Ynnis were quick to distance themselves from Daffyd and his followers. Informants led the peacekeepers to the rest of Daffyd's small band, who began rounding them up.

To his surviving attackers, Devlin offered a choice. They could face Caer justice, which demanded that anyone who offered violence while under an oath of hospitality be stripped of all kin ties and exiled. Or they could face Jorskian justice, which called for the death of any who attacked the Chosen One.

Fist and Heart chose Jorskian justice, and Devlin sentenced them to be hanged on the following day.

It was bitterly cold that morning, and Devlin shivered inside his fur-lined cloak as he stood in the square in front of the army garrison, waiting for the sentence to be carried out. He stood on the steps that led into the garrison, a few feet from the fortress wall, from which projected a half dozen gibbets. The two closest had new ropes attached to them and a small wooden platform below.

On his right side stood Lord Kollinar. In the courtyard, on the left side of the gibbets, stood Chief Mychal and the lawgiver Peredur Trucha, who leaned heavily on the arm of his apprentice. They were there as witnesses only and had no official presence, for what was being done today was according to Jorskian law.

At the foot of the stairs stood Stephen and Didrik. Devlin looked down, ostensibly surveying the onlookers, and saw that Didrik was pale but composed. He had insisted on bearing witness, despite Devlin's protests and against the advice of his healer. Fist had been aptly named, for he had broken three of Didrik's ribs before Didrik had knocked him unconscious. A healer of the first rank had been summoned, and he had used his power to fuse the ribs back together. The ribs were sore, but now there was no risk that they would puncture a lung. Still, he had urged Didrik to rest in bed for a full day after the healing, advice Didrik had ignored.

Devlin had nearly ordered him to stay behind, but then relented. He, too, was prone to ignoring the advice of healers when it suited him, and he could hardly fault Didrik for doing the same.

The prisoners had already been brought to the raised platform under the wall, their hands bound behind them. Dozens of soldiers formed a human wall around the gibbet and the official dignitaries, in case of trouble. But there were no signs of disturbance, and only a handful of folk had come to witness the executions.

Devlin forced himself to watch impassively as the linen ropes were affixed around the necks of the two rebels. There was a moment of fumbling delay as Heart's long hair became entangled in the noose, but eventually all was arranged to the executioner's satisfaction.

He was close enough to see their faces. Fist had apparently availed himself of the numbing drug offered by the soldiers, for his eyes were glassy and his expression slack. It was not clear if he knew what was about to happen to him, and Devlin supposed that was mercy, of a sort.

It was more mercy than Fist had shown Ensign Annasdatter, for after his capture, Fist had boasted of being her killer. As Fist told the tale, he had interrogated the Ensign for hours, while she gave him information in exchange for the promise that she would be released. But as a man with no honor he'd never had any intention of sparing her, and when he was finished with his questioning he'd strangled her and left her mutilated corpse to be discovered by the watch.

Heart was defiant to the last and had apparently refused the drug. She kept her composure well enough, until the executioner tied back her hair, at which point tears began to roll down her face and her legs started to tremble. Only the soldiers on either side of her kept her upright.

She looked even younger than she was, an apprentice metalsmith who had yet to see her twentieth winter. And now she never would. It was hard not to look at her and think of her as a disobedient child. But in the eyes of the law she was an adult, and responsible for her actions.

The prisoners were forced to take two steps forward until they stood at the very edge of the wooden platform. The executioner looked over to where Devlin and Lord Kollinar stood.

"It is time," Lord Kollinar said.

Devlin drew a deep breath. He forced himself to remember that Fist and Heart had freely chosen the manner of their lives and their deaths. He had met with them in all honor, but they had betrayed their oaths by attacking him. And if he had not stopped their rebellion, they and their leader might have unleashed untold horrors upon his people.

Better that these two should die than the thousands they might have led to their deaths.

"Crevan and Larena," he said, giving their true names, "you have been found guilty of the crime of high treason and sentenced to death by hanging, in accordance with the power granted me by His Majesty King Olafur."

His words were but a formality, for the official sentence had been issued and recorded yesterday.

"One day justice will find you *fearnym* and when it

does my death will be repaid tenfold," Heart declared. It was a brave speech, if one ignored how her voice shook.

Crevan, who now called himself Fist, said nothing.

Devlin waited several heartbeats, until even the murmurs of the onlookers fell silent. Then he nodded to the executioner.

"Let it be done," he said.

As the soldiers relinquished their grasp on her arms, Heart summoned her composure and leapt from the platform. There was a dull crack, and her body jerked as the rope caught her weight. Fist, his wits dulled by drugs, was pushed from the platform by the executioner. His body, too, jerked, then twisted as it swung from the rope.

Devlin forced himself not to look away as the pair stopped twitching, their limp bodies swaying at the end of the long ropes. The executioner had been as skilled as Lord Kollinar claimed, for the specially knotted ropes had killed the prisoners instantly rather than leaving them to endure a slow, suffocating death.

Devlin waited, unblinking, until the executioner confirmed what he already knew.

"The prisoners are dead," the executioner said.

There was a cry of anguish that rose suddenly, then was cut off. Devlin turned, and over the heads of the soldiers he could see an older man being comforted by his son.

Devlin turned back toward the gibbets.

"Justice has been done. Now their bodies will serve as a warning to all others who would contemplate such treason," Lord Kollinar said.

Devlin shook his head. "Cut them down."

"What?"

"Cut them down," Devlin ordered. Bad enough that the image of their dangling bodies would now be added to the horrors that infested his dreams. He did not need to dream about their corpses slowly rotting and falling to bits.

"It is the custom—"

"It is the custom to do as the Chosen One orders," Devlin barked. "Cut them down," he said, his voice raised.

The executioner and his assistants moved swiftly to comply.

Devlin climbed down the stairs, and went over to Chief Mychal.

"See to it that their bodies are returned to their families," he said. "Daffyd's as well, if you can find anyone who will claim him."

"They may not wish to come forward," Chief Mychal said.

It was not as if there was still any doubt as to who the rebels had been. Within hours of their capture all three had been identified and the names of their families recorded. Devlin had promised that he would not seek retribution against their kin, but they might be reluctant to put his word to the test.

"Larena, at least, has a father, if my ears do not deceive me. The others have families as well. They may have failed to teach their children wisdom, but the least they can do is see that they have the proper death rites and pass peacefully into the next realm. See to it that the bodies are claimed or take care of it yourself."

"As you wish," Mychal replied.

After a last disapproving look, Lord Kollinar and his aides disappeared inside the garrison. Peredur was helped to climb into a litter, and he and his apprentice were dispatched to the peacekeepers' compound, along with Chief Mychal. Devlin waited until the bodies of Fist and Heart had been taken down, and then he and his escort made their way across the city.

Once again he stood in the peacekeepers' barracks room, but this time he was a mere witness, as others passed judgment and ensured the sentence was carried out.

To his surprise, Muireann had chosen exile over death. She stood in the center of the room, facing a long table at which seven lawgivers sat. As the most senior, Peredur read the writ of the judgment while the others prepared to record it in their scrolls. Copies would be sent to every corner of Duncaer, so that all would know to shun her.

"Muireann of Tannersly, you have heard the charges against you. Have you anything to say in your defense before I pass judgment?"

"I say again that I had no knowledge of what the others planned. I gave my oath in all honesty. I did not know that they were armed," Muireann said.

It was most likely true. Muireann, alone of the party, had been carrying no weapon. It seemed the others had not trusted her. Questioning the remaining members of Daffyd's band had yielded the information that Muireann had been on the far edges of the group, a known sympathizer, but hardly a member of the inner circle.

Still that did not excuse what she had done.

"Your statement is noted," Peredur said. "But regardless of what was in your heart when you swore the oath, you betrayed that oath when you chose to join the others in their treacherous attack. With my own eyes I witnessed your crime. Do you deny this?"

She shook her head, but did not speak.

"Muireann, we have found you guilty of breaking one of our oldest and most sacred traditions. You have shown yourself to be a person without honor and are no longer fit to live among our people. I declare you kinbereft and order that your name be stricken from the rolls of your clan. You will be given three pieces of silver and must make your way into exile. After three months from this day, if you are found anywhere within Duncaer, you will be summarily executed. Do you understand?"

"I understand." Her voice was steady as the last of the ties that bound her to Duncaer were stripped away.

"So let it be written," Peredur said.

There was a moment of silence, broken only by the faint scratching sounds of pen against parchment.

"Where will you go?" Devlin asked.

"Does it matter?" her voice was sharp.

"I suppose not."

He watched as she picked up the bundle next to her feet, and two peacekeepers escorted her from the room. They would make sure that she left Alvaren without incident, and accompany her for the first seven days of her journey, to ensure that she did not try to turn back.

He wondered what would become of her. She could make her way to the southwest and risk the hardships of the Endless Mountains—the great peaks that made the mountains of Duncaer seem like mere hills. Or she could head north into the Kingdom of Jorsk and try to make her way among the people she despised.

There was a third choice. She could try to remain in Duncaer, hoping not to be discovered. But such would be nearly impossible, for none would offer hospitality to one known as an oathbreaker. At best she could live the life of a wild animal, lurking in the forests, catching only the occasional glimpses of a society that she could never rejoin.

In many ways, it would have been kinder if he had hanged her.

Didrik eased himself down onto the floor, leaning against the wall of the arms' salon. He told himself it was because there was no reason for him to remain standing, but he suspected that he should have paid more attention to the healer's warnings. His legs were tired, and he wondered if he would be up to the long walk back to the governor's residence.

Just a little rest, he told himself, then he would be himself. For the alternative would be the humiliation of a litter, and that he would not endure.

The day had begun before dawn as he dressed and joined the others as they made their way to the garrison to witness the execution of two of Devlin's attackers. Justice had been served, but it was no pleasant thing to watch. Then, over Devlin's protests, Didrik had insisted on accompanying him and Stephen to the peacekeepers' compound to watch as Muireann's sentence was passed.

It still seemed to him that she had gotten off lightly. After all, she had stabbed Devlin, intending to kill him.

And then she had broken her oath and joined with others when they attacked him. Mere exile hardly seemed sufficient punishment for such crimes. Yet watching the faces of the Caerfolk as her sentence was pronounced, he knew they would disagree.

Stephen had been quiet all morning, and afterward had made his excuses, saying that he needed to return to the governor's mansion to prepare for their journey.

Devlin had elected to stay behind, for one last discussion with Chief Mychal, and Didrik, not trusting his legs to carry him back to the residence, had chosen to remain as well. He had listened as Devlin and Chief Mychal discussed the plans for rounding up those members of the Children of Ynnis who had so far escaped the citywide search and what was needed to ensure lasting peace in the city.

It was dry talk, and neither man seemed to have the heart for much discussion. When Chief Mychal asked if Devlin had tried out his newly found sword, Devlin had eagerly accepted his suggestion that he do so, using the peacekeepers' training room.

Didrik followed, and watched as the two men stripped off their overtunics and began to limber up. At first Devlin practiced alone, running through the patterned sword drills. The first time through his strokes were tentative, but the second time through the patterns were swifter, and by his third pass he was executing the patterns with near-perfect form. His face was serene, and his breathing unlabored as he lost himself in the discipline of the ancient forms.

Didrik envied his ability to wipe out the events of this morning with the discipline of practice. Were it not for his injury, he, too, would be trying to work off his anger with exercise. As it was, he could merely watch in envy.

After a half hour of drills, Devlin and Chief Mychal began a friendly bout. They began by simply feeling each other out, in a time-honored rhythm of attack and parry, followed by a pause for the opponents to regroup. It was an interesting match. Mychal was a trifle shorter than Devlin, but he was heavily muscled and wielded the two-handed broadsword as if it were made of wood. His years of experience showed in his controlled movements. Devlin was taller, with a longer reach. The Sword of Light was longer and narrower than a broadsword, and Devlin held it easily in a one-handed grip, as if he had drilled all his life with this weapon.

By now a small crowd had gathered. He heard someone come up beside him, and as he turned he recognized Saskia, his guide from the other day.

"Your master is good," she said, as Devlin's sword slipped under Mychal's guard and came to rest against his throat. "I never would have recognized him."

Didrik winced. Only the most skilled of swordsmen dared duel that closely with sharpened blades. And he knew Devlin was crippled, even if Devlin seemed to have forgotten that fact. But Chief Mychal merely grinned and stepped back, saluting his opponent.

Devlin raised his own sword in salute, then they began to circle each other again. He tossed the sword from his left hand to his right, and back, dazzling the eye, before whirling around and countering Mychal's high stroke with his own. Sparks flew as the two blades met.

"I stand corrected. He is not merely good," Saskia

said, sinking down onto her heels next to him. "Mychal is among our best, and yet Devlin is easily keeping up with him. It is no wonder that he was able to out-duel your Duke Gerhard."

There was a flurry of movement, almost too fast for the eye to follow, and then the participants separated. There was a long vertical slash on the front of Devlin's shirt but he appeared unharmed. The cut seemed to have inspired him, for the next time they met, he sent Chief Mychal's blade flying.

Didrik's head swam with dizziness, and he wondered if he could blame it upon his injuries. But it was more than that. He had just seen a heavy broadsword sent flying as if it were a mere dueling rapier. It should have been impossible. But apparently it was not.

"Gerhard should have killed Devlin," Didrik said. "Devlin was skilled, but Gerhard was our very best. Undefeated. He could have killed Devlin easily in the first minutes of the duel, but instead he decided to make him suffer. To inflict the death of a thousand cuts rather than making a single killing blow."

"A nasty fellow," Saskia said.

Didrik nodded in agreement. He remembered that moment, and how only Captain Drakken's grip on his shoulder had prevented him from violating law and custom and charging to Devlin's defense.

"Gerhard's overconfidence proved his undoing, for when he finally went for the killing stroke, Devlin turned into it and was able to disarm the Duke. The rest you know."

His eyes returned to the dueling pair. Mychal was saluting Devlin, which meant that Devlin had won another round while Didrik's attention was elsewhere.

"Then Devlin has learned much since the duel," Saskia said. "I would not want to stand against him were he to fight in earnest."

He watched as Devlin held the sword in his right hand, executing a riposte that would have been impossible for him only a few days before. No man with half a hand could wield a sword so well. And yet neither the sword nor Devlin himself seemed to remember that he was crippled.

Indeed he had never seen a sword that accommodated itself so well to both one and two-handed grips. It was almost as if the hilt changed itself to be whatever Devlin needed. Though such a thing was surely impossible.

He remembered all the times Stephen had insisted on reciting the heritage of the sword and telling the story of how it had been crafted by a son of the Forge God Egil. Like Devlin, he had scorned such tales, but now he realized that there might be more than a grain of truth in them.

At least it looked like a normal sword. Unlike the first time Devlin had held it, the blade did not glow with white light, nor did the gem in the pommel shine with ruby fire. No doubt such effects were saved for when the Chosen One was fighting for his life, as opposed to mere sparring practice.

Thinking about the sword only intensified the aching in his head, and he decided it was time to change the subject.

"Tell me, do you think the threat is over? Will the Children of Ynnis crawl back into their holes? Or do we need fear others trying to take the place of this Memory and his band?" Didrik asked.

Saskia shrugged. "From what we can tell, there were

only a handful of dedicated fanatics who followed this Daffyd and knew what he intended. There were a few dozen others who sympathized with the cause of liberation, but had no notion that he intended armed rebellion."

"With so few followers how was he able to amass stockpiles of weapons? Even Commander Willemson in Kilbaran had heard of the Children of Ynnis and grown wary."

"With enough money, smugglers will bring in anything. If you want to seek out the real troublemakers, you must find Daffyd's foreign paymaster. Whoever gave him the gold is your true enemy."

But Daffyd had taken his secrets to his grave, as he had no doubt intended. None of the other members of his band had any inkling as to the identity of their foreign patron. Indeed, they had all appeared horrified to realize that Daffyd was using arcane magic rituals to communicate with someone from outside Duncaer.

"Hopefully your people will be less willing to trust foreigners who come bearing gold," Didrik said. "Daffyd was a fool, for if he had succeeded in rebelling, he would have led thousands to their deaths."

"Agreed." Saskia ran one hand through her spiky hair. "But do not expect us to shed any tears on the day that this unseen enemy finally strikes at your heartland."

Her grin was as sharp as a knife, and he felt pleased that she trusted him enough to speak honestly.

"The enemy of your enemy is not necessarily your friend," Didrik warned her.

"True. But that does not make him our enemy either," Saskia said. "If they leave us in peace, we will do the same."

Twenty-eight

AFTER THE PRACTICE BOUT WITH CHIEF MYCHAL, Devlin accepted his invitation to dine with the peacekeepers, and it was late that evening when he and Didrik finally returned to the governor's residence. He spent a few moments speaking with Stephen, who was subdued by the day's events and eager to begin the journey home.

Lord Kollinar had already retired for the evening, and when Devlin tried to see him the next morning, he found that the governor had already left for the garrison. The governor seemed to be avoiding him, and Devlin knew that Kollinar was still angry that his orders regarding the rebels had been overruled. He would have to deal with Kollinar before he left the city.

Putting aside the problem of the governor for the moment, Devlin next sought out Didrik. The lieutenant moved with a stiffness that indicated he had overexerted himself on the previous day, though he claimed to be well enough to see to his duties. But there was no sense in taking chances, so Devlin ordered him to rest and personally oversaw the final preparations for their journey. They had four new mountain ponies, courtesy of the army stables, along with dried meat and fruit for themselves and grain for the horses. Worn tack had been replaced and the ponies newly shod. Saddlebags lined with oilcloth would protect their gear from the winter rains, and new fur capes would keep them warm in the coldest snows.

Satisfied that they were as prepared as they could be for the exigencies of the road, Devlin left orders that the ponies were to be saddled and brought to the residence at first light on the following morning. Then he left the stables and made his way to Lord Kollinar's office.

The past weeks had shown him that while Kollinar was an able administrator, he was unwilling to consider anything outside the narrow realm of his responsibilities. He lacked the imagination necessary to respond to the threats now facing Jorsk. Worse, his troops showed distressing signs of complacency and lacked the discipline that wartime demanded. As a leader of garrison troops, Kollinar was adequate, but in a crisis he would be woefully lacking.

One had only to witness how he had mishandled the outbreak of grain madness. At the first outbreak he should have acted swiftly to identify the source of the contamination and eliminate the tainted grain. Instead the sickness had been allowed to spread until it threatened the very stability of the province.

Not to mention all those who had needlessly died, simply because Kollinar had no wish to report his failings or to beg the King for the permission needed to open the emergency grain stores. Once Devlin realized that such stores were available, he had swiftly given the necessary orders. With luck the new grain would reach the stricken areas in time to stave off more deaths. But such a disaster must never be permitted to happen again.

It was unfortunate that he could not simply replace Kollinar, but there was no one suitable to take over as Marshal in charge of the occupying troops. And only the King could name a new Royal Governor. For now, it would be up to Devlin to make clear what he expected from Kollinar and the troops under his command. And when Devlin returned to Kingsholm, he would use every scrap of influence he had to persuade King Olafur to appoint a new governor for Duncaer.

As the governor's aide ushered Devlin into his office, Lord Kollinar rose hastily to his feet. "My lord, I did not expect to see you until this evening. Is there something amiss?"

"I have just finished the preparations for our journey and wished to speak with you before I left. In private," Devlin added.

Lord Kollinar nodded at his aide, who left, closing the door behind him. He waited until Devlin sat before resuming his own seat.

"You mean to leave tomorrow then?" Lord Kollinar asked.

"Yes."

"And your man is well enough to travel? If not, he is welcome to stay as my guest and leave here when he is fit."

"Lieutenant Didrik is well enough," Devlin said. It would take time for Didrik to regain his full strength, but he could ride, and he refused to be left behind.

Kollinar picked up a scroll from his desk. "Chief

Mychal reports that they have captured the last member of the outlaw band."

Devlin nodded. Mychal had sent a messenger to him as well.

"So I had heard. I suggest that you leave the rebels to the lawgivers for judgment," Devlin said.

"I had planned to do so. Such has been the custom, and it will reassure the people that all will go on as before," Kollinar replied. "I still don't know what this Daffyd hoped to accomplish by killing you. He must have known such an act would turn his own people against him and his followers."

"War," Devlin said flatly. Memory's dying words had revealed as much.

Kollinar looked at him blankly, and Devlin elaborated.

"He knew the army would be forced to avenge my death. He hoped you would see this as an act of war and unleash the full force of the army against the Children of Ynnis. Faced with open warfare, he expected the masses would rally to his cause."

"Even though it was a war they could not win?"

"Even then," Devlin said.

It was the scheme of a madman, made all the more frightening because it might well have worked. Each person that the army arrested or killed would leave behind a web of family and friends who were honor-bound to avenge them. It would take only a few dozen deaths to involve the whole of the city. And then, from there the entire country would be drawn in. And once such a bloody conflagration had begun, it would be nearly impossible to end it.

"Let us hope we have struck a crippling blow by

cutting off the head of the group, and that the rest of these rebels will melt back into the dark corners from whence they came," Lord Kollinar said.

"At the very least we have set back their plans and bought time," Devlin said. "You should have a peaceful spring."

Would that he could say the same for the rest of the Kingdom of Jorsk. It had been weeks since he had had reliable news of the capital, and it would be many more weeks before he returned. The search for the sword had taken him far longer than expected. When he had conceived the trip, he had expected that by this time he would be halfway home. Instead he had yet to start on his return journey.

But he was returning in triumph, and his hand dropped to his side to touch the scabbard that held the Sword of Light. Already it was so much a part of him that it seemed he had never wielded any other blade. Though skeptical by nature, he had begun to suspect that Stephen's tales might well be true. Surely magic had gone into the crafting of the sword, for how else to explain how well it fit Devlin's grip? When he held the sword it was as if his missing fingers had been regrown. Even one-handed, all of his old skills had come back to him, and he had easily defeated his sparring partners.

Surely there could be no better proof that Devlin was indeed the Chosen One, Champion of the Kingdom, and blessed by the Gods. Even his bitterest enemies would be forced to acknowledge his office, and to accept his leadership of the King's Council. Now, finally, he would have the power he needed to defend the Kingdom.

And it was not too late. With hard riding they might

well make the opening of the spring court. Or, if not the opening ceremonies, they would certainly arrive before the council began its true deliberations.

"Before I leave, I have new orders for you and your troops," Devlin said. Given Kollinar's shortcomings, he was leaving nothing to chance. He reached into the pouch at his side and pulled forth a scroll, tied with red ribbon and stamped with the seal of the Chosen One. Kollinar took the scroll in his hand but did not open it.

"If Jorsk is invaded," Devlin began, though privately he thought it was a matter of when, not if. "If invasion comes, and matters are grave, you are to turn over control of the granaries and the garrisons to the peace-keepers. Then you and your troops are to make all haste to Jorsk to join in defense of the homeland. You are not to wait for orders from the capital, but rather to make all haste once you hear of the invasion."

Lord Kollinar's eyes narrowed. "My orders are to hold Duncaer at all costs. Would you have me betray them?"

"If Jorsk falls, you cannot hope to hold Duncaer. Not without the food imports, which will by then be in enemy hands. You will be trapped in the mountains, and if my people do not kill you first, then starvation will."

Kollinar continued to stare at Devlin, as if he suspected some hidden meaning in Devlin's words.

"It will not come to that," Kollinar said.

"So I hope as well," Devlin said. "But it has been many long years since you were in the capital, Lord Governor. Things have changed. Raiders from Nerikaat cross the border with impunity, and when the spring thaws come, we may well lose Ringstadt. Pirates have decimated the shipping that forms Myrka's lifeblood, and only this past summer we fought off an invasion force that sought to land in Korinth. And those were but mere skirmishes. I fear our enemy has yet to show his true strength."

"I do not believe matters are as grave as you paint them."

"So speaks a man who was only a hairbreadth away from an armed uprising that would have destroyed this very city," Devlin said.

Kollinar flushed. "I would never have let it come to that."

Such arrogance was incredible. "It still might. The peacekeepers will be on their guard, but you must be as well. Daffyd's paymaster is still out there. He may have failed this time, but that does not mean he has given up. Until we have achieved a decisive victory, none of us can rest."

"Then I must hope that you are able to fulfill your task and defeat this unseen enemy of ours," Kollinar said.

It was impossible to tell from his expression whether he was in earnest or mocking Devlin's concerns.

"I will do my duty and trust that you will do yours," Devlin said.

"I will obey my orders," Kollinar said.

He had done what he could. Kollinar had his orders. And he was not a stupid man. He would do his best to ensure that Duncaer remained quiet and that Devlin had no reason to ask the King to replace the governor. It was the best he could hope for, for the present.

But Devlin promised himself that when the crisis was over he would revisit the question of who should govern Duncaer and see if he could find someone who would take the time to learn about the people he governed. Someone flexible enough to respond to new challenges, whatever form they took.

"I thank you for your assistance in retrieving the sword. I will be sure to mention your helpfulness to the King when I return to Kingsholm," Devlin said.

"I am pleased that I have been of service," Lord Kollinar said. "I wish you safe journey and look forward to hearing of your future successes."

No doubt he looked forward to getting rid of the troublesome Chosen One, who had so disordered his existence and stirred up the Caerfolk. With Devlin gone, the governor hoped that life in Duncaer would return to its usual ordered paths. For all their sakes, Devlin hoped for the same.

Devlin hastily swallowed the last of his kava and handed the mug to a servant, who handed him his cloak. He shrugged it on and fastened the brooch that held the neck closed.

His right hand dropped down and briefly touched the scabbard that held the Sword of Light. It felt good to be leaving this place. True there were weeks of hard travel ahead of him, and he had no illusions that his return would put an end to all his difficulties. There would be nasty political battles to be fought on the council and perhaps even uglier battles on the field. But regardless of what awaited him, Jorsk was where his duty lay. His visit to Duncaer had shown him that much. For it had been a visit, not a homecoming. There was a part of him that would always belong to Duncaer, but Devlin was the Chosen One. He had grown beyond merely caring for his own people. Now his responsibilities lay beyond those he called kin. Now he had an entire Kingdom to protect, and Duncaer was just one small piece of it—though it would always hold a special place in his heart.

He glanced over at Stephen, who grinned at him. Stephen had his own reasons for being glad to leave.

The main door swung open, and Didrik entered.

"Devlin, the ponies are here. Along with our escort," Didrik said.

Devlin turned to Lord Kollinar, who had risen at this early hour to bid them farewell. The governor had offered Devlin an escort, but Devlin had refused.

"I gave no such orders," Kollinar said quickly.

"Come and see for yourself," Didrik said.

Curious, Devlin made his way through the open door, then stopped on the steps. Grooms from the army held the leads of three saddled ponies and one laden with their baggage. Next to them were seven mounted soldiers.

Devlin blinked as he realized that they were not soldiers, for they wore off-white woolen cloaks and carried transverse bows slung across their backs. Peacekeepers.

As he descended the stairs, their leader dismounted. When she tossed back her hood, he recognized Saskia's features.

"What is the meaning of this?" Devlin asked. Had they come to wish him farewell? Or was there some new threat?

Saskia drew herself to attention and stomped the heel of her right foot in salute.

"Lord Devlin. I am in charge of your escort," Saskia said.

"And it takes seven of you to see me safely to the city gates?" he asked.

They must be expecting a small riot at the very least.

"My orders are to see you safe till the Kenwye River," she said, naming the river that marked the border between Duncaer and Jorsk.

He wondered what had prompted Chief Mychal to order this escort. By any measure it was a generous gesture, for the peacekeepers could ill afford to lose the services of seven of their own for the length of time it would take for them to journey to the border and return. But it was generosity he did not need.

"Tell Chief Mychal I thank him for the gesture, but I need no escort. My friends and I will be safe enough on our own," Devlin said.

"No," Saskia said.

"You do not say 'no' to the Chosen One," Kollinar said, coming to stand behind Devlin.

Saskia grinned and shook her head. "I am not speaking to the Chosen One," she replied. "Devlin of Duncaer has shown himself a man of honor and courage. The peacekeepers have declared him kin, and it is our right to protect our family. Even if they do not wish it."

He felt a lump in his throat and blinked his eyes rapidly, chasing away what felt suspiciously like tears. "You honor me beyond all measure," he said, with only a slight hitch in his voice. "But I say again, I do not need an escort."

"And how do you propose to stop us? You can hardly order the army to arrest us, not after we have claimed you as kin," she said.

He had been neatly boxed into a corner.

"Devlin, the ponies are growing cold standing here, as am I," Didrik said. "We can discuss this as we ride."

He should have known that Didrik would take Saskia's part in any argument. The two of them had seemed quite friendly, and Didrik, ever mindful of his responsibilities, would be glad to have someone he trusted to help guard the Chosen One.

They mounted their horses and rode off, the peace-keepers falling in behind him. As they passed through the northern gate, he murmured a private farewell to Alvaren and the friends he was leaving behind. Devlin did not know what dangers he would face when he finally reached Jorsk. But no matter what they were, with the strength of his friends and kin behind him, he knew he would be equal to any challenge.

About the Author

PATRICIA BRAY inherited her love of books from her parents, both of whom were fine storytellers in the Irish tradition. She has always enjoyed spinning tales, and turned to writing as a chance to share her stories with a wider audience. Patricia holds a master's degree in Information Technology, and combines her writing with a full-time career as an I/T Project Manager. She resides in upstate New York, where she is currently at work on the next volume in The Sword of Change series. For more information on her books visit her Web site at www.sff.net/people/patriciabray.

Be sure not to miss
the thrilling conclusion to
The Sword of Change

Devlin's
Justice

Coming in summer 2004

Please turn the page for a special preview

KING OLAFUR SURREPTITIOUSLY RUBBED HIS DAMP palms against the sleeves of his silken robe. A lesser man might have shown his impatience by fidgeting, or given in to the urge to pace, but Olafur was beyond such temptations. The blood of great rulers flowed in his veins. Thorvald, his father, had conquered Duncaer and expanded the reach of the empire from sea to sea. Olaven, his grandsire, had brought glory to Jorsk as the hub of a trading empire. And his great-grandsire was King Axel, whose brilliant diplomacy had enabled him to forge an alliance with Emperor Jeoffroi of Selvarat, after two hundred years of enmity between their peoples. King Axel's skill at diplomacy had been equaled by his prowess as a war leader, for the combined might of Selvarat and Jorsk had crushed the Nerikaat alliance that had threatened both their realms.

His forebearers had left him a mighty kingdom, along with the responsibility to preserve it. Since his father's death, Olafur had done what he could, in the face of nearly insurmountable odds. Even Axel had faced only one enemy—and the Nerikaat alliance, for all their viciousness, had been an honorable foe who attacked openly. By contrast Olafur had been fighting a series of faceless enemies who melted away as soon as they were confronted. Border raiders, pirates, and internal unrest had bedeviled him, along with crop failures, plagues, and a host of monsters that had claimed the lives of the Chosen Ones with predictable regularity.

Olafur knew that no other man could have held the kingdom together for so long. But even he could only do so much. Help must be had, if the kingdom was to survive. It was time to call upon the ancient alliance once more, and to ask the Selvarats to honor their promises of friendship and mutual aid.

His eyes swept the receiving room, ensuring that all was in readiness. On his left side stood Lady Ingeleth, the leader of the royal council. Ranged beside her were a half-dozen high-ranking nobles, carefully chosen so that each region had a representative. If this had been a formal reception in the great throne room, his entire court would have been in attendance. But a mere ambassador did not rate such an honor, regardless of the importance of his mission.

Standing on his right side was Marshall Erild Olvarrson, who now led the royal army in the absence of the Chosen One. While the marshal would never inspire the strong feelings of devotion that Devlin invoked in his followers, his loyalty to the throne was unquestioned. As was his obedience.

And while no one could question the Chosen One's loyalty to his oaths, Devlin continued to see matters in the most simplistic terms. He had yet to learn the value of political compromise. It was for the best that Devlin's journey to Duncaer had taken longer than expected. His presence here would needlessly complicate matters.

Not to mention that it would give Olafur great pleasure to be the one who ensured the security of his kingdom. He, and he alone, would be hailed as the savior of his people. Devlin's heroics and his strange ideas about the place of the common people would be forgotten.

Once the kingdom had returned to normalcy, Olafur would see about making other changes in his court. Devlin had served ably as Chosen One, and such he would remain until his inevitable death. But it might be time to appoint another as general of the army. Olvarrson, perhaps, or another scion of a noble family who owed him a favor.

But those were considerations for another day. Now he must focus all his energies on his meeting with the ambassador and the negotiations that would take place in the days to come. Only in his private thoughts would he admit how relieved he had been when word was brought that Count Magaharan and his party had arrived in the city. He had expected them some time before, the ice on the river Kalla having been clear for nearly a month. But it would not do to give any hint of his impatience, so in a show of politeness, Olafur had given instructions that they be welcomed and shown to their quarters so they could refresh themselves after their long journey.

Having given them a chance to bathe and dress in their court finery, he could welcome his guests. A nervous man might have resorted to a formal diplomatic reception, trying to overawe his visitors. But Olafur was too subtle for such tactics. He did not need to wear a heavy crown or be seated upon the royal throne in order to demonstrate his power. Instead he could greet the ambassador as a friend, setting the tone for the discussions to come. He would treat him as an equal, not as a beggar. Misfortune might have plagued Jorsk in these last years, but he was still ruler of a powerful kingdom. The aid he sought had been paid for tenfold by the blood Axel's forces had shed on behalf of the common alliance.

Indeed the last letter he had received from Empress Thania had been a carefully worded assurance that she was prepared to assist Jorsk in defending itself against the foreign aggressors. Now with the return of her ambassador, he could negotiate on what form the aid should take. Devlin, along with the barons of the coastal provinces, insisted troops were needed to stave off a possible invasion. He argued that last year's landings in Korinth had been but a feint, and that their enemies would strike Korinth in force before the summer was over.

A few of the army officers shared Devlin's views, but

Olafur himself was not convinced that they faced a land invasion. In his opinion the sea raiders from the Green Isles were as much a threat as any possible invasion. The raiders destroyed coastal villages, but they also wreaked havoc on shipping, which was the lifeblood of the kingdom. A few well armed ships from the Selvarat navy might well be worth more than a regiment of soldiers.

He wondered just how generous Thania was prepared to be. His earlier requests had fallen on deaf ears, but it seemed last summer's aborted landing in Korinth and the events surrounding Duke Gerhard's execution, had convinced her that Jorsk was indeed in need of assistance. It chafed to be put in the position of supplicant. He reminded himself that the aid he asked for was no more than his rightful due, promised by long-standing treaties and paid for by years of mutual alliance. If Selvarat had been the one to fall into danger, he himself would do no less.

But he knew better than to suppose that the help would come without a price. Treaty or no, there was always a cost. He would have to rely upon his own cunning and skill at diplomacy to ensure that the price of salvation did not beggar his kingdom.

His musings were cut short as two guards swung open the doors, and then clicked their heels and bowed their heads in respect.

Count Magaharan was the first to enter. Tall and lean, even in his brightly colored court robes, he had an ascetic look more suited to a scholar than a veteran courtier. The count had been Selvarat's ambassador to Jorsk for the past two years, and he appeared completely at ease as he strode into the receiving room.

Following Count Magaharan was his aide Jenna, a young woman who called herself a commoner, though rumor claimed she was a bastard offspring of the royal house. Behind her were two men whom he immediately dismissed as minor functionaries by the plainness of their dress.

Just as the guards were getting ready to close the doors, a

man stepped through, trailing so far behind the others that it was not immediately clear that he was a member of the ambassador's party. His presence seemed almost an afterthought.

Or perhaps he had deliberately chosen to make an unconventional entrance. Olafur's eyes narrowed as he studied the newcomer. The man was plainly dressed. His court robe showed only a narrow band of silver brocade, but he carried himself with utter confidence. And as he approached the others, Olafur noticed that the count's aide stepped aside so the newcomer could take her place.

The ambassador bowed deeply, extending his right hand in a flourishing sweep before him. His companions followed suit.

"Count Magaharan, it is a pleasure to welcome you and your companions, and to offer you the hospitality of my court."

The ambassador drew himself erect. "On behalf of myself, and in the name of the Empress Thania, whom I have the honor to serve, I thank you for your courtesy. The empress sends her greetings to her friend Olafur of Jorsk, along with her wishes for your continued health and the prosperity of your kingdom."

"Empress Thania is gracious indeed, and we count ourselves fortunate in her friendship," Olafur replied.

"May I present my companions? You already know my aide Jenna, and this is Vachel of the house of Burrel, and Guy from the house of Saltair."

As they were named, Vachel and Guy each stepped forward a pace and made their bows, which Olafur acknowledged with a polite nod. Burrel and Saltair were mid-rank houses in Selvarat, and this confirmed his impression that the two were mere advisors. Worth keeping an eye on, but they would defer to Magaharan in all matters of importance.

"And this, your majesty, is Karel of Maurant."

"Your majesty," the late arrival said, with a deep bow, and an even more elaborate hand flourish than Magaharan had made. His manners showed that he had traveled little outside his own land, for while this might be the fashion in Selvarat, here such a display might be taken as mockery.

New to diplomacy he might be, but this man was not one to be taken lightly. Maurant was not just any noble house, it was the house of Prince Lenexa, the royal consort of Empress Thania. And while he could not quite remember the intricacies of the imperial family tree, it would be wise to err on the side of caution. Simply because no title had been claimed did not mean that this Karel was without rank.

"Lord Karel, I welcome you to my court," Olafur said. "I would make known to you my chief councilor, Lady Ingeleth, and Marshal Olvarrson of the Royal Army."

Karel acknowledged the introductions with studious politeness. As Lady Ingeleth introduced the remaining Jorskian nobles to the ambassador's party, King Olafur took the opportunity to study their visitors. He thought he saw a certain resemblance between Karel and Jenna, in the shape of their noses and their unusually small ears, which gave further credence to his belief that Jenna was a member of the royal family.

Olafur had been disappointed when his equerry had reported that there was no senior military officer among the ambassador's party. If the empress intended to honor the treaty, then surely she would have sent along a general or a marshal at the very least, someone who could discuss the disposition of the Selvarat forces and how they could best aid in the defense of Jorsk. But perhaps his disappointment had been premature. Sending a member of the royal family, however distant his connection to the prince, must be taken as a sign of favor.

But whatever their intentions were, he would have to wait. He knew better than to expect that Count Magaharan would immediately reveal the messages he had been entrusted with. There were certain rituals to be observed. And it would not do to give the impression of desperation.

Need, yes, but desperation would be taken as a sign of weakness and exploited accordingly.

"A feast has been prepared in your honor," King Olafur said. Though feast was perhaps too strong a word, since royal kitchens only had hours to prepare for their guests. Still whatever was served was bound to be better than journey fare. And he had ordered the remaining Myrkan red brought up from the cellars, so there would be no cause for complaint there. "If you would join us?" Olafur asked.

"It would be our pleasure," Count Magaharan replied.

Captain Drakken buckled the scabbard of her sword over her dress tunic and then tugged at the hem of her uniform until it hung straight. Seldom used in the winter months, a musty odor arose from the garment and she made a mental note to have words with the servant who oversaw her quarters. With the court about to commence its annual session, it would not do for her to discover that her dress uniforms were moth-eaten or rotted from neglect. King Olafur was known to be a stickler about such things, and her place in court was tenuous enough without incurring his wrath over such a trifle.

He was also insistent on punctuality. A glance at the sand clock showed that she needed to leave soon if she was not to be late for the dinner honoring the Selvarat Ambassador. But she did not want to leave before Lieutenant Embeth had made her report, and wondered what could have delayed her.

There was a sharp knock and the door to her quarters swung open before she could respond.

"Captain, your pardon," Lieutenant Embeth paused to gasp for breath. Her face was flushed and she was panting as if she had just run a race.

"Wait. Breathe," Captain Drakken said. There was no sense in listening to a report made incomprehensible from lack of breath.

"Report," she ordered, when Embeth had gained control of herself.

"Captain Drakken," Lieutenant Embeth drew herself to attention. "As you know, Ambassador Magaharan and his party arrived by ship just before the noon hour. They were met by a royal equerry who escorted them to the palace. In addition to the ambassador, there was his aide Jenna, two noblemen named Vachel and Guy, and a man called either Karel or Charles whose status I could not confirm. He was accorded his own chamber, so he may be another aide."

Strange that Count Magaharan would have brought not one but two aides, along with a pair of advisors who had never visited Jorsk before, but then again this was no usual visit. Drakken knew full well that King Olafur was hoping for a renewal of the ancient alliance, and an agreement for Selvarat to supply troops to defend Jorsk's borders. The dinner tonight would serve to introduce the ambassador's party to the court, but it would do no harm to also check with Solveig, to see if she knew anything of their visitors.

"There were also four clerks, a priest, a half-dozen servants, and the ambassador's personal honor guard."

"Is that all?"

"That is the party that arrived at the palace. But we kept watch on the ship that carried the ambassador, and at dusk six persons left the ship and took rooms in the old city. They were dressed as sailors but they had the gait of landsmen, and at least one of them was wearing a sword under her cloak."

"Soldiers," Captain Drakken said. "Or mercenaries."

"So I suspected. I stayed long enough to confirm the report and then ordered a watch kept on the inn where they were staying."

"You did well. Make sure the watchers know to be discreet, and that they are to make a daily report of what these people do and who they meet. And if they see anything suspicious they are to notify me without delay."

"Understood, Captain."

She dismissed Embeth with a nod, and the lieutenant saluted before making her departure.

A glance at the sand clock showed that she would have to make haste to avoid a late entrance at the dinner, but instead Captain Drakken crossed over to her desk and unrolled a parchment scroll which showed a map of the kingdom. Along the Southern Road was a small spot, so faint that it might be mistaken for a flaw in the parchment. But in truth it was the latest position of the Chosen One, as verified by the soul stone only this morning. He had made good time since leaving Duncaer, but in the last days his pace had slowed. By her reckoning Devlin was at least a fortnight away from Kingsholm. She glared at the map, but all her wishing could not make the leagues any shorter, and with an angry curse she rolled it back up.

Devlin had been gone too long. He should have returned over a month ago, but his errand in Duncaer had taken longer than expected. Now he was on his way home, presumably bearing the Sword of Light. But they could not wait another two weeks for him. They needed him here in the capital. Now.

The court was beginning its spring session. The ambassador from Selvarat had arrived, bringing with him the Empress Thania's response to King Olafur's request for military assistance. Intelligence indicated that the empress would respond favorably, but intelligence could be wrong. And even if she sent troops, it would take skill to deploy them to the maximum advantage.

Now was the time when decisions would be made that would secure the kingdom's safety, or see it fracture under the competing pressures from within and without. It was a time for bold leadership, but such was noticeably lacking. Devlin's few friends at court had no influence with either King Olafur or his council. Marshal Olvarrson was neither a strategist nor a leader. He would do as King Olafur instructed, heedless of the long-term consequences.

She knew that many were expecting great things from

the Selvarat alliance, but she herself was wary of strangers offering gifts. Ancient treaties or no, if Empress Thania was prepared to have her soldiers shed blood on Jorsk's behalf, then it was safe to reason that she was expecting to receive something of equal value in return. Depending on what concessions the Selvarats might win out of King Olafur, the cure might well prove worse than the disease.

And if politics were not enough for Drakken to worry about, she now had six mysterious strangers who would have to be closely watched. Not to mention that she had yet to discover who had sent the assassins after Devlin last fall. For all she knew their paymaster might well be among those nobles who were even now arriving in the city for the spring council.

There were plots among plots, and very few people whom she could trust. For these past months she had done what was needed, to ensure that Kingsholm would be ready for Devlin's return. She had held her tongue, ensuring that she gave the king no cause to relieve her of command. But she could no longer afford inaction. Now she owed it to herself, and to those whom she served, to make her opinions known. And she knew Devlin's other friends, including Lord Rikard and Solveig of Esker, would be facing similar dilemmas.

Only Devlin's voice could balance the conservative forces of the court. She prayed to the gods that his errand had been successful. If Devlin returned bearing the Sword of Light, it would be impossible for King Olafur and the courtiers to ignore him.

"Hurry back," she said aloud. "We cannot hold on much longer."

King Olafur led the way into the great dining hall, with Count Magaharan at his side. The rest of the party followed, and from the corner of his eye he saw Lady Ingeleth speaking to Lord Rikard. Rikard, who had been intended to sit on the main dais, found his way to a seat at the head of the center table along with Vachel and Guy, while Lady Ingeleth escorted Lord Karel to a place at the dais.

The main doors were opened and the rest of the court filed in, along with the members of the ambassador's retinue who had been too lowly to be presented to the king, but were too important to be consigned to the servants' hall. Only a third of the tables had been set, for with winter just ended, most of his nobles were only now beginning to make the long journey to court. Still there were enough courtiers who had wintered over in the capital to make for a lively gathering.

Conversation at dinner was general, as he had known it would be. Affairs of state were too delicate a matter to be discussed in such a public setting. Instead they spoke of trivialities. Count Magaharan described his journey on the newest ship in the imperial fleet, and how it was so comfortable one could scarcely believe they were on a ship instead of on dry land. Olafur, whose own memories of sailing ships included misery and wretched discomfort, kept his doubts to himself.

For his part he spoke little, content to let Lady Ingeleth play the role of hostess—a part she was well suited for. Knowing the ambassador's love of culture, Lady Ingeleth reported that a new poet had come into favor at the court over the winter, and offered to arrange a private performance for the ambassador and his party.

Such trifles kept them occupied until the last course had been removed, and the final toast drunk. King Olafur dismissed the diners, then invited Count Magaharan and Lord Karel to join him in his private chambers. Lady Ingeleth and Marshal Olvarrson accompanied them.

He waited with seemingly endless patience as the party settled themselves, and the servants served glasses of ice wine and citrine. At his signal the servants placed the pitchers on the sideboard, then took their leave, bowing low as they closed the doors behind them.

Ambassador Magaharan lost no time in coming to the point. "Empress Thania has sent a letter of greeting which I will give to your secretary. But I am authorized to tell you the gist of her message, which is that she honors the alliance between our peoples and has sent the troops from our armies to assist in the protection of Jorsk."

Olafur nodded gravely, though he felt nearly dizzy with relief. This was no more than he had expected, and indeed the last letter from Selvarat, received before the winter ice locked the harbor, had strongly hinted that this aid would be forthcoming. But much could change in three months time, and only now did he realize how much he had feared that she would have found some reason to refuse his request.

"When friends stand together there is none can divide them," Olafur said. "As it was in the time of Axel and Jeoffroi, so shall it be with Empress Thania and myself. Just as our enemies are your enemies, we pledge that your enemies will be ours as well."

It was speech that he had rehearsed for days, yet had never quite been sure that he would have the opportunity to say.

Marshal Olvarrson cleared his throat, drawing all eyes to him. "If I may, your majesty," he said. "Count Magaharan, did I hear you say that the empress had already sent the troops? Are they on their way here even now?"

"Better than that, they have already landed," Count Magaharan replied with a small smile. "Two hundred horseman and a thousand foot soldiers have already disembarked on the coast of Korinth. Our ship accompanied the transports and witnessed their landing. By now they have secured the whole of the eastern coast."

Lady Ingeleth's eyebrows rose. "This is indeed unexpected," she said.

It was more than unexpected. It was presumptuous, to

say the least. True, Thania had been generous in the number of troops she sent, but he should have been consulted before they arrived.

"I appreciate the Empress Thania's loan of her troops, but I had expected to be informed before they set sail. My commanders will want to make best use of them," King Olafur said. His pride was stung by the highhanded way in which this had been done, but he could not afford to offend those who represented the empress. He needed those soldiers.

"Of course, but such consultations would take time, and the empress wished to send her aid with all possible speed," Count Magaharan said. "She did not want you to be caught unprepared, if there should be an invasion this spring. We knew of your concern over Korinth from our discussions last fall, and felt it was best to send the troops where they needed without delay."

He allowed himself to be mollified. Help that came too late was no help at all. The journey between Selvarat and Jorsk could take several weeks, depending on the weather. Having asked for help to be sent with all speed, he should not quarrel if his allies had used their own judgment about the method of fulfilling his request.

"And now that we have arrived, we can discuss the disposition of the next wave of forces with you and Marshal Olvarrson," Lord Karel added. "Our general staff recommended that our troops be used to secure the eastern provinces, which are the closest to Selvarat. You could then use your own units to secure your northwestern border. But this is just a proposal. Naturally you will want your advisors to review these plans to see if you agree with our suggestions."

"Naturally," he echoed.

Marshal Olvarrson rubbed his chin thoughtfully. "I would have to see the plans, but there is sense in what he proposes. Major Mikkelson has been complaining for months that if an attack came he could not hold the east coast on his own."

Mikkelson. Now there was a man who was nearly as much trouble as his mentor Devlin. Mikkelson had pleaded that the troops be released from their central garrisons, not seeming to realize that trouble was just likely to come from the west as the east.

"It seems you have thought of everything," Lady Ingeleth said drily. From the tone of her voice Olafur knew that she was not pleased. "And what precisely is it that you expect from us in return?"

Treaty or no, there was bound to be a cost.

"The empress seeks a pledge of friendship. And a gift to seal the alliance."

Olafur had a strong suspicion that he knew what the gift was to be. He had had months to resign himself to this, though he had not yet told Ragenilda of her probable fate. Fortunately she was a biddable girl and would do as she was told.

It was a shame that he had only one child. Ragenilda would rule Jorsk after him, and whomever she married would be the father of the next king or queen. Still it was a small price to pay if it meant ensuring there was a kingdom for her to inherit.

"My daughter Princess Ragenilda is young—"

"Not too young to be pledged," Lord Karel interrupted.

Lady Ingeleth hissed at this breach of court etiquette.

"Prince Nathan is just turned sixteen, and would be a fitting match for your daughter, when the time comes. But Ragenilda's future is a matter for another day," Karel continued.

"Then what is it you want?" Olafur asked.

"The Chosen One," Lord Karel replied. "We want Devlin of Duncaer."